Whiplash

ALSO BY CATHERINE COULTER

THE FBI THRILLERS

KnockOut (2009)

TailSpin (2008)

Double Jeopardy (2008):
The Target and *The Edge*

Double Take (2007)

The Beginning (2005):
The Cove and *The Maze*

Point Blank (2005)

Blowout (2004)

Blindside (2003)

Eleventh Hour (2002)

Hemlock Bay (2001)

Riptide (2000)

The Edge (1999)

The Target (1998)

The Maze (1997)

The Cove (1996)

Whiplash

CATHERINE
COULTER

**Doubleday Large Print
Home Library Edition**

G. P. PUTNAM'S SONS

New York

This Large Print Edition, prepared especially for Doubleday Large Print Home Library, contains the complete, unabridged text of the original Publisher's Edition.

G. P. PUTNAM'S SONS
Publishers Since 1838
Published by the Penguin Group
Penguin Group (USA) Inc., 375 Hudson Street, New York, New York 10014, USA • Penguin Group (Canada), 90 Eglinton Avenue East, Suite 700, Toronto, Ontario M4P 2Y3, Canada (a division of Pearson Penguin Canada Inc.) • Penguin Books Ltd, 80 Strand, London WC2R 0RL, England • Penguin Ireland, 25 St Stephen's Green, Dublin 2, Ireland (a division of Penguin Books Ltd) • Penguin Group (Australia), 250 Camberwell Road, Camberwell, Victoria 3124, Australia (a division of Pearson Australia Group Pty Ltd) • Penguin Books India Pvt Ltd, 11 Community Centre, Panchsheel Park, New Delhi–110 017, India • Penguin Group (NZ), 67 Apollo Drive, Rosedale, North Shore 0632, New Zealand (a division of Pearson New Zealand Ltd) • Penguin Books (South Africa) (Pty) Ltd, 24 Sturdee Avenue, Rosebank, Johannesburg 2196, South Africa

Penguin Books Ltd, Registered Offices: 80 Strand, London WC2R 0RL, England

ISBN 978-1-61664-340-9

This Large Print Book carries the Seal of Approval of N.A.V.H.

ISBN 978-1-61664-340-9

This is a work of fiction. Names, characters, places, and incidents either are the product of the author's imagination or are used fictitiously, and any resemblance to actual persons, living or dead, businesses, companies, events, or locales is entirely coincidental.

[illegible]

[illegible]

Acknowledgments

I would like to thank:

Lisa Amoroso for yet another incredible jacket.
Karen Evans for her excellent discrepancy-spotting in the manuscript.
Dorian Hastings for all her excellent catches in copyediting.
Chris Pepe for her special enthusiasm about this book.
Erin Vollmer for always keeping all the balls in the air.

I'm very lucky to have you all in my corner. Thank you very much.

TO A GREAT GROUP OF WOMEN:

Ingrid Becker
Lesley DeLone
Karen Evans
Catherine Lyons-Labate
I'm glad you're in my life.

Whiplash

1

STONE BRIDGE, CONNECTICUT
Late Sunday night

Erin used her third-generation lock picks. She knew each one intimately, having successfully, and in excellent time, learned to unlock by the age of six and a half whatever her father hid under her pillow. Her hands didn't shake, though her heart felt like it would pound out of her chest. Crouching in a dark maintenance closet for three hours with two bottles of water and a PayDay candy bar hadn't been fun, but surely it wasn't all that illegal. What she was doing now, though, it was the real deal. She wasn't just twisting the law, she was stomping on it. She was breaking and entering. She could go to jail for the rest of her youth, which would be a real shame since she hadn't yet produced the fourth generation of lock pickers.

It wasn't the first time she'd gone through the back door to make things right for a client, but she prayed with all her heart it would be the last. Maybe if she'd been able to speak to the CEO, Caskie Royal, if only she could have tried to reason with him—no, that was a load of bull.

The lock snicked open. She slid her grandfather's picks back into the pocket of her black jacket, checked the corridor both ways, and opened the door just enough so she could slip inside the CEO's office. She turned on her penlight to get the lay of the land. It was a large square room, business-opulent, she'd call it, with a rich dark burgundy leather sofa, a love seat, and a huge matching chair with ottoman. A fine antique mahogany desk dominated the office. She flicked off the penlight, locked the door, and walked to the wall-wide window behind the desk, to make sure no one was out there.

Mr. Royal had a lovely view of a large park-like lawn, now moonlit, lined with plants still bursting with blooms at the very end of summer. The maple and oak woods behind the lawn stretched a good quarter of a mile into Van Wie Park. Since she didn't see a single soul out there, she didn't close the draperies. She stepped to the computer sitting on the big desk and turned it on.

Of course it was pass-coded, but she was prepared for that. Her list had failed her only once, but that was years ago, and she started in on it now. Number 3 on her list—his third wife's birthday, that was the one she was betting on, but it was Number 4—the family dog, Adler, named after Schiffer Hartwin's director, Adler Dieffendorf. She was fairly certain Caskie Royal's boss wasn't aware of this honor—that his namesake was a happy brainless Dalmatian she'd seen belly up, legs waving, on Jane Ann Royal's website. Maybe it meant Mr. Royal had something of a sense of humor, since Herr Doktor Adler Dieffendorf's photo in Schiffer Hartwin's glossy annual report showed an older man with a lovely head of white hair, a thin patrician nose, and intelligent gray eyes.

She was in. Thanks, Adler.

She began searching his files. She felt queasy and ignored it. *Get it done, get it done. If you're caught and go to trial, maybe the jury won't convict you given what these greedy yahoos are doing unless you get a crappy lawyer*—there it was, no doubt at all in her mind—a file titled "Project A."

She began reading what were obviously Caskie Royal's notes on what Schiffer Hartwin was doing with the drug Culovort. He'd detailed his instructions complete with a To Do list, all neatly bulleted, beginning with the near shutdown of Culovort production at the U.S. Schiffer Hartwin manufacturing laboratory, Cartwright Labs, in Bartonville, Missouri. Next came instructions to their distribution plant, Rexol, also in Bartonville.

She was so deep into disbelief at what she was reading, it took her a moment before her brain processed the sound of a car driving around to the back of the building, right beneath the big window of the CEO's office. She dashed to the window and looked down to see a big silver Lexus. It was Caskie Royal's car.

What was he doing here, late on a Sunday night?

Doesn't matter, he's here. If he caught her, she'd soon be wearing a neon yellow jumpsuit, PI license or not. She plugged in a flash drive, and ran into another password, this one corporate. *He's here, he's here. No choice.* She pressed Print File and watched as page after page flowed out of the high-speed printer.

She hadn't checked the file size. What if there were a zillion pages? What if what she needed to have didn't print out in time—no, she had some time, it would be all right. Even Mr. Royal had to stop by the guard in the lobby and sign in before coming up.

The printer stopped. Thank goodness there were only nineteen pages in all. She quickly slid the pages inside her black jacket, zipped it up tight, turned off the printer, slipped the flash drive into her pocket, and closed down the computer. She straightened the chair, checked to see it all looked the way it had when she'd come in, and hurried to the office door to listen. She heard voices at the end of the long corridor. Royal and a woman coming her way.

Not good.

It was time for Plan B. Always have a Plan B, her father had drummed into her head, and she had one. It sounded like they were arguing. She pressed her ear against the door, heard the woman say clearly, "I still can't believe you've made me a part of this, Caskie. What do we need it for?"

"Carla, the money is rolling in so fast there's barely time to even count it. They're looking at a windfall profit of about, conservatively, one and a half billion dollars. They've already racked up nearly a billion in sales in the last six months. And it's a freebee, like manna from heaven."

"It's unethical and you know it. And it's dangerous and illegal."

"Just back me up on this one, and I'll see to it you get a six-figure bonus in your pocket, Carla. And don't fret. There's no danger here, nothing bad can happen."

"But—"

His voice was impatient. "You gotta admit, with Culovort off patent, the profits are hardly enough to fill a nut cup. What is it? Fifteen bucks a chemo session? *Fifteen bucks?* Get real. It'll take the FDA so long to get their act together, we'll all have cashed in before the pressure's too great.

And so far, you know as well as I do there's hardly been any pressure at all, just a letter of inquiry from the FDA and a couple of newspaper articles about the shortage."

They were coming closer. That wasn't good, but she couldn't help herself, she stayed at the door. What a bit of luck, good and bad. It had to be Carla Alvarez, the production manager. So Carla hadn't been part of it for long, but she wouldn't blow the whistle, either.

"Hey, babe, let's forget this stuff. You look so hot I can't wait to put my mouth on you."

Good grief, Alvarez and Royal? Lovers? She hadn't picked up a whiff of that when she'd done her research on Royal and his management team. Did anyone else know?

Carla said, "Maybe it won't take the FDA long to jump on Schiffer Hartwin. You'd have to be an idiot to believe the shortage of Culovort is just poor planning and—how did they put it—connected to an expansion of our production facilities? Couldn't they come up with a more believable excuse? Aren't they worried we'll soon be hated as much as bankers?"

They were close now, not ten feet from his office door. Any moment they'd be waltzing in, headed toward that big leather sofa. “That’s the beauty of it,” she heard him say, chuckling, “Even if it’s our production and distribution labs in Missouri that are having the expansion problems, it’s Schiffer Hartwin who’ll get all the blowback, if there is any—and they’re way the hell over in Germany. Carla, stop worrying about it tonight. We don’t have that much time—”

“But what about—”

There was a whoof of surprise from the woman, the sound of scuffling, then a low moan.

She heard hard breathing, a suck-air kiss, and raunchy groaning. Evidently the time for business talk was past, a pity. She’d studied the floor plans, knew her escape route if disaster struck. Disaster was readying itself to strike in under a minute unless they decided to have sex against a corridor wall. She ran to the adjoining bathroom, slipped inside, and quietly closed the door again. She stepped into the glass-block shower and looked up at a small window near the top that had looked larger and lower on the plans. How the devil would she get up there? She heard the office door open.

2

Showtime.

She sucked in a deep breath and jumped. She managed to grab the windowsill with one hand, the window latch with the other, and pulled herself up. The window was cracked open enough for her to grab the rough stone edge of the building outside the bathroom window. She shoved at the latch with her other hand, but the sucker didn't budge. Not good. As her heart thumped louder and faster, she heard her father's voice in her head, *"When you're butt-deep in trouble, you focus and you get it done."* She shoved as hard as she could on that latch, once, twice. The window flew outward.

She eyeballed the opening above her. It wasn't very wide, but on the other hand, thank the good Lord and the gym, she wasn't either.

She heard Royal and Carla Alvarez fumbling with each other not twenty feet away, laughing, kissing, sex-walking, she knew, toward that sofa. She had to be quiet.

She got both hands outside, one on the edge of the outside wall, the other on the window frame, and pulled herself up and through the opening. She hung upside down, looking at bushes a galaxy away.

She heard Caskie Royal say something, then his footsteps coming toward the bathroom.

No choice. She wiggled through and did a lovely tuck into the bushes.

She landed on her shoulder, the shrubbery cushioning her fall, and lay there, breathing slowly, querying her body parts. She was okay, she hoped.

She turned her head and looked up. Would he notice the wide-open window? Would he wonder? Would he be suspicious?

With her luck, he and Carla would probably take a pre-sex shower. She heard them still laughing and talking, coming closer. The shower was small, but not that small.

She rolled off the bush, bent nearly double, and took off running toward the dark woods of Van Wie Park at the back of Schiffer Hartwin's American headquarters.

She ran faster when she heard a yell coming from the bathroom.

Okay, so they knew someone had gone through the window, but they'd have no clue who it had been. It was okay. The cops would want to know if anything had been taken. Royal would search his files and see the date stamp on the Project A file. He'd know someone had read it. Would he know it had been copied? Would he tell the cops? No, he couldn't risk it. On the other hand, if he thought it through, he'd realize that someone probably had those files, and there'd be no way to keep the fabricated Culovort shortage from getting out. There'd be hell to pay.

For that, she couldn't wait.

She hoped it scared the crap out of him.

If the cops were called in, they'd know

only one thing for sure. The thief was a small boy or a female, because no male over the age of twelve could have squeezed through that window.

Once inside the Van Wie Park woods, she went down on her knees, sucked in air, and looked back. Lights now flooded the bathroom and the office.

She heard what she hoped was a cop car screech into the parking lot in front of the building. In that moment she knew the guard had called the cops, not Caskie. *What are you going to say, Caskie?*

She was grinning as she ran through the trees and out the back to the back road that led to the main highway that ran through Stone Bridge. *No sex for the wicked tonight, Caskie*.

With the cops there, Caskie would have to go on record. On record with what, that was the question. He'd also have to explain to his wife what he was doing in his office late on a lovely Sunday night with Carla Alvarez.

Once she'd hiked half a mile to her baby, a muscular light blue Hummer H3, she fastened her seat belt and turned the ignition. She loved the sound of the powerful engine. She drove slowly down the road for a bit, realized her heart was still pumping too fast and her hands were still shaking. She pulled over to get herself some time to calm down. She sat back, closed her eyes, and thought back to her client, Dr. Edward Kender, professor of archaeology at Yale in New Haven. He'd been a friend of her father's, someone she'd known from her earliest years. Dr. Kender wasn't an emotional man, but she could imagine him grinning from ear to ear in excitement when he read the Culovort files she had tucked in her jacket, as he recognized the power the contents of the files gave him. The media blitz could even force Schiffer Hartwin to start up full production of Culovort again. She'd done good.

It was because he'd known her father that he'd come to her small office the previous Wednesday afternoon. It was nearly three years since she'd seen him, since her father's funeral in fact. He'd arrived unannounced at her small office on Birch Street in Stone Bridge, and told her that, just like her father, his father was undergoing chemotherapy, not for the lung cancer that had killed her father, but for Stage 4 colon cancer. In the middle of it all, he'd been told by his oncologist that the supply of Culovort had been drastically cut. Dr. Kender didn't know what she could do to help him, but he'd been trying to pressure Schiffer Hartwin Pharmaceutical to start up full production of Culovort again.

"Culovort isn't a cancer drug, but it's used in conjunction with other chemo drugs for a wide range of cancers," he'd explained to her. "The kicker is that Culovort is critical in treating colon cancer. It's used along with another cancer drug, Fluorouracil, or 5-FU, as it's commonly called. Think of 5-FU as a grenade that masquerades as a component of DNA and explodes inside the cancer cells. Culovort is an accomplice that helps it get past the guards. Without the Culovort, you've got all the toxic poison of 5-FU, but fewer cancer cells getting killed."

He steepled his long thin fingers together, and looked over them as he spoke. "The problem is, Culovort is off patent and therefore it's cheap."

Erin said, "That's a problem? Oh, I see."

Edward Kender nodded. "Schiffer Hartwin Pharmaceutical makes only a negligible profit off it. Without it, the people suffering from colon cancer are the biggest losers, like my father. With no Culovort, they'll be forced to use the new oral drug—Eloxium. Some believe the oral drug is better—but the thing is, Eloxium can cost twenty thousand dollars for the treatment course.

"Most insurance companies do not cover the oral treatment, or only a small part of it, which means that many colon cancer patients will have to come up with thousands of dollars to pay for the Eloxium. Dad's oncologist is furious about it because she'll have to force patients over to the oral medication. There'll be simply no choice once there's no supply. Even worse, if a patient begins the Eloxium, there's no going back, even if Culovort becomes available again."

Erin said slowly, "So mortgage your home to pay for the treatment of a life-threatening disease, and have a nice day."

"Can you imagine, Erin, not only dealing with chemotherapy and all the brutal side effects, the possible prospect of dying, your family's grinding fear, the unending stress, and then being told that one of the major components of your chemotherapy course isn't available anymore because of unexpected production problems? And, oh, yes, sorry, but on top of all that, it's going to cost you a bundle out-of-pocket to switch over to a new chemo drug."

Oh, yes, she could imagine it. She remembered all too well her father's final months, the soul-draining helplessness they'd all felt watching her father become a frail old man, so ill he couldn't eat, so weak he could barely stand. She remembered how he'd told her late one night that this damnable cure made you forget the disease, you felt so rotten. She swallowed down tears, shook her head. "What I really can't picture is a group of people actually sitting down and deciding to simply stop making an important medicine for cancer patients, people who may already be staring at death from the doorway and trying to deal with it."

Dr. Kender smiled at her, a charming smile that for an instant erased the terrible fatigue and worry from his eyes. "Ah, you're forgetting the bankers on Wall Street. They purposely set out to make all the money they could, and they didn't seem to give a damn about the consequences."

Erin sighed. "I'm beginning to wonder if greed has any limits at all."

He said, "We are the ones who have to set those limits. Controlling and manipulating access to drugs for profit is wrong, but at least it affects a finite number of people. The bankers have damaged the entire world."

He drummed his fingertips on the arm of his chair. "At any rate, Erin, I went to see Mr. Caskie Royal, the CEO of the U.S. subsidiary of Schiffer Hartwin Pharmaceutical, located right down the road in Stone Bridge. He agreed to see me because he fancied I was some sort of big-wig professor from Yale."

"You are."

He tried to laugh, but only dredged up a small smile. "Disease is the great leveler, Erin. If you're facing death, nothing else exists—money, fame, power all cease to be important. As for Caskie Royal, he said he was sympathetic, then actually threw his hands in the air. Told me he was trying his best to solve the unexpected production line problems brought on by overenthusiastic expansion, was the way he put it." Dr. Kender lowered his eyes to his clasped hands. "As if any moron would believe that. I mean, a company wants to expand and it doesn't determine the effects of said expansion on its current production of drugs?

"It's a lie, of course. I'll admit it, I wanted to pull him out of his big executive chair and choke the life out of him.

"There is another Schiffer Hartwin production laboratory for Culovort in Spain. Their PR folk came up with a new reason for aborting production—quality-control issues, they said, and even the possibility the production line might have been sabotaged. It will take them some time to ramp up production again, blah, blah, blah."

"What about the media?"

"The fact that a cancer drug isn't available isn't sexy enough for the national media to make a big issue of it, since there's a different drug on the market. *The Wall Street Journal* and *The Washington Post* reported on the shortage and Schiffer Hartwin's response, but that's it. No digging, no real questioning of the company, and those two newspapers usually take an interest in medicine."

Dr. Kender looked like he was at the

end of his rope. There was anger in his gaunt face, but more than that, there was a sheen of hopelessness. He said on a sigh, "My dad, you never met him, Erin. He's old school, tough as nails, determined to take care of himself. We've discussed going on the oral cancer drug, but he's heard too many horror stories about the side effects, and he can't afford it in any case. If he's forced to go on it, he'll probably sell his house, and he's already told me there's no way he'll let me help. I've wanted to choke him for his misplaced pride, even though I completely understand it."

He paused a moment. "I hate that he's suffering, and now this worrying about having to come up with twenty thousand dollars when the Culovort runs out. It's breaking his will. I don't want him to die like this." He looked down at his tasseled loafers, his shoulders bowed, like a man who's gone up against the giant and gotten smashed. Erin wanted to weep.

He said quietly, "Do you know that in the U.S., about one hundred and fifty thousand people are diagnosed with colon cancer every year? I've written letters, sent e-mails, made phone calls to my elected representatives, to the FDA, until all I wanted was to shoot myself. No one seems to care except for the oncologists, the patients, and their beleaguered families, and they're powerless. I don't really know why I'm here. I knew you'd understand, Erin, but what can you do? What can anyone do to force the drug company to start up Culovort to full production again?"

"What we need," Erin said, drumming her fingertips on the little banged-up desk she'd bought from Goodwill in her sophomore year at Boston College, "is to get hold of solid proof they know damned well what they're doing, and that they are profiting from it. Then the media will sit up and pay attention. They love drug company scandals, but they like them much more when they're presented on a nice big platter complete with fines of hundreds of million dollars."

She rose, took both his hands in hers. "I don't know yet what I'm going to do, sir, but I do know that I'm going to try my best to find something that will help. Let me think about this, all right?"

She knew he'd left without much hope,

but she was fired up, her brain cooking. She spent three hours that evening on the Internet searching out everything on the Culovort shortage, but found little more than Dr. Kender had already told her. Everywhere the same thing, in other words, the company line: *Production line problems, overexpansion, it was being worked on, but it would take time.* It was when she read about how the oncology departments at major university medical schools were beginning to ration Culovort that she kicked her desk.

Why didn't someone in power question what the drug company said? Didn't any of these vaunted medical reporters remember the drug companies' record of gross misconduct—hiding negative data from the FDA, practically bribing physicians, failing to publish negative results, ghostwriting journal articles—and start waving red flags immediately, when it might make a difference? Didn't they remember the Vioxx scandal? How many people had died before Merck was forced to pull that drug?

Was this simply the way all drug companies operated worldwide? Come to think of it, was this the way politicians operated? Was self-interest the only driving force?

She was depressing herself.

What she needed was rock-solid proof that Schiffer Hartwin was doing this knowingly, and for profit. By midnight, she'd decided her old lock picks were her best shot at getting proof and forcing the Culovort production line to get up-and-running again.

3

STONE BRIDGE, CONNECTICUT
Monday morning

As Erin chewed on her English muffin, she reread the nineteen pages she'd photocopied from the Project A file. There was plenty there, even explanations the PR people were to give for the breakdown in Culovort production they knew would impact cancer patients. Caskie Royal had been wonderfully thorough in his To Do list, including one bulleted sentence that summed it all up: *Given current worldwide Culovort supplies and current production levels at our facility in Spain, we estimate it will require four months for Culovort shortages to develop in the U.S. Shortages will force many oncologists to switch to Eloxium.*

And then they shut down production in Spain!

Erin frowned. She realized all of this would make much more sense if Schiffer Hartwin also owned the patent for the enormously expensive oral drug Eloxium.

But they didn't. A French pharmaceutical company, Laboratoires Ancondor, produced Eloxium. Dr. Kender had told her one hundred and fifty thousand people in the U.S. were diagnosed with colon cancer each year. The income from Eloxium would end in more zeros than she could count.

But why would a German pharmaceutical cut way back on its Culovort production in its U.S. and Spanish facilities so a French pharmaceutical company could reap the profits?

Clearly, antitrust laws wouldn't allow them to profit directly. Was there some other way they were scratching each other's backs? Were there payoffs involved? Swiss bank accounts? Or were they so arrogant as to believe there would be no legal action if they violated the antitrust laws?

Erin smeared more crunchy peanut butter on her English muffin as she read about Serono, a Swiss biopharmaceutical company, that had tried to bring an AIDS drug to market "by concocting a dubious medical test," U.S. Attorney General Alberto R. Gonzales had alleged. The company "put its desire to sell the drug above the interests of patients." Serono had even offered doctors an all-expenses-paid trip to France to prescribe the drug.

Did she have to add doctors to the growing list of endlessly greedy professions?

She laid aside the stack of printouts that documented incredibly creative bad deeds by the pharmaceutical companies. What she needed now was to act. She began to refine her list of media people to contact with the papers she'd copied off Royal's files. It was going to be tricky since she didn't want to go to jail for breaking into Caskie Royal's computer. She finally selected Paul Bradley at *The Wall Street Journal* and Luther Gleason of *The New York Times,* as both had reported on the

Culovort shortage. None of the major TV stations had reported on the Culovort shortage and its consequences to colon cancer patients. When this story broke in the newspapers, though, Katie Couric, in particular, would be all over it.

Her head snapped up when she heard a TV reporter say, "The body of a man was discovered two hours ago in Van Wie Park—"

Van Wie Park was right behind Schiffer Hartwin's American headquarters. She grabbed her cup of tea and sat down in front of the TV. A reporter shoved his microphone into a man's face. "This is Special Agent in Charge of the New Haven field office, Bowie Richards. Special Agent, what do you know about this death? Was it murder? Why is this in the hands of the FBI and not the Stone Bridge police department? Have you identified the victim? Do you believe it connects to the break-in at the U.S. subsidiary headquarters of Schiffer Hartwin last night?"

Agent Bowie Richards looked both pained and grateful at the reporter's shotgun approach, Erin thought, since it allowed him to pick and choose. "The FBI was called in because the victim was found in Van Wie Park, which is federal land. The FBI and the local police department will be working together to solve this brutal crime. That's all I have to say at the moment." He turned and nodded to a portly middle-aged man the reporter introduced as Police Chief Clifford Amos, who didn't seem at all happy that the victim had the bad judgment to get whacked on federal land.

"Chief, have you identified the victim?"

Police Chief Amos said, "The FBI wishes to withhold his identity until the family is contacted. As Special Agent Richards said, my department will be closely involved in this case."

Yeah, sure you will, Erin thought. If she were Bowie Richards, she'd keep the local cops as far out of the loop as possible. *A dead guy murdered in Caskie Royal's backyard and I was there, or maybe close by, when it happened. I could have stumbled over the body, maybe run headlong into the murderer. They'll find out I was in Caskie Royal's office, lifting documents from his computer, and they'll think I murdered him. I'll go to jail and Dr. Kender's father will have to sell his house to pay for the Eloxium and—* Slow down, slow down. Was the murdered man an employee of Schiffer Hartwin? The way the world worked, she'd bet the last bite of her English muffin on it, with an extra spoonful of peanut butter smeared on top.

Could it be possible the dead guy had nothing to do with Schiffer Hartwin? Maybe he was just an unlucky out-of-towner, here to visit his mother, who managed to get mugged and killed? That was too good to believe. And if he was connected to Schiffer Hartwin, did his death have anything to do with her being there?

Fact was, she hadn't seen a thing, hadn't heard a thing, hadn't stumbled over a dead body, not, of course, that a single soul would believe her.

Then it hit her hard. How could she give all the documents from Caskie Royal's computer to the media now? She'd have her butt arrested within an hour.

Whatever she did, from this moment on, she was going to have to be very careful she wouldn't be connected to the murder.

When the doorbell rang an hour later, Erin was just beginning to organize her notes, Royal's Project A file, and her printouts and clippings.

As was her habit, she looked through the peephole instead of flinging open her door to avoid welcoming in a vampire or other miscreant. Good grief, hadn't she just seen that face on TV? She felt her heart fall to her toes. They'd found out about her so soon? No, impossible. She had to get a grip. "Who is it?"

"My name's Bowie Richards. May I speak to you, Ms. Pulaski?"

"Why?" But she knew why. They'd found a witness who'd gotten the license plate number off her Hummer, or the guard had somehow seen her on a camera she hadn't known was there and she'd been identified by Carla Alvarez, who'd recognized her from the gym or—

"It's personal, Ms. Pulaski. It's about my daughter, Georgie."

What? Georgia Richards—Georgie—was the daughter of an FBI agent? No, more than that—Bowie Richards was the big-cheese FBI agent in New Haven. Why hadn't anyone said anything? She felt a huge black cloud moving swiftly toward her and she wondered in that moment if her family's legendary good luck was fast heading south.

She didn't want to, but she opened the door and stepped up to block the doorway.

Bowie Richards looked different in person—bigger, and harder, and to her panicked eyes, the Agent of Doom embodied in a dark suit, white shirt, red and blue tie, and black wingtips. He was young to have the position of Special Agent in Charge in an FBI field office, no more than early thirties. He was olive-complexioned, his hair dark brown, his eyes light blue, with a lean, rangy runner's body.

She didn't move from the open doorway. "You're Georgie's father?"

He stuck out his hand and she automatically shook it. A really strong hand that could twist her small .22 around her fingers, and laugh. "Bowie Richards. Ah, do you have a few minutes, Ms. Pulaski? It seems I'm badly in need of your help."

She couldn't let him in, he'd see all the Culovort pages, all the stuff she'd copied off the Internet about drug company scandals. All her work sheets were still spread out haphazardly on the dining room table.

It wouldn't take him more than two seconds to realize he'd walked right in on a potential murder suspect. Five minutes later and all those damning pages would have been in folders and tucked away. Her good luck was indeed now traveling south at warp speed.

Erin said, "Sorry, but I can't let you in. I just sprayed for bugs and the smell's toxic. I'm sure you can smell it from here so don't breathe deeply. I just took off my mask. Let me step out into the hallway." She closed the door behind her.

Erin smiled at him brightly. "What about Georgie?"

Bowie wondered what was going on here. He hadn't smelled a thing. If she'd worn a mask, where were the marks on her face? Why didn't she want to let him in? Ah, there was probably a guy in there, and she didn't want him to be seen. But why? Maybe because the guy was married?

He leaned against the hallway wall, crossed his arms over his chest. The pose was intimidating, only he didn't realize it. Erin stood in front of him, her hands stuck in her jeans pockets, wondering what demon convinced her to work at home this morning, and prayed.

"My daughter is always talking about you, Ms. Pulaski. She told me you walked in the first day of class and announced to all the children and their parents that your name was Erin Pulaski and you were a Polish-Irish-American. I laughed at that, and so Georgie kept repeating it, at least half a dozen more times. I believe she's repeated every word out of your mouth. I suppose I feel like I know you and so that's why I came to you. I know I can trust you."

What? Talk about a leap. If only he had a clue.

He said, "You know, I really didn't smell anything. Surely it would be okay now inside your apartment."

Not going to happen, buddy.

When she said nothing, he plowed onward. "Well, I guess the hallway is just fine. I am Georgie's dad, not an imposter."

"I know who you are. I recognized you from TV. You're an FBI agent."

He nodded, then raked his fingers through his hair. "Oh, yes, I forgot how many TV guys were at the crime scene."

"A dead guy found behind a company

headquarters surely isn't an everyday occurrence in Connecticut."

"That's for sure. It also means it's going to be very difficult for a while, which is why I'm here. Like I said, I desperately need your help, Ms. Pulaski."

"With Georgie? Is there a problem? Can't she make her ballet class tomorrow?"

He shook his head. "No, it's not that. Frankly, I've run out of options. I could be called away on this case at any time, and I was hoping, praying, actually, that maybe you could help me take care of her for a while when she's not in school, maybe come to my house for a few days. Georgie always talks about you being a dancer, like that's what you do for a living, and I thought—"

At her utterly bewildered look, he said, "Ah, you're not only a ballet teacher, are you? You also have a full-time job, and you don't have the time or the inclination to take care of a little girl?"

"That's right. Teaching ballet is a hobby for me, Agent Richards."

"What do you do for a living, Ms. Pulaski?"

"I'm a private investigator, Agent Richards."

He looked at her like she'd suddenly sprouted devil's horns. She supposed he'd expected her to say anything but that. She knew what she looked like, a beanpole in jeans and a white T-shirt, boots that brought her to nearly six feet, and nearly to his eye level, her plain brown hair in a thick French braid. Long silver hoops dangled from her ears.

"You know," she said patiently, "as in people hire me to solve difficult personal problems? Don't you know any private investigators, Agent Richards?"

"Well, yes, one guy in New York City. I think he was beat up last month by a husband who caught him spying on him and his mistress."

She didn't rise to that juicy bait. "Then you know we're self-employed and work long hard hours if we want to feed ourselves. Unlike you, I don't have a government job that pays me whether or not I show up. Sorry, that sounded snippy. What's wrong with Georgie's mother?"

"She died some time ago."

Erin had known that. Oh dear. "I'm sorry. She has a nanny, right?"

"Yes, but Glynn's had surgery and her

mother came and took her back to Boston until she's well again."

"And you made no plans for this?"

"I should have said it was emergency surgery. Of course I have backups, but none of them is available."

And I'm dead in the water, she could read that conclusion plainly in his eyes. "I have no one to take care of Georgie. Actually, Glynn mentioned you, said you liked Georgie and dealt really well with her. I thought maybe, since you weren't married and Georgie really likes you that—sorry."

And he tipped his head at her. "Forgive me for bothering you." As he turned and strode off down the hall, Erin called out, "Wait. Wait a minute, let me see what I can come up with."

He jerked around on his booted feet, a look of hope on his hard face.

"Wait out here a moment, let me straighten up."

I will shoot myself later, a nice clean head shot, get myself out of my misery once and for all.

4

CHEVY CHASE, MARYLAND
Sunday night

"That's got to be the weirdest thing I've ever seen," Sherlock whispered against Savich's ear.

They stared at something filmy white floating through the trees, not quite opaque, not quite transparent—"otherworldly" was the word the senator used, Savich recalled and dismissed the thought immediately. He very strongly doubted it was anything like ectoplasm manifesting itself in the small knot of woods at the back of Senator David Hoffman's backyard in Chevy Chase, Maryland. With all the wickedness in the world, it was far more likely the senator's specter was what he'd described to them—a swatch of carefully cut feathery material about the size of a standard pillow.

They watched the white object move slowly toward the house, pausing every few seconds, as if the person feeding out the wire it was attached to was having some difficulties. *Open mind,* Savich thought, since he really couldn't tell what it was.

"It appears outside my bedroom window," the senator had told him and Sherlock that morning as they sat in front of his impressive desk in his elegant home office, his voice low, strained, as if he knew even saying this out loud would bring ridicule down on his head. He cleared his throat, his eyes darting to Sherlock's curly red hair, then beyond her to the bookcases that lined the wall. Sherlock followed his gaze. "You see something, Senator?"

"What? Oh, no, Agent, I was just thinking I should read some of those books. Do you know they came with the house? I've never touched them." He shook his head. "This house has been my local residence for nine years now. That's not right."

Savich said, "Senator, this thing you see dangling outside your bedroom window, what exactly does it do?"

"It simply flitters around," the senator said. "Back and forth, then it sometimes just floats or billows a bit. The first time I woke up and saw it, I thought I was having some sort of weird hallucination, but it just kept dancing around. I got out of bed and walked to the window, I was scared, I'll admit it. Whatever it was just continued to float up in front of me, then it was gone, from one moment to the next"—he snapped his fingers— "it simply vanished. I stood there and waited for it to come back, but it didn't. I was convinced I'd dreamed it, that, or it was the consequences of too many oysters—until it happened again."

"How many times has this thing appeared?" Sherlock asked.

"A dozen times now, I've counted them. Actually, I've written each occurrence down in this notebook." He tossed a small brown leather notebook back into his desk drawer. "If I was going crazy, I wanted to be able to show the course of my mental deterioration." He gave a quiet laugh. "Now, I simply lie in my bed and watch the thing dance around until it disappears after ten minutes or so. I've timed it. And every single time, the thing is there one instant, gone the next."

Savich asked, "How does it wake you up?"

"I'll be dead to the world, then I hear this sort of huffing noise, like a person trying to suck in a breath, and it's loud enough, insistent enough, to wake me up. The draperies are open and there the thing is, dancing outside the window. I really can't give you a simpler description of how it acts."

Sherlock said, "Can you see through it?"

He shook his head, his eyes again on her hair. Sherlock cocked her head at him.

"Sorry," Hoffman said. "My wife—her hair was red, not as beautiful as yours, Agent Sherlock, but it was bright and warrior fierce, even curlier than yours."

Warrior fierce, Savich liked that.

"Thank you, Senator," Sherlock said.

"The thing is, I can't exactly see through it in the dark, but it isn't exactly solid either. It's sort of filmy, like one of those very fine old linen nightgowns or a thick wedding veil, and like I said, about the size of a pillowcase."

A pillowcase certainly makes it sound earthbound. Savich said, "Senator, have you tried sleeping in another bedroom?"

He shook his head, his deep voice austere. "It has never been in me to run and hide, Agent Savich. This is my bedroom, my house. No ridiculous manifestation or whatever it is, is going to scare me away. I will, however, admit to taking sleeping pills once. It still woke me, that huffing noise, it went on and on."

"Have you told anyone about this manifestation?"

"Yes, my aide, Corliss Rydle. Corlie won't say anything to anyone for the simple reason that she doesn't want the crazy squad to come cart me away. That would mean temporary unemployment for everyone, including her.

"She insisted on spending several nights, in a sleeping bag right by the window. The thing didn't show. She then took her sleeping bag outside, maybe fifteen feet from my bedroom. Again, it didn't show.

"She talked me into hiring a private investigator to watch the house at night, telling him I was concerned about being stalked. Nothing out of the ordinary happened when he was there, either."

"Who else besides Corliss Rydle knows?" Sherlock asked as she put a check in her small notebook beside the woman's name.

"My two sons. I called them both over here after it had appeared about a half-dozen times. I told them about it, all very straightforward I was, because, to be honest here, I wanted to see their reactions. I remember they looked at each other like, *The old man's losing it, and what the hell are we going to do?* But they also insisted on camping out several nights in the backyard, but again, the thing didn't appear. I think they believe I'm teetering on the edge."

Savich said, "Have you ever gotten a sense of why this is happening, any signs of any sort to alert you to the meaning of all this? And the huffing sound that wakes you, have you ever heard it without the manifestation appearing?"

The senator shook his head, then paused. He raised pain-glazed eyes. "Oh, yes, I've heard that sound. When my wife was very ill, she couldn't breathe well. She made that same huffing sound. I'd sit by her bed and listen. I often counted how many times she had to make that sound in a five-minute period to stay alive. It was horrible, and this has brought it all back." He paused a moment. "The sound disappeared when she slipped into a coma and the respirator breathed for her."

Savich continued, "Have you ever felt this thing, whatever it is, was trying to communicate with you?"

Hoffman's dark eyes cut to Savich's face. He grew very still. Slowly, he shook his head. "I'll tell you, after the sixth or seventh time it appeared, I wasn't so freaked out. And I started talking to it. I asked it what it was doing here, asked if it wanted anything. All it ever did was move around, near the limits of my vision. I'll tell you, I felt like such a fool. I never approached it again, simply watched it from my bed."

Sherlock asked him, "Have you investigated it in any other way?"

"Do you mean have I climbed in the oak tree beside my window to see if there are any remnants of rope or footprints or broken branches? Yes, the private investigator did that. He found nothing. Neither did Corlie or my sons." He began turning the elegant gold Mont Blanc pen over and over between his fingers, frowning at it. "I did tell another person, my best friend outside of politics, actually. We're both avid golfers. We play golf every Saturday we can get together."

"His name, Senator?"

Hoffman's dark eyes slid over Sherlock's bright hair a moment, then he said, "Gabe Hilliard. He owns half a dozen security firms around the country, one of them here in D.C. I've known him forever. He's an excellent friend, rock-solid. He'll never tell anyone about this. Like me, he has no clue what's going on, but he's concerned."

Sherlock wrote down his name and particulars.

"I told you about Gabe just because you want all names of those I've confided in. You're thinking it makes sense that one possible explanation behind all this is someone gaslighting me. Maybe, but I can't think of anyone with a motive."

Savich asked, "Are both your sons financially secure?"

The senator said, "They assure me their finances are in order for the moment, even though their wives wiped the floor with them. I haven't personally checked their portfolios. I can't imagine their lying to me about money since if either of them had financial problems, they'd come running, you can bet your Porsche on that, Agent Savich. Beautiful machine, by the way."

Savich smiled.

Sherlock said, "Unfortunately, Senator, both of your sons *are* hurting financially. Yet you say neither has come asking for help?"

"No, neither of them. I should have assumed you'd know everything about me and my family before you set foot in my house. So the little blighters have run through the interest on their trust funds, have they? And their quite generous salaries? Thank God for their families that my lawyer convinced me to protect the principal until they're both fifty." He tapped the pen on the beautiful mahogany desktop. "Three years ago, I told them they were adults, and it was time they acted like adults. There would be no more handouts, they were to be responsible for themselves and their families, it was past time for them to be men.

"You're thinking they may have rigged up a ghost to scare me out of my wits? So they could declare me incompetent, get their hands on my money? I'm enough of a cynic to be effective in the world, Agent Sherlock, but I can't believe that of my sons. In fact, I wouldn't be at all surprised if they haven't told others about their crazy old man over an expensive glass of white wine. Neither of them could keep a confidence if their marriages depended on it. Let me say they're both divorced, twice, so I rest my case."

The sons, Savich knew, Aiden and Benson, had grown up with too much money and not enough boundaries, and, as Sherlock had noted on her background check before they'd come to the senator's home, they both appeared to be dogs when it came to marital constancy.

"And my sons certainly have a solid motive, I can see that. I guess there's no one else besides Aiden and Benson with any kind of motive." He sat back in his big chair, steepled his fingers.

"Agents, my sons are both prosaic thinkers. They see something they want and they think, 'I want that,' and they head for it like a guided missile. This situation—it is inventive, creative, wouldn't you say? Shows resourcefulness and ingenuity?"

Savich nodded.

"To be brutally honest here, my sons couldn't hatch up a creative idea between them no matter how much money was at stake."

Savich said, "You're saying then that if your sons were broke and had to have money, they'd simply come over here and shoot you in the head?"

The senator laughed. "Quite an image, Agent Savich. But that isn't what they'd do either. They would probably come over and beg. If they're behind this manifestation, believe me, someone else came up with the idea, someone else is driving them, telling them what to do." He shook his head decisively. "Neither of them is fashioned in the right mold to pull this off."

"The right mold?"

Hoffman nodded to Savich. "All they like to think about is sailing, eating clams on the beach with as many scantily clad women as they can attract, and jetting off to Milan to buy their next Armani suit or sports car. They have jobs because the presidents of both companies are longtime friends of mine. As far as I can tell, their lives are pretty much a waste. I say that with great sadness. As their father, I must bear the responsibility, and I do. My wife and I did try, we did. What went wrong? What could we have done differently? I've asked myself that question many times, but I just don't know."

No boundaries, too much money, Savich thought again, and wondered why the obvious answer didn't hit the senator between the eyes.

"Their saving grace is that between them, they've produced three smart kids, all by their first wives, two boys and one girl. All three are hard workers who'll amount to something." The senator sat back and sighed. "However, I have to stand by what I said. This simply isn't like my sons, and their well-developed survival instincts wouldn't allow them to hire anyone to do it."

Savich asked, "Has this manifestation appeared anywhere else, sir? Like outside your office window in the Hart Office Building?"

The senator laid down the pen and raised his eyes to Savich's face. "No. Only here. Only around midnight, only outside my bedroom window. I will be honest here, Agents, I have no more thoughts or suspicions, no more obvious avenues to try."

Hoffman sat back in his big chair. "Like all my legislative colleagues, I have made a great many enemies, as well as a great many friends. I imagine that a couple dozen of my political opponents would gladly see me retired, but to try to drive me crazy? Hmm." He grinned as he shook his head. "Nah, not at all likely.

"That's why I called you, Agent Savich. You were recommended to me by Director Mueller because you've studied things, even experienced things, that can't be easily explained, and dealt with people and events that are frankly—bizarre.

"If there's the possibility that this—thing—is, well, otherworldly, I thought you might be the best person to help me."

Savich knew Hoffman sat rock solid in the center of the political spectrum, always trying to draw the extremes toward him. *I represent the great intelligent American majority*, he'd say. He knew Hoffman was smart, something of a hardnose. He was rarely mealy-mouthed or equivocal when asked a question, like the vast majority of politicians. He wasn't known to spin an answer or evade or immediately blame someone else. Not the kind of person you would expect to start hallucinating or have a mental breakdown.

He was a tall man, slender and fit, and had celebrated his sixty-eighth birthday two months earlier. His eyes, a bit slanted at the corners, were a foggy gray, intense eyes that bespoke power, the doling out of favors as well as punishments. He imagined Hoffman looked quite natural and in complete control of his world in that big executive chair before this happened. But today, this morning, he looked bone weary, a man on the edge. He couldn't keep his hands still.

Savich rose. "I'd like to see your bedroom."

5

As the three of them walked up the wide oak staircase, Savich said, "Have you told anyone about our coming to see you this morning, Senator?"

Hoffman shook his head. "I told Corlie I had a meeting with some friends at the house. I said nothing to anyone else. I suppose Director Mueller knows, since I spoke to him about you, but that's it."

Savich nodded. "I'm relieved you haven't been intimidated, Senator, that you refuse to be frightened out of your own bedroom, because I very much want you to sleep in your own bed tonight."

"I was thinking you and Agent Sherlock would want to sleep in my bedroom."

"No, we'll be in the backyard. We're going to try to come in unseen. Do you have any staff living in?"

"No. The housekeeper, Mrs. Romano, and the cook, Mrs. Hatfield, both leave at five unless I'm entertaining, then they stay."

"Be sure they don't know anyone will be coming tonight, all right?"

Senator Hoffman nodded.

The master bedroom looked like a monk's cell, big, white, stark, and sparsely furnished. *Too much empty space,* Sherlock thought as she ran her fingers over the black leather easy chair in the sitting area, which was dominated by a television large enough to service a small theater. The king-size bed had a simple dark blue coverlet over it, no pillows or accessories of any kind. There was a large plain dresser, and one additional chair, perhaps used by the senator when he put on his shoes in the morning. There wasn't a single painting on the stark white walls, not a single knickknack in view except for a beautiful, very feminine jewelry box on top of the dresser. She watched Dillon walk over to the windows, and brought the senator's attention back to her. "The jewelry box, sir, was it your wife's?"

He started to say yes, then swallowed and simply nodded. Dreadful pain there still, it hadn't faded, even after three years. When she'd first met Dillon and someone would mention his deceased father, Buck Savich, she remembered the same flash of pain in his eyes. She wanted to tell him it would fade into soft memories, as hers had with her sister Belinda. She asked, "How long were you married, Senator?"

"Thirty-nine years. Her name was Nikki. She was only sixty-one when she died. She promised me she'd make her birthday, and she did, barely. But you know this already, Agent Sherlock. The director told me the two of you never went into anything blind if you had a choice. And, yes, I've heard of MAX, Savich's laptop that he's programmed to do pretty much everything but call the Redskins' games. I'll bet if I wore toenail polish, you'd know the color and the brand."

"I'm very glad that you don't," she said, and smiled up at him. Again he looked at her hair and his breathing hitched. She lightly laid her fingertips on his forearm, offering, she hoped, some hope and comfort.

He wasn't big and muscular like Dillon, but she'd bet he was stronger than he looked, this aristocratic man who was older than her father, a federal judge who still terrorized defense attorneys. He seemed both very human and infinitely sane. She liked him.

When Dillon came away from the window, he smiled at her and nodded toward the door. "We're done here, Senator."

"Did you see anything, Agent Savich?"

"A very nice backyard, Senator. The woods, how far back do they go?"

"They're not that deep. The brick wall continues all the way around the property. There are two gates, one in the front and a smaller one in the back for the garbage people and repair people who come in on a narrow access road running alongside it."

A perfect place, Sherlock thought, drive right in, and pull out your gate key—oh, yes, whoever was behind this had a gate key—and set up this elaborate gaslight charade. She gave the senator's bedroom one last look. She realized now what he'd done. All the bareness, all the absence of any mementoes of their life, except for his wife's jewelry box, he'd simply moved everything out, and not replaced it with anything of himself. After three years, it was still too soon.

Sherlock and Savich stopped a moment on the wide front veranda of the colonial mansion and enjoyed the morning sun shining down on the colorful flowerbeds lining the front of the house. It was early September and the trees were still full and lush.

Sherlock asked him, "Sir, are you seeing anyone socially?"

He looked startled, and then she saw a tightening around his mouth. "Not really," he said, again looking at her hair. "Well, yes, occasionally, I see Janine Koffer, she's Lane Koffer's widow, you know, the former secretary of state? He died two years ago. Prostate cancer."

He slept with her, Savich thought, and it made sense. Washington, he'd learned over the years, was a very lonely place, despite the scores of young people bursting its seams with their undisciplined boundless energy, their still unfocused ambitions.

If you were smart, you took your comfort where it wouldn't come back to bite you in the butt.

Savich and Sherlock shook Hoffman's hand. "Please do what you normally do, Senator," Savich said, "and remember, don't breathe a word of our coming tonight to anyone, Corliss Rydle, your cook, Mrs. Koffer, anyone."

"All right. When will you come tonight?"

Savich shook his hand. "I'd just as soon you didn't know any more than you do now, sir. But we'll be here."

6

"I saw it come from behind those oak trees," Sherlock said, pointing, "moving slowly, hesitantly, like it didn't know where it wanted to go. But look now, it's moving fast, in a straight line to the senator's bedroom window."

Savich said, "I'd hoped it would come down from the roof."

"Easier to yank up, you mean? For the instant vanishing act?"

"It seems the easiest way for human hands to control it." Savich raised his cell phone, zoomed in, and snapped several pictures of the apparition fast approaching the second-floor bedroom window. They watched it close in, then simply hang there a moment before it began moving about, billowing, then dancing up and down.

"You know it's got to be human hands, Dillon, given that enthusiastic performance," Sherlock whispered. "I'd say a standard-size pillowcase, like the senator said, a whole lot of thread count, very fine material, probably Italian."

"Let's go find how they're doing this," Savich said, took her hand, and turned into the woods. They stopped cold at odd huffing sounds from behind them, like someone trying to breathe, Savich thought, like the senator's dying wife trying to breathe. It seemed to be coming from the house. The senator had nailed the sound.

"There must be some wires, something." Sherlock adjusted her night-vision goggles. She always kept her feet planted on terra firma. "I'll bet you're thinking it's someone in the family, too, admit it. Family—it's depressing. Cursed money, it's behind too much bad in this world.

"I'm glad whoever's behind this believed it was just fine to perform tonight. I don't see a wire or anything, do you, Dillon?"

They stood quietly at the spot where the apparition had floated out of the woods, staring up, looking for a wire, anything. "Not yet," he whispered.

As she scanned the trees, she whispered back, "I wonder how the person responsible for this ghost performance plans to get the senator's money? Surely he or she doesn't expect the senator to die of fright or run screaming to an asylum, so they can pronounce him incompetent? And why would he flip out now if he hasn't already? Why keep it up? Sounds like a real long shot to me."

They combed through the oak and maple trees. No wire in sight.

"So it's a very fine wire, or could the whole thing be radio controlled? But it has to originate from somewhere, somewhere in sight," she said.

Savich opened the back gate that gave onto the small access road at the back of the property. When they'd left the senator's house that morning, they'd checked the area behind the property. They saw only the same two crushed empty beer cans, the same half-dozen cigarette butts.

There was no sign of anyone or any sort

of vehicle, no sign of any mechanism they could see orchestrating the flight of the dancing pillowcase.

"I don't get it," Sherlock said. "Where is it?"

Savich paused, became perfectly still and focused. He heard the sounds of the night—a single owl hooting, crickets and cicadas clicking, rustling bushes as small animals moved through. He became aware of the air, warm and soft against his skin, an early fall feel to it, promising change, but not here just yet. Then suddenly the air seemed curiously charged, like a live wire sparking against his cheek. The air seemed to have tangible weight now, physically pushing against him. Now what was this all about? Then the air stilled and became warm once again, and he would swear the sounds of the small varmints scurrying around in the woods became louder.

They walked back toward the house, but saw nothing. It was gone. He whispered against Sherlock's ear, her curly hair tickling his mouth, "I'm thinking this whole thing has nothing at all to do with the senator's wastrel sons. I think it's about something else entirely."

"You think it's maybe some sort of hologram? But who's projecting it, and from where?"

He shook his head against her hair. "No, our manifestation isn't a hologram."

"Please, Dillon, don't tell me you think it's really woo woo."

"Well, there's something different happening here," Savich said, and kissed her ear. "We'll just have to see."

Sherlock rubbed her arms even though the night was warm. "You think it's the dead wife, don't you? You think it's Nikki?"

He nodded. "I felt as if something or someone is trying to communicate. It would seem the senator isn't able to understand. But it keeps trying. His wife, Nikki? Maybe."

Sherlock said, "But we're here and it was here as well. If it is Nikki, you think she came because she thought you could help? You'd recognize who and what she was?"

"All good questions. It's been over fifteen minutes, and there's nothing here now. Let's go home."

"Dillon, there's something I don't understand." She was frowning toward the senator's bedroom window.

He waited, his fingers rubbing the back of her hand.

"I would expect you to see it. But what about me? I've never seen anything. But I saw it too, clear as day."

"So did the senator."

7

GEORGETOWN
WASHINGTON, D.C.
Monday morning

Savich was wide awake at two a.m., listening to Sherlock's even breathing, wondering if a ghost was going to come tell him a story.

Nikki, where are you? I saw you, you let both Sherlock and me see you. Were you trying to tell me something about the senator? Is there some sort of trouble heading his way?

There was nothing from Nikki.

He finally fell into a surprisingly deep sleep and didn't stir until the alarm went off at six-thirty a.m.

He opened his eyes to see Sherlock, on her elbow above him, staring down at him. He shook his head. She leaned down to kiss him when—

"Papa, Mama, you're still in bed! Gabby will be here soon and I've got to be ready for her to take me to the Gumby Exhibition."

The Gumby Exhibition at the Throckmorton Center didn't open until ten o'clock. Sherlock grinned at her son standing in the doorway wearing only SpongeBob SquarePants pajama bottoms, his black hair as tousled as his father's. He was so beautiful it made her heart ache. "I'll be right in to help you, Sean. Go brush your teeth."

When she heard him whoop down the hallway, Sherlock kissed her husband, and cupped his face between her hands. "Stop worrying about it. Things always happen when they're supposed to."

He surely hoped so.

What he didn't expect was anything to happen in the middle of an emergency meeting that morning with Mr. Maitland and

Eurydice Flanders, known as Dice to her federal lawyer colleagues, a fifteen-year veteran of FBI headquarters here in Washington.

"Dillon, how's tricks?"

Savich shook her hand and sat down beside her. He thought about the wonderful nine and a half minutes he'd had that morning with Sherlock before Sean came back, his teeth brushed, and raring to go. "Tricks are good, Dice. What's up, sir?"

"Early this morning a pair of runners found a murdered man in Van Wie Park, in Stone Bridge, Connecticut. That's federal land and makes it ours. The dead guy's name is Helmut Blauvelt, and he's a German national. We haven't released any information on him yet to the media. He's been employed for the past ten years by Schiffer Hartwin Pharmaceutical, reports directly to the director, Adler Dieffendorf."

Dice asked, "What do you know about Schiffer Hartwin Pharmaceutical, Savich?"

"They're one of the largest drug companies in the world. Family owned, established back in the late nineteenth century, in Hartwin, Germany. Very profitable."

Dice nodded. "They're also very powerful and well connected locally. They employ close to forty thousand people worldwide."

Mr. Maitland rubbed the faint black stubble on his chin. "Bowie Richards, our New Haven SAC, called me this morning after he'd identified the man, asked me if we had any interest in him or his employer, the Schiffer Hartwin Pharmaceutical company.

"We didn't until I found out about this Herr Helmut Blauvelt. Okay, Dice, tell Savich what we know about him."

Dice was tall and leggy, with blond hair cut in a sharp wedge, and was smarter than she probably deserved to be. She sat forward and sniffed. "You smell very hot, Dillon. Did Sherlock buy you some new cologne?"

"Dice, focus, please," said Maitland. "Hey, my wife bought me some new cologne and you didn't say anything."

"Very fruity, sir. I like it." She gave him a big grin, then sobered, and continued in her slow sweet southern drawl that camouflaged a knife-sharp brain. "Okay, Dillon, here's the deal. Helmut Blauvelt wasn't just any employee, he was Schiffer

Hartwin's main problem-solver and troubleshooter, their Mr. Fix-It, for over a decade now. The directors sent him all over the world, wherever there was a possible threat to the company, whether it was local union problems, suppliers reneging on contracts, or politicians asking for kickbacks. He was apparently very good at it, that is—poof—problems gone. His methods included bribery and violence. Of course, there's no real proof, especially since he rarely spent much time in any one jurisdiction or country. But there were enough questions asked for Interpol to have a file on him."

"But is he a killer, Dice? And if so, how come there's no proof of that?"

"Not as such, but the word is, folks have disappeared—in Africa, in Egypt, in England. Mostly we think he strong-arms, intimidates, and strikes deals the company can't publicly avow. And now he's dead, murdered on our soil. As of yet, his bosses in Germany haven't made a peep. Bowie called them a couple of hours ago. I suppose they've got to figure out how to respond to the murder of their Mr. Fix-It right here in the U.S. of A.

"We naturally wonder what he was here to fix. Or who. And how this ties in with the company. And that is why you and I are both here at the get-go, Dillon."

Savich said, "Tell me you have some ideas."

"Well, no, sorry," said Dice. "This murder is wide open. But believe me, the director wants to find out, and that's why Mr. Maitland brought you into it."

Maitland said, "Dice said they hadn't let out a peep. Well, they did, a loud one, just before I walked in here. They called Bowie back to inform him they're sending over a German Federal Intelligence Service agent from the BND to represent them in the investigation."

"Sounds like the corporate office wants to put a lid on it," Savich said.

"I would like to agree with you," Maitland said, "but our Legat in Berlin says this guy—Agent Andreas Kesselring—has the reputation of being a straight arrow in Germany, and he has an exemplary record.

"He'll be arriving at JFK tomorrow afternoon. Bowie Richards will be sending a car to fetch him."

Dice's left eyebrow shot up. "Don't you

want Savich to pick up Kesselring, since he's going to head the investigation in Stone Bridge? Get an up close and personal feel for the guy?"

Maitland said, looking over Dice's left shoulder, "Savich isn't really going to head up the investigation."

Dice went on red alert. "Why, for heaven's sake?"

"You should know that Bowie Richard's family and Vice President Valenti's family are close. Really close."

Just dandy, Savich thought, a SAC with juice and a German federal agent, both. Not to mention a multinational pharmaceutical house with as much money and resources as the FBI.

"Look, guys, it's the hand we've got to play. I know you'll deal well with Bowie Richards, Savich. Here's a couple of photos of Helmut Blauvelt." Maitland slid over two five-by-sevens.

Dice took one look at the photo and quickly closed her eyes. "Eeew, he's got no face left. Why would someone do this to him?"

The dead man looked middle-aged from the clumps of bloody brownish gray hair still on his head, Savich thought, and Dice was right, someone had whaled on him and hadn't stopped. And why was that?

Dice kept her eyes on Maitland's face. "This overkill, it makes no sense. One blow and he's dead. Was it to keep him from being identified? That might have been true fifty years ago, but give me a break. Surely the murderer had to know we'd still be able to identify him."

Maitland said, "In addition to smashing his face beyond recognition, the killer also cut off his fingers, so no fingerprints. It wasn't as if the killer didn't try.

"Savich, I called Bowie, told him I was sending you and Sherlock. He wasn't all that happy. More resigned, I guess you'd say. Do you know him?"

"I met him once at Quantico, maybe three years ago. I remember he's got a little girl who's about two years older than Sean."

Dice carefully turned over the photo of Helmut Blauvelt. "Now I think about it, I remember hearing his wife died a few years ago. Wasn't she killed driving drunk, something like that?"

Maitland nodded. "Let's just say it was

bad and leave it at that. Bowie's a cracker and a bulldog. Try to work with him, Savich, not go through him. I don't want to hear about any calls from Vice President Valenti to Director Mueller."

Dice Flanders shoved her tortoiseshell glasses up on her nose. "When you and Sherlock bring down the bad guys, sugar, you be sure and ask them what the devil Schiffer Hartwin's bad boy was doing here, won't you?"

"You can count on it, Dice," Savich said.

"Well, if that's it," Maitland said, motioned for Savich to take the photos, and stood. "Any questions, funnel them through me. Savich, hang on a minute."

As Dice Flanders passed him, she patted his face. "I sure liked hearing you play your guitar at the Bonhomie Club last week. Your new country western tune nearly made me weep. If I weren't old enough to be your mama, I'd give Sherlock a run for her money."

Savich laughed. "Sherlock wrote it."

"Talented girl, curse her," Dice said, and gave a little wave as she walked out of the conference room. "You guys take care of this mess, all right? And be careful."

The air changed around Savich, became heavy, pressed against his face, as if charged somehow, just as it had the previous night in Chevy Chase in the senator's backyard. *Nikki? Please, not just yet. Come back later.*

The air immediately softened. Savich was aware that Mr. Maitland was talking to him. "Savich, bring your brain back to the party. Where'd you go?"

Savich shook his head, smiled, wondering how he'd looked in those seconds. Had his lips moved? Surely not. "Just an errant thought, sir."

Maitland said, "Savich, you and Sherlock need to be on an FBI helicopter in two hours. Pack some clothes, I don't know how long you guys will have to be there. You'll be staying at the Norman Bates Inn in Stone Bridge proper—yeah, someone's got a twisted sense of humor there, but it's the closest lodging. Schiffer Hartwin's U.S.A. headquarters is located at the edge of Stone Bridge, Van Wie Park right behind it. You need anything, call me or Dice. Keep us in the loop, every step."

Savich barely made it back to his office when he picked up a faint jasmine scent.

He turned his back to his office door and looked out his open window to the small park across the street. He smiled at the sight of Old Sal feeding her pigeons. She must have gotten her Social Security check. He said, “Tell me what’s going on with your husband, Nikki.”

There was no answering voice in his mind. But he felt a pressure in the air against him. He didn’t speak again, he thought, *Why were you coming to your husband, Nikki? What’s wrong?*

The answer came high and frantic. *Danger. David’s in such danger. He doesn’t understand, doesn’t realize what will happen to him. You’ve got to stop it, you’ve got to, he can’t—*

His office door opened and Ollie Hamish, his second in command, stepped in. It was as if the air itself whooshed out of the room.

“Savich, I—hey, I’m sorry to disturb you, I can leave.”

It didn’t matter, she was gone. Savich said easily, “No problem, Ollie. I just wanted to tell you Sherlock and I are going to Stone Bridge, Connecticut, to investigate the murder of a German national.”

"Yeah, I heard."

"This place is five million square feet," Savich said, shaking his head, "but when it comes to buzz, you'd think you were in a tree house, word gets around so fast. I just found out about it myself."

Ollie grinned. "The good stuff always spreads like a grease fire, you know that. Ruth was in the women's room and in comes Dice Flanders, humming the song you sang at the Bonhomie Club. Ruth asked her what she was doing on the fifth floor and Dice told her a bit about this Helmut Blauvelt mutilation murder."

Savich had to smile. "The men's room is gossip central too. Okay, before Sherlock and I head out, let's talk about the Hoven killings in Jefferson City."

8

STONE BRIDGE, CONNECTICUT
Monday afternoon

Special Agent in Charge Bowie Richards, too young for his position, some said, stood beside Savich and Sherlock and the M.E., Dr. Ella Franks. Together they looked down at the devastated corpse of a middle-aged man laid out on the morgue table in a stark white room in the basement of Stone Bridge Memorial Hospital. His face and head were a bloody pulp. Dr. Franks had pulled a green sheet down to his chest.

Savich said, "Tell us what happened to him, Dr. Franks."

"This was no crime of passion. Whoever killed this man was cold-blooded and methodical. He used the proverbial blunt instrument and swung with a great deal of power, one hard hit first, to the back of the head, the kill blow. His skull was crushed in and he was dead before he hit the ground. But the killer didn't stop there." She pointed to various shattered bones on the man's smashed face. "You can see how the blows are carefully placed to the same areas on both sides, to destroy the facial bones and eye sockets." She lifted the sheet to show his arms and hands. "His killer cut off his fingers as well, in clean strokes with a smooth metal blade. It was probably to keep us from identifying him, but as it turns out, it wasn't a problem. We managed to get his identity fast because of Bowie." Ella gave him a fat smile, and nodded at him.

Bowie said, "I recognized the dental work wasn't American and called a dentist friend of mine who'd served a tour of duty abroad. He came over and immediately recognized the dentistry as German. We started searching through the middle-aged males who'd come into the country from Germany during the past three days, and Blauvelt popped up right away. The German BND helped us access his digital X-rays, and they were a match."

Sherlock said, "Good work, Bowie. Dr. Franks, have you done a tox screen on him? Any drugs on board?"

Dr. Franks said, "No, not a single aspirin in his system. That's a bit of a ha-ha since he worked for a drug company. Now, I have learned a number of interesting things about him. First, his stomach contents revealed that Helmut ate a lovely dinner about three hours before his death—oyster and caviar appetizers followed by stuffed venison, julienned potatoes and carrots and radicchio, accompanied by red wine. There's only one restaurant in our immediate vicinity that serves all that stuff under one roof."

She gave them a big smile.

Bowie said, "That would be Chez Pierre in Monmouth, ten miles west of Stone Bridge. I was hoping Helmut dined with his killer."

Dr. Franks lowered the pale green sheet. "Now look at this." They stared down at an inflamed, five-inch scar low on his abdomen. "Helmut Blauvelt's bosses didn't even give him a chance to heal from an appendectomy before they shipped him over here. I'd say his appendix didn't come out more than five days ago."

Sherlock said, "I wonder what was so urgent that it couldn't wait another week or so?"

"There was obviously something he had to fix," Bowie said, "something he had to fix immediately. Tell them what else you have, Ella."

Dr. Franks said, "Helmut didn't die in situ, there wasn't enough blood. I found threads of wool on his skin, which means that whoever killed him stripped him, then wrapped him in a blanket and moved him."

Bowie said, "Which means the killer hauled him out and dumped him in those thick bushes in Van Wie Park, took all his clothes, his shoes, anything that identified him."

Sherlock said, "Herr Blauvelt is good-sized. I can see a strong woman bashing him, but carrying all that dead weight? Not likely. But I don't get it—why didn't the killer simply bury him deep in the woods, where he wouldn't be found, if keeping his identity a secret was so important?"

They all pondered that. Bowie said, "Maybe he didn't have the time or the opportunity. When we get him, we'll ask."

Savich said, "I wonder what the killer did with his clothes."

"I've still got agents out looking. Nothing yet."

"Any clue where he was staying?"

"Not so far. Agents are checking all the hotels, inns, and motels within a ten-mile radius. So far, nothing on Helmut Blauvelt checking in anywhere. Of course, he could have used an alias, a fake credit card. Or he could have been staying with someone, maybe the same person who killed him. And that means starting interviews with all the Schiffer Hartwin executives."

Savich said, "Yeah, it sounds reasonable he might have been staying with the big muckety-mucks here in Stone Bridge. You've spoken to the CEO, Caskie Royal?"

Bowie nodded. "Which brings up the break-in of Caskie Royal's office late last night. Some coincidence, huh? Well, it turns out Royal showed up while the thief was there. The commotion alerted the guard, and he was the one who called the cops, not Royal. I wonder if Royal would have called at all since he wasn't alone. His production manager, Carla Alvarez, was with him. To work, he told me. The guard, when I spoke to him, didn't say a word about it, stayed stone-faced. I haven't spoken yet to Alvarez, but I've seen a picture. I'd guess they were there to visit his sofa.

"Royal was insistent when I spoke to him this morning that nothing was missing, and that he has no idea who it was. He claims his arrival must have thwarted the thief from taking anything."

"I wonder who broke into his office," Sherlock said. "Was it Helmut? Did Caskie Royal figure it out and confront him? Kill him? And then he didn't have time to bury Helmut, so he just dumped him behind the building?"

"Admittedly I've met Caskie Royal only briefly, but to be honest here, I really can't see him obliterating anyone's face, much less chopping off fingers."

"Jingle Bells" played at full volume. Bowie reached into his jacket pocket, came out empty. Dr. Franks pointed to the cell phone that sat atop the cabinet across the room. Bowie grabbed up his cell, frowned at the name of the caller. "Excuse me, I've got to take this," he said, and walked out of the room.

Dr. Franks said, "I know, 'Jingle Bells' is four months early. The thing is, Bowie can never seem to return his cell phone to the right place, like in his pocket. When anyone hears a Christmas carol, they know it's his cell, and can point him to it." She beamed at them as if to say, *Isn't he about the cleverest person you've ever met?*

Sherlock said, "I gather you work a lot with him?"

"Oh, yes, Bowie makes sure I do all the autopsies under federal jurisdiction in Connecticut."

She pulled the sheet over Mr. Helmut Blauvelt's destroyed face, then stripped off her gloves. "This is a mess. Since you two are here, I realize it isn't even a down-home mess, but a big honking international mess. If I find anything else that could help, Agents, I'll contact Bowie."

"Or us," Sherlock said, and gave her a sunny smile and each of their cards.

When they stepped into the long dim hospital hallway, Sherlock said, "She wishes he were her son. The maternal pride nearly bursts right out of her."

Savich nodded. "Before we left Washington, I spoke to another couple of agents who know Bowie. They both agreed Bowie's building himself a reputation as a real ass-kicker. When he was appointed SAC of the New Haven field office last year, there was a lot of grumbling about bringing in an outsider—an agent from L.A.—rather than promoting from within, complaints of nepotism, which could, as a matter of fact, have a grain of truth, given his family's connection to Valenti, but his record in L.A. was sterling and his record here in New Haven is, to date, quite good."

Sherlock said, "He's not happy we're here, but he's sucking it up, so that says something about him. At the same time, he looks at you like he's sizing you up for combat, Dillon."

"I might oblige him when this is over. Christmas carols," he added, shaking his head. "It seems like he thinks outside the envelope. Bottom line, it's likely he can help us."

Bowie laid his cell phone on a desktop beside him when he finished the call, then frowned, slipped it back into his jacket pocket, and waved them over. "That was Agent Ivan Izbursky from my office. He says the German agent, Andreas Kesselring, is indeed arriving tomorrow. It's confirmed." He paused, looked down at his boots, then back up at both of them. "Look, I know the brass in Washington think I'm too inexperienced to deal with this, but—"

Savich interrupted him smoothly. "What's important is we find out what happened to Helmut Blauvelt. So we put all our respective brains together and we catch ourselves a murderer. Personally, I can't wait to find out why this guy Helmut was sent over here. The three of us will figure it out, and that will tell us why he was killed. And then, Bowie, all of us have more experience."

Bowie let it drop, he had no choice. "I was thinking we could have dinner at Chez Pierre tonight, enjoy the food and speak to the staff who were there last night. I got us a reservation for nine, the earliest available. That okay with you guys?"

"When you made the reservations, did

you ask who Blauvelt dined with last night?" Sherlock said. "Seems to me that person could very well be his killer."

"When I went by Chez Pierre before I met you guys, the owner, Paul Remier, was there. He showed me the reservations page for last night. There was no Helmut Blauvelt listed."

"Which means, I hope," Savich said, "that he was there with someone, and the reservation was under that someone's name."

"Nope. I spoke to the maitre d'. He told me there was a last-minute cancellation and just as he was hanging up the phone, in walked this single middle-aged gentleman. Well-dressed, spoke with a slight accent. Couldn't say if he was German or not.

"Then I got hold of the waiter. He said no one came near the guy the whole time he was there. But he also said they were really busy and he could have missed something.

"The same waiter will be at Chez Pierre tonight, so you guys can talk to him yourselves. I'm still hopeful someone there can help us. I asked all of them to think about it."

Sherlock said, "You've covered a lot of the bases, Bowie." She sighed. "Wouldn't it be nice if something in this life was easy?"

Bowie gave them a small salute, patted his jacket pocket to be sure his cell was safely inside, and started to leave. He called out over his shoulder, a big grin on his face, "I sure hope you enjoy Norman Bates Inn." There was a slight pause, and a waggle of dark eyebrows. "Most do."

They were shown to an antique-filled large corner room on the second floor of the Norman Bates Inn, with a dozen framed posters from *Psycho* on the walls. Savich said, "I need to call Senator Hoffman. He's probably wondering what's going on after last night, and I did tell him I'd get back to him soon."

Sherlock was studying the classic image of Janet Leigh being stabbed in the shower, when she heard Dillon say into his cell, "Senator, Sherlock and I are in Connecticut. We're here to look into the murder of a German national. But first, I wanted to give you an update on what happened this morning."

Sherlock listened in as Savich repeated

to Hoffman what he had already told her, and watched Savich fall silent as he listened to Hoffman's utter disbelief flow over him, followed by a dozen questions.

When Senator Hoffman finally ran down, Savich said, "Yes sir, I do know how difficult this is to accept. I know it sounds like madness, but it really is Nikki. On the other hand, seeing something float outside your bedroom window most every night sounds pretty nuts too.

"Do you know what Nikki is talking about? What it is you don't understand? What is this danger you're facing?"

Savich listened to Senator Hoffman huff and deny there could be any danger—"I mean, who, Agent Savich, would want to hurt me?"—and nearly hyperventilate, then hang up.

Savich looked at Sherlock, who was smoothing a pair of black pants onto a wooden hanger, and gave her a crooked grin. "Understandably, the good senator is shaken and disbelieving, and wishes he'd never contacted us. He says he has no clue what his dead wife could be warning him about." Savich shrugged. "Nothing more to be done, I suppose, until something really bad happens or I get a chance to talk to Nikki."

"You think you will?"

"I have no idea."

When they left Norman Bates Inn, Savich patted the black Pontiac G6's roof in the inn's parking lot. "Nicer wheels this time. What do you say we pay a visit to Carla Alvarez and Caskie Royal after we visit Milo's Deli right down the street?"

9

SCHIFFER HARTWIN U.S. HEADQUARTERS
STONE BRIDGE, CONNECTICUT
Late Monday afternoon

When Sherlock and Savich stepped out of the third-floor elevator into the Schiffer Hartwin executive reception area, they saw three assistants, their heads close, no doubt buzzing with speculation about the murder and break-in. The reception space was good-sized, but not particularly plush. The chairs looked comfortable enough, the magazines on the tables not too ancient. Behind a counter there was a well-equipped work station, on the wall behind it a half-dozen framed black-and-white photographs of nineteenth-century Stone Bridge.

At the sight of the two strangers, two of the three assistants slithered away. After they showed their creds to a dimpled young woman who looked both worried and excited, Sherlock was directed to the second door on the right, and Savich to the last office on the left.

Sherlock paused at a big door emblazoned in gold lettering: *C. Alvarez, Production Manager*.

An assistant sat at her work station in front of that impressive door. She was a young woman who sported blond hair in a brush cut maybe a half-inch long all over her head, and bright red lipstick. She looked, Sherlock thought, both clever and hip, like she could toss down a few straight vodkas and remain standing.

"I'm Special Agent Sherlock, FBI, Ms. Riker," she said pleasantly. "I would like to see Ms. Alvarez."

Lori Riker jumped to her feet. "Oh dear, I mean, Ms. Alvarez is in a meeting with Mr. Drexel, ah, that's Mr. Turley Drexel, he's the accounting manager, and it's their monthly meeting to go over—"

"It's all very important, I know," said Sherlock, "but given the murder last night of one of Schiffer Hartwin's German employees right in your backyard and the break-in into the CEO's office, I think I trump just about everything, don't you?"

"The dead man is German? I didn't know that. But who was he? I mean—oh goodness."

Sherlock stepped toward the big shiny door. She heard the angry voices before she even had the knob in her hand.

"No, wait, Agent Sherlock, I mean, really, let me tell them, inform them that—"

Sherlock flashed Lori Riker a sweet smile and opened the door to see a seated man and woman, their faces just inches from one another. The air was thick with acrimony, and sudden silence.

The woman straightened like a shot and moved quickly away from the man, going to stand behind her very modern glass-and-chrome desk. Every inch of it was covered—by stacks of papers, a sleek computer, printer, and two phones. She was tall, in her mid-thirties, with an athlete's body, hair dark as sin and nearly as short as her secretary's. She was wearing a navy blue suit and white blouse with a mannish blue tie, and plain dark blue pumps. Her eyes, also very dark blue, and as cold as ice, were narrowed on Sherlock's face. She should have looked severe and masculine in her getup, but, oddly, she didn't. She looked forbidding and angry. But just for an instant, Sherlock saw fear leap into her dark eyes.

Sherlock looked back and forth between the two of them. "I believe you're Carla Alvarez, production manager, and you are Turley Drexel, accounting manager. Have I got that right?"

"Yes," Carla said, voice clipped. But Sherlock saw another flash of fear in her narrowed eyes before she wiped her expression clean. Her chin went up and the power player was back, full force. She asked, her voice steady as a rock, "You are a police officer? Here to question us about the murdered man in Van Wie Park?"

"I'm FBI—Agent Sherlock." She handed Carla her creds, then she handed them over to Mr. Drexel, who was looking at Carla Alvarez, eyes flat and hard. He didn't even bother to glance at Sherlock's ID. Finally, he nodded to her, and remained seated, looking hard again at Alvarez, mouth tight.

Alvarez asked, "Why is the FBI here and not the local police?"

"The body was discovered in Van Wie Park, and that's federal land, which makes it our case."

It was obvious neither Alvarez nor Turley had known that. Hadn't they watched the news? The murderer hadn't known it would draw in the feds either, Sherlock would wager. Sherlock decided she was going to rock and roll with this woman who was struggling to look so formidable.

Sherlock gave them both impartial smiles. "What were you fighting about?"

Turley Drexel was fifty-two years old, and cursed with a round baby face he'd hated for as long as he could remember. He answered her in the tone of a prim, tightly wound bureaucrat used to juggling numbers. "See here, Agent, we were simply having a business discussion, of no concern to you, I assure you, nothing at all to do with that dead man found out back. We don't even know who he is. No one's bothered to tell us. Was he a transient?"

Sherlock said easily, "No, not a transient, Mr. Drexel. Actually, I'm very sure both of you knew him. He was an employee of Schiffer Hartwin, from their headquarters, a German national. His name was Helmut Blauvelt."

Mr. Drexel paled, then quickly lowered his eyes to his black loafers and muttered something under his breath.

As for Carla Alvarez, her hand went to her throat. She said slowly, "Helmut Blauvelt? No, surely that's not possible, surely—you're certain?"

"Very certain."

"We didn't know, I mean, sure, we've met Mr. Blauvelt, but we didn't realize—we just thought it was some stranger who was mugged and killed in the park. This is unbelievable, Agent. Mr. Blauvelt—it just doesn't seem possible."

"He was identified very quickly." She gave them no details. She turned. "Mr. Drexel, if you would please return to your office, I would like to speak with Ms. Alvarez alone. I'll be in to speak with you soon."

After Turley Drexel nearly ran from the office, Sherlock turned back to Carla Alvarez, studied her a moment, and said, “Men are dogs, aren’t they, Ms. Alvarez?”

“Dogs? What is that supposed to mean?”

“I mean, Caskie Royal is married, he’s got kids, and here he is sleeping with you. I wonder how many women, how many employees, he’s talked onto his sofa? Surely you realize you’re not the first.”

“That’s insulting. If I were a man, you’d never say anything like that.”

“Depending on where I happened to be, and what I happened to find, sure I would. Ms. Alvarez, I understand you and Mr. Caskie Royal interrupted a break-in last night, in his office, and I was thinking it really strange that neither of you called the police, that the security guard did it some minutes later, with no prompting from you. Why is that?”

“What does it matter who called the police? They were called, weren’t they?”

“Why don’t you tell me why that wasn’t the first thing you and Caskie did.”

Alvarez shrugged. “We were anxious to see if the thief got away with anything valuable, like confidential files or e-mails. So the guard called. I repeat, who cares?”

"I'm thinking you guys didn't call because you were afraid the first question put to you would be why the two of you were there alone on a Sunday night."

"We were working on the budget—we had adjustments to make, production dates to change—"

"That doesn't sound all that urgent. So how long have you been sleeping with Mr. Royal?"

"I am not sleeping with him!"

"What did the thief take, Ms. Alvarez?"

"Nothing, as far as I know. That's what Mr. Royal told me last night. He hasn't said anything different to me today."

"How many times did you meet with Mr. Blauvelt?"

"Only once, when he was here three, four months ago, his first visit to our office, I believe."

"No, he's been here many times. All right, what was your meeting about during this visit several months ago?"

Sherlock saw Alvarez's face go utterly blank, then watched her brain snap to. Alvarez said, her voice ice chips, "Not that you'd understand, but we spoke of the reasons behind some budget overruns on drugs we distribute. It's all very involved. After our discussion, he met briefly with Mr. Royal, then, so far as I know, he returned to Germany, pleased that we had resolved the situation."

"You're lying to me, Ms. Alvarez, and I do hate that. You know as well as I do that Mr. Blauvelt wouldn't know a budget overrun from a *Gesundheit*."

"I am not!"

"Why did Mr. Blauvelt come here this time?"

"I have no idea. I didn't even know he was coming."

"You must know Mr. Blauvelt was Schiffer Hartwin's enforcer, their messy-problem solver. Whenever he showed up, it meant there was a screw-up that needed his brand of fixing. This always involved people, Ms. Alvarez, not production problems. Who was he here for this time? Who was the problem, Ms. Alvarez? Were you the one he came to see?"

10

CASKIE ROYAL'S OFFICE

Savich studied Caskie Royal, sitting erect and confident in his executive leather chair behind his equally impressive mahogany desk, and watched him thread a Cross pen through his large blunt fingers. He knew Royal had been first string quarterback in his senior year at Florida, and he still looked fairly buff, though living well was starting to thicken his waistline. His hair was thick, dark brown with flecks of gray at the temples, the politician's *You can trust me* look. Savich knew about his tomcat reputation and imagined Sherlock could tell him what it was that made women look his way. His dark eyes were intelligent, but Savich saw cunning lurking in them too. At first he looked decisive, a man at the top of his game, sure of his place in the sun. But his hands were the giveaway—nervous hands, fiddling with the pen, his fingers tapping. Savich imagined he'd been instructed to make nice and to get this mess shut down cleanly. He doubted Royal could be intimidated, at least not here on his own turf. A laid-back, more conciliatory approach, then.

Royal asked, "May I ask why the FBI is visiting me, Agent Savich? It was a break-in, probably some competitor looking for some advantage, new and exciting to them, no doubt, but nothing more. I know poor Helmut Blauvelt was found murdered in Van Wie Park, but I will tell you right now I know nothing about that." He looked down pointedly at his Rolex.

Savich smiled to himself. "I realize you're a busy man, Mr. Royal, and we will make this as quick and painless as possible. Did your employers at Schiffer Hartwin call you from Germany?"

"Yes, of course they did. We are all very upset by this. They want me to help you as much as possible, but as I said, I don't know how I can." Royal shrugged.

"Helmut Blauvelt was here to see you, Mr. Royal?"

"No, I have no idea why Mr. Blauvelt was even here in the U.S." Royal sat forward, folded his hands in front of him. He looked serious and concerned, the picture of cooperation.

Savich sat back in the chair, crossed his ankles, and said easily, "Mr. Blauvelt was a man to be reckoned with, Mr. Royal. He took care of people who were causing problems, as I'm sure you know. He was a fixture at Schiffer Hartwin when you first came on board five years ago as CEO. He possibly did your own background check."

"I heard rumors, nothing more. Believe me, I didn't know what, if anything, he was here to do."

"When was the last time Mr. Blauvelt came to see you, Mr. Royal?"

Royal's eyes never left Savich's face. He splayed his wide palms on the desktop. Nice manicure, Savich saw.

"I don't remember. Wait, oh, yes, it was

maybe a year ago. We discussed cost overrun problems with a new drug. We resolved questions and he left."

"Actually Blauvelt was here three and a half months ago. Why was he here then, Mr. Royal?"

"He was? I'm sorry, Agent Savich, but I don't believe I saw him. Perhaps he was here on vacation."

Savich merely continued to look at Royal. Clearly he was an ambitious man who enjoyed his perks, a man unlikely to let any morals or ethics impede his progress toward his goals. Surely he was bright enough to come up with a better answer than that to suit Savich. "Why don't you look it up in your appointment book, Mr. Royal. It will only take a moment."

Caskie Royal turned his chair to the credenza behind him where his computer sat next to a photo of a pretty blond woman in a white summer dress with two boys, one standing on each side.

"Your family, Mr. Royal?"

"What? Oh, yes, that's my wife, Jane Ann, and my two sons, Chad and Mark."

He raised his hands to the keyboard, then shook his head at himself. "Sorry, I forgot." He swiveled his chair toward the desk again and opened a drawer, withdrawing a datebook covered in beautiful Moroccan leather. He looked up after a moment. "Here we are. Yes, I remember now. He came over to speak to me about one of our employees. A manager at Rexol, our distribution plant in Missouri. Blauvelt was here to discuss problems with his performance. He wanted me to fire him.

"I, ah, I talked him out of firing the employee, Mr. Rink, who is a good man, very experienced. I explained to Mr. Blauvelt that we could trust Rink to turn things around. He was having personal problems. I told Blauvelt I'd speak to Rink, oversee his work more closely. Blauvelt agreed and left. There was nothing more to it than that."

So Royal had quickly come up with a nice fleshed-out story on the fly. Savich was impressed. "You are a very important man in the Schiffer Hartwin hierarchy, Mr. Royal. Why would corporate in Germany send Blauvelt over to speak to you about the performance of one of your own employees?"

Royal continued to smile, looking more

sincere than the pope. He said, "I recall they sent a message through him, Agent Savich, giving me their ideas and expectations. Not a big deal."

"All right, Mr. Royal. You're certain Mr. Blauvelt wasn't scheduled to meet with you on this trip to the U.S.?"

"No, he wasn't."

"Would you mind telling me what you had on your computer that might tempt a thief?"

"E-mails mostly, and endless reports, Agent Savich. A great many reports are copied to the CEO, reports on programs in research and development, reports on our cost structure, reports on the status of drug production and distribution, you get the idea."

"No reports that were particularly critical? That might be of interest to a competitor?"

"That's hard to say, Agent Savich. There were so many reports, I don't think a thief could have located a specific one. But whatever the thief was after, he was out of luck." He smiled.

"I see. I'm something of a computer expert. Would you like me to look through your files? Perhaps I could locate files that were accessed before you and Ms. Alvarez interrupted the thief."

Royal shook his head. "I cannot do that, Agent Savich. I assure you, no files were disturbed. We interrupted whoever it was before anything could be taken."

"You yourself checked your computer to see what file or files were accessed?"

"Of course I checked immediately, nothing was opened. Look, Agent Savich, I told you, we interrupted the person before anything could be touched. I even took my hard drive to our IT department this morning, had them install a new one. They are checking it again to be sure nothing was uploaded or accessed."

Now that was well done, Caskie. You're not a dummy, are you? Savich said pleasantly, "So the files that were on your computer last night are gone, destroyed?"

"That's right. No big deal, Agent. I do it several times a year."

"I read in the police report that the thief escaped through a small window in your connecting bathroom, which means your thief was very probably a woman. Do you know anyone who might fit the bill?"

Royal shook his head slowly. "It's bizarre, the break-in. I wouldn't have thought any of our competitors would break into our headquarters."

"Of course, given how important a cog Mr. Blauvelt was in Schiffer Hartwin's vast wheel, I would assume he would have had the access and passwords to all the management computers. Could he have hired a woman to break into your computer for something specific?"

Royal looked bewildered. "I'm sorry, but I can't imagine what."

Savich said, "Well, we know it wasn't Ms. Alvarez, since she was with you. I guess in a small town like Stone Bridge, you can't be discreet getting a hotel room. That sofa doesn't look all that comfortable."

"I was not here last night to sleep with her! I do not have sex with my managers. We were having a business discussion, that's all."

Savich looked down at his fingernails, buffed them on his sleeve. He said, "A man like you—you earn a good living, you support your family, you provide for all their needs and wants." Savich splayed his hands in front of him. "Of course I understand how a man like yourself wouldn't want to admit that you sometimes get bored. That you would want, even need, some variety to liven things up now and then. After all, don't you deserve it?" He gave Royal the man-to-man look he'd seen on DEA agent Joe Monroe's face when he talked about his girlfriends at the gym.

"No, really, it's just that I—" Royal saw that look, recognized it immediately, gave Savich a shrug, and said finally with a smirk, "What the hell. Carla's hot, you know? She loves sex, unlike my wife, and knows more ways to do it than I do. She had a bad divorce a while back, so there's no chance she'd want more than sex and some laughs."

"A pity you had to deal with the break-in and the cops instead of enjoying yourself."

"Yeah, that's the truth."

"You must have some idea of who broke in last night and why."

"No, I'm sorry, I don't."

"Mr. Blauvelt's body was found behind your building, at the edge of Van Wie Park, an area few people ever go since the undergrowth is so thick. Come now, who could Blauvelt have sent to break into your office? Was he here in the building with her? Did you or someone here come in on him, kill him, then panic and dump him out back?"

"No, that is ridiculous! I am trying to cooperate with you, Agent Savich. You have no right to treat me like a criminal. I should get one of our lawyers in here."

"Would his name be Bender?"

Royal froze. Slowly, he took his hand off the phone. "Yes," he said, "it would. We call him Bender the Elder."

Savich said easily, "We are nearly done here, Mr. Royal. I don't believe Bender the Elder is needed, do you?"

Royal chewed that over a moment, then drew in a deep breath, and nodded.

"Tell me, how long have you been having an affair with Carla Alvarez?"

"If you must know, not all that long. Maybe four months. I was getting tired of her, truth be told. You know how it is, you screw an older woman, and she gets ideas." He shrugged.

Older woman? Savich had seen a photo of Carla Alvarez. Caskie Royal had at least seven or eight years on her. He looked hard at Royal. He looked just a bit shaken, but still well in control. Savich said easily, "No, I can't say I've had that experience, Mr. Royal."

11

CARLA ALVAREZ'S OFFICE

Sherlock asked again, "If Helmut Blauvelt wasn't here to see you, was it Caskie Royal? There was something in Royal's files Blauvelt wanted to see, something Mr. Royal had done, right? I find it strange Mr. Royal didn't mention Blauvelt to you last night when the two of you were together. Royal had to be worried that Blauvelt was here, and terrified of what he'd find out. How about you, Carla? Were you terrified too? Were you part of—what? A cover-up, maybe some profit skimming, some doctored financial reports? Something your German bosses found out about and sent their Mr. Fix-It to take care of?"

Carla said quickly, "No, no, they've been quite pleased, our profits have been unexpectedly high, and now— No, there was nothing like that, look, I have no idea about any of this, Agent, none at all."

Unexpectedly high profits? What was that slip all about? She pressed on. "So Blauvelt came over here to work with Mr. Royal because of this windfall?"

"No, there is no windfall that I know about. I misspoke."

"So Mr. Fix-It is murdered his very first night on our soil. If you and Mr. Royal didn't kill him, who did, Ms. Alvarez?"

"I'm telling you, I don't know."

"How long have you been sleeping with Mr. Royal?"

"My private life is my own affair! Just because I'm a woman, even you, another woman, immediately suspect me of sleeping my way to the top." Carla Alvarez drew herself up. She stared straight through this obnoxious FBI agent with her cool leather jacket and her curly red hair. "You have been listening to gossip, Agent Sherlock.

I'm surprised that an FBI agent would listen to meaningless gossip."

"Ah, we listen to all sorts of things, Ms. Alvarez, and sooner or later we learn just about everything that's important. Do you know, I'd bet your beautiful leather briefcase that his wife already knows about the two of you.

"If I were you, I'd update my résumé, Carla. You're divorced, right? For nearly two years now? Your ex burned you to your heels, and on top of that you have to pay the loser alimony."

"Yes, that miserable—I resent this. My personal life has nothing to do with the death of Helmut Blauvelt, Agent, and nothing to do with the break-in in Mr. Royal's office. I could be sleeping with half the staff here and it would still have nothing to do with any of this."

"Actually, it does, since you and Mr. Royal were here about the same time Mr. Blauvelt was getting himself murdered and dumped in the bushes in your backyard. Tell me, what was copied off Mr. Royal's computer files, Ms. Alvarez?"

"As I already said, Mr. Royal told the

two officers he saw that nothing was accessed, nothing erased or disturbed."

"Of course he'd lie to the police, but not to you, Ms. Alvarez. I suppose since you're sleeping with him, you're very likely a part of this. You were with him when he discovered the thief. Mr. Royal must have been really upset because of what was copied. What was it?"

"No, the thief ran off, we ran him off before he could get to Caskie's computer."

"What was the thief after?"

"I don't know!"

Sherlock said, "I agree it wasn't Blauvelt who was in Royal's office, even though he could have walked in and accessed anything he wanted. The thing is, he couldn't have fit himself through that small bathroom window. So he hired someone. It had to be a woman. Do you know who she could be?"

"No, I have no idea!" Alvarez looked battered. The well was dry, Sherlock thought. She said gently, "I sure hope Caskie Royal is an excellent lover, Ms. Alvarez, because meeting him here was a very bad decision on your part."

Alvarez looked down at her nails, frowned at the hangnail on her thumb. She didn't look up as she said, "No, not particularly. Like you said, Agent, men are dogs."

"You're a smart woman. You should clean up your act. Now, tell me how you see this going down, Ms. Alvarez. Don't give me the tired old line about a mugger. Who do you think murdered Helmut Blauvelt?"

Carla Alvarez sagged against her desk. "I wish I knew, Agent. I'd tell you. Then I'd never have to see you again. You're a bitch."

"And proud of it," Sherlock said, gave her a smile, and left her office.

12

STONE BRIDGE POLICE STATION

Sherlock and Savich sat in wooden chairs across from the ancient desk Bowie had been temporarily assigned in the local police department.

Sherlock said, "I agree with Dillon. Let's get Caskie Royal in here tomorrow and have at him. No more kid gloves like you used today, Dillon, we'll catch him by surprise. Bring on the lawyers, it'll be fun."

Savich said, "If I were his boss, I'd lawyer him up and dare us to connect Blauvelt's death with Schiffer Hartwin." He paused a moment. "You know, I would like to go a couple rounds with Bender the Elder." He smiled a smile that would make the Devil rethink things, Sherlock thought. He continued, "What you found out, Sherlock, about this unexpected profit. I have a gut feeling you're on to something. *Unexpected profit*. It's worth looking into. I think I'll get MAX started on this. It could be someone in Schiffer Hartwin is involved in something unethical and illegal that's dumped money in their laps, and that's what Alvarez was referring to."

Bowie said, "A windfall profit. I like the sound of that."

Savich said, "I'll call Dice, see if we have any whistleblowers from Schiffer Hartwin who've come forward."

Bowie said, "Since that landmark criminal and civil fine last year of two point three billion dollars levied against Pfizer, I wouldn't doubt it. I wondered how much of that money the six whistleblowers split among them."

"Enough for a whole lot of encouragement," Sherlock said. "Admittedly, though, their lives couldn't have been fun for most of a decade, but in the end, it paid off big-time for them. That two point three billion dollars represents about a year of profits for Pfizer. Do you think it's enough to make some of the drug companies clean up their act?"

Bowie said, "Don't know. I'm rooting for Health and Human Services myself. I know they'll be monitoring Pfizer for the next five years, since no one trusts them to keep to a straight path." Bowie looked down at his watch. "I've got to go. I'll pick you guys up for our date at Chez Pierre, at eight forty-five, okay?"

They watched him dash out of the small makeshift room where he and four other FBI agents were temporarily housed. The Stone Bridge police chief, Clifford Amos, obviously wasn't happy about the feds invading his police station, and the accommodations he'd provided them showed how he felt about it.

Agent Dolores Cliff leaned forward in her ancient creaky chair, behind an even more ancient desk than Bowie's. "Bowie's got to pick up his daughter from school and take her to the new babysitter."

13

Erin came down on her knees to look Georgie Richards in the face. “You wanna stay with me for a couple of days, Georgie? Your dad and I decided it’d be more fun to stay here rather than me trucking over to your house. What do you think?”

Georgie was looking toward Erin’s colorful living room, with bright pillows tossed on the green-and-white-striped sofa, a huge red beanbag in the corner, and framed posters of Degas ballet dancers on the walls. “I don’t know,” Georgie said, taking a step toward the living room. “Maybe you’re not such a good roommate.”

"Hey, anyone who can teach smart-mouthed kids how to demi-plié has to be a good roommate."

Georgie said, "You are a good dancer."

"Yep, I can dance up a storm. My grandmother told me my second arabesque was the most graceful she'd ever seen. Hmm, I think she told my mother the same thing. Anyway, maybe I could give you extra pointers. For free. I've got a surprise for you in your bedroom."

"A surprise?"

That got the kid's attention. "All surprises are better if you have to wait awhile."

Georgie was nearly humming with excitement. She'd scored a point on that one, Erin knew, and tried not to smile. Then Georgie said as she touched her fingertips lightly to the leaves of an African violet, "Can you cook?"

"Hard to get, aren't you? Sure, nearly as well as I can dance. Wait'll you taste my Nutcracker Brussels sprouts and Swan Lake cabbage salad."

The little girl grabbed her stomach. "Eeew! Daddy, tell her I can do the cooking, I know some great recipes. Daddy loves them."

Bowie laughed. "Her hot dogs with chili and grated cheese on top and her famous Special K with sliced baked apples stirred in are the best I've ever had."

"That does sound good," Erin said. "Hmm, maybe we could work something out."

"Daddy washes my clothes for me when Glynn doesn't. Will you, Erin?"

"Okay, maybe I could do that."

"And ironing—?"

"That's pushing it, kid. Your dad can iron for you before he goes to bed, how about that?"

"I just don't know, Erin. Daddy says he's got some real heavy stuff to do. I don't know if he'll ever go to bed until he catches these bad guys."

Erin didn't want to, but she looked up at Bowie Richards—Special Agent Bowie Richards, SAC of the New Haven field office—and recognized him for the predator she knew he could easily be. She wasn't fooled for a minute by the thankful father who saw her as his salvation. If only he knew. She'd already cursed herself from here to Bratislava thinking this over. She'd done it for Georgie, but she'd also realized if she was careful, she could work with this. Just maybe when he came over to visit his daughter, she could be subtle enough so he'd never know she was easing information out of him. She could do subtle well, her case successes told her that. The huge ball of fear she'd felt since this morning dissolved a bit in her belly.

She saw Bowie Richards look at his watch. She got to her feet and shook his hand, a big hand, callused. "I'll even iron her clothes, but I draw the line there. Georgie, you've got to make up your own bed."

The look of absolute relief on his face nearly made her laugh. "Georgie's been making her own bed for two years now, haven't you, baby?"

"I'm seven years and six months old now, Daddy, I'm not a baby."

"How could I be so blind? Forgive me." He went down on his haunches and hugged her, breathed her in. "I'll come visit whenever I can, but like I told you, I'm up to my earlobes in a big gnarly mess right now."

"Will you come back for dinner tonight?"

"No, sweetie, I'm sorry. I've got to have dinner with two hotshot FBI agents the bosses sent up from Washington."

"And they need you to show them what to do, right?"

She believed in him absolutely, Bowie thought, looking at that precious face and huge dark blue eyes, her mother's eyes. He nodded. "Yes, sweetie, they need my help."

He kissed his daughter again, told her to mind her manners, ruffled her dark brown hair, his hair, and rose. "Thank you, Ms. Pulaski, I owe you big for this."

Erin prayed she'd never have to collect on the debt.

And so it was done. Erin had a roommate for two days, then they'd reevaluate, Bowie had said in a hopeful voice.

Georgie shook her head and said in a too-adult voice, "He's worried, I know he is, but he doesn't say anything. Some German man got killed in Van Wie Park, and Daddy's got to figure it all out. He said he found out who the man was because of his teeth. He didn't have any ID either. I heard Daddy say that on the phone. I hope the agents from Washington will be able to help."

So the man who was killed was German? If he was German, he was almost surely connected to Schiffer Hartwin. He didn't have any ID? Bowie figured out he was German from his teeth? So that meant Bowie recognized German dentistry? Well done. What about his fingerprints?

She'd have to find out about that. She smiled down at Georgie. "We'll eat in an hour, that okay with you?"

"Will we have Nutcracker food?"

"Nah, not tonight. I've got a macaroni and cheese casserole in the oven. Now, kiddo, let me show you your room."

"What's my surprise?"

"It's in your room. Let's take a look."

Erin opened the door and Georgie charged in to see a barre set against a long glass wall. "Now you can practice and practice," Erin said. "I even lowered it for you. What do you think of that?"

Georgie had obviously nourished higher hopes, but the kid was polite. "It is a beautiful barre, thank you, Erin," and that little voice told her another surprise would be a lovely thing for Erin to produce. Long day for the little girl, she thought, and so full of change.

Erin said, "You know, if you don't want the mac and cheese, I could fry us up a mess of liver and put Cool Whip all over the top."

The little girl laughed and laughed as she walked over to lightly run her fingertips over the smooth wooden barre.

When, Erin wondered, did little girls, seven years and six months, usually go to bed? She had a feeling if she asked Georgie, she'd lie to her, clean.

They had a successful meal of mac and cheese, obligatory green beans, and a small salad thrown in. After an hour playing on the barre and two TV shows, Erin looked over at the droopy-eyed Georgie, who'd sworn her daddy never made her go to bed until *very* late, and dialed Bowie Richards's cell.

"Richards. Yeah?"

He sounded harried.

"It's Erin Pulaski. When does Georgie usually go to bed?"

There was an instant of stark silence. She could see him firmly bringing his brain back to the mundane. "An hour ago, at seven forty-five. She got you, huh?"

"Oh yeah." And she hung up.

Bowie laid his cell next to himself on the car seat. Sherlock eyed it as it slid into her. She picked it up and handed it to him.

"Oh, thank you," he said, gave it a baffled look, and stuck it in his pocket. "That was Erin Pulaski, she's my temporary babysitter, taking care of my daughter. She's, ah, a private investigator here in Stone Bridge, as well as my daughter's ballet teacher." He shook his head, flipped on his left-hand turn signal. "Some combination."

Savich said from the back seat where he was working on MAX, "Her name's Georgie, right?"

"Yeah, today she told me she was seven years and six months and not a baby anymore." He shook his head, grinned. "I'll tell you, it seems like she was wearing diapers and drooling just last week. Tell me about your little boy."

They spoke to him of Sean and their dog, Astro.

"Georgie wants a dog, what kid doesn't? We'll have to see."

The evening was cool, the moon at half-mast, the sky clear and studded with stars. Bowie said, "The restaurant is just down this road. I had their lobster the one time I ate here and it's great. Another thing, the owner, Paul Remier, wasn't too happy to be hosting three cops in his fine upscale restaurant tonight. I think he's afraid we'll slap handcuffs on someone and march him out."

Sherlock grinned. "Then let's keep him guessing."

He looked over at her, appreciated the nice black dress she was wearing, the sexy open-toed shoes that showed off her bright red toenails. She'd pulled back all that beautiful red curly hair and fastened it behind her ears with gold clips. He'd never take her for a tough-as-nails FBI agent, which is what she was.

He glanced over at Savich, who was wearing a conservative black suit, nearly a match to Bowie's. He liked them both, but he still wished they weren't here, wished they were back in Washington playing with their kid. Why did Disneyland East always think the field offices were incompetent? At least Savich and Sherlock had excellent reputations. He'd heard some talk that Savich was into psychics, or something, which sounded ridiculous to Bowie, not that he was going to ask Savich about it. What did one do? Have séances?

The FBI didn't deal with ghosts. It just wouldn't work.

It was nine o'clock on the nose when they walked in. The maitre d' stood by a podium near the front door, along with the owner, Paul Remier, a very short rotund man with jet-black hair and black eyes. Neither of them looked particularly welcoming.

Sherlock gave them both a high-voltage smile. "Dr. Ella Franks tells us you serve the best oysters this side of the Atlantic."

"Ah," said Paul Remier, unbending just a bit, "this is true. So you know Dr. Franks? A fine lady. Do allow me to seat you myself. We hope you have a lovely dinner. Our chef's oysters *à la maison* are exceptional. I have arranged for last night's waitstaff to be available for you to speak with, discreetly, here at your table. Will that be convenient for you?"

Once they were seated, with their water poured in crystal glasses, fine virgin olive oil in a small bowl, and a warm baguette laid in a white basket on their lovely corner table, Bowie raised a brow at Sherlock. "How did you do that? I thought Remier would prefer to serve me for dinner rather than feed me oysters when I saw him this morning."

Sherlock grinned at him. "I found out Paul Remier is a neighbor of Dr. Ella Franks. Dr. Franks calls him Paulie."

14

Dillard Shanks, known to the Chez Pierre patrons as Estafan, told them he'd happened to overhear Mr. Blauvelt speaking on his cell phone, something simply no one did at Chez Pierre, and he actually sniffed. However, no one had bothered the gentleman since he was sitting at a back table, wearing an expensive English suit and Italian loafers; but still, Monsieur Remier had believed it exceedingly rude.

"Tell us what you heard him say," Bowie said.

They could tell Estafan didn't want to admit to eavesdropping, but when Bowie added, "You'll make us the happiest people in Stone Bridge if you heard something," Estafan said, "Well, as a matter of fact, I did stop and listen because the gentleman had a bit of an accent, German, I believe. I heard him say he'd made up his mind and to leave him alone. He said something about flying home, but I didn't hear enough to be certain. He listened for a couple of seconds, then nodded, just like a person was sitting across from him, and said there were always difficulties but he was good with overcoming them. Then he switched to German, laughed a little bit, then hung up." Estafan frowned at a fork beside Sherlock's plate, picked it up and rubbed it vigorously on the napkin over his forearm. "I guess he got more difficulties than he'd counted on, since he's dead."

Sherlock smiled up at him. "Thank you for the information and my shiny fork. You ever need a parking ticket fixed, you call Agent Richards."

Estafan said, "Could that include my boyfriend, who's a maniac on his motorcycle?"

"Not a problem," Bowie said, and wondered what the odds were of Chief Clifford

Amos's making good. Bowie sat back in his chair and watched Estafan lean over a client four tables away, nod solemnly, and wend his way gracefully to the kitchen. "My question is, if Blauvelt was speaking to his boss in Germany, then why was he speaking in English? And what did he mean about he'd made up his mind and leave him alone?"

They enjoyed a further bit of luck with Claude—just Claude—the sommelier, who confided that the foreign gentleman at table eleven obviously had a lovely trained palate, and money, since he'd ordered a bottle of Blanklet 2004 Paradise Hills Merlot, Napa Valley, a very fine wine indeed.

"Did he drink the entire bottle?"

"Oh, yes, he did," Claude said to Sherlock, admiring the lock of red hair curling around her ear. "It costs nearly two hundred dollars a bottle here."

Bowie said, "Was he tipsy when he left?"

"I wouldn't say tipsy, no. He ordered another bottle, then paused and appeared to think about it. He changed his mind, waved me away. I didn't notice him after that."

"Okay," Savich said when the dapper Claude was out of earshot, "Dr. Franks did indeed say he'd had red wine with his venison. An entire bottle—did that make him slow, less careful?"

"Well, he certainly realized another bottle might impair him," Sherlock said. "Speaking of wine, does anyone want a nice dry chardonnay for dinner?"

Bowie shook his head, smiling. "None for me, I don't drink."

Sherlock's left eyebrow hoisted itself. "Health reasons?"

"No, not really," Bowie said, and nothing more.

They enjoyed a lovely sauced scampi over rice, crème brûlée for dessert, and rich dark French espresso.

It was nearly midnight when Bowie dropped them back at the Norman Bates Inn. Fifteen minutes later, they were tucked into a soft bed with Janet Leigh's silent earsplitting screams on the wall behind them. Sherlock said against his shoulder, "The espresso was a mistake," and sighed.

"Maybe not," Savich said, and turned to her. After a couple of minutes, she whispered against his mouth, "Well, another dessert is always nice."

15

Tuesday morning

Erin let a well-dressed, heavy-eyed Bowie Richards into her apartment the next morning at seven thirty.

"You don't look good, Agent Richards. You on an all-night bender with those wild agents from Washington?"

"All I can hope is they had as miserable a sleepless night as I did. We all drank espresso, and the stuff was so strong it could have blasted a rocket into space. That and thinking about this gnarly murder kept me up until nearly three a.m."

Erin cocked her head to one side, tried to look uninterested, but polite. "And what did you decide after all that thinking?"

He eyed her, realized he liked the oversized white shirt over the black leggings, the ballet flats on her feet. Her hair was pulled back in a French braid, big dangly hoops in her ears. She looked all dancer this morning, not a whiff of P.I. "About what? Oh, the murder. It's interesting, we found a waiter at Chez Pierre last night who'd heard the murdered man on a cell phone saying he'd made up his mind and to leave him alone—" Bowie stopped, frowned, shook his head. "Forget I said that, I shouldn't have. Shows you my brain is still singing the espresso blues. Where's Georgie? We've got to leave for school pretty soon."

Yeah, sure, I'll forget it. It's already emblazoned on my brain. Erin said, "I heard the murdered guy's name on the news this morning. Helmut Blauvelt."

"Yeah, I forgot we let out that information."

"It's lucky the waiter at Chez Pierre understood German, isn't it?"

"Oh, he didn't. Blauvelt spoke in English,

only a slight accent, Estafan told us, until the end, then Blauvelt switched to German—what's wrong with me? Keep that confidential, okay?"

Erin said easily, "Not a problem. Georgie! Your dad's here."

"I'm eating oatmeal," Georgie called out from the kitchen. "You want some, Daddy?"

Bowie rubbed his eyes. "Oatmeal? She never eats oatmeal. How'd you manage that?"

"I've got a special recipe passed down from my great-grandfather. Georgie took one bite and blissed out. She doesn't want to let the oatmeal out of her sight. Have you had breakfast yet, Agent Richards? Maybe Great-granddad's oatmeal will glue things back together again in your brain."

"Call me Bowie, please."

"All right. Call me Erin."

"Erin." He took a quick look at his watch. "I really don't have time, I've got so much stuff to do and—your great-grandfather's recipe, you say?"

"Yep. He was Polish, but he always claimed he'd learned how to make it when he lived in Inverness for three years. Come on, Bowie, come into my kitchen. It'll just take a minute. Believe me, Georgie isn't going to budge from the kitchen table until she cleans out her bowl, and it's a big bowl."

Erin eyed him as he took a tiny bite, nodded, then went to work on the oatmeal with brown sugar sprinkled on top, nodding some more as his daughter spoke nonstop to him, at him, really—about how she took a running start and landed right in the middle of the red beanbag in the living room, and then Erin tried it but she was too big and fell off the side, before switching to Erin's bedtime story about a ballet dancer who hated wearing a tutu.

Erin knew Bowie's nods were automatic—he was thinking about Blauvelt's murder, she knew, that or he was thinking about falling back into bed and sleeping around the clock. How to get more information out of him? Like, did they have any witnesses who'd seen her fall out of Caskie Royal's bathroom window? If so, had these witnesses described her?

She took a sip of her tea. "Georgie, you've told your father everything, down to the color of your socks. And you've eaten every stick of oatmeal."

"Oatmeal is gooey, Erin, there aren't any sticks."

"Hmm. Okay, you're stalling. Go brush your teeth and get your sweater, it's cool today." She waited until Georgie had cleared the kitchen door, then went for it. "That break-in at the Schiffer Hartwin headquarters, did it have anything to do with the German guy's murder? Wasn't he found right out behind the building?"

Bless her Polish great-granddad. It was the best oatmeal Bowie had ever eaten in his life. Actually, now that he thought about it, this was probably the only oatmeal he'd ever eaten. His mom hated the stuff, never made it for him or his siblings. "Break-in? Oh yeah, that was weird, truth be told."

"Why?"

He said after a moment of chewing and savoring, "I keep forgetting, you're a P.I. You've got terminal curiosity, don't you?"

If only you knew. She nodded easily. "You've got a point. Come on, Bowie, what was weird about the break-in? What was taken? Do you have any ideas who it could have been?"

Shut your mouth—too many questions, don't make him suspicious.

"All we know is it was a woman."

Had someone seen her running from the Schiffer Hartwin building? Not good, not good. "How do you know that?"

He took a last spoonful of oatmeal, sat back in the kitchen chair, and crossed his arms over his chest. "I do believe I've got my hundred-watt bulb back. That was delicious. Thank you, Erin. She went out a bathroom window that's too small for a guy."

How could I forget that wretched window was small? It's okay, then. Not a big deal. Was that all they knew?

Bowie rose when Georgie came skipping back into the small kitchen. "Thanks again for feeding me, Erin. I'll have Georgie work on you for the oatmeal recipe. Hey, you ready, kiddo?"

Georgie nodded and took his hand. "You look tired, Daddy. If you went to bed at eight o'clock like me, you wouldn't be."

"That's a fact," he said. He smiled at Erin. "Thank you for taking Georgie in. I hope she didn't give you any grief after you called me last night at bedtime?"

"Not a bit, particularly since it was well after eight o'clock when I found out when her bedtime actually was. Well, maybe I did threaten to make her do barre exercises if she wanted to stay up so late." Erin head-rubbed Georgie, and the little girl laughed and ran out of the kitchen.

"I'm going to have the strongest legs in ballet class!"

Erin waited a moment until she heard Georgie at the front door. "This murder and break-in deal, you think you'll get it solved pretty soon?"

"Oh, you're wondering how long you'll have to keep my kid as a roommate?"

No, you idiot, Georgie can stay here forever. "Yeah, I stewed about it all night. She's such a trial. No, of course not, Georgie's just fine. Forget reevaluating tomorrow, okay? Unless you think you'll have everything figured out by noon, hotshot that you are?"

"Maybe, we'll see. The big fed hotshots sent to run the investigation, turns out they're pretty okay."

"That's lucky. Now there are three hotshots cleaning things up here. Do you know, I ran into a fed once on a case and I would have sworn he wanted to pull off his wingtip and bash me with it."

He grinned, as she'd meant him to. "Did you smart-mouth him?"

"Nah, well, maybe a little bit. The jerk. So these guys are smart?"

"There are two of them, they're married of all things. The guy, Dillon Savich, he's big and tough-looking, and he's got a look about him that would scare anyone with a brain. Sherlock, his wife, she's pretty, sweet smiles she uses very effectively, but you know in your gut she'd kick your butt all the way to Vermont if you crossed her. I'm meeting them at the police station now to talk things over."

He looked better, she thought, his eyes clear, back straighter, more focused now. Yeah, Mr. Hundred-Watt was back.

"What's wrong? Do I still look like crap?"

"No, I was thinking you look human again—the wonders of Scottish oatmeal. Have a good day, Bowie. Will you be coming by tonight before Georgie's in bed?"

"I'll try." He looked down at her, but not that far down. In her ballet flats she was about five ten, maybe eleven. In heels, they'd be eye-to-eye. "You teaching a ballet class today?"

"What? Oh, because of my getup. Yeah, this afternoon. I'm working at home until then."

"Are you working on a case yourself?"

"Yeah, but it's no biggie. Have a nice day."

"Some guy hire you to follow his wife around?"

She gave him a smile to freeze his lungs. "Oh yeah, I might even get to hide in a bedroom closet and take a video." Then, to his utter surprise, she drew back her fist and smacked him in the arm, hard.

He was rubbing his arm when Georgie shouted, running right at him, "Daddy, I'm ready! Let's go or I'll be late."

Call him Mr. Smooth. "I guess that was a kind of stupid thing to say, wasn't it? Sorry. Bye, Erin."

"Bye, Erin. I'll see you at ballet class this afternoon." Georgie gave her a huge grin, and shook her finger at her. "Don't be late. Daddy, what did you say to Erin that was stupid?"

Erin closed the apartment door and latched the chain. She pushed the red beanbag back into the corner and paced. So they knew a woman had broken into Caskie Royal's office, no surprise there since the small window made it pretty obvious, but they couldn't have a clue it was her. She wasn't anywhere near their radar, and why should she be? They also believed the murder was connected to the break-in, but she was safe—unless she sent all her evidence, all the Culovort papers she'd copied off Royal's computer, to the media. Then they'd track her down and fry her.

But what if I get the Culovort documents to the media anonymously? I'd be safe then, wouldn't I? Dr. Kender would get to nail the bozos and we'd both walk away.

It could be done, but it was scary. Thank God there was time to think about it. She wondered what Dr. Kender would have to say.

Erin put the few dishes in the dishwasher, swiped down the kitchen, and got to work.

16

Savich was clipping his SIG to his belt when Elton John sang out "Candle in the Wind" on his cell.

"Savich."

"Bowie here. A guy called the field office in New Haven. I've got a lead on the woman who did the break-in at Schiffer Hartwin," and Bowie gave them an address not three blocks from the Norman Bates Inn.

"Sherlock and I are on our way."

Eric Tallman was a runner with insomnia who was also a sports writer and stay-at-home dad. He waved them into a small toy-strewn living room. He leaned down to scoop up a stuffed golden retriever as he waved them to the red-and-green plaid sofa. “Sorry for the mess. I haven’t cleaned up after Luke yet this morning.” He checked his watch. “He’s taking his morning nap, but it’s going to be close. Believe me, if he wakes up, conversation will cease. Sit down, sit down.” He checked the baby monitor on a side table. “Since Luke came, I can’t run now during the day, only at night after he’s in bed. As I told Agent Richards on the phone, I was running in the woods near the Schiffer Hartwin building on Sunday night, a little after midnight. I nearly fell over a hedge because my eyes were on this woman I saw shimmying out of a small window on the side of the building, some fifteen feet up. She landed on a mess of bushes then rolled off and ran for Van Wie Park behind me.”

Bowie looked wired. “What did she look like, Mr. Tallman?”

“She was slender, had on a dark jacket, zipped up, jeans, sneakers. I think she was wearing a black baseball cap, but she had a ponytail bouncing out the back, you know?”

"Yes," Bowie said. "What else?"

"I don't think she saw me, she was focused on getting out of there. She wasn't a runner, didn't have that natural runner's gait, but she was really graceful, I remember thinking that. She moved fluidly, I don't know how else to put it."

Sherlock sat forward. "Interesting way to put it—fluidly. Could you try to describe that more to us?"

"I don't know, really, like I said, she wasn't a practiced runner, didn't have those natural moves, but the thing is—" Tallman paused, shook his head. "Damned if I know, it's just that I know an athlete when I see one and that's what she was. She was in really good shape, you could tell. I could see she was scared but not panicked. Smooth, she looked smooth, controlled."

Sherlock pulled a stuffed bear from behind the sofa and stroked its soft fur. Sean still had his own white rabbit, but it only had one ear now. "Did you see the color of her ponytail, Mr. Tallman?"

Tallman thought about that. "It was thick—the tail was flopping around when she ran, I can see that clearly. The color—hmm, not black like mine, not red like yours,

Agent, brown, I'd have to say. Her skin was very white in the moonlight."

Bowie sat forward, clasping his hands between his legs. "You said her jacket was zipped up?"

"Yeah, it looked kind of weird since it was pretty warm Sunday night." He frowned a moment. "Do you know, now that I think about it, maybe she looked a little thick through the torso, a bit on the bulky side."

"Like she'd maybe zipped up something beneath that jacket she was wearing?" Sherlock asked.

"Yes, perhaps."

Bowie said, "Do you remember her size? Tall? Short?"

"That's tough since I didn't have any perspective. I guess I'd have to say pretty tall. I didn't have my cell phone with me or I might have called the cops. When I got home, Luke was sick and it fell right out of my mind. Then Monday morning I heard about the break-in at the pharmaceutical company on the news, and that someone was murdered in the park Sunday night. That shook me, I'll tell you, I mean, I saw the woman who was the thief. My wife Linda said I had to call you guys right away."

Savich spoke for the first time. "You're sure she was alone, Mr. Tallman? No one was there in Van Wie Park, waiting for her?"

"No one I saw. I'm always glad I don't see anyone when I run because it's dark and it's late and someone else might not want to just wish me a good evening, you know?"

They repeated the same questions, giving them a slightly different slant, but Eric Tallman didn't know any more.

Bowie rose about the same time as a baby's loud cry came over the monitor. He smiled. "You've given this lots of thought, we really appreciate your calling. Have fun with Luke."

Tallman rose to shake their hands. "This woman who broke in, do you think she also murdered that man?"

"We'll see," Bowie said.

Luke yelled again from the bowels of the house.

Tallman said, "The little champ's better than an alarm clock. It's ten on the button, and Luke is ready to suck down formula, burp, and gnaw on his stuffed dog's ears."

"What's his dog's name?" Savich asked him.

"Maynard the Brave. He's getting so tatty I'm afraid he's going to fall apart every time I wash him."

Savich smiled. "My little boy has a one-eared rabbit named Goober. We never found the other ear. As for the tail, we've reattached it a good dozen times."

As they were walking to their cars, Bowie said, "Georgie's all-time favorite stuffed animal is a crocodile named Rufus, not that she pays him all that much attention anymore since she's discovered the glorious world of dolls. Do you guys know there have got to be a thousand different Barbies and all of them have cars and planes and a thousand pairs of shoes?"

Ten minutes later, at Luther's Big Bite, they were drinking coffee, Savich tea. After Bowie took a grateful sip he said, "I'll check the photo IDs of all the female Schiffer Hartwin employees. If any of them look promising—tall, slender, brown hair—I'll show Mr. Tallman some photos. I don't think a police artist could get anything useful out of him."

Sherlock said as she sipped her coffee, not bad for a diner, but not nearly as good as Dillon's, the prince of the coffee bean,

"What struck me was a guy, who's a runner himself, saying the woman ran gracefully, fluidly, even though he said she looked scared. Interesting description."

They thought about this.

Bowie sipped his coffee. "Maybe she's used to moving gracefully—maybe at one time our girl was a model? Or a dancer?"

"Possible," Savich said.

Bowie said, "My agents in New Haven found out Blauvelt's air ticket was paid for on his personal account, not a company card. The Schiffer Hartwin travel staff told the BND, who told us they didn't even know he was coming to America. He rented a car at JFK, a dark blue Ford Taurus, license RWI 4749. Still no sign of it. As for where he was staying, no luck yet with that either, but he probably used an alias, paid cash."

"It would have to be a motel off the highway," Savich said, "a lodging that wouldn't care who or what he was. On the other hand, maybe he was staying with his murderer."

Bowie said, "Agents have checked the residences of all upper management Schiffer Hartwin employees, looking for the blue Taurus, speaking to neighbors. Nothing yet. Oh, yes, I meant to tell you the most important news this morning: our local police chief, Clifford Amos, has agreed to let us use his conference room for interviews, though he'd just as soon kick all our federal butts to Alaska. I asked Caskie Royal to come down at eleven."

Sherlock saluted him with her cup. "That's good, Bowie, take him out of his comfort zone."

Savich said, "Being close to a jail cell just might make him reevaluate his talking points." He smiled. He couldn't wait to have Royal on cop turf.

Sherlock said, "He knows exactly what the woman copied, he's afraid of it getting out, and so he's not cooperating, murder or no murder. The file or files she copied, that's got to be the key. And there were enough pages zipped into her jacket that she looked a bit bulky, Mr. Tallman said.

"Whatever she took, I'll bet my sneakers it shows something Schiffer Hartwin very much wants to keep quiet. I'll bet whatever it is, it's pretty big. I wonder what she's planning on doing with the file?"

Bowie said, "I was wondering that myself. It could be anything from extortion to espionage to someone trying to be a Good Samaritan."

Savich said, "Question is, what does she do with the files now that Blauvelt got himself murdered right out back at about the same time? Even if she didn't have anything to do with Blauvelt's murder herself, she's got to be scared. She's got to be praying we'll find the murderer soon so she'll be free to act."

Bowie said, "Or maybe she murdered Blauvelt, before or after she copied some files."

Savich said slowly, "She knew what she wanted, that's for sure. She wouldn't risk breaking in on a fishing expedition. I'll bet the German bosses are very well aware of what she copied by now, but without a direct link to the murder, we don't have a chance of talking anyone into a warrant." He swished the tea leaves at the bottom of his cup, and looked thoughtful.

Sherlock knew that look and smiled. "We've got to find her, see what's she's got before we arrest her for breaking and entering. I'm thinking once we know that, we'll know why Blauvelt was here."

Bowie looked out the window to see an ancient pink Cadillac cruise down High Street. "I'm not so sure about that. There doesn't necessarily have to be a tie-in."

"Maybe not," Sherlock said, "but somehow, it just feels right, like it's all part of the whole." She looked down at her watch. "Bowie, what about that German policeman? Andreas Kesselring of the German intelligence agency? Isn't he due in at JFK about now?"

Bowie grinned. "Yep, he surely is. I sent Special Agent Dolores Cliff to pick him up. She's got quite a talent for prying information out of people. Give her an oyster and she'll come away with the pearl. By the time she gets him back here, he'll have told her the color of his underwear and what he bought his wife for her birthday."

When they pulled into the parking lot of the Stone Bridge Police Department five minutes later, Bowie was rubbing his hands together with anticipation. "Caskie Royal's got to be scared spitless at this official invitation to cop central."

"Particularly since that woman has material that could fry his butt as well as the collective butts of the higher-ups in Schiffer Hartwin," Sherlock said. "But you know, it's Blauvelt who's the key. It all comes back to him and why he was here."

17

STONE BRIDGE, CONNECTICUT
Tuesday morning

Savich watched Caskie Royal come into the conference room, two Schiffer Hartwin lawyers following close on his heels. If the older man had worn a robe and sported a beard, he'd have looked like some medieval alchemist. His eyes were intense, his look resolute, ready to take on the devil himself. It had to be Bender the Elder, Savich thought. As for the younger lawyer, he was an interesting mix of apprentice and hip professional in his electric yellow tie and conservative suit. Royal looked like the successful CEO he was, in a lightweight gray suit, pristine white shirt, and sharp Italian loafers, the look both understated and expensive, sure to impress those lower on the food chain. He looked both angry and harried.

The alchemist took a pair of aviator glasses from his breast pocket and put them on his long narrow nose, adding at least fifty IQ points to the package. Savich watched him lightly touch a white hand to Royal's shoulder, lean close to whisper something in his ear. Royal jerked, gave the lawyer a searching look, then nodded slowly.

There was no hand-shaking, only curt nods to accompany the introductions, the barest sheen of civility. Both Harold Bender and Andrew Toms settled in, each withdrawing a yellow pad from their leather briefcases, expensive pens at the ready.

Bowie took papers out of his own briefcase, ignoring them for a good minute. He smiled when he finally looked up at Caskie Royal and his lawyers. "We appreciate you gentlemen coming in on this fine day." He leaned forward, and the smile fell off his face. "We are, as you all know, investigating the murder Sunday night of Helmut Blauvelt, an employee of your company. We are making the reasonable assumption, for the moment, that his murder may be tied to a break-in at your office that same night. We have reason to believe that if we can find the woman who broke into your office, Mr. Royal, we might find out who killed Mr. Blauvelt, and why.

"It seems, sir, that she intended to copy one or more of your sensitive passworded files. That means either someone in your office managed to find out your password, or you used a password that could be easily guessed. What is your password, Mr. Royal?"

"My dog, Adler, but no one knows what my password was, not even my executive assistant."

Bowie said patiently, "Anyone who knows what they're doing has a list of most common words or dates people use for passwords. Any dog in the household usually makes the list."

Royal said, "Look, I'll admit that was sloppy on my part, but I've since changed the password. As I've already told you people, Ms. Alvarez and I interrupted the thief before anything on my computer was even accessed. Maybe the thief tried, but didn't have time to work through the list of passwords."

Bender the Elder said, "The fact that Mr. Royal used a password a thief could guess means nothing. Mr. Toms personally examined Mr. Royal's computer before the hard drive was removed by the IT department. There was no attempt to access anything of value."

Andrew Toms's electric yellow tie blasted back the sharp sunlight pouring through the conference room window, making him either a sartorial masterpiece, or colorblind, Bowie couldn't make up his mind. "That is correct," Toms said, his pen on the table. Tap, tap, tap.

Bowie said easily, "I'm only pointing out that given the simplicity of your password, Mr. Royal, we can't assume your thief necessarily works inside your company or has everyday access to your office. I'm thinking of a possible whistleblower."

"Whistleblower, Agent Richards?" Bender the Elder arched one of his eyebrows a good inch. "Do you have any evidence of that?"

Bowie leaned forward. "Tell us, Mr. Royal, who do you think broke into your office Sunday night?"

"I have given this a lot of thought, naturally," Royal said, voice dripping sincerity, "and I can think of no one at all, either working for me or outside my business. It makes little sense, as I have already told Agent Savich. And I will say it again, there was nothing all that sensitive on my desktop computer. There is far more valuable information on our servers, but that is highly restricted."

Bowie said, "It's really past time for you to turn away from your lawyers' script and step into the light, Mr. Royal. Your computer was accessed, you know it, we know it. Now, what was in the file or files that were copied?"

Apprentice Toms said, "Mr. Royal has told you the truth, Agent Richards. He has also told you it doesn't matter to your murder investigation."

Toms, young though he was, was blessed with the mellifluous voice of a seasoned vicar. Maybe that was why he'd become the alchemist's apprentice. Bowie mowed right over that beautiful vibrant voice.

"Surely you realize that your problems are just beginning, Mr. Royal. The thief, this woman, she's got copies of files you obviously shouldn't have had on your computer, given that they could be accessed by anyone who could type in your dog's name. I don't imagine your masters in Germany are very pleased with you, Mr. Royal, just as I have no doubt Mr. Bender here is keeping them fully informed about what's happening across the pond."

"Agent Richards," Toms said, "Mr. Royal isn't here to be insulted. As for calling our corporate executives in Germany his 'masters,' you are merely baiting him, and, I might add, showing your jingoistic prejudices."

Bowie never took his eyes of Royal. "Any prejudices on my part are the least of your problems. The fact is, Mr. Royal, regardless of what that woman took, no matter if it is related to Mr. Blauvelt's murder, your future is in this woman's hands. If these two crimes are connected, and you impede our investigation, you can be indicted for murder as an accessory after the fact."

Royal shot a look at Bender the Elder,

but kept his mouth shut. Bowie wanted to smack him.

Bender the Elder cleared his throat. This aristocrat of lawyers had worked for Schiffer Hartwin over a decade, five years longer than Caskie Royal had been CEO. He cleared his throat again to draw all attention to him, even making Savich look up finally from MAX. He straightened his aviator glasses. "I will say this once, Agent Richards. Mr. Royal has no idea who the thief was or what the thief was after. What was on Mr. Royal's computer that night is irrelevant, and we cannot help you tie this break-in to the unfortunate murder of Mr. Blauvelt, as you persist in trying to do, with no proof whatsoever.

"Now, Agent, is there anything else you would like to ask Mr. Royal to justify your asking him here, to the local police department?" He looked around the spare conference room with its functional table and dozen uncomfortable chairs, as if expecting a roach or two to scuttle across the floor.

Sherlock spoke for the first time, her eyes locked on Royal's face. "Actually, we're close to locating your thief, Mr. Royal.

You see, we found a witness who saw her. And once we have her, we may not need you or your company's help any longer. That would not be in your best interest, Mr. Royal.

"I do not believe either you or Ms. Alvarez murdered Helmut Blauvelt. You don't seem to me to be murderers. But he is dead nonetheless, and he had an appointment to see you yesterday."

"No! I told you, I didn't even know Mr. Blauvelt was in the U.S.!"

"Mr. Royal, a waiter at Chez Pierre overheard Mr. Blauvelt speaking on his cell phone Sunday evening. He spoke of you, seeing you on Monday morning. Come now, Mr. Royal, as I said, I don't believe you killed him, so why not tell us the truth? Don't you want to help us catch Mr. Blauvelt's murderer?"

Bowie went still at her smoothly delivered lie.

Bender the Elder opened his mouth, but Royal shouted over him, "All right! It doesn't matter anyway. So I knew Blauvelt was coming, but only the day before he arrived, and it was he who called me, not the directors in Germany. Mr. Blauvelt gave me no indication why he was here, and I did ask him, but he said it would wait for our meeting. I was mildly alarmed because I know his reputation. I did not see him before his murder and that's the truth. That's all I know. It doesn't help you at all because he's dead."

"Whatever it was that led to the break-in, could it be that Mr. Blauvelt was here to deal with the situation, or the person responsible?"

"I don't know."

"His death could mean someone was desperate, about to be exposed. Have you thought about the fact you might be next?"

18

Apprentice Toms and Bender the Elder talked over each other, Bender winning out with his booming cauldron-stirring voice. To Sherlock's delight, he actually smacked his fist on the tabletop and lost it, his breath coming harsh and fast. "You baited Mr. Royal into saying this. I don't like your unnecessary scare tactics, Agent Sherlock, that insult both Mr. Royal and Schiffer Hartwin! And your name—Sherlock!—it's absurd, you made it up, right? It is meant to be funny?"

Sherlock gave him a sweet smile. "Maybe it is funny. I'll tell you, though, it gives some people pause, Mr. Bender. Does it give you pause, sir?"

"I am not the bad guy in your silly plot, Agent Sherlock!"

"No sir, I'm sure you're a fine, honorable man. However, Mr. Royal did, finally, admit he'd been lying. He knew Mr. Blauvelt was here, knew he was coming to see him. We're past that lie, aren't we, Mr. Royal?"

Royal didn't say anything, only nodded.

Sherlock looked over at Dillon, who had his head down, working on MAX. She knew he'd heard her questions, knew he'd heard her lie that pushed Royal into some truth about Blauvelt. The small smile on his mouth gave him away.

She looked back at Bender the Elder to see him shooting his cuffs in a practiced movement. He was regaining his control. He eased back his querulous voice, filling it again with authority, and hints of sarcasm. "I apologize, Agent Sherlock. It was not right of me to insult your name, no matter how—unusual."

Savich looked up now at Bender, whose jaw was still so tense Savich was surprised it didn't crack. Sherlock had pushed a major leaguer nearly to blows. He looked over at Caskie Royal, sprawled back in his chair, trying to appear relaxed and indifferent, but not quite managing it. Was he still not telling the whole truth? Had he also known why Blauvelt wanted to see him? Why Blauvelt was murdered?

Savich hit a final key on MAX's keyboard, read silently for a moment, then looked up at each of them impartially, shaking his head. "Maybe this is easy, so very easy."

"What's so easy?" Andrew Toms frowned, his pen tapping against the table in double time.

Savich said, "It's on the Internet, for all to see, right up front in articles in *The Wall Street Journal* and *The New York Times*."

"What is, Agent?"

Savich closed MAX's lid, bringing all eyes to him. "Mr. Royal, I could be wrong, but from just the little bit I've read online, the stakes might be high enough."

Royal frowned, rearranged himself in his seat.

"The drug is called Culovort, and Schiffer Hartwin has been the sole manufacturer of the drug at Cartwright Labs, in Bartonville, Missouri, and in Madrid, Spain. Lately there's been a shortage of the drug, and the cause of the shortage came to light in March."

Bender said, "This drug has nothing to do with anything."

"So you know all about Culovort, do you?" Savich studied each of their faces. "This drug has been off patent for many years now, which means its yearly income doesn't add much to Schiffer Hartwin's bottom line. Still, there has been quite a stir on some of the medical blogs related to cancer and among colon cancer support groups. Enough to cause quite a stir in the organization, no doubt. Enough to interest Helmut Blauvelt?"

Toms said in his deep magic voice, "Agent Savich, there have been production problems at Cartwright Labs because of a planned expansion that didn't take into account the full impact on the worldwide supply.

"Schiffer Hartwin is working to remedy the problem and get the supply of Culovort back up to demand levels. There has never been, nor will there ever be, any hint of wrongdoing on their part."

Bender's face was flushed again, his eyes behind his cool glasses hot and hard.

Savich waved him off, never even looked at him, something he imagined would enrage the man, and addressed Royal. "I find it interesting, Mr. Royal, that production of the drug in Spain has also ceased."

There was a frozen silence until Royal burst out, "I can't—"

Both lawyers were on their feet now. "You are skirting perilously close to libel, Agent Savich. Mr. Royal has nothing to say."

Through it all, Caskie Royal sat quietly, head down. His hands, however, were clasped tightly in front of him on the table, his knuckles white, his attempt at playing the lazy lizard long forgotten.

Savich continued, never looking away from Royal. "It's past time for you to let us help you. Do you actually believe your lawyers here—both of whom are paid by Schiffer Hartwin—have your best interests at heart? Surely you can't be that naïve, you know who pays their freight."

Bender shouted, "That is quite enough, Agent! We are leaving! This inquisition has gone on long enough!"

Bender put his arm on Royal's sleeve, spoke low in his ear, trying to pull him up, but Royal didn't rise.

Savich said, "Come on, Mr. Royal, tell us the truth before Schiffer Hartwin hangs you out to dry, or sends another Mr. Fix-It over here to deal with you. I fear for you, I fear for your family as well. This may be your last chance to let us help you."

Toms and Bender were on either side of Royal now, Bender's voice booming out, "There is absolutely no reason for you to fear for your safety!" They actually pulled Royal out of his chair.

"It's your life, Mr. Royal," Sherlock said. "Not theirs. You'd be wise not to forget that. Whoever killed Mr. Blauvelt knows who you are and what you know, and what danger you may pose to him. You do realize that, don't you?"

Caskie Royal looked ready to lay it all out. His face was dead white, his mouth working, like that humongous whale that swallowed Jonah.

Royal tried to jerk away from his lawyers, but they wouldn't let him go. "Look, I can't believe this is happening, and all because Blauvelt got himself murdered and that damned woman broke into my office! I didn't realize, I didn't know that—"

At that moment the conference room

door creaked open and a veritable man-god strode into the room, followed by a short plump woman with a heart-shaped face and very pretty dark hair—Agent Dolores Cliff.

Objectively the man really was quite beautiful, Sherlock thought, if one happened to like perfectly chiseled features, razor-sharp cheekbones, thick brown hair, and eyes greener than just-mowed summer grass. He looked to be in his mid-thirties, with a rangy, fit body covered with a well-tailored light blue suit. Arrogance seemed to pump off him in palpable waves. Agent Cliff looked besotted. Evidently the ride from JFK hadn't been long enough for her to get her fill.

"Sorry, Agents," Dolores Cliff said. "Agent Kesselring insisted we come in, wouldn't take no for an answer." If Sherlock had had her SIG out, she might have shot him, Agent Cliff as well for not keeping him out. They had been so close, but Caskie Royal had laid eyes on Kesselring and slipped his neck back into his leash.

19

So this was Agent Andreas Kesselring of German foreign intelligence, the BND, Savich thought, looking at the man, wishing he could kick him through the window. If not for Kesselring breaking the moment, Caskie Royal would have cracked, laid it all out. His lawyers knew it too. Both of them were looking at Kesselring as if he were the sheriff who'd ridden into town and shot the bad guys.

Kesselring looked at each of them dispassionately, gave a slight bow, then said in perfect English, "Agent Cliff and I have been listening from the hallway. You are

Special Agent Dillon Savich of the Federal Bureau of Investigation, are you not?"

Savich nodded. He wanted to take Kesselring down a notch for what he'd done, but Royal and his lawyers were still there.

Bender never loosened his grip on Royal's arm. "Agent Kesselring, we understand you are here to help solve Herr Blauvelt's murder. We have finished for today, and are leaving. Good day to you." Bender and Toms, Royal between them, hustled out the door in about two seconds.

Savich said, keeping his voice calm with effort, "You screwed things up already, Kesselring. Royal was very close to telling us the truth when you barged in."

Kesselring stared after the lawyers and Royal before turning back to say to Savich, "Yes, so it would appear. It seems I must apologize for my inopportune entrance. I had no idea things had reached a boiling point. I am Agent Andreas Kesselring of the German BND."

Bowie couldn't help himself, he had to add his two cents. "Kesselring, your timing sucked. Royal was this close"—Bowie snapped his fingers—"to laying his soul bare. Now his lawyers have got him back under control, and we may not have another chance."

Kesselring's face froze. He gave Bowie a stiff bow. "I have apologized, Agent Richards. I can do no more. You are Agent Bowie Richards, the Special Agent in Charge of the New Haven field office, are you not?"

"Yes, I am." Bowie saw that the usually hard-nosed Dolores was staring at the man like he was a Krispy Kreme. All right, so the guy was good-looking, no doubt about that, but Dolores was tough, curse her, he'd seen her bust badass drug dealers and yawn. Now she looked for the world like her hormones had taken over her brain. If Georgie ever looked at a man like that, Bowie would lock her in a closet until she was thirty. He'd have to think about assigning Dolores to cleaning the men's room for a week, see if that settled her hormones down.

Bowie waved to two chairs, but Agent Kesselring remained standing. He smiled at Agent Cliff and pulled out a chair for her, politely bowed her into it.

Savich said, "Kesselring, your coming in without even a knock—" Savich stopped himself, put away his mental whip. The man was standing stiff as a poker, his face expressionless, his hands fists at his sides. No need to belabor the point, Kesselring knew they were pissed. Savich doubted more haranguing would do any good since Bowie had laid it on with a trowel. He said, "Very well, Agent Kesselring. Apology accepted. Tell us what you know about the slowdown of production of the drug Culovort."

Kesselring said slowly, "I had no idea this drug Culovort was important to this case."

"It may be," Savich said shortly.

"I must apologize again, Agent Savich. I know little about the Culovort production problems, probably no more than you do, namely the company seems to have had problems both here in America and in Spain, and they have occurred at roughly the same time, which sounds like poorly timed coincidence to me. However, the situation in the Spanish plant is a bit different. The Spanish police are looking into the possibility of sabotage."

"Did you also find out the plant outside

Madrid isn't going to be reopened?" Savich asked.

Kesselring looked taken off guard, but only for an instant. "No. If this is true, it is a very recent decision."

"No, it isn't," Savich said, an eyebrow arched. "Why do you think anyone would sabotage a drug production plant in Spain?"

Kesselring said, "There are miserable people in the world, Agent Savich, you yourself deal with them on a daily basis. Many times they have no tidy motives to explain their actions.

"In the case of Spain, I'm inclined to agree with the Spanish police that it was a saboteur, perhaps a person who reacted badly to a drug produced at the plant or who had a loved one harmed by a drug. Who knows? It is unfortunate, to be sure."

Savich said, "Both production facilities down at the same time, in two different countries. It sounds like sabotage, you're right, Agent Kesselring. It also sounds like it was carefully coordinated. Two unrelated occurrences? What are the odds of that happening?"

"You are a cynic, Agent Savich."

"In our line of work, I would say that major doses of cynicism keep us grounded in the real world, don't you agree?"

Kesselring looked at Savich more closely now. Odd, Savich thought, how the man could become still so quickly, and make his face utterly expressionless, giving nothing away.

"Perhaps it could seem so, but I happen to know personally several of the directors at Schiffer Hartwin. I have always believed them to be good men. They have never given me reason to doubt them.

"As you must know, we in Germany are as concerned with proper conduct of our pharmaceutical houses as you in the United States. Schiffer Hartwin is an excellent pharmaceutical house, usually well managed.

"Schiffer Hartwin operates worldwide and has done so for over one hundred years. The Culovort production problems, they appear to be inopportune, nothing more. However, in light of this murder, I will closely look into the situation again, to see if there is anything going on behind the scenes that could possibly be related to this drug."

Savich said, "I just read on the Internet

that because of extraordinary pressure, Schiffer Hartwin has instituted a lottery system for oncologists. If the oncologist is lucky, the patient gets Culovort, and if the oncologist isn't lucky, his patient loses it. It's sad to be diagnosed with colon cancer and be subjected to that."

Kesselring said, "If it were I with colon cancer, or someone I loved, I would be very distressed. I would probably do a lot of yelling. I doubt, though, I would turn to violence."

He stood tall, shoulders back, and addressed them as if from on high. "Of course the immediate task at hand, Agent Savich, the task I have come to help you with, is the murder of Helmut Blauvelt."

Bowie wanted to clap. "Perhaps you can start by telling us why Helmut Blauvelt was sent here, and who he was sent here to, ah, visit."

Kesselring gave a shadow of a smile. "Ah, I see you know Herr Blauvelt's unfortunate reputation. That aside, the directors at Schiffer Hartwin tell me he was here on personal business. Indeed, they informed me they knew nothing of his plans to come to America."

Sherlock said, “He was here on personal business? Mighty dangerous business since Blauvelt got himself brutally murdered. Tell us, then, Agent Kesselring, how you plan to help us straighten this out.”

20

"I wish I knew that precisely, Agent. Looking into this murder is the task assigned me, as it is yours. You must know from the files we sent you that Herr Helmut Blauvelt was never arrested for any crime. He has never been shown to be consorting with any criminal organizations or abetting any fraudulent schemes, despite the rumors about him, which you yourselves, of course, have heard. I have heard them as well. They are, I am forced to say, groundless, even if they are delicious tales. We are opening this case with an open mind, simply as the murder of a German citizen on foreign soil.

"According to the company, Herr Blauvelt was their special emissary, a trusted employee of some talent whose job was to collect information and report back the exact nature of any problems he uncovered. He did, upon several occasions, discover evidence of local malfeasance, both within and against the company, but he was never authorized to take action against any individual. That was neither his job nor his responsibility.

"Schiffer Hartwin is very concerned about his vicious murder and that is why they specifically asked my agency that I be sent here, to assist you in discovering the truth."

Sherlock said, "You were not introduced to me, Agent Kesselring. I am Special Agent Sherlock."

"I know who you are, Agent Sherlock." For an instant, Kesselring looked directly at Sherlock, and his eyes went hot and dangerous. Savich went on red alert. What was that all about? Then Kesselring blinked, nodded, his eyes calm again, assessing her.

"Tell me, Agent Kesselring, what problem, specifically, could be so pressing here in Stone Bridge, Connecticut, U.S.A., that required Blauvelt's presence here? Surely you don't believe it was some personal business of his, as Schiffer Hartwin claims?"

He said to her, professor to student, "My superiors sent me here to assist in the apprehension of the person or persons who killed Herr Blauvelt. As for his reasons for being here, the nature of his business, again, Agent, I have no idea yet beyond what Schiffer Hartwin management has told me. Mr. Royal didn't help you?"

"Only that Blauvelt had made an appointment to see him," Bowie said. "Do you have any theory about this, Agent Kesselring?"

"Have you considered that Herr Blauvelt might have been murdered by one of your American muggers, a rather obvious possibility I would think, since his clothes and wallet were taken. He could have been, simply, in the wrong place at the wrong time. Even in Germany these things occasionally occur, to everyone's chagrin and regret."

Bowie said, "Perhaps you could tell us

why this American mugger beat Mr. Blauvelt's face into pulp, Agent Kesselring, and cut off his fingers, if all he wanted were his possessions?"

Kesselring went still a moment, taking this in. He said, "A crude attempt at hiding his identity. Occasionally a thug is also a psychopath. Then there is violence, ugly and vicious. We may be searching for such a man, gentlemen—ladies—a man who may be listed in your NCIC—your National Crime Information Center. I doubt this is the only time he has taken a life, and in such a repugnant manner."

Sherlock said, "Why do you think Herr Blauvelt's body was found in Van Wie Park, right behind the Schiffer Hartwin building? Another coincidence?"

Kesselring turned to look at her. Again, his eyes went hard and hot. "That is a curious thing, I will admit. It's the kind of thing that makes our lives crazy."

An attempt at humor? Sherlock didn't think so. His voice was flat, almost without expression. Those eyes of his when he looked at her, she couldn't begin to understand what was behind his beautiful eyes.

At that moment, Bowie would swear he

heard Agent Dolores Cliff sigh. He nearly sighed himself, reminded that her brain was temporarily off the planet. He rose and walked over to Agent Kesselring. "I'm assigning Agent Graham Painter to work with you whenever you are in need of assistance. Agent Painter will get you settled at our local B-and-B." Bowie heard Dolores make a small distressed sound, but didn't acknowledge the sound or Dolores. He was going to keep Dolores and Kesselring as far apart as he could. As for Graham, he was a perfect foil, a good old boy from Little Rock, so easy in his manner and speech you'd think his IQ was about as high as that of the hamburger he was eating. But Graham was sharp and steady and wouldn't get taken in, like Dolores. He could get along with Godzilla, if he had to, and might even get a kick out of Kesselring. Better still, he would keep Kesselring out of their hair.

Bowie said to the group, "I'll be back shortly, after I introduce Agent Kesselring to Agent Painter. He can tell Agent Painter how he wishes to proceed finding this psychopathic mugger. Agent Cliff, you will remain here."

Dolores looked like she was going to say something, but under Bowie's cold eye, she slowly nodded.

When the conference room door closed behind the two men, Sherlock said quietly, "This isn't good, Dillon, not good at all. Do you think it's possible Kesselring is in Schiffer Hartwin's pocket? Here to sweep whatever he can under the rug?"

"Oh, no," Agent Cliff said, sitting forward. "Andreas feels so badly about all this. I know he wouldn't—"

Sherlock said, "Get it together, Agent Cliff, or I'll have to deck you."

Dolores jerked back. "I don't think you have any right to say that to me." Her surprise gave way to insult and then to sheer mean. "You don't look all that tough. I don't think you could do it."

Sherlock couldn't help it, she laughed. "Keep that attitude, Agent Cliff, really, you need to, particularly around Kesselring."

"Easy for you to say, married to him."

Sherlock had to agree. "You got me on that one."

Savich, who'd been on MAX again, looked up. "There's a French pharmaceutical house, Laboratoires Ancondor, that owns the patent on an oral chemotherapy drug called Eloxium. It appears to have different side effects from the usual 5-FU with Culovort. Some of the side effects of Eloxium can remain with the cancer patient for life.

"Here's the kicker—if an oncologist has to switch the patient to the new oral medication, even if Culovort were to subsequently become available, there's no switching the patient back, at least from what I've read. And the oral drug is very expensive since it's not off patent like Culovort."

"Hmm," Sherlock said. "Makes you wonder if there might be some sort of collusion going on between Schiffer Hartwin and Laboratoires Ancondor? Shutting down Culovort production so patients are forced to Eloxium? Remember Carla Alvarez talked about a windfall profit. You don't think—"

Savich said, "I don't know but I'll call Mr. Maitland, have him contact Dice, see what she can dig up."

Dolores Cliff said, "I know drug companies do crappy things, but to stop producing a drug for people with life-threatening cancer to force them to another, very expensive drug? That would be disgusting."

Savich said, "Yeah, it sure would. So please take your blinders off, Dolores. We need to know how to play this. I've got to say from what I've heard this morning, and what I've read on MAX, this doesn't look good to me."

Dolores Cliff didn't say a word. She popped her gum and began chewing viciously.

21

Tuesday afternoon

Erin looked down at her orange Day-Glo watch, a gift from her nephew. She had another hour before she picked Georgie up from school. Then it was back here to straighten the apartment and make sure both she and Georgie looked decent, since Bowie was coming over with take-out Chinese for dinner and bringing along two visiting Washington, D.C., FBI agents. Three FBI agents in her apartment. *Three*. And here she was, a freshly minted criminal. What had she done in life to bring three FBI agents to her dining table?

You took in Georgie, that's what, idiot. When life gives you lemons, add vodka. No, no, make lemonade.

She'd deal, no choice. If she was smart, they could be three major-league sources for her.

She also had to decide what she was going to say to Dr. Kender at lunch tomorrow. He had to be in agreement with whatever she planned to do with the files from Caskie Royal's computer. He was, after all, the client, and she couldn't be certain she could keep his name buried deep if the files went public. The feds would be all over her about Helmut Blauvelt's murder.

Erin could almost see the doomsday tsunami rolling toward her.

The doorbell rang. She slipped her cell into her shirt pocket and glanced through the peephole to see a woman she'd never seen before, a woman who'd make any breathing man grab his heart. Long streaked blond hair, wide brown eyes—ah, maybe a new client?

"Yes?" she said as she opened the door.

"May I speak to you, Ms. Pulaski?"

Lovely low voice, honey smooth.

"Yes, of course. Did you call my office?"

"Office? No."

So not a client. "What can I do for you?"

"I'm a friend of Bowie's and I would like to see Georgie."

Erin looked at the female treat with her buttercup yellow sundress, high-heeled sandals, pretty French pedicure, and lovely thin nose. Her very nice social smile disappeared as she stepped into the apartment and looked around.

"I'm Erin. And you are . . . ?"

The woman turned back to face her. "I'm Krissy Canter. As I said, I'm a friend of Bowie's."

"I see," and Erin did indeed see. She was facing one half of a couple. So why hadn't Bowie asked her to take care of Georgie?

"Actually, I'm here to take Georgie back to my apartment."

"Have you spoken to Bowie about this?"

"Yes, of course. Well, not precisely about that, but she'd want to be with me, Bowie would want that as well."

"Georgie's still in school."

Krissy looked down at her watch, frowned.

"I forgot the school hours. I'll go pick her up, take her back to my place."

"I can't allow that, Ms. Canter, not unless Bowie tells me this is what he wants. It's his decision."

And everything went downhill from there.

When Bowie showed up with his married FBI agents in tow, delicious Chinese food smells wafting from two big brown bags with *Feng Nian* emblazoned on the side, Erin was wearing nice black slacks and her favorite pale blue cashmere sweater, Georgie standing beside her, in a clean pair of jeans and a pink polo shirt.

Krissy Canter had, mercifully, left after speaking tersely to Bowie on her cell phone. When she rang off, she'd said to Erin, "Once Bowie and I have a chance to talk this over, I'll be back for Georgie." She strode out of Erin's apartment without another word, looking as mean as a mud wrestler in beautiful sandals.

Bowie gave Erin a quick once-over. "You look really nice, Erin. Thanks for having us over. Savich and Sherlock here—" He didn't get out another word because his daughter launched herself into his arms.

He laughed, hugged her close, kissed her ear, and set her back down. “Okay, kiddo, put on your company manners. I want you to meet Agent Sherlock and Agent Savich.”

Sherlock came down on her knees, took the little girl’s hand between hers. “You can call me Sherlock. And this big guy is Dillon. I’m married to him. He and I have a little boy, younger than you. His name is Sean. Unlike you, Sean can’t dance.”

If there was any ice that needed breaking, that broke it. Erin stood back, watching the four of them. Bowie looked over, met her eyes.

“Sorry I didn’t give you any warning about Krissy, but I wasn’t expecting her back for another couple of days. We’ve been dating when she’s in town, but she’s never taken care of Georgie before, and when she asked me where Georgie was, I didn’t think, I just told her. I’ve told her Georgie needs to stay with you this time.”

“Krissy was really steamed at Erin,” Georgie said, sounding very pleased, which made Bowie frown. “She was at school when Erin came to pick me up. She gave me a big hug and told me I would stay with her soon. I could tell she really wasn't happy when we left. She gave Erin the evil eye."

Erin said, "Everyone come to the table. I'll get the wine and warm up the Chinese."

"Krissy said she was going to talk with you again, Daddy. She said she was going to be in town for three days before she has to fly back to London."

Bowie said carefully, "Did you tell Krissy you wanted to stay with her?"

Georgie shook her head. "I told Krissy Erin was my ballet teacher and I want to get on her good side." She turned and gave Erin a huge smile. "I told her Erin even ironed my clothes for me."

"I did not iron your clothes, just a light press. You're a brat, and a player—and you're only seven years and six months old."

"Okay," Bowie said. "I'll call Krissy, tell her again it's best if you stay where you are, to sweet-talk your teacher."

Married FBI agents, Erin thought, looking across the table at the dark tough-looking man and the sweet-as-a-daisy woman with her vivid red hair and beautiful blue eyes.

She imagined their little boy Sean, if he looked at all like them, would be a heartbreaker some-day. She knew she'd have to be on her toes, really careful how she wormed information out of them. It was going to be difficult to even get a word in edgewise since they were already telling Georgie stories about Sean and his best friend Marty, a little girl who could shoot more free throws than Sean could. Then Georgie told them a story about that jerky boy Aaron at school who tried to steal her lunch. Georgie said, "Today I had to eat the peanut butter and banana sandwich Erin made me really fast, because Aaron sniffed it out from six feet away." She followed that with ballet class stories where Erin was featured prominently—stuff she'd said, stuff she'd done. The kid remembered everything. It was scary.

". . . and then Erin told Molly Heckler to get her sucker out of her sneaker and stand it up against the window."

As the adults looked over at her, Erin said, "It wasn't a totally happy ending since I was the one who had to clean sucker-sticky off the window. You didn't tell them that, Georgie. You want another moo shu pork pancake?"

"Daddy calls them moo burritos. Can I fill it myself, Erin?"

Sherlock watched the easy camaraderie between the woman and Bowie's little girl. She said, "You guys have known each other for a very long time, right?"

"Just about forever," Georgie said. "Erin's been teaching me since I was a little kid, not even five. But she just met my daddy yesterday."

Interesting, Sherlock thought. "I've never met a ballet teacher before."

"I'm from a long line of dancers and teachers," Erin said as she handed Georgie the bowl of moo shu pork. "Both my grandmother and my mother are beautiful dancers, both of them still teach ballet, my grandmother in St. Petersburg, Florida, and my mom in Grand Haven, Michigan."

Sherlock rolled up a moo shoo pancake. "Is your father also in the arts?"

"No, Dad died of cancer three years ago. He couldn't dance a step even after a dozen Arthur Murray dance lessons with Mom. She finally gave up. He was a Navy SEAL."

And he could pick locks and strategize how to break into places where you shouldn't be. He taught me everything he knew— "Well, that's enough about me, isn't it?"

Bowie bit into an egg roll. "Erin's primarily a private investigator."

"Whoa," Savich said. "That seems an odd combination. How did you pick investigation as a field, Erin?"

"I'm good at finding out things," she said, "always have been. As a kid, my friends would ask me to help them find missing candy bars, video games, schoolbooks, whatever. I got better and better at it. Dad was always giving me hints on how to track things down. Then their folks started coming to me when they lost something or they had a problem with their kids, like a fight at school or something, and they needed information, or wanted to know what really happened. I could usually find out what they needed. And they'd give me a buck. My mom was embarrassed."

"And your dad?" Sherlock asked.

Erin laughed, couldn't help it. "He was very proud of me, said I was earning my college fund."

"What exactly did your dad do?"

"He was a security consultant," Erin said. "By the time I went to college, I knew what I wanted to do. My degree was in forensic science, lots of options there. I moved to Stone Bridge five years ago, got my license, and set myself up in business. I've supported myself very nicely, at least after my first two years or so in business. Most of my income came from teaching ballet in the lean years. Now, it's become more a hobby, something I enjoy and it keeps my hand in. Or my feet," she added and gave them a fat smile.

Georgie said, "Erin found my house key once. I looked and looked. I nearly called you, Daddy."

"That wasn't a biggie," Erin said. "You'd stuffed it inside your sock and tossed your sock in the waste basket because you found a hole. My dad told me all about how to find where missing keys were hiding."

Bowie waved his glass at her. "Thanks."

Erin grinned at him, waited a beat, and gave the agents a bright interested look. "Enough about me. Bowie told me you guys were sent here to assist him in his investigation into this Helmut Blauvelt's murder."

Sherlock shot Bowie a look, saw that he was concentrating on helping his daughter stuff moo shu pork into her burrito. Well, Erin was a professional, and she seemed smart and savvy. Evidently Bowie thought so. Why not use her brain? Sherlock said, "We've got a witness who saw our girl wriggle out of Caskie Royal's bathroom window, land in the bushes below, bounce right up, and take off running into Van Wie Park."

22

Erin nearly fell off her chair in a dead faint. She cleared her throat. “Did the witness give you a description?”

“Yes, he did. Longish hair flopping up and down out the back of a baseball cap. Probably brown, like yours, Erin. She was tall and rangy, the guy said. Slender. He said she didn’t look like a runner, but he was struck by how gracefully she moved. Fluidly, smoothly, he said. Isn’t that interesting?” And Sherlock held her eyes.

She can’t know, she can’t know, she can’t— Erin laughed to keep the terror out of her voice. “That is an odd thing to say. I wonder who she is.”

Bowie said, “Whoever she is, she’s got Caskie Royal’s fate in her hands, and he knows it. His lawyers sure know it, and I’ll bet now his bosses in Germany know it. He’s scared, but not enough to let us help him yet, the idiot.”

Sherlock added, “We also had a gorgeous German agent added to the mix today. Dolores Cliff, one of Bowie’s agents, thinks he looks like Adonis. He’s not Dillon, but I’ve gotta be honest here—he’s a pretty close second.”

Bowie said to Georgie, “You remember Agent Cliff?”

“Oh, yes, she kicked my soccer ball clear out of the field. It took Coach and a bunch of parents to find it. She showed me how to do the splits. I’ll bet Erin does the splits better than anybody.”

“Don’t kiss up,” Bowie said. “Yeah, that’s Agent Cliff, a real hardnose. Only thing is, she’s acting like you’d better not act when you turn thirteen, kiddo, and discover Y chromosomes.”

“What’s Y chromosomes?”

“Y chromosomes give fathers nightmares." He ruffled his daughter's hair. "Boys," he added.

Erin said, "You mean this guy, this Adonis, bowled her right over?"

"Yeah. I had to team him up with a guy who wouldn't care what he looked like."

"Why does he look like Adonis?" Georgie asked.

It was left to Sherlock to describe Kesselring, and she did him justice.

Georgie thought about this as she took another bite of her moo shu pork burrito. "I bet Krissy would really like him."

Bowie blinked. "Why do you think Krissy would like this foreign agent, sweetheart?"

"I heard Krissy tell you that she really likes your sexy stomach muscles. I'll bet this guy has sexy stomach muscles like you."

Bowie looked appalled. Erin thought he looked like his heart had seized.

Savich said easily, "This makes me wonder if Sean has passed along any phone conversations he's overheard. Scary, isn't it, Sherlock?"

Sherlock laughed. She leaned over to Georgie. "Do you know, I've probably said the same thing about Dillon. Hmm. I have to say that Agent Kesselring does look like a real dish. But you know what? Even though he looks like a chocolate sundae, I don't like him much. He isn't a straight shooter like Dillon or your dad, and that's something super important. I don't think he's got much respect for us women, either."

"A woman's got to be honest too," Bowie said. "Even if the woman is still a kid," he added, looking at Georgie.

Georgie spooned on some more sauce and took a big bite of her burrito. "Daddy's always honest except when he lies to Krissy."

Another heart stopper.

Bowie eyed his daughter. "I don't lie to Krissy. Why'd you say that?" Why had he asked that question, he, the well-trained FBI agent?

All the adults watched Georgie chew and swallow, and take a drink of her water. "I heard you tell her once that you were head-over-heels with work and couldn't see her. Then you took me out for pizza and a movie."

"Okay, but it wasn't a lie, not really," Bowie

said. "I worked after you went to bed." *Talk about lame. Well, he had checked his e-mails.*

"What about when she wanted to give me a movie-star Barbie birthday party and you told her my birthday was going to be at Grandma's?"

"That was very nice of her, but something came up. Hey, I threw you a party, remember?"

Georgie said to Sherlock, "I was Wonder Woman. I looped all my friends with my lasso of truth so they'd be forced to tell me what was written on the card in their hand—Daddy wrote down stuff—and they had to tell me if it was a lie or not. It was totally fun although the lasso didn't work very well. Well, Billy Bennett did tell me he'd stuck his finger in the frosting on my birthday cake."

"What did Wonder Woman do about that?" Sherlock asked.

"Billy helped me climb up to where Daddy hid the cake and I got a swipe too."

Bowie stared at his daughter, who looked very pleased with herself, the center of attention. "I wondered why the cake was all smeared."

"Billy and I tried to smooth out the frosting," Georgie said. "With our fingers."

After dinner, Sherlock dried glasses in the small kitchen while Erin washed. "Imagine, both guys tucking Georgie in."

Sherlock buffed up a dish and set it in the cupboard. "Dillon told me he'd like to see how it works with a little girl as opposed to a boy. He's very good at reading bedtime stories."

Erin handed her a plate to dry. "She's precocious. I'm reading her Nancy Drew's *Mystery at Lilac Inn* right now."

"I remember I always had a Nancy Drew under my pillow," Sherlock said. She added after a moment, "I know Bowie's wife died in an automobile accident. Do you know what happened?"

"Sorry, I don't. Georgie told me once that her mama was in Heaven, but I didn't want to ask her what had happened. And as I said, I only met Bowie yesterday."

"Looking at the three of you, it seems like much longer. You're all very comfortable around one another. Are you working any interesting cases right now, Erin?"

"Yes, one," Erin said without thinking as

she washed a fork. She shot a look at Sherlock. "Well, it's not all that important, not really."

Sherlock didn't change expression. "I hope it's not following a cheating husband?"

"Oh, no, I don't do those sorts of thing, at least not anymore. When I first started out, I did half a dozen to feed myself. No, this is about a man whose father is ill and—he's asked me to look into a—financial problem with his drugs."

Sherlock cocked an eyebrow.

Shut up, shut up, do you have a hole in your head? She was facing a real professional who could smell something crooked in the next county.

"What do you think about this murder?"

Relieved, Erin stopped scrubbing the shine off a fork. "From what Bowie's told me, it sounds like this guy Blauvelt went all over the world for Schiffer Hartwin, and cleaned up messes for them, silenced people who were causing problems, that sort of thing, right?"

Sherlock nodded.

"So maybe it's the CEO of Schiffer

Hartwin here in Stone Bridge who killed him, maybe in self-defense. What's his name?"

"Caskie Royal. Or maybe whoever killed Blauvelt is planning on killing Caskie Royal too."

Erin said, "You know, I think I'd speak to his wife. Wives know every secret, every sin."

"Her name's Jane Ann Royal. She's on my To Do list for tomorrow," Sherlock said. "Turns out, Caskie was sleeping with one of his executives. I guess the night of the break-in, they didn't make it to the couch."

Yeah, I sure wrecked their fun. Erin said, "I'd shoot the louse if he were my husband. Why is his wife putting up with it?"

"I'll ask her," Sherlock said. "Interesting that you're working on a case about drugs. Tell me about it."

Unfreeze your brain. "Well, I promised the client to keep it confidential, you know?"

Erin was saved by the two men walking into her small kitchen, Savich saying, "The kid's got Nancy Drew memorized."

Bowie laughed. "That's the truth. She said Savich read okay, but she likes your voice better, Erin. She said you should go to Hollywood. I think she really wants you to do her ironing."

Erin was still lying wide awake in her bed around midnight, with Georgie asleep and her apartment quiet, wondering if she'd looked guilty when Sherlock had asked her about her case. Sure she had.

No, she was being paranoid, about all of it. None of them would ever begin to guess it was she who'd dived out of Caskie Royal's bathroom window. Graceful or not, long brown hair or not, they knew her in an entirely different context. They had no reason to suspect her, none at all. She wasn't on their radar, she wasn't on anyone's radar.

Tomorrow, she was driving up to New Haven to have lunch with Dr. Edward Kender at the Berkeley College dining room.

She realized she'd told Sherlock she was having lunch in New Haven with a client at Yale, but that was it. Sherlock probably wasn't even listening.

Erin finally went to sleep and dreamed of the eight-hundred-pound gorilla sitting under the red beanbag in the middle of her living room.

23

BERKELEY COLLEGE DINING ROOM
NEW HAVEN, CONNECTICUT
Wednesday

Erin gazed around the huge dark-wood-paneled room as she chewed on a pork sparerib, the meat falling off the bone it was so tender. She waved the rib toward the large buffet. "I've never seen such a delicious display of food in one place in my life, and it's a college dining room. Amazing."

"Wait until you taste the garlic mashed potatoes, my father always calls it his forbidden treat when he eats here with me. It's been a while now."

Dr. Kender paused a moment, swallowed.

"I have the papers with me, sir. I think you're going to be very pleased. I know I am. It's all laid out, everything we want and need. Whenever you would like to look at the pages—"

He raised his glass of spring water and clicked it to hers. "Congratulations, Erin. That was well done of you, but far too dangerous."

"As I already told you, sir, I couldn't think of anything else to do. But please don't congratulate me for breaking the law, though in this case, I think it was worth it. On the bright side, I'm in the clear."

"Then we'll drink to your being in the clear." He tapped his glass to hers again. "I am happier than I can tell you that we have the goods on those unconscionable bloodsuckers. Yes, I would like nothing better than to study the papers in detail, but I invited you here for lunch. Let's eat first." He looked around the vast dining hall with its long tables and benches and the scattered group of students. He and

Erin sat at one of the small tables favored by the faculty. "I spent many happy hours here when I was a student. It seems like an eternity ago. Life continues to happen, doesn't it?"

"Yes sir, it does."

He sighed, ate a final bite of green beans, then slowly placed his fork neatly across his plate. "I can see something's happened since we last spoke. Before we go over the papers, tell me if I'm right."

Erin said honestly, "I'm scared. For you. Please tell me you had nothing to do with killing Helmut Blauvelt."

She watched a flash of fear cross his face, and then she saw anger, deep anger at her, and she saw something else in his eyes, some reaction she couldn't grasp, though she was usually very good at reading people. She watched him pick up his fork again and push a cherry tomato around in his salad plate. Then he looked at her and said smoothly, "I see you're serious, so I will answer you seriously. No, I did not kill Helmut Blauvelt. After you told me who he was, I paid more attention to the newspapers and the television reports. That isn't to say that if I'd run into him in a dark alley and I'd had a gun, I wouldn't have been sorely tempted."

"Good, that's answered. Thank you, Dr. Kender. To be honest, I was afraid you'd made contact with him in some way, that perhaps you were on the list of people he was here to see. If you had killed him, it would have been in self-defense in any case." *Except for bashing his face in and cutting off his fingers.* She wasn't about to tell him that. Those details hadn't been released by the FBI, probably never would be, except to a grand jury.

"Thank you for believing me to be such a man of action."

"I think most anyone could be a man of action if pushed hard enough, if, for example, someone you love is placed in danger."

Dr. Kender stared at her. "Do you really think the man could have been here to see me? Me, as in archaeology professor at Yale University? An academic right down to my tweed jacket?"

"And a very persistent one, Dr. Kender. I'd like for you to tell me exactly how far you went with your complaints and questions to Schiffer Hartwin. Both here and in Germany."

"I pestered them nearly every day from the day after Dad's oncologist told us about the unexpected Culovort shortage, until I came to you last week. I helped support the post office, one registered letter after the other, maybe a few dozen if you count all the members of the board of directors in Hartwin, Germany. I don't remember if I told you I called. The first couple of times, the assistant put me through to the head of the whole shebang, a Dr. Adler Dieffendorf. The conversation was not cordial, especially after I told him cutting back on the production of Culovort was criminal, that he was killing my father. I asked him if it was his wife or one of his children who needed the drug, would he have allowed this to happen? I told him I was sure they could start production up quickly again if it was worth more money to them. I told him I would soon have proof of that, and I planned to go to the media once I had all the facts. I might even have intimated I'd key his Mercedes before he lost his calm and threatened me with their cadre of lawyers. Then he hung up on me."

Erin said, "Did you tell him where you were going to get the proof?"

He looked down at his elegant hands. "Well, I might have mentioned the American headquarters in Stone Bridge."

Wonderful, just wonderful. "Did you imply that an employee here in the Stone Bridge headquarters had ratted them out?"

"I made up any number of things, any threat I could think of. Yes, I might have suggested that someone would roll on them. I remember he snorted when I mentioned a whistleblower. A pity, but he didn't seem to believe that.

"It got harder and harder to get through to anyone after that, though I did manage a few calls to some of the other directors. They all spoke English quite well, a good thing since I can't think all that fast in German."

He gave her a crooked smile that was really quite charming, but Erin didn't smile back. "So you've been a real pain in the butt, sir?"

"I certainly tried to be. There were also e-mails, and I've contributed to several blogs and public forums on the Internet. I'm just one voice among many out there."

"Okay, here's what I'm thinking. Suppose someone actually believed you about getting your hands on proof, believed that an employee at Stone Bridge was going to spill the beans. I'm thinking you might have scared someone into action, and they sent Helmut Blauvelt over here to see exactly what you had and who you were talking to at Schiffer Hartwin."

Dr. Kender sat forward, laid his hand on hers. "Listen, Erin, I'm truly nothing to Schiffer Hartwin, just an irritant, someone hardly worthy of their attention. When it comes down to it, all I ever did was yell and write letters. Surely they wouldn't see me as a threat."

"Sir, stay with me here. The game has changed. Blauvelt is dead. Not just dead, he was brutally murdered. Someone in Schiffer Hartwin has stepped way over the line. My guess is, because they're guilty of a real crime this time, that would mean jail time, not just a fine for pulling something unethical."

"Erin, who could possibly connect me to the break-in, and why would they even think of it? Schiffer Hartwin has undoubtedly gotten a truckload of furious complaints from patients."

She leaned close, lowered her voice.

"Listen, everyone now knows the person who broke into Royal's office was a woman. Obviously they don't know who I am, at least not yet, but if they find me, they can and will connect me to you. The FBI will investigate the loudest voices against the company, if they don't solve this murder quickly."

Erin looked at him steadily. "Did Helmut Blauvelt contact you, sir?"

Dr. Kender shook his head. "No, he did not contact me. I have had no communication at all, either from Blauvelt or from anyone else at Schiffer Hartwin."

On the other hand, why would the snake warn his prey before sinking in his fangs? "Listen to me, you're not taking them seriously enough. What some of the drug companies have done curdles my belly. Until now, they've played corporate fun and games over patent extensions, skewing the data they present to the FDA to get new drugs approved, misleading the public about side effects. When asked about it, they defend the indefensible because billions of dollars are at stake. They seem to be willing to do just about anything to keep the money flowing in. But not murder,

Dr. Kender. This is a whole different level of serious."

"You're wrong, Erin. Take the antidepressant drug Paxil. GlaxoSmithKline did not disclose that Paxil was ineffective or could be dangerous when taken by children. How many children might have become suicidal or even committed suicide as the result of lies and cover-ups like that? Wouldn't their deaths be the same as murder?"

She shook her head. "I'm sure no one at any of the drug companies wants people to die, Dr. Kender."

"That's a circular argument, Erin. The fact is, people have died. And so what? No one gets indicted, no one goes to jail. The drug companies simply pay out huge fines and go about their business. Like Pfizer. They were so blatantly unethical, last year our government fined Pfizer two point three billion dollars, yet no one was held responsible and charged, no one was sent to jail. Nothing happened that might have made a difference. I'll tell you, sometimes I think we're a failed species."

He shook his head. "Do you know that

while negotiating this huge fine, Pfizer was being charged in another case in Nigeria alleging they'd done illegal drug studies on hundreds of children? That there were claims that Pfizer didn't tell parents their children were part of a trial? And claims that the Nigerian approval on which Pfizer relied was a sham?

"My bet is they'll get away with paying out a half billion dollars to the families and to government officials, of course—shareholders' money."

Erin reached out her hand and laid it over his. "All of that may be true. However, what's important is what's in front of us to deal with now. Schiffer Hartwin know they've got big problems here, and both they and the FBI are looking for the woman who broke in, looking for me. They could be watching us right this minute." Both of them looked around the dining hall.

"Everyone's a teacher or under twenty-two," Dr. Kender said. "Stop worrying. Caskie Royal, he's the one who should be worrying. He's the one who left the damning information on his computer. May I read the documents now?"

She leaned down to retrieve the pages from her ancient black leather briefcase. "Read, then we'll talk about what to do."

When he finished, he looked up, eyes glistening, grinning like a maniac. "You've got them! There's enough here to show reckless disregard, enough to lose them a great deal of money and force them to start making Culovort again. I can take this material to the media, and at the same time, get it sent to the Justice Department. I can tell all of them these documents were sent to me anonymously. You'd be safe then."

"Maybe for thirty minutes," she said. "Neither of us is invisible, Dr. Kender, and I'll have a bull's-eye painted on my chest. Even if the FBI were willing to keep my identity a secret for a while—and there is the small matter of breaking and entering—Schiffer Hartwin would eventually find out who I am. Neither of us is sitting in a good place here, Dr. Kender. Don't forget we'd also be suspects in Blauvelt's murder, and we don't know who killed him. I'd like to ask you to hold off going public with these papers, even anonymously. I want to give the FBI a chance to solve this murder first."

Dr. Kender took a drink of his now tepid tea, gave her a crooked grin, and patted his mouth with his cloth napkin. "I've always believed cops were fascists. But maybe the FBI are the ones to help us now."

Erin said matter-of-factly, "You're a professor at an East Coast university. Of course you believe cops are fascists, it's hard-wired into the walls here, but they're not. I know three of them who only want to catch criminals."

"You mean us?"

24

WASHINGTON, D.C.
Early Wednesday afternoon

Veteran lobbyist Dana Frobisher cut the huge fried shrimp and lovingly laid it on her tongue. She didn't particularly like shrimp, but it was deep-fried, beautifully spiced, and the fact was, shoe leather would taste delicious if it was fried. She savored the taste, ate another shrimp, then opened her eyes to smile at Senator David Hoffman, Chairman of the Appropriations Committee, a long-time powerhouse on the Hill. She'd met him half a dozen times over the years, but she'd never sat across a private table from him, and, wonder of wonders, at his invitation. When his head staffer, Corliss Rydle, had called her executive assistant, Jeremy Flynn, and said Senator David Hoffman wanted to ask her to lunch, she could hardly believe it. And here she was, less than a week later, eating fried shrimp with the great man. He was fit and good-looking. He didn't look as old as she knew him to be, not that it mattered since he didn't, according to Jeremy, screw around with his aides or anyone else. What mattered was the senator could give her clout and influence with a flick of his pinkie finger.

"I've never eaten at the Foggy Bottom Grill before," she said, ate another shrimp, and saluted him with her water glass. No wine at lunch, a longtime promise she'd made to herself when she'd first arrived in Washington fifteen years before. She was pleased to see he was drinking fizzy water as well, a slice of lemon perching on the edge of the glass.

Hoffman raised his glass and smiled at her. "I see you like the shrimp. I usually order the shrimp myself, astronomical fat content be damned. I figure stuffing the fat-covered shrimp in my mouth once a week isn't going to clog my arteries. I'm pleased you're enjoying it."

"Oh, yes, it's nearly a spiritual moment." She ate another shrimp, patted her mouth with her napkin, and leaned back. The time had come to go beyond pleasantries. She was through with her shrimp now, good as it was, and she was ready to hear what he had in mind. Dana gave him a lovely sweet smile, tried to keep the excitement out of her voice. "Now, if I can do anything for you, Senator, I'd like to hear it. Otherwise, I have a couple of matters of my own that might interest you—"

"Actually, it's about my wife, Nikki. You worked with her at one time, didn't you?"

He wanted to talk to her about his dead wife? What was this all about? Dana said, "Yes, and I liked her very much. It was a huge loss to all of us when she died." That sounded good, she thought, and it was the truth, at least way back then. She saw a spasm of pain cross his face. He was still grieving? She ate a bit of organic salad, and waited for him to speak. But the salad didn't taste very good, more like a TV remote with vinaigrette on it. Had he asked her to lunch for a trip down memory lane about his dead wife? Wasn't this about the advice she could provide him on the miserably low funding currently under discussion in committee for children's diseases?

"I believe you and my wife were involved in one of her favorite charities—spinal meningitis? As I recall, you were just a baby lobbyist at the time, full of passion, wanting desperately to move up in your lobbying firm. Weren't you with Patton and Associates at the time? Nikki was very impressed with the work Patton did."

Dana nodded automatically. She couldn't believe it, he'd asked her to talk about his damned wife? And her damned charities? She felt deflated, a bit angry at his deception.

Hoffman suddenly sat forward, his lunch, a small Cobb salad, untouched in front of him. "I still miss her, Dana. I suppose you could say she even speaks to me."

Speaks to him? Was he crazy?

"There was something I wanted to ask you about, something she told me about the two of you—"

Dana Frobisher heard his deep mellifluous voice, the words nearly resonating, a master's voice, she thought, but oddly, she couldn't seem to understand the words, what they meant, ah, but they were so beautiful, his voice so mesmerizing. There were two shrimp left on her plate and she forked one up, but as with the salad, she couldn't taste the delicious fried fat anymore. She stopped chewing the shrimp when she felt a hard pounding over her right eye. Oh, no, not a headache. The last thing she needed was a headache while she was sitting not two feet from one of the most powerful men in Washington. She never had headaches, but she knew this wasn't just a headache, this was something more, this was fast becoming excruciating, vicious. She closed her eyes and swallowed, felt suddenly nauseated.

"Dana?"

She opened her eyes, tried to concentrate, but she couldn't quite focus. She realized she couldn't seem to swallow, and she started to hear her own breath in her throat. She rubbed her palms over her neck, working the muscles, but everything seemed to be backing up inside her, not just her precious breath, but something black and rancid and vile. She tried to scream with the sudden terror of what was happening, something she couldn't begin to understand, but nothing came out of her mouth. She fell over onto the floor, vomit heaving out of her mouth. In another moment, she went into violent convulsions. She heard the shouts of those around her, felt hands touching her, and she saw Senator Hoffman's face over hers, a pale blur, and she heard him say over and over, "Tell me what's wrong, Dana. Talk to me. Tell me what to do."

What to do? Her stomach was ripping apart and he wanted her to tell him what to do? He was shaking her shoulders, still speaking, but now it didn't matter because her mind spasmed with horrible, unspeakable pain and then something inside her brain seemed to pop, and she didn't know she was convulsing anymore, or that foam was billowing out of her mouth.

Her heart stopped at exactly one-thirty p.m.

25

Wednesday afternoon

Savich stepped out of the black FBI Bell helicopter at exactly five p.m. Special Agent Dane Carver waved him toward his Jeep. As Dane pulled out of Andrews Air Force Base, he said, “Everything’s still in an uproar. The body of the lobbyist who was poisoned at the Foggy Bottom Grill is already with Dr. Branicki at Quantico. The paramedics who showed up a few minutes after she died said it looked like arsenic to them. We already know they were right. Of course, they've closed the place down and it's all over the news."

Savich said, "Where is Senator Hoffman?"

"Back at his home in Chevy Chase, with Mr. Maitland. He's shaken, as you can imagine. Look, Savich, Mr. Maitland told us you'd been working with Hoffman, that you told him his wife was trying to warn him—do you think the poison was meant for him? That Dana Frobisher was poisoned by mistake?"

Savich looked out the Jeep window at the sun baking the sidewalks, radiating enough heat to make you sweat just looking. Here it was mid-September and nearly ninety degrees. There were still tourists wandering around, families with tired children in tow. Wasn't school back in session? He remembered Dane's question. "To swallow a bullet meant for someone else, to die because of a mistake. That's tough, Dane."

Dane turned onto K Street. He spotted staffers thick on the ground, off for the day, heading for the local bars, maybe for home. He pulled the Jeep into a parking slot in the underground garage at the Hoover building.

Dane said, "According to Senator Hoffman, she'd had only a few bites of the salad, but she'd really plowed into the fried shrimp. I guess the poison was probably in the batter coating the shrimp. It's all being analyzed as we speak."

They walked through security, took an elevator to the fifth floor, and walked down the impossibly wide hall to the CAU, Savich's Criminal Apprehension Unit.

Ollie Hamish, Savich's second in command, was speaking to Ruth Warnecki, gesticulating as he always did. Agent Cooper McKnight, only three months in the unit, stood close, listening intently. Shirley, their unit assistant, sat on Dane's desk, chewing on an apple, listening as well.

Everyone turned when Savich and Dane walked into the large room. Ollie called out, "Mr. Maitland just phoned. Arsenic poison was all over the shrimp, in the batter, and she ate five of the six shrimp they served her. That's why she died so quickly. He said it wasn't elemental arsenic, but an arsenic compound—arsenic trioxide, to be exact. Get this—arsenic trioxide is approximately *five hundred times* more toxic than elemental arsenic. A lethal dose of pure arsenic in adults is about a hundred milligrams. The woman ate about four hundred milligrams of the arsenic trioxide. Dr. Branicki said she'd have died from just one shrimp.

"It literally exploded her system. She was dead within minutes, maybe less. The senator is in shock.

"Ruth here personally interviewed the waiter. Tell him, Ruth."

Ruth Warnecki said, "Mr. Graves is a twenty-year veteran waiter at the Foggy Bottom Grill. He told me the senator always orders the fried shrimp every week when he comes in. This time he didn't. Mr. Graves said he was surprised, but the senator told him, laughing, that his waistline was begging for only a salad today, and Mr. Graves recommended a small Cobb salad. He remembers the senator told his companion about how great the fried shrimp was, and she ordered it.

"When he brought their plates, Mr. Graves said he accidentally placed the shrimp plate in front of the senator, only to be reminded that Ms. Frobisher had ordered it. He said he remembered thinking that it was a forgivable mistake on his part, since he was used to serving it to the senator, and usually it was the ladies who ordered small salads."

Savich said, "Okay. Ruth, I'd really like to speak to Mr. Graves myself."

Ollie gave him a big grin. "Ruth and I figured you would. He's in the conference room with Lucy."

When Savich walked down the hall into the conference room, he saw Agent Lucy Carlisle sitting beside an older man who was squeezing the life out of a Coke can. He was long in the torso, thin as a plasma TV, and was trying to grow a beard that had, so far, produced only patches of hair on his chin and cheeks. Lucy looked up, smiled at Savich. "Ollie said you'd be here in twelve minutes. Ruth said ten. She was right." She turned. "Mr. Graves, this is Special Agent Dillon Savich, my boss. He'd like to speak to you."

Mr. Graves raised tired eyes to Savich. Savich saw his right eye twitch. He'd finally crushed the Coke can, and now he was tapping it up and down on the tabletop. The man was a mess.

Savich sat across from him. "Mr. Graves, I appreciate your waiting for me." He shook the man's hand, wishing he could calm him. "I'm Agent Dillon Savich. Now, I know this must be very difficult for you, a huge shock. I know you've probably told what happened at least a half-dozen times by now, but I hope you would tell me. Please go slowly, all right?"

". . . When I first saw it, the shrimp plate was under the warming lights, the table number and order tucked beneath it. The Cobb salad sat beside it, not under the warming lights. You never put salads under the warming lights." Mr. Graves blinked, cleared his throat. "I took both plates to Senator Hoffman's table and automatically put the fried shrimp plate in front of Senator Hoffman. He laughed, told me not today, he had to lose an inch, but the lady was fit as a fiddle and so it was for her enjoyment today. I was embarrassed, I'll admit it. To make a mistake like that with Senator Hoffman, but as I said, he only laughed, wasn't put out or anything, not that he ever is. He's been coming to the Foggy Bottom Grill for maybe ten years now, once a week, like clockwork, and he always orders that shrimp plate—" He looked at Savich and his eye twitched again. "That poor woman, it was horrible, Agent Savich. One of the busboys pulled my arm, and I looked up to see her holding her throat. I remember thinking she looked more confused than anything, like she didn't know what was happening to her. It was so fast, it's hard to remember, but then she toppled off her chair and onto the floor and she was vomiting and writhing and then she just seemed to freeze. White foam was pouring out of her mouth, I can see it so clearly, that white foam just gushing out of her mouth, so much of it, then she lay there perfectly still, and I just knew she was dead.

"Senator Hoffman was with her, talking to her, trying to find out what was wrong, shaking her, but it didn't do any good. She was gone. It was horrible."

Mr. Graves put his head on his folded arms on the table. His shoulders were shaking. Lucy reached over and patted him.

Suddenly Mr. Graves raised his face, now white and drawn, his eye twitching again. "What if Senator Hoffman had ordered the shrimp? What if I'd given him the plate? He would have died." He stopped cold, as if appalled at what he'd said. "It didn't matter, did it? No matter where I put the plate, one of them would have died."

"I know, sir. Mr. Graves, do you have any idea how the poison got into the shrimp batter? Are there any new employees?"

"Yes, I already told Agent Hamish. There are a couple of young kids working in the kitchen, busing, washing dishes, that sort of thing. It's a low-paying job, but enough to give high school kids walking-around money. All the waitstaff, we've been there for years. It's a good job, and we have our own clientele, really, who come in and ask for us specifically."

"I want you to think back, Mr. Graves. Picture the kitchen in your mind after you placed Senator Hoffman's lunch order. That's right, think about it. Just relax. Now, tell me what you see."

Mr. Graves said slowly, "I see Gomez, he's one of the sous chefs, a real mean little pisser, chewing out one of the new kids because he dropped a pan of sautéed mushrooms on the floor. There's lots of commotion because the mushrooms were going on the filet mignon Senator Reinwald had ordered. The chef's screaming for quiet, the dishes are getting scrambled around, everyone's on edge." He paused a moment, then shook his head, opened his eyes. "I'm sorry, Agent Savich, but I really can't recall anything else. Just the chaos. Do you think those mushrooms were spilled on purpose? The kid said someone bumped him, he didn't see who, so it wasn't his fault. You think that person could have slipped into the kitchen and put the arsenic in the shrimp batter?" He closed his eyes again.

"Who normally prepares the shrimp batter?"

"One of the sous chefs, always. The chef himself sometimes. Today? I honestly don't remember."

"Thank you, Mr. Graves," Savich said, and put his hand on his shoulder. "I know this is very hard for you. You've been a great help."

26

STONE BRIDGE, CONNECTICUT
Wednesday afternoon

At two o'clock, Sherlock and Erin pulled into the Royals' impressive tree-lined circular driveway on Maple Lawn Drive. Sherlock knew Caskie Royal was at the office, probably being worked over by the Schiffer Hartwin lawyers trying to ensure he stayed with the program and kept his mouth shut.

The house was a huge white Colonial, at least eight thousand square feet with a four-car garage, its newly painted white doors glistening in the September sun.

The grounds were beautifully groomed with thick full bushes and well-spaced maples and oaks.

There was a new black Audi coupe in the driveway, a motorcycle beside it, and a bicycle propped against the garage.

Sherlock knew Erin was psyched, nearly jumping out of her skin, but trying hard not to show it. She'd called Erin a short time after Dillon had left for Washington and asked if she'd like to come with her to interview Mrs. Royal, saying it might help to have another woman with her, even if it was official FBI business. The truth was that in her gut Sherlock knew there was something going on with Erin, something she didn't understand yet, something Erin knew and she didn't. Her interest in this whole case seemed excessive. Sherlock wanted to find out more about Erin Pulaski, P.I. And what better way than to invite her along to interview Mrs. Royal? She hadn't told Bowie.

Erin said, "You're sure Mr. Royal isn't here?"

Sherlock pulled the key out of the Pontiac's ignition. "Nope, Caskie's at the office, either being pounded by the Schiffer

Hartwin lawyers or huddled with Ms. Carla Alvarez, or all of the above. Nice spread, isn't it?"

Erin, who'd driven by the Royal house several times on Sunday evening, merely nodded. "It would appear there's lots of money in drugs."

Sherlock grinned. "Sure enough."

A young Hispanic woman with beautiful glossy hair answered the door. She was wearing an actual uniform. Sherlock gave her a big smile and showed her FBI creds. She watched her study them carefully before she said, voice wary, that Mrs. Royal was playing tennis. Well, Sherlock thought, of course there were tennis courts. The maid handed back her ID, and led them through an immense entry hall, through an equally impressive family room, through glass doors into a large covered patio. Jasmine wove in and out of white beams overhead, scenting the air, and baskets of flowers spilled out of Italian pots lining the patio, their scent mixing with the scent of the jasmine. Sherlock said to Erin, "This is beautiful. Sean would really like that swimming pool."

"Georgie would, too." Erin shaded her

eyes with her hand and looked toward the tennis court some twenty yards beyond them, then on to the woods behind the six-foot gray stone fence that separated the woods from the property. At one time the fence had enclosed the entire property, but now gray stones lay scattered in small piles along a section of it, probably left there on purpose to add atmosphere. "So would I, actually," and Erin grinned.

"I would, too," the maid said, smiled, and left them. They skirted the pool area and walked down a flagstone path to the tennis court. A double, of course, not a single. One for family, one for friends.

"I wonder why the original owners built that fence all around the property," Sherlock said. "It would make this place feel like a prison. Just look at the height of that back wall."

Erin said, "I wonder why they left that last piece. Surely not for protection. Walk around it and you're inside."

"Probably to keep the woods from encroaching. It's stark but beautiful, isn't it?"

Erin nodded. "I'll bet you there are alarms all along where the fence used to be."

"That was good, Erin."

"Yeah, well, I saw an alarm box on the back of the house. Wow, look at her move. She's got a great backhand."

They stood alongside the court watching Jane Ann Royal playing a vicious game of tennis with a hunky young guy, probably her instructor. When she aced her serve, she tossed her racket in the air and did a victory dance. The young man, perfectly tanned in his tennis whites, called out, "Very nice game, Jane Ann. You really got some heat on that last serve. Sharp English, too. Well done."

"Yep, that's a teacher, not a friend," Sherlock said. "A friend would be properly pissed at losing."

"Lover too?" Erin wondered aloud.

"We'll soon see. She sure seems like a happy camper, doesn't she? All caught up in winning the game, not a single worry to her name. You'd think her husband hasn't spoken to her about any of the trouble camping at their door."

Jane Ann Royal saw them and waved. When she trotted to them, short blond hair shining in the bright sunlight, long lean tanned legs covering the ground at a fine clip, she was smiling, flushed with victory, not a care in the world. "Hi, who are you? Alana brought you back so I suppose you're not jewel thieves."

Sherlock handed over her ID.

Jane Ann Royal studied her creds more thoroughly than Alana. She looked up, frowning. "FBI? Oh, yes, Caskie told me you people were in town to investigate the murder of that German guy."

Sherlock's eyebrow went up as she slipped her creds back in her pocket. "Didn't your husband tell you who the German guy was?"

"No, he was busy, on his way out to some meeting. I heard on TV the dead guy worked for Schiffer Hartwin. I asked Caskie if he knew the guy the next morning, but he said he'd only heard of him, didn't have a clue why the man was even here. What's up?"

"I'm Agent Sherlock and this is Erin Pulaski. We'd like to talk to you, Mrs. Royal."

"You're kidding—Sherlock? That's very cool."

"Thank you," Sherlock said, and smiled. She felt a tug of liking for Jane Ann Royal.

"Come over to the patio, we'll sit down, and Alana can bring us some iced tea."

She turned to wave at the tennis instructor, who waved his racket back at her and disappeared around the front of the house. A few moments later, they heard the motorcycle fire up.

"Your instructor?"

"Yes. Mick Haggarty. Quite a cutie, isn't he? He couldn't make it in the pros and so he teaches at the Glenis Springs Country Club over in Millstone. Actually, Mick wants to go to Hollywood and see his name up in lights, poor schmuck. I've seen him perform in summer stock at Belson College. He's not a bad actor, but everyone knows it's all about who you know and who you are in L.A. And no, we're not sleeping together." She grinned. "Well, not yet. I'm still evaluating. His form on the tennis court is excellent, he's got a good sense of humor, so who knows?"

Sherlock said, "I would imagine your husband doesn't have much time for you, what with the FBI all over him since the murder. Thing is, Mrs. Royal, Caskie did know Helmut Blauvelt."

"Caskie never has much time for anybody, particularly his sons. He knew Blauvelt? That sounds interesting. All he said to me about it was that he met with you guys yesterday at the local police station, in a grungy conference room, his words, to talk about what he knew about Helmut Blauvelt, which wasn't much, he told me. He wasn't happy about it, I can tell you that. So, you caught him out? How did you manage that? Fry his butt?"

"We singed his butt," Sherlock said. "Only singed."

Erin said, "Did he seem worried when he spoke to you?"

Jane Ann shrugged, accepting Erin as another cop. "Caskie's always been a worrier, it's really what he does best. I'm forgetting—he's really smarter than he has a right to be, excellent at planning and sniffing out the marketplace, and that's why he makes the big bucks. The bonuses are quite lovely." She waved her hand around the house and grounds.

"I see he's many thousands of square feet smart," Erin said.

"Nearly nine thousand, as a matter of fact," Jane Ann said. "And that's just the house."

The tea arrived and both Erin and Sherlock turned down sugar. Jane Ann Royal loaded in three envelopes of Splenda, raised her glass, and gave them a toast. "To this beautiful September day. Now, Agents, what can I do for you besides telling you about Caskie's birthmark? It's like a little sea horse on his left buttock, kind of neat, really, very unexpected. When we first got married, I liked to lick it."

"And now?" Sherlock asked. She felt a tug of liking again for this woman with her spectacular topaz eyes, colored contacts, she assumed.

"Now, not so much. I'll tell you what I can, though it's very little. My husband never talks about work to me."

Sherlock said pleasantly, "We'd like to know what you think about your husband sleeping with Carla Alvarez."

27

Jane Ann Royal didn't blink. She took another deep drink of her tea, threw back her head, and laughed, a healthy laugh, loud and full. When she got herself together again, she saluted both Sherlock and Erin with her glass. "What do I think? Nothing much, one way or the other. Carla isn't the first. And yes, I've always known about all the women. Caskie's a cheater, always has been. The first time, I was pregnant with Chad."

"Why do you put up with it?" Erin asked.

"Ah, do I hear a bit of judgment in your voice, Agent? A bit of contempt for the pitiful weak female? Don't concern yourself about me. I like my life, thank you very much, my children like their lives, I believe Alana likes her life, and my husband certainly likes to flaunt his Don Juan image. You saw my tennis instructor. Mick Haggarty, a lovely Irish lad. He's young, has a nice flat stomach, and very well defined muscles. What's not to like?"

Sherlock regarded Jane Ann Royal over the rim of her glass. "Is Mick Haggarty your first tennis instructor?"

An eyebrow flew up. "You can't be serious, Agent Sherlock. He's maybe the fourth, fifth. One forgets. I always hire them young, not over twenty-five. Unlike my husband. Caskie tends to like women closer to his age, which seems against stereotype, but there you have it. After seeing him naked nearly every night for fifteen years, after putting up with him in bed when he's hit a dry spell, it's my never-ending pleasure to have a twenty-two-year-old tennis pro strut around. Surely you can understand that, Agent."

"Well, actually, I can't," Sherlock said. "You said your husband never talks to you about work?"

"That's right. Look, I'm sorry, but I don't see how I can help you. Wait a minute, there's something, isn't there, something you've heard? Did you hope I'd fall apart when you told me about my dear spouse screwing another woman and pour out my guts to you?"

Erin said. "Mrs. Royal, you live with a man who's up to his eyeballs in bad stuff. Come now, surely he's let something drop, something that might help us protect you."

Jane Ann Royal smiled at them, studied her lovely French manicure, then slowly shook her head.

Sherlock said, voice a bit harder, "Caskie is in very deep trouble, Jane Ann. Like Erin said, we're talking bad stuff here, real danger. He's playing hardball with people who won't hesitate to do whatever necessary to win. One man's dead already. Help us. Help yourself and your family. Tell us what you know about what's been happening at Schiffer Hartwin."

"Danger? Me? My kids? Come on, what could possibly be the danger? Good Lord, he works for a pharmaceutical company headquartered in Germany. As I said, he gets great bonuses. He's treated well. Danger, from Schiffer Hartwin? I can tell you what he's been doing for them—he's been selling drugs, coming up with new marketing strategies, for heaven's sake."

Sherlock said, "We think someone at your husband's company has broken the law, Jane Ann, and on a global scale. I guess Caskie didn't tell you about the woman who broke into his office Sunday night and copied documents off his computer, documents that may prove he and Schiffer Hartwin are knowingly engaging in unethical, perhaps even criminal, practices?"

"If you want to make me believe you, you've got to be more specific."

"All right, then." They weren't one hundred percent certain, but close enough. Sherlock continued. "It involves a drug called Culovort, which is used with the common 5-FU chemotherapy formula, a very critical drug for cancer. Culovort is now in very short supply and we believe it's because of Schiffer Hartwin's manipulations."

Jane Ann Royal had straightened in her chair now, shoulders square, focused on Sherlock. Her voice lowered. "Listen to me, I know nothing at all about this Culovort shortage. I wasn't lying to you, I know very little about Caskie's work. He doesn't bring it home, never has, so how would I know what Schiffer Hartwin is doing?"

Sherlock waited a bit, then said with deadly calm, "Caskie's involved big-time in this, Jane Ann. He's in deep trouble. The stolen documents will come to light very soon now, and everything will blow wide open, with Caskie in the center of it. After all, he's the one here at the U.S. Schiffer Hartwin headquarters. Germany's far away.

"It's just a matter of time before he gets hauled off to jail or Schiffer Hartwin sends over someone to keep him quiet. Don't you know the murdered man, Helmut Blauvelt, was the main Schiffer Hartwin enforcer?"

She saw the flash of knowledge in Jane Ann Royal's eyes, and for the first time, fear, but again, she shook her head. "No, I didn't know. This Blauvelt, you're saying he was here to shut Caskie up? But how on earth does that make any sense?"

"No, you're right, it doesn't," Sherlock said, "for the simple reason that Caskie's papers hadn't yet been stolen. So, why, exactly, was Blauvelt here? Who was he here to see? To shut up? We don't know yet."

Erin said, "What we do know is Schiffer Hartwin has to respond. As we speak, their lawyers are with your husband, trying to convince him to keep his mouth shut."

Sherlock said, her voice hard as flint, "Do you think Caskie will keep quiet?"

Jane Ann slowly shook her head. "I really don't know. Caskie's always been something of a maverick, plots his own course, sometimes contrary to what others in his company have laid out. He's always coming up with ideas no one else ever thought of. He's proud of that." She rubbed her fist over her eyes. Sherlock hoped she wouldn't dislodge the topaz contacts. "I had no idea about any of this."

Sherlock said, "I really hope you're telling us the truth, Jane Ann, but I gotta tell you, I doubt it. Yesterday, all your husband did was lie, and it was really tiring. No, don't deny more, it just pisses me off. Now, you need to think hard about this. Tell me, where were you this past Sunday night, between ten p.m. and three a.m.?"

Jane Ann Royal jumped to her feet,

splayed her lovely tanned hands on the tabletop. She was visibly shaking. "You think I had something to do with that German's death? No, no way, not a chance."

"Please tell us where you were," Sherlock said matter-of-factly, "or I will take you to the local police department, to that grungy conference room, and grill you in your tennis whites until your lovely tan fades."

"This is ridiculous nonsense," but she sat down again. At last she looked scared. *About time,* Erin thought, and looked through her lashes at Sherlock. She was good, excellent in fact.

Erin leaned toward Jane Ann. "Talk to us, Mrs. Royal. Believe me, these are powerful people."

"Listen to me, both of you! I don't know anything! I was in bed two nights ago, watching a stupid movie on TV, then I went to sleep at maybe midnight."

Erin said, "Since your husband wasn't with you, you really don't have an alibi, do you?"

"You told me he was with Carla." She shook her head, diverted. "Poor bitch, to have to settle for him. She divorced a jerk and now she's sleeping with another one. Look, I don't have an alibi, but I wouldn't leave my kids alone, I wouldn't! And I never sleep with another man in my own house, not with my children here. Caskie probably would, he's simply never had the opportunity. At least as far as I know."

Jane Ann Royal, whatever she knew, if there was indeed more, wasn't going to spill. Sherlock knew it. But they'd primed the pump well. Sherlock rose, Erin followed suit. She said, "We hope you have an excellent security system, Jane Ann. I strongly suggest you speak candidly to your husband about this. You might want to ask him how he plans to prevent his kids from getting hurt. He's up to his neck in alligators here. Encourage him to come clean with us, and we can help him. You might also want to give more thought to coming clean yourself. Good day."

After a few steps, Sherlock turned back. "You might want to consider visiting your mom for a while, with your kids."

Sherlock and Erin both nodded to Jane Ann Royal, who still sat at the wrought-iron white painted café table, the glass of iced tea in her hand. They walked around to the front of the house, just as the tennis instructor had done.

They heard Jane Ann shout, "Alana! Come here, now!"

"You really shook her," Erin said with a good deal of satisfaction. "She said so much, contradicted herself. To be honest, Sherlock, I couldn't tell the truth from the lies."

"I'm thinking she just might call me tonight. Don't think we failed, Erin. Thing is, we accomplished our mission. The woman is now seriously rattled."

She paused a moment as she opened the car door. She looked at Erin over the roof. "You said the wife always knows, but this was so blatant, so accepted, and Jane Ann has this ironic perspective about it.

"Dillon knows to his toes if he ever slept with another woman I'd shoot him dead, not the woman. Her I'd just rough up some." Sherlock shook her head. "To make promises, then to break them for no good reason I can think of, and you've got kids at home looking up to you, that's simply pathetic." She sighed as she opened the car door and slid in. "All too common, I guess."

Erin slid in beside her. "To be honest, I don't understand it either, not that I have all that much experience. I was married for a total of two months and twenty-seven days when I was twenty-two, not yet graduated from college. My husband was a grad student in economics. He didn't sleep with my friends, nothing like that, he simply didn't want to take his turn at washing the dishes and doing the laundry, that was my job, and so he told me. He said he had more important things to do than be a stupid drudge. Can you beat that?"

"Please tell me you took a whip to him."

"I should have, but I didn't. By the time eight weeks had passed I was so disillusioned with the jerk I didn't really care what he said, I just wanted him out and gone. But Jane Ann, she's different."

"Yes. I wonder if Caskie knows she sleeps with her tennis pros?"

When Sherlock's cell phone rang two hours later, she looked at the screen and pulled over. "It's Dillon, Erin. Let's see what's going on down there."

Sherlock listened as she unfastened her seat belt and stretched. "You're already on your way to see Senator Hoffman? This is wild, Dillon. His wife sends him a warning through you from the vast beyond, and he discounts it. Or maybe he didn't, just didn't realize he could die in a public restaurant.

"I bet he's really shook now. Yes, call me later. Then I'll tell you about Jane Ann Royal."

28

CHEVY CHASE, MARYLAND
Late Wednesday afternoon

Savich drove his Porsche through Senator David Hoffman's old established neighborhood, Ruth beside him. "A longtime lobbyist dead of poison with a United States senator sitting across the table from her, and he's probably the one meant to eat the arsenic. This is going to be pretty wild, Dillon. Good thing wild is our unit's middle name."

"Actually, our middle name is Apprehension."

Ruth punched him in the arm.

"'Wild' is the word Sherlock used when I called her."

"Great minds usually run in parallel," Ruth said.

Savich was grinning when he turned the Porsche smoothly into Senator Hoffman's driveway. He saw a TV van parked across the street. "They're fast. We've got to hurry." He and Ruth did a fast jog up the flagstone path to the senator's front door.

An agent stepped out. "Agents. Get inside before the locusts swarm onto the yard. Look at that yahoo running up here to get to you, waving his camera guy forward. The idiot, I'll deal with him."

Savich closed the door firmly behind them and turned to look around the large entrance hall. It was empty and dead silent. They waited a moment, but no one appeared. There didn't seem to be anyone inside the house. Since Savich knew the way, he led Ruth to Senator Hoffman's study, down the hall and to the right. Another FBI agent stood beside the door. He nodded to them.

The senator was seated behind his desk, his head back against the comfortable headrest, his eyes closed. His senior aide, Corliss Rydle, stood in front of his desk, arms crossed over her chest, yet another guard dog. Savich had seen two FBI agents. He wondered how many more Mr. Maitland had assigned to guard the senator. Corliss Rydle stared at them hard. *Message received,* Savich thought, *we'll have to go through you first to get to the great man.* She was closer to a guard poodle, he thought, petite, probably had to stretch to reach five-foot-two. She had short black hair and an olive complexion, probably some Mediterranean blood lurking around in her background somewhere. She was dressed in a stark black suit, white blouse, and a glossy pearl necklace. She all but growled at them.

Senator Hoffman opened his eyes, sat forward. "It's all right, Corliss." There was a hint of humor in his voice. "This is Agent Savich, and he's—very important."

Savich introduced himself and Ruth to Corliss Rydle, watched her step down a bit. He asked her to leave.

She didn't move, shot her dark eyes to her boss. Hoffman said quietly, "It's all right, Corlie. If I'm not safe with these people, then I should simply hang it up. Go finish drafting that statement for me. We've got to move on this, and as soon as Agent Savich brings me up to date, we're going to proceed."

When they were alone, Hoffman eyed Ruth. "Where's Agent Sherlock?"

Savich said, "Sherlock's up in Connecticut working on the murder of that German national."

"Oh, yes, I heard about that. What the devil is going on up there?" He stopped, shook his head at himself. "What am I blathering on about? Dana Frobisher is dead. I asked her to go to lunch with me and she ate my favorite dish—the fried shrimp—and died right there in front of me, seizing on the floor, foaming at the mouth." He shuddered, swallowed, then whispered, "It was meant for me, wasn't it, Agent Savich?"

"Could have been," Savich said matter-of-factly. "We're certainly looking at that as one possibility."

Hoffman stared at Savich like he was nuts. "You're telling me it's possible a middle-aged woman who happens to be a lobbyist had enemies who hated her enough to take the incredible risk of poisoning her in the Foggy Bottom Grill?"

"The same could be said for you, Senator. You're a middle-aged man who just happens to be a United States senator, and someone took the incredible risk of trying to kill you. What's the difference?"

"Well, that's a point, Agent Savich, but there is a world of difference between the murder of a lobbyist and what could have been an assassination attempt on a United States senator.

"My wife told you—*warned you*—but I refused to take it seriously. Even if I had taken her warning seriously, I wouldn't have questioned having lunch at one of my favorite eating places. But it happened there. Now, you're not going to tell me Dana Frobisher's ex-husband paid someone in the kitchen to poison her lunch? The woman isn't—she wasn't—rich, she wasn't particularly savvy or charismatic, she wielded very little power, hardly a person worth killing for any reason other than a personal one."

Ruth said, "Actually, sir, Dana Frobisher did very well financially. Her experience and contacts have given her a certain power, a certain cachet, if you will. I'm told she was a very effective negotiator.

"So far we have not found anything out of the ordinary—no stalkers, no angry neighbors, no seriously pissed-off clients. Her ex-husband is a farmer in New Mexico. He was distraught when we spoke to him. She left one grown daughter, in her third year at Brown, and an extended family, who are in shock. But of course we'll keep looking on her side of things, to see if she could indeed have been the target."

Savich said, "Let's back up a minute, Senator. Tell us why you invited a lobbyist to lunch."

"My wife worked with her years ago, admired her for her energy, her commitment to charities focused on raising money for childhood diseases. I wanted to make use of her expertise in this particular fund-raising area because it is my intention to rekindle Nikki's charities, particularly for spinal meningitis, the charity closest to her heart since her own sister died of that disease when she was six years old. I remember Nikki told me if Dana Frobisher really believed in a cause, she'd throw all her energy into it. I was eager to get her commitment."

Savich said, "Senator, I've told Ruth we have it on good authority—namely, from your wife, Nikki—that danger was coming in your direction. I agree, it seems more likely you were the target. An assassination attempt? I don't know, but it simply doesn't feel like that to me."

Hoffman said, "Over the years you learn to expect a lot of things on the campaign trail and on the Hill. Lies about your record, distortion of the facts, thinly disguised attempts to buy influence, even attempts at extortion—but that someone would try to kill a senator for personal gain? I will tell you, it gives me pause. It certainly felt to me like an assassination attempt."

Hoffman slowly rose, splayed his hands on his mahogany desk. "I think you are wrong about this. I also hope you haven't told anyone about my dead wife contacting you, asking you to warn me. Dear God, man, if the media picks that up, I'll look like a major fool on every TV screen across the United States. It could end my career."

"Only three people other than Sherlock and I know about your wife, Senator, and they are FBI agents I trust to keep things close to the vest. What about the people you've taken into your confidence—Corliss Rydle and your two sons? Are there others you confided in?"

"I told you about my nonpolitical friend, Gabe Hilliard, who owns several security firms. He knows, but believe me, he has no axe to grind. He doesn't want to kill me, he only wants to beat me at golf. Listen, if I can't trust him, I can't trust anybody." The senator looked down at his watch. "Corliss told me Gabe's coming by anytime now. She told him he might have to run the gauntlet through the media. You can meet him if you like."

Savich thought that would be a good idea. "Your aide knows Mr. Hilliard personally?"

"Oh, yes, they're great friends. You know, maybe one of the house staff overheard something, but no one else. All right, I see your point. There are lots of possible leak sites."

Savich said, "I suspect your aide, Corliss Rydle, could have her fingernails yanked out and still not tell anyone about this. I gather you've told your sons you'd cut them off at the knees if they let this thing out?"

"Cut them off at the neck, more like it."

Savich added, "You're sure the investigator has no clue about Nikki?"

"No, Corliss told him we were worried about a stalker, not a ghost. Listen, Savich, a media leak still concerns me."

Savich said, "The media is not what I'm worried about. The fact is, everyone who knows, whether innocently or not, has a tie to this. We have to find out if this was personal, or, as you believe, an assassination attempt, before they have a chance to try again. Now I want to hear everything that happened from the moment you stepped into the Foggy Bottom Grill until Dana Frobisher was taken away by the paramedics."

29

Hoffman jerked his fingers through his hair, and looked both ashamed and embarrassed. “Here I am thinking about myself, and how all this will affect me. That poor woman is dead because I called her to ask her to lunch.

“All right. When she arrived, we chatted about things in general, you know, nothing important, one doesn’t discuss business right away. . . .” He paused a moment. “Then we ordered. I had just begun telling her why I’d asked her to lunch, when she became ill and—died.”

Ruth asked, "Did your office call her office?"

"Yes, Corliss usually makes my calls."

"Did Corliss tell her the reason for the lunch invitation?"

Hoffman frowned down at his clasped hands. "No, I don't think so. Corliss was after me about an upcoming vote, and I needed some more information, and so I don't think we did. She accepted my invitation, and that was that."

Savich said, "Did your office make the reservations, Senator? And when?"

"Yes, my staffer, Al Pope, always gives them a heads-up even though I'm there like clockwork every single week, usually with a colleague. It's only polite to let them know how many people will be coming. I believe he made the reservation five, maybe six days ago."

"Which of you arrived first, Senator?"

"I did. I always arrange to get there first, say hello to everyone, shake hands with the diners I know. Dana Frobisher arrived some ten minutes later, if I remember correctly. My waiter—the same waiter I've had for years, Mr. Graves—he would know for sure."

"Did you order something to drink while you waited for her?"

"Yes, mineral water, lemon slice. Mr. Graves always brings it without my even asking."

Savich said, "Did you suggest she order the shrimp, Senator?"

Again, Hoffman paused, looked over at the draperies covering the long windows at the front of the house. "Maybe I did, or maybe Mr. Graves did. Isn't it odd? I don't remember Mr. Graves's first name, never used it. In any case, Mr. Graves might have mentioned to her that it was excellent, that it was the dish I always ordered, or I might have. She told me this was her first visit to the Foggy Bottom Grill.

"As I said, I always order the fried shrimp. It's my one dietary sin for the week. Everyone who works there knows that, it's sort of a joke, you know, they batter up the shrimp extra thick for me, fry it in a skillet with two inches of hot oil. But I wanted something light, as my weight was up this morning, so Mr. Graves suggested I order the small Cobb salad. Can you believe that? I over-indulge at dinner last night and that saves my life? Something so insignificant, so arbitrary. It's hard to deal with this, Agent Savich."

Ruth asked, "You're sure Mr. Graves told her you always ordered that dish, Senator?"

"Yes, I think so. I remember how I also told her it was the best thing on the menu. And we laughed about fried food and how delicious it was. I really can't remember anything else, my brain feels a bit scrambled right now.

"I remember the look on her face when she ate that first fried shrimp—sheer bliss. I think she said something about having a spiritual moment. I remember I laughed, and wished I'd ordered it too, I could diet the next day." He paused a moment, swallowed, then he rubbed his hand over his throat.

"What?" Savich asked.

"She was doing that, rubbing her hand over her throat. I didn't know why, really didn't think about it, but now of course I realize it had to do with the poison beginning to act, she must have been having trouble swallowing.

"I reminded her she'd worked with Nikki, easing into what I wanted to ask of her—now that I think about it, she didn't say anything. Listen, Agent Savich, it all happened so very fast. One minute she was eating shrimp and we were talking and then she turned silent, working her hands against her throat, then she fell out of her chair and onto the floor, and she vomited, and went into seizures." Again, he shuddered, seeing it clearly, Savich thought, knowing it could easily have been him on the floor, wracked by seizures, spurting out foam as he lay dying.

"And then she was dead. Just dead, gone."

Ruth said, "So she never knew why you'd asked her to lunch?"

He drew back a bit, looked impatiently at Ruth. "No, I don't suppose so." He fanned his hands in front of him. "Who cares?"

Savich said, "Mr. Graves initially set down the shrimp plate in front of you, didn't he, sir?"

"Yes, he did, and I told him it wasn't for me today, and he apologized, moved the plate in front of Dana. I don't remember if he said anything else. Obviously you've spoken to him. What did he say?"

Savich merely smiled. "Did you have

time to eat any of your salad before she became obviously ill?"

"Maybe a bite or two. As I said, it all happened very fast."

Ruth said, "The M.E. said she'd eaten five shrimp, and yet you only ate a couple of bites of salad?" Her voice was a bit sharp, a bit disbelieving. Savich never changed expression. For a moment he thought Senator Hoffman looked at Ruth like he'd just as soon she jumped out the front window. But when he spoke, his voice was deep, disarming, his words self-deprecating. "It was probably because I didn't have time—I was doing most of the talking." He gave both of them a tired smile. "Agent Savich knows how much I like to talk," he added to Ruth. He rubbed his forehead. "Maybe I ate more than a couple of bites, it's hard to remember. I close my eyes and see her lying dead on the floor, everyone standing over her, horrified, and all I can think of is that it should have been me eating that fried shrimp, not Dana Frobisher. It should have been me lying dead on the floor. I should have listened to you, Agent Savich, when you told me about Nikki."

Savich was on the verge of asking him about the work Dana Frobisher and Nikki shared, when there was a knock on the study door, and Corliss Rydle stuck her head in. "Gabe is here, sir."

"Show him in, Corliss." Hoffman rose to walk around his desk. "Gabe, thank you for coming."

Savich and Ruth watched the man squeeze Corliss's hand, then he walked to Hoffman and the two men embraced. Hilliard stepped back. "I was scared out of my mind, Dave, are you all right?"

"Yes, yes, I'm fine, just rattled."

"No wonder." Gabe Hilliard turned his attention to Savich, who'd slowly risen from his chair.

He was a block, Savich thought, nearly as wide as he was tall. He was about Hoffman's age, and perfectly bald. His features were as blunt as Hoffman's were refined.

"Gabe, these are two FBI agents. Agent Savich, Agent Warnecki, this is Gabe Hilliard, a very longtime friend. Incidentally, his son, Derek, knows Corliss."

Gabe Hilliard grinned. "Maybe there'll be an announcement from those two pretty soon."

They all shook hands. Ruth had to admit she was impressed when Hilliard offered her his hand as well. She gave it a good shake. He was shorter than she was.

"Sit down, sit down, Gabe. We were talking about what happened today and that poor woman's death."

Gabe Hilliard pulled up a chair beside Ruth's, sat down and crossed one leg over his knee. "If you want to, tell me everything. I've got a brain, maybe I can help."

"From your lips to God's ear," Hoffman said.

30

Ruth was on her cell phone as Savich negotiated the heavy traffic back into Washington, wondering what Sherlock was doing, praying she was keeping herself safe.

Ruth punched off. "That was Ollie giving me the results of his last interview. He said he got statements from all the staff who handled food in the kitchen at lunchtime today."

"Talk to me."

Ruth thought briefly of her husband of one month, Dix, and the boys, and realized she wasn't going to be in the stands for Rob's Friday night high school football game. It was the beginning of the season, but still . . . "There were eleven employees in and out of the kitchen today at the Foggy Bottom Grill: the chef, two sous chefs, three dishwashers, two busboys, and three waiters all had easy access. The owner, Raul Minsker, was also in and out of the kitchen, but he doesn't think he was in there during the time the poison had to have been introduced into the shrimp batter, but who knows? We're not going to discount him.

"I was there when Ollie spoke to the chef—Carlysle is his name, Carlysle Boyd—and he said he always prepares Senator Hoffman's shrimp personally, and he did this time as well. He said he thought it was for the senator's usual order. The batter was mixed by one of the sous chefs, Jay Luckoff's his name, from the usual ingredients as far as he knew. Luckoff said he let the batter sit because he was preparing three other dishes at the same time, so anyone could have stirred something into it.

"Ollie's doing an in-depth check on Luckoff, nothing so far. Elliot's doing checks on all the other kitchen employees. One of the busboys has a few juvenile offenses, nothing horrendous, joy riding in a stolen car, some marijuana. He was shaking so hard when Ollie spoke to him, Ollie doesn't think he could have pulled it off.

"To be honest here, Dillon, it could be any one of them. Ollie's setting all of them up for lie detector tests."

"That'd be too easy."

"Show me some optimism here, boss."

"All right then, I'm hoping by tomorrow we'll have nailed him," he said as he smoothly swung around a big black SUV.

Ruth felt the wind tear through her hair. "Let's hope." She laughed. "Ah, this is wonderful. I'm thinking I'll talk Dix into a Porsche. What are my chances?"

Savich shot her a grin. "I'd like to hear what he says."

"Are you going back up to Connecticut?"

"Tomorrow, if Mr. Maitland agrees. I want to see the results of the lie detector tests, use them to recreate where everyone was in the kitchen." Savich shrugged. "I've got some serious thinking to do."

Back in his office, Savich shut his door, turned off his cell, pulled off his tie, and sat down. He closed his eyes and he concentrated. *Nikki, David nearly died today. I really do need you.*

He pictured her from the photo Senator Hoffman had showed him and Sherlock. A solid woman, she had thoughtful brown eyes, "handsome" was the word, he supposed. She looked fit, a gym lover probably, lightly tanned, her hair beautifully styled and red as a sunset. And an appealing smile, at least in the photo. She stood alone, a big star jasmine bush trellised behind her, white blooms so thick they nearly covered the trellis. He pictured her, tried to feel her. *Nikki, please come. There's trouble here, and I know you can help me.*

He waited, tried to relax, and opened his hands on his desk. He made her face as clear in his mind as he could, as if she were right in front of his nose.

He felt nothing at first, and then it seemed her face was floating, but it wasn't clear anymore. It was swallowed up by what seemed like a fog, cold and gray. Suddenly the fog was churning in front of him. It seemed substantial, and yet he knew he could put his hand through it, knew it would be wet if he did, but she wouldn't really be there to grasp his hand. There would be nothing. *Nikki, make yourself clear*.

The swirling fog thinned, and he saw a vague outline, blurred, then clearer, but never clear enough, as if she were a prisoner behind the thick veil, unable to come through. He concentrated hard on trying to see her face, but there was nothing but a vague outline he could hardly make out. He thought he heard her voice, faint and hollow, her words indistinct and distant, as if she were retreating, farther and farther away.

Savich's eyes opened slowly. He looked at Dane Carver, who stood in the doorway of his office, stone still, watching him. Dane asked calmly, "You get anything from the wife?"

Had Dane knocked and he hadn't heard him? Very probably. Savich had to grin. There was no doubt in his mind the whole unit knew now about Senator Hoffman's dead wife. There was no doubt in his mind either that not a word about it would get out. "No, well, she couldn't seem to come through to me. Very weird, actually. What's going on, Dane?"

"You need to switch gears back to Connecticut. Maitland just told me the top-dog director of Schiffer Hartwin, Adler Dieffendorf, and one of his subordinates, Werner Gerlach, marketing and sales, are on their way here from Germany."

"Isn't that a nice surprise? It seems this is very important to them if they don't trust their lawyers to handle it. When are they arriving?"

"Tomorrow afternoon at JFK."

Savich picked up his cell from his desktop. "I'll give Sherlock and Bowie a heads-up. Things are going to happen fast up there now."

31

STONE BRIDGE, CONNECTICUT
Early Wednesday evening

"Hot diggity," Sherlock said. "The mountain's coming to Mohammed. I can't believe it. I've got Bowie right here, I'll tell him." Sherlock rang off, gave Bowie a fat grin. "Guess what? Dillon told me the big German guns are coming here, all the way from Hartwin, Germany, the managing director, Dr. Adler Dieffendorf, and Mr. Werner Gerlach, director of pharma marketing and sales."

Bowie made a victory fist. "Here I was

picturing us going to Germany and having them slam the door in our faces, the German cops kissing us off, and here they come, right into our open arms."

Erin was spooning taco meat from a skillet into a bowl on the table. Her heart was pounding hard, but she tried to look only mildly interested. She had to be cool, had to keep her excitement under wraps, well hidden from these two pairs of sharp eyes and sharper brains. "That's great, right? And even better, they'll speak English."

Sherlock smiled at her. "How do you know that, Erin?"

Erin's spoon dashed taco meat onto the table. "Oh, rats, look what I did. How do I know they speak English? Well, all the higher-ups in the big corporations in Europe speak English. They'd have to, wouldn't they? I thought everybody knew that."

"I didn't," Bowie said, and helped her spoon up the meat. "Is the placemat clean?"

"Yes. In any case, don't forget the five-second rule. Georgie," she called out, "come to dinner."

"I didn't know that either," Sherlock said. She knew something was up here, knew it to her red toenails.

Erin gave them both a distracted smile. "Now you won't underestimate us private investigators in the future. We know lots of stuff." She turned to Georgie, who looked adorable, Sherlock thought, dressed in jeans and a red, white, and blue T-shirt that had Wonder Woman emblazoned across the chest. "Hey, kiddo, your hands clean?"

Georgie held up her hands, palms out.

"Good. Tacos, Georgie. You said you could match me. Come and prove it. You really think you can eat a dozen?"

Georgie came skipping into the small dining room. "Not twelve, Erin. Daddy can't even eat twelve tacos."

"So now you're trying to welsh on the bet?"

Bowie looked from one to the other. "You've got a bet? Twelve tacos?"

"We didn't actually specify a number," Erin said, and motioned Georgie to her chair. "You get your homework done, sweetie?"

Bowie did a double take. He watched his daughter slip into her seat, shake her head at Erin. "You're nagging, Erin. I got nearly all of it done, but Daddy needs to help me with the grammar part. We have to put in commas and periods. Okay, Daddy? After dinner?"

Bowie nodded. Georgie had been living with Erin for only two days, and here Erin was acting like her mother? The thought stopped him cold. He had to bring this case to a close so he could get his daughter out of here, away from Erin. He didn't care that Erin Pulaski was smart and nice and sincerely liked his daughter, and liked him too, he thought; there was no way he was traveling down that road again, not after Beth. His brain froze as it always did when he thought of Beth, like he'd stepped to the edge of a black hole and leaped back. At least the memories no longer burst through into his dreams to give him nightmares. And that made him think of Krissy, which was odd. He and Krissy had been friends, with benefits, for nearly four months, but neither of them wanted anything more, at least he had thought that. He said easily to his daughter, "I got a call from Krissy today. She sends you her love. She wants to bring you something from Harrods in London. Is there anything in particular you'd like?"

"What's Harrods?"

"It's a big, gorgeous department store," Erin said, "with more cool stuff than you can imagine, including this huge floor just for food, with everything from candy to filet mignon. Me, I love their stuffed olives."

"Okay, tell Krissy we'd really like some olives. I don't know about stuffing them, though."

Bowie's eyebrow shot up. "What is this, Georgie? You're ordering food all the way from England? Erin doesn't have enough to share? You won't be here long enough to worry about that. Glynn will be better soon and home again. Don't forget, Erin has that big important client, right, Erin?"

Does he suspect something isn't right, like Sherlock? She stared down at her taco, her tongue stuck to the roof of her mouth.

Sherlock said when Erin didn't reply, "You remember, Erin, your case dealing with drugs, right?"

Erin said, "You can tell Krissy any of the candies would be great, okay, Georgie? Candy will travel better than stuffed olives. Whatever she brings will make you dance on the ceiling, something I haven't yet figured out how to do. Big case? Well, really, it's not big at all. No, it's not about drugs."

Hmm. Sherlock said to Georgie, who was all ears, "By any wild chance did you hear us talking before dinner?"

"Well, maybe I heard some things, Aunt Sherlock."

Bowie nearly dropped the handful of lettuce he was spreading on top of his taco. *Aunt Sherlock?*

Georgie continued, "You know, I might have heard some stuff when I got real close to the door. Erin's walls aren't very thick, you know. It's an apartment, and Daddy says apartments have crappy construction."

"Well, I didn't say exactly that," Bowie said. "Don't say 'crap,' Georgie."

"I didn't say 'crap' exactly, Daddy."

"Close enough. Whatever."

Georgie gave her father a sweet smile and continued, "Erin knows lots of neat things. She's known people in Europe speak English for years and years. I think I knew it too."

God bless this wonderful child, Erin thought, as she spooned taco meat into a tortilla shell, carefully handed it to her, and waved at the bowls of lettuce, tomatoes, and cheese. "Add whatever you want.

Years and years? That makes me sound about a hundred."

"No, Grandma's about a hundred," Georgie said, and sprinkled cheddar on her taco.

Bowie was looking at her, too many questions in his eyes, and so Erin proceeded to lie, clean as a whistle. "It wasn't years and years ago. When I was twenty I took off a year to bum around Europe. I began to notice that business people, especially in international companies, sometimes spoke three, four different languages, English included. I decided it must be a requirement for upward mobility." She never raised her head, concentrated on her own taco. "Except in France, of course. I think if you speak English in France, you can be guillotined as a traitor."

Bowie was diverted, just as she'd intended. He laughed, couldn't help it. "Sherlock, should I send Dolores Cliff back to JFK tomorrow to fetch the two Schiffer Hartwin gentlemen?"

She said, "It appears they're going to control our access to them much better than that. Dillon told me they're being transported here in a proper big limo, one of those eighteen-foot jobbers, I bet. I wouldn't be surprised if the lawyers will already be in the limo to brief the bigwigs on the drive here to Stone Bridge."

Bowie said, "I'd sure like to be in that limo with them. I'm thinking they've got to be really concerned to come here themselves to try to defuse this."

Sherlock said easily, "I hope they're really scared. Dillon called and got the DOJ to look into the Culovort shortage, so things may get even scarier for them sooner than they know."

"We could phone Jane Ann, see if her husband will be with the lawyers in the limo. You think she'd tell us, Sherlock?"

Erin? What did she have to do with Jane Ann Royal? He said, "I want to hear about your meeting with her, Sherlock," Bowie said, and shot Erin a look.

"Erin and I met with her this afternoon. We'll tell you all about it after dinner, Bowie, after you've helped Georgie with her commas and periods."

Sherlock continued, "I'm wondering what their lawyers will be cooking up for Dieffendorf and Gerlach to tell us."

Georgie said, "Lawyers are a pain in the ass."

"*What?*" Bowie said, his second taco halfway to his mouth.

"I've heard you say that, Daddy, several times. You were pretty pissed off."

"You listen to me, kiddo, you do not say that word either. Nor do you say 'crap.' Okay? It's not polite, particularly for a kid. You've got to be eighteen before you can say those things."

"All the kids at school say them, and lots more stuff. I even heard my teacher tell her ex-husband to piss off just outside the classroom. All of us heard her. And he was really mad. He stomped off down the hall, we heard that too. When Mrs. Reems came back in, her face was red."

Bowie looked ready to laugh and yell at the same time.

Erin took Georgie's face between her hands. "Listen to me, Small Person, your dad's right. Eighteen is the magic number in your future. Until you're eighteen, you have to try to have the cleanest mouth in Stone Bridge, okay?"

"But all the kids talk like that, Erin, it's no big deal."

Bowie said, "Georgie, if you talk like that, everyone will think I'm a lousy parent."

Georgie's lower lip fell.

"*All* the kids, Georgie?" Sherlock asked. "Surely not. Sean doesn't, nor do his friends." She crossed her fingers. He was two years younger.

Georgie nodded vigorously.

Bowie said quietly, "Georgie Loyola Richards, you will not say bad words," and he looked at her straight on, in silence.

Georgie took a big bite of her taco and chewed hard.

"Her middle name is Loyola?" Sherlock grinned at the little girl. "I like it."

"It's was for her grandfather, Sean O'Grady, and yes, he graduated from Loyola, valedictorian of his class. Story goes he downed six shots of Irish whiskey and passed out in a closet."

Erin said, "I remember when I was Georgie's age, there was a Mr. O'Grady—he lived one street over—but he was a gambler and a bad one. He had what my dad called negative luck. He pawned his wife's wedding ring and the poor woman thought she'd lost it. She hired me to find it and I tracked down the pawn stub in Mr. O'Grady's dresser drawer. Mrs. O'Grady didn't speak to him for months, as I recall."

Everyone laughed, and the tension disappeared.

Sherlock started telling them about the case in Washington, D.C.

Georgie, all ears, ate three tacos.

32

It was Sherlock who tucked Georgie in that evening and read her the next chapter of her Nancy Drew mystery. Erin and Bowie cleaned up the dishes in Erin's small kitchen.

Erin cupped her hand to her ear.

"What?" Bowie asked.

"I can't seem to hear Sherlock reading to Georgie. And her bedroom is only one crappy-thin poorly constructed wall away."

Bowie vigorously dried a cup. "Sorry about that, but you know it's usually true."

"Yeah, yeah, I know. You're off the hook." She tossed him a dry dish towel.

Bowie stared at a wet glass. "Sherlock

was out of line to take you to see Jane Ann Royal."

She grinned at him. "Is that snark I hear? Why would you care if Sherlock took me along?"

"You're not FBI, Erin. You're a civilian. She shouldn't have taken you anywhere related to the investigation, and this interview was official."

Erin threw a handful of soapy water at him.

"Hey!" He wiped off his face and frowned at her.

"Sorry, but you deserved that, Bowie Richards. I'm good, and you're supposed to have the brains to know to use good people whenever you can. You and your precious FBI—like Agent Cliff got all that much information out of Andreas Kesselring?"

How did she know about that? He had no smart reply ready. Because he wasn't stupid, Bowie shut up. He dried another glass. "I was with Agent Kesselring most of the day."

"If I tell you about our meeting with Mrs. Royal, will you tell me about what you and Agent Kesselring did?"

He dried two plates before agreeing.

After Erin told him her impressions of Jane Ann Royal and what the woman had said, with many questions thrown in by Bowie along the way, he nodded. "So both you and Sherlock think she knows quite a bit about what her husband's doing, and she's just playing dumb. Sort of like Madoff's wife did a couple of years back?"

"I don't know how much Jane Ann actually knows, but I'll tell you, she puts on a good act, all straightforward and open, but she knows more than she lets on. And Sherlock, the consummate professional, agrees with me."

"All right, all right, I'll drop that if you will. The tennis pro, did you speak to him?"

"No, he just waved and left. Mrs. Royal said she hadn't decided to sleep with him yet. Evidently he wouldn't be the first tennis instructor she's bedded. She likes them young and hard. She said her husband prefers women nearer to his own age, like Carla Alvarez. An interesting reversal. I wonder if she's right. His name is Mick Haggarty and he really wants to be an actor. If what she says is true, he may not know much."

"Neither you nor Sherlock trust her, either. We'll see. I'll check out the tennis pro."

"Mick Haggarty. He's a tennis pro at the Glenis Springs Country Club right down the road."

Bowie nodded, put another glass in the cupboard. He was building a military-straight line of glasses.

She said, "Georgie was telling me about your long commute, how you get home tired a lot of nights. She said you were thinking about leaving Stone Bridge and moving to New Haven."

"The commute's not all that bad, really, but she's right, I am thinking about putting my house up for sale." He paused, frowned. "I don't know how she knew that."

"The kid's precocious, reads people, particularly you, very well, and she's a great eavesdropper. Actually, now that I remember back, I started early as well. I was a champ by Georgie's age. No one said anything I didn't pay attention to."

"That's what's in my future? Whispering whenever I'm in the house? Maybe it was a mistake to settle here in the first place, but given the current market, I may not have a lot of choice. Thing is, Georgie's school was highly recommended by a friend of mine in L.A., and that's what locked me on target. Georgie really likes her school, likes the kids, sure likes her dance class and teacher."

"Tough decision." Erin wiped her hands on a dish towel, found herself twisting it over and over. "Well, maybe it's not all that great a distance. I made it up to New Haven today to see my client, did it in under fifty minutes."

"What client?"

Big mouth, big mouth. Didn't matter. Who cared? "He's a professor at Yale, an old friend of my dad's. We ate in the Berkeley dining room, his college when he went there thirty years ago. Quite a place."

"What are you doing for him?"

Shut up, shut up. "Confidential, Agent Richards. Pull out my fingernails, you still can't make me talk. Tell me about Kesselring."

Why doesn't she want to tell me? He said, "Kesselring wanted to see Blauvelt's body today and that was when I decided to deal with him myself. I called Dr. Ella Franks and she met us at our local morgue, in the basement in the Stone Bridge Memorial Hospital. I have to admit he asked her good questions, and he said right off he didn't believe the killer obliterated his face to prevent identification. We've all been wondering about that."

Bowie thought back to the cold sterile room, standing across the autopsy table from Blauvelt's body. Bowie had watched Kesselring carefully as he stared down at Blauvelt's ruined face. "Dr. Franks, you said the killer struck a half-dozen blows to his face?"

Dr. Franks nodded. "Yes, exactly half a dozen, like his killer counted the hits. It was postmortem. Why do you think the murderer did this to him?"

Kesselring never looked away from Blauvelt's face. He said with complete certainty, "Rage, psychotic rage. Someone was really over the edge, so wound up he just didn't stop. He wanted to—how do you say it—erase the man, yes, that's it, the killer wanted to erase him, and he did."

And Bowie had said to him, "If the killer didn't care about his being quickly identified, then why did he cut off Blauvelt's fingers? Why not cut off his feet?"

Kesselring was silent a moment, chewing this over, and admitted it was strange. "Perhaps the psychotic rage had burned itself out, perhaps the killer heard someone coming. Perhaps he planned to come back and bury Blauvelt, but he was prevented from doing so."

All of that made sense, Bowie thought, and cursed under his breath.

Bowie had noticed that Dr. Franks, who admired *him*, dammit, respected what *he* said, was looking at Kesselring with something of the same expression he'd seen on Dolores Cliff's face. It burned his gut.

Bowie shook his head at the memory of his own conceit. He said to Erin, "Then Kesselring asked to visit the Schiffer Hartwin offices. The lawyers were camped out there. Caskie Royal refused to see us, sent us a message to talk to his lawyers. Kesselring and I met briefly with Bender the Elder. He was cordial to Kesselring, but of course offered no help at all.

"Then Kesselring wanted to speak to Carla Alvarez. We were both surprised when she agreed to see us, but then she simply smiled at us, and said she had no comment on the advice of their legal staff. And she didn't budge. I think she saw us just to rub our noses in it."

Erin asked, "What about the guy who's manager of accounting, Turley Drexel?"

"What do you know about Turley Drexel?"

"Didn't Sherlock tell you? She said when she walked into Alvarez's office the morning Blauvelt's body was discovered, she interrupted Alvarez and Turley Drexel in a loud and nasty argument. She didn't know what it was about, but could there be something there?"

"I'll check on that." He ran his fingers through his dark hair, making it stand on end. "This is precisely why there should be only one team working a case. This could be important, yet I didn't know about it."

"It's called debriefing, Bowie. I'll bet you haven't told Sherlock all about Kesselring yet, have you?"

"That's beside the point, I—well, smack me in the head. Okay, you're right. And you can stop that now."

"Stop what?" He was standing two feet away from her, staring at her hard.

"Stop being such a smart-mouth, even if you're right. It burns me."

Erin gave him a fat smile. Without thinking, she took a single step toward him, leaned up, and kissed him, fast and light and easy, and stepped back. She laughed. "Suck it up, Agent Richards," and she snapped his thigh with the towel.

"Georgie's almost asleep," Sherlock said from the kitchen doorway. "Since the walls are so thin in apartments, you know, I heard most of what you guys talked about." She raised an eyebrow, looked from one to the other. "Interesting."

"What's interesting?" Bowie asked, lips seamed.

"What you said about Kesselring. Where's he at this evening?"

"He's dining at Chez Pierre. He wanted to see where Blauvelt had his last meal. He wanted to speak to Estafan, see if he could find other witnesses. I wonder what the owner Paul Remier thinks of him."

Sherlock frowned. "Seems like a waste of time to me. He could read the reports, they're very thorough. Why is he rewalking in all our steps?"

"Maybe he doesn't think the FBI is thorough enough," Erin said. "Or more likely, he thinks you're holding out on him."

Bowie looked thoughtful. "Or maybe Kesselring knows more than he's told us and wants to see if anyone else does too."

33

STONE BRIDGE, CONNECTICUT
Thursday morning

Why hadn't Dr. Kender called? Surely he'd had plenty of time to think things through. Erin looked over at her fireplace, at the two loose bricks she'd dug out to stash a copy of Caskie Royal's papers. She'd awakened that morning feeling urgent, wanting to get something rolling or—or what? She didn't know, but she felt restless and unfocused. She felt something bad was coming, and it was driving her nuts.

Fifteen minutes later, Erin gave up and

dialed Dr. Kender's number. She got his voice mail. She checked the schedule he'd given her, and sure enough, he was teaching a graduate class on Ahmose I, first ruler in the Eighteenth Dynasty, who finished the campaign to expel the Hyksos rulers from Egypt, something she knew since she'd read the course syllabus. If he didn't call her by noon, she'd try again. She was anxious to talk over taking the next step, releasing the papers, come what may. What was holding him up?

She grabbed her car keys and decided to see for herself. She drove past the Schiffer Hartwin corporate headquarters outside Stone Bridge, past the local police station with its American flag flying outside in a nicely planted flowerbed. She admitted she'd hoped to see a sign of Bowie, but she only saw two uniformed officers walking purposefully toward their patrol car. She knew Police Chief Amos had to be hating every minute the feds were there.

She turned her beautiful Hummer right on Munson Avenue, just five minutes from the interstate. In her rearview mirror she could see a car she recognized turn right some twenty feet behind her.

It was the same car that had been with her since she'd left her apartment.

She couldn't make out the license plate. Her grandfather hadn't believed in coincidences, nor had her father. Genetically, she wasn't predisposed to, either.

Time to test it out. She pressed her foot down on the gas and took a quick right onto Marple Drive, her tires screeching.

The car turned a moment later, its tires screeching as well, even accelerated, gaining on her now.

Coincidence would have been nice. This wasn't good.

She tried to make out who was driving and how many were in the car but she couldn't tell because the windshield was darkly tinted, and who did that? No one on the up-and-up, that's for sure. It was time to do a U-turn, though her Hummer H3 didn't like them very much, and drive as fast as she could back to the police station.

No, not yet. She had to find out who was after her. She speeded up again, turned a sharp left and another sharp left, and came out again on Munson Avenue. She was only a half-mile from the police station, so she slowed down, hoping the car would close with her, when she heard a sound like a gas stove lighting and saw a glimpse of flames from the corner of her eye outside the left rear door. She unclipped her seat belt, hit the brake hard, flung the door open, and threw herself out of the car. She hit hard on her shoulder against the asphalt, and rolled just as the explosion ripped through the roof of her Hummer, burst out the side windows and the windshield, sending shards of glass flying out everywhere and waves of boiling air and shooting flames into the sky. She curled into a ball, covered her head with her arms, and prayed. The noise deafened her, made her ears ring, and the smell made her gag as she curled tighter. She tried to suck in air, but the explosion had eaten it all up. She felt something strike her back, and shook it off. She saw it was part of a car seat, burning brightly beside her. She didn't know how badly it had burned her, but she didn't hurt, didn't even feel it yet.

She staggered to her feet and ran behind an oak tree at the edge of someone's front yard, and watched the lighter debris raining down. The road behind her Hummer was empty, her pursuer gone. But her car was a torch, and she felt the air boil hotter now than it had just a moment before. How was that possible? She was watching a nightmare, but it was real and it was happening here, right in front of her, in a nice middle-class neighborhood with no one around, thank God.

Her beloved baby, her Hummer H3, that she'd proudly owned for three years since she bought it from a gentleman from Cabot, Vermont, who made cheese and whose fiancée had hated it. It was light blue and so beautiful all the guys envied it, and now it sat in the middle of the street, only its frame intact, a flaming, stinking, smoldering mess.

Someone had meant for her to be in it.

She heard a woman scream.

Then a guy was yelling, "Go inside, kids. You heard me, Get inside. Jennifer, Todd, get inside now!"

She looked at the still burning jagged piece of car seat that had struck her back, felt the sharp impact again, but it still didn't hurt. But the moment Erin heard sirens in the distance, a pain in her back detonated just like her car had and burned her all the way through to her backbone. Air whooshed out of her as she fell to her knees, and bent over on her hands and knees, sucking in big gulping breaths to keep from yelling.

Someone leaned over her, she could see his shadow. “Miss, are you all right?”

Her brain was mired in a wasteland of pain, throbbing hot pain.

“No, she’s not, Rick. Call an ambulance. How’d she blow up her car?”

“It isn’t a car, it’s one of those big-ass Hummers. It exploded right in front of my house. Jeez, it smells bad.”

“What’s she doing driving a Hummer?”

“Call freaking 911!”

Their voices washed over her, not really touching her. She was focused on the vicious pain in her back.

34

STONE BRIDGE MEMORIAL HOSPITAL

Dr. Henry Arch said, “I hope you’re not vain, Ms. . . . ?”

A long pause, then Erin said, “I don’t remember if I’m vain or not.”

“You might end up with a bit of a scar on your upper back, near your right shoulder, Ms. . . . ?”

Erin was lying flat on her stomach, drifting along in a cloud of morphine. She grinned up at him. “The way I’m beginning to feel, I really don’t think I care.”

She heard a man’s voice outside the

cubicle. It was Bowie arguing with a woman. She'd lose, Erin would bet her currently fairly healthy bank account on it. Then he was there, beside her, and Dr. Arch said, "You her husband?"

"No, I'm FBI Agent Bowie Richards. She's my daughter's ballet teacher."

"I had no idea teaching kids how to demi-plié was so hazardous. You wouldn't think parents would get that pissed at her."

Bowie looked down at her back and swallowed. The burn looked really bad—fiery red, oozing and angry. Thank the good Lord it wasn't all that big. He drew a deep breath and asked, "How serious is it?"

Dr. Arch said, "If she's a back sleeper, she'll have to find another way for a couple of days. Almost all of the burn is second degree, but I'll admit, it looks like misery. Fortunately, the jacket she was wearing protected her from a truly critical burn. There aren't many deep spots, and all of it should heal without a graft. What's her name? Her purse wasn't with her when she was brought in."

"Erin Pulaski."

"I'm an Irish-Polish-American."

"Me, I'm a Russian Swede." Dr. Arch

was laughing as he lightly touched his gloved fingertips to her back.

She reared up. "It doesn't hurt much but I think I'd be yelling without the morphine."

"Sorry," Dr. Arch said.

She felt Bowie's hand on her shoulder, lightly pushing her down. He leaned next to her face. "You hang in there, kiddo. I'm here and I'm not leaving."

"What happened, Bowie? I sort of left the planet when the paramedics picked me up."

"The paramedics got there fast and brought you in, that's all. Since there were half a dozen 911 calls, the whole police station knew about it real fast. I didn't realize it was you until I heard one of the patrol officers talk about 'Erin's poor Hummer' still burning on the street. Are you together enough to tell me what happened?"

Erin didn't want to remember, she didn't want to think about anything, except maybe humming a nice chorus of "Forever Young" with the morphine playing a smooth bass. She closed her eyes and saw herself hurtling out of the Hummer door, and crashing against the curb. "Am I hurt anywhere else?"

Dr. Arch said, "I haven't had time to check you as thoroughly as I'd like. I'll do that again as soon as we get your back taken care of, but from what I can see, so far you've just got a few bruises and scrapes. You won't even need any sutures."

Her mind was fuzzing over. It felt bizarre and comforting at the same time. She said, "I don't suppose you caught the creeps who did this?"

"Not yet," Bowie said. "Talk, Erin."

". . . I remembered my dad telling me a car on fire was a rolling bomb and believe me, I didn't even pause a nanosecond, I just slammed on the brake and threw myself out the driver's side door. My baby, Bowie, my Hummer exploded maybe three seconds later."

There, it was said. Erin wasn't aware that tears were streaming down her dirty face until she felt Bowie's fingers wiping them away.

"I'm sorry. You'll be okay, you heard Dr. Arch. Damn me for an idiot, I never seriously thought you'd be in danger because we let you get connected to the investigation—"

"I'm fine, Bowie. It's not me, it's my Hummer, she's gone. Someone blew her up. She cruised all over town like a rock star, taking bows at every red light. I'd come out of the dry cleaner's to find guys draped all over her, but she was mine."

"You survived, Ms. Pulaski," Dr. Arch said as he dabbed ointment on her back. "Suck it up."

"You're a dolt, sir. You never saw my Hummer, never rode in her. All the guys in Stone Bridge were jealous of her, Bowie included, he just pretended he wasn't."

"Yeah, yeah, poor me," Dr. Arch said as he did this and that to her back, better not to know, she thought. "Here I am stuck with a plain old three-year-old Ferrari F430, a boring bright racing red, U.S. specs put it zero to sixty in three point six seconds, and I've been too chicken to let it loose on the highway. My son, now, he's chomping at the bit. I told him he had maybe twenty more years to get himself prepared. Hold still now, I'm going to give you some more morphine."

Bowie said, "You're alive, Erin. You'll replace the Hummer. I'll help you find one. Please don't tell me you're really crying for that car."

"Okay, I won't." Erin closed her eyes again, and felt, all of a sudden, that she was floating some six feet above herself, nearly up to those removable tiles in the ceiling, and it was so lovely and calm up there next to the light fixture, where nothing bad could happen to her.

Dr. Arch said thoughtfully, "Come to think of it, if my Ferrari exploded to smithereens, I might shed a couple buckets of tears myself. I take it all back, Ms. Pulaski, you go right ahead and weep." He was working on her shoulder now but she felt only a whisper touch against her skin. She vaguely heard him say to Bowie, "Would you look at that bruise. Well, it's no big deal in the great scheme of things. I don't think anything's broken, but we'll check her out with an X-ray. Say, if someone tried to blow her up, you're a federal cop, why don't you protect her from now on?"

"That's my plan," Bowie said. She felt blessed warmth when he took her hand, but his fingers against her skin brought her right down from above and she didn't know if it was worth it.

35

Erin usually hated lying on her stomach, but with the lovely morphine, she could have been standing on her head and not felt uncomfortable at all. "It was a light brown sedan, a Mitsubishi, I think, not very old. It looked like one of those rental cars—nondescript, butt-plain. I've always wondered why they even make cars like that. I mean, who'd want to buy one? I couldn't make out the license, they'd dirtied it up."

She'd have some pain for the next couple of days, Dr. Arch had told Bowie, but nothing a bit of Vicodin wouldn't handle. Her hair was still mostly in its thick French braid and they'd washed her face and all the rest of her he could see. She was lying on her stomach, her head to the side, looking like she didn't have a care in the world.

He lightly smoothed back a hank of hair that had fallen across her face and tucked it back into the braid. "That's good, Erin. The tinted windows give us something to work with."

She peered up at him with sudden interest. "It occurs to me that you look sort of cute, Bowie—all sorts of worried and mad."

"What? Oh, well, thank you, but that's the morphine talking."

"Nope, it's me."

He said, "Well, I am worried and mad."

"You wanna know something else?"

"Ah, maybe."

"You've got a really nice smile, nearly as nice as your butt."

"What? My—oh, well, thank you, but again, Erin, that's the morphine talking."

"Hmm. You mean I won't like your finer points when the morphine is no more?"

"I, ah, well, I don't know."

"I might, you know. What are you going to do if I still like those gorgeous white teeth of yours and those big feet?"

"I'll smile at you a whole lot with my bare feet up on the coffee table."

"That was really smooth, Bowie," she said, and closed her eyes. "You're a great dad. Georgie does nothing but brag about you. I keep telling her you're just a plain old garden-variety sort of dad, but she won't have it. That's quite an honor."

"Yes, it is, and nice to hear." He waited just a moment, to see if anything else outrageous would come out of her mouth, but she was still again. "Now, Erin, don't go under again just yet. Try to remember, did you see who was in that car?"

"Nope. Hey, wait a minute. Even though the windshield was darker than usual, I remember I didn't see anyone in the passenger seat, yes, I'm sure of it. There was one guy driving but I didn't see him well at all. Rental cars don't have dark windshields, do they?"

"I doubt it, but we'll soon see." When he punched off his cell a minute later, he said to her, "Agent Cliff will check it out. Okay, now, it's time—"

"Georgie told me you liked Krissy but she wasn't a keeper. Georgie said she didn't think there would be any keepers for you since you really loved her mommy and then she died and your heart broke in two. Is that true?"

"What? Georgie said that?" He was beginning to believe Georgie didn't keep any thought from Erin.

She could see he didn't want to answer her, sensed a deep, longtime resistance, but then he said, "No, it isn't true."

"I think morphine is the greatest stuff. I can say anything I want and it doesn't seem to matter and you can't get mad at me because I'm down and out."

He laughed.

"Georgie's got talent. Any dancers on your side? Was her mom a dancer?"

"No, Twinkle Toes is all on her own, genetically speaking."

Sherlock came running into the room. "Erin! I heard your Hummer exploded. The nurse told me you'd be all right, but I want to hear it from you."

"I'm okay, Sherlock, really. I'll be down for a while. It's a burn on my back, but you know, I'm a fast healer, so say a couple of days and I'll be good to go again. Don't worry."

"She's also loopy from the morphine so

don't take it seriously when she tells you your hair is glorious."

"Of course I'll take it seriously." She patted Erin's arm. "Dillon said you loved your Hummer more than he loves his Porsche. Let me tell you that's not possible."

"I loved my Hummer a whole bunch," Erin said, and squeezed her eyes closed. Sherlock studied her too-pale face, her eyes trying for bright but clouding over from the drugs, and slowly nodded. "I'll make it a tie then, okay? Now, tell me what happened. Don't leave anything out."

Sherlock never said a word until after Erin had stopped talking and closed her eyes. She looked limp and exhausted. "Thanks to Mom, who nagged at me for a solid three months, I got good health insurance last year. I've got good insurance on my Hummer too."

Bowie said, "Thank God for mothers. Tell me your company and I'll handle it, both your medical and your car."

Erin sighed. "Bowie said he'd help me find a new Hummer, but even if it's pale blue, it just won't be the same thing."

"Dillon's Porsche got blown up a while back, just like your Hummer. He's got a new one, looks exactly the same, but sometimes I see him looking at it, all sorts of wistful, and I wonder if he's thinking about his old baby. When I asked him about it, he said time heals all wounds."

"I sure hope he's right," Erin said.

Sherlock stood back while Bowie stepped close, pen and notebook in hand, to take down all the insurance information Erin remembered. As she looked at Erin's vague drugged eyes, she realized the suspicions she'd had were inescapable, all the seemingly random points connecting right up. Had Bowie made any connections from everything Erin had let drop?

She smiled at him when he left the room to deal with hospital administration.

"You've got the neatest hair, Sherlock. Bowie's right, it's glorious. The color is like the Olympic flame."

"Thank you."

Erin grinned. "All those curls, I'll bet Dillon thinks you're edible."

"Edible? Hmm, now that sounds interesting. Erin, as much as I like hearing Ms. Morphine pay me compliments, it's time we talked." Sherlock pulled a chair close to the bed and said very quietly not three inches from Erin's nose, "I know you're right in the middle of this, Erin. The fact that someone tried to kill you today clinches it. It's time for the truth. I don't want to give whoever is behind this another chance to kill you."

Erin felt the velvet fist behind the words. She whispered, "You can't know—can you?"

Sherlock said matter-of-factly, "You've dropped lots of things since we've met. You also tend to speak before you think. With you, if one really listens, everything is right up front."

Erin shut her eyes. "It's true, I have the biggest mouth. I always have. My dad would say my big mouth was fine by him, I couldn't get away with anything."

"Does Georgie beat you at poker since everything you're thinking troops right across your face?"

"Haven't tried poker with her yet. You know, I lied once to a boyfriend in college, and you know what he did? The jerk laughed at me. It was so depressing."

Sherlock waited.

Erin felt fatigue wash over her, both fatigue and an overwhelming sense of failure.

"I can't tell you, Sherlock, since he's a client. It's confidential. I'll have to speak to him first, see what he says."

"Since you were nearly murdered, it seems to me this client's answer should be obvious unless he's in this mess up to his eyeballs, unless he knows who's behind the attempt on your life, or unless he's the one who tried to kill you."

"He's a very nice man, but it's all very complicated. I'm in so bloody deep. I'll probably go to jail."

Sherlock lightly stroked her fingers over Erin's pale cheek. "Don't be dramatic, it'll be okay. Believe me, nothing's simpler than the truth. Spit it out. We'll deal with it, trust me."

"No, Sherlock, I simply can't, not until—"

"Until you speak to your client who's a professor at Yale University?"

"See? A fine example of my big mouth, but you've got to let me talk to him myself."

"You really should tell me now, Erin, so we can clean this mess up without your getting killed in the process."

Erin wished the morphine would knock her out again, but it didn't. She was even feeling some mild throbbing in her back. It wasn't fair. "Can I have more morphine?"

"Yes," Sherlock said, and left her to speak to the nurse.

Half an hour later, Sherlock and Bowie were sitting side by side watching Erin sleep the peaceful sleep of the drugged.

"Well, damn and blast," Bowie said. "She'll have to tell us soon, Sherlock."

"When she wakes up, I'll get it out of her. I'd rather have the truth when she's alert and willing."

But what could Erin possibly know? Nothing important, he was sure of that. "Are you going to tell me what you think she knows?"

"No, let's wait."

36

MERRITT PARKWAY REST STOP
Thursday afternoon

Caskie Royal zipped up his pants, walked to the rusted sink with its dulled mirror, and stared at a face he hardly recognized. In only four days, fear had leached the color from his skin, and his jowls looked pale and saggy. He looked ill, terminally ill. That thought brought a ghastly smile to his face.

He was afraid, more afraid than he'd believed possible ever since that woman had broken into his office on Sunday night. He'd asked himself over and over how she'd known about the Culovort files, but he still had no clue how she'd known or why she'd copied them or who she was, but then again, neither did any of those agents who'd been stomping on him ever since. Was she a cancer patient? Or maybe it was her husband who was the patient? There were scores of patients very unhappy with him and the company since the Culovort shortage began, but still, that didn't ring true. If someone had merely wanted to make the papers public, why didn't the newspapers, or even the FBI, already have them? If she was a blackmailer, why hadn't she called?

He shook his head at the stranger in the mirror. Nothing made sense anymore. He had no idea if she was the one who'd murdered Blauvelt, not that he cared.

Caskie started to wash his hands. He turned on the warm water faucet, but the water was cold. He pressed down on the soap pump and lathered up, automatic after all these years. Jane Ann had nagged him to do it since the day he married her. *His wife.* He wasn't about to worry about her now, but his boys, Chad and Mark, were another matter entirely. How could he protect them? Protect their future? He felt a shaft of pain deep in his belly. It wasn't indigestion, it was grief.

Caskie knew he was going to be sucked down into the swamp where all the hungry alligators waited. Unless he was real careful, he'd end up in jail, or dead. Who would have thought that any of this would end up as anything more than a fine for the company at worst, maybe an early departure for him as CEO if it all hit the fan. If he'd thought jail was a possibility, would he have turned all this down? Maybe, he thought, sure he would have. No one in his family had ever gone to prison. He wasn't a young man any longer, he wouldn't be able to protect himself from all the predators in prison and he knew the predators were there, everyone knew that.

He turned his head slowly from side to side as he watched in the mirror. No, he thought, honest in that moment, the thought of jail wouldn't have deterred him. There was so much money, quite a lot of it already in his private accounts in the Grand Cayman.

What he'd done, it hadn't been all that bad. Just look at what those clowns at Pfizer had finally been nailed for, they'd deserved the huge fines. They'd deserved prison too, but that didn't happen. Fines for criminal behavior, not jail. Wasn't that a kick?

The party's over, he whispered to the deathly-pale face. The coffin lid was inexorably closing over him. He'd escaped for the moment to the men's room in the rest area, Toms with him at first, but Toms, who'd hummed while he'd peed, had finished and left. He hadn't washed his hands. Had he come back? Was he waiting outside the door? He wouldn't put anything past him, the bastard.

They'd told him, not asked him, to sit on the backward-facing rumble seat with Toms, facing Bender, Dieffendorf, and Gerlach. He'd tried to act dignified, tried to act the consummate CEO.

Dieffendorf hadn't bought it. He disliked Dieffendorf, always had, but the fact was, he hated Werner Gerlach now, hated what was in his eyes every time Gerlach looked at him. It was his own death he saw there if he couldn't convince them to trust him. And he saw in those eyes that he had failed. Caskie was nothing more than a pawn to Gerlach, he knew it to his soul. Gerlach had always been a priggish little man, barely five-foot-six in his elevator shoes—pathetic, really, when he wouldn't stop bragging about his sexy young wife, Laytha. What man in his right mind would want to be married to a woman younger than his daughter? Did she talk about getting zits? About going to bars and listening to music Gerlach hated? Caskie wondered whether Laytha cost Gerlach so much in maintenance that Gerlach had no choice but to keep coming up with new schemes to make more money. He had to keep up with Laytha's new shoes. He was brilliant at market strategies, at innovative ways to get around rules, and was endlessly greedy. Caskie supposed he'd recognized himself in Gerlach the moment the two men had met five years ago.

Gerlach and Dieffendorf had known each other forever, it seemed to Caskie, had run Schiffer Hartwin for close to twenty years now. They had always shown a united front to the world, just as now, the second in command accompanying Dieffendorf to face the latest battle.

Yet they couldn't be more different.

It was odd, Caskie realized, but he was as afraid of Dieffendorf as he was of Gerlach, and Dieffendorf didn't even have his guard dog Blauvelt to solve all his problems any longer.

Caskie saw Dieffendorf's calculating, emotionless eyes staring back at him in the mirror. He could still hear his accented voice as he'd said, "I sent Helmut here to get to the bottom of this Culovort shortage you have helped to create. He was coming to see you for explanations yet you claim you didn't see him, Mr. Royal. Is this true?"

"Yes," Caskie had said, his voice steady, the ring of truth bright and shining. "I did not see him. He was murdered Sunday night. I was to see him Monday morning."

Gerlach said, "And you were busy Sunday night, were you not? With your current lover, I understand. And thus you say you could not have killed Blauvelt. I hope your family is holding up under this painful scrutiny. It must be especially difficult for your boys. Their names are Chad and Mark?"

"Yes, they are holding up well. They don't know anything. I thought that was best." Message received, Caskie thought, loud and clear.

He looked at Gerlach's small hands clasped together in his lap. Caskie hated to shake his hand, the skin was dry and hard, desiccated like his face, like his soul. Gerlach crossed and recrossed his legs, showing off his Italian loafers with their nearly two-inch lifts.

As the limo cruised smoothly east on the Merritt Parkway, Dieffendorf said, "I must tell you, Mr. Royal, when I was informed you had arranged to shut down the Culovort production in Missouri without consulting me, I was not happy, but I was not overly concerned since the drug doesn't add much to our bottom line. But when the plant in Spain went down recently—due to sabotage, mind you—and it became clear that worldwide supply of our drug Culovort would dry up completely, well, suddenly what you'd done took on a new significance. Would you agree?"

"It was very unfortunate, more than unfortunate, tragic—but no one could have anticipated that, Mr. Dieffendorf."

"If you know nothing about that, Mr. Royal, can you tell me why you left such detailed information about the effects you anticipated from the Culovort shortage in the United States on your computer? Did I make a mistake in hiring you, Mr. Royal?"

Caskie sat forward, hands clasped between his knees, just the right note of sincerity in his charming voice, "I cannot tell you how I regret I did that, sir, but you see, no one is allowed in my office except my assistant and even she doesn't know my computer password. But this woman, she managed to—"

Dieffendorf interrupted him smoothly as if what he was saying was not worth spit, "Is there anything as yet to point to the identity of this woman who broke into your office?"

Caskie shook his head. "I know the FBI are trying very hard to find her."

"Helmut would have located her by now." Dieffendorf sighed. "How I miss him. To hear he was murdered in such a brutal fashion, I cannot comprehend who would have done such a thing. Do you know, Mr. Royal?"

"I have no idea, sir. I wish I did. Evidently it was close to the time the woman broke into my office. Perhaps she was involved. Like I said, the FBI is looking hard for her."

Dieffendorf said slowly, "I am not certain I want the American FBI to find her. What would she say? I am here, Mr. Royal, to ensure that Schiffer Hartwin does not suffer from your negligence. I have promised the family that I will discover everything that is going on here and fix it. Do you understand me, Mr. Royal?"

Gerlach said, "Actually, Adler, the FBI doesn't need to find her to have the axe fall on the company's head. She has but to give the papers over to the media. I sincerely hope she plans to blackmail us instead. What with the unfortunate sabotage of the Spanish plant, the hungry media here would crucify us. Isn't this correct, Mr. Royal?"

Caskie nodded dumbly. He thought about grabbing a plane to South America, getting lost in Patagonia.

Dieffendorf said, "Mr. Bender tells us you are thinking about speaking frankly to the FBI, Mr. Royal. May I ask what you would say to them?"

The spit dried in his mouth. Caskie shook his head, back and forth. "No, Mr. Bender is quite wrong. I would never do that, never."

Caskie saw from the corner of his eye that Bender would speak, but Dieffendorf raised his hand to keep him silent.

"I really am curious what you would say if you decided to speak to them."

Caskie ran his tongue over his dry lips.

"Listen, sir, no one was more shocked than I was to hear about the closing of the Spanish plant. I owe my loyalty to Schiffer Hartwin, my livelihood, you know that. I've worked for you for five years now, five excellent years."

"I found myself wondering why on earth it would be important to anyone to have a major shortage of such a simple drug as Culovort. It didn't take long to think of the CEO of Laboratoires Ancondor, the paltry unethical little hypocrite who produces the oral cancer drug Eloxium. Do you know Monsieur Renard? Did you perhaps make a deal with him? Stocks and cash in exchange for help cutting off our Culovort production, and forcing our patients to his high-priced oral drug?"

"Sir, I have never met Monsieur Renard." It was the truth, he thought, but still, his armpits were wet. Could they smell his sweat?

"If I discover that you have been lying to me, Mr. Royal, I will make a call. You will find yourself wishing for Helmut Blauvelt's tender mercies. Do you understand me?"

"I understand," Caskie said at nearly a whisper. "I am guilty of nothing, sir, except bad luck. Our plant in Missouri will be much more profitable once our production problems are behind us. The papers on my computer, they were an exercise in thinking outside the box, something you encourage, nothing more."

Dieffendorf slowly nodded. "Schiffer Hartwin will see to that, Mr. Royal." It was then that Caskie looked for the final time into Gerlach's eyes.

Caskie washed his hands again, stared at himself once more in the old mirror over the ancient sink, maybe to reassure himself that he was really here, and not the ghost of a man who would shortly be dead.

He knew what he had to do. He had to get home, gather his passport and some cash and his private bankbooks, and disappear. This rest stop was in the boonies of western Connecticut, thick woods all around, and very few people. He could get away here, but not through the restroom door, Toms or Bender might be there. He had to do something else. He looked up at the windows, not small like the window in his office bathroom, thank God. He judged the distance from the floor, wondered if he was strong enough to pull himself up.

If he wanted to live, he'd do it. He was alone in the restroom for now, but Toms could open the door at any time, or anybody who wanted to take a leak. He had only a minute. He drew in a deep breath, climbed up over the sink, and managed to grab the windowsill.

Now, pull yourself up—

Caskie pulled and heaved, felt sweat slicking his hands, felt his muscles shake. He couldn't fail, or he'd be dead, Gerlach, Dieffendorf, it didn't matter which. Living in South America would beat any jail here in the U.S. Surely if he was gone, his boys would be all right with their mother. The FBI would blame him for everything, surely that would be what Dieffendorf would want as well.

Caskie managed to heave himself through the open window. It was only about five feet to the ground and he managed to turn as he pushed himself out and land on a roll. He felt a sharp pain in his back, but he dismissed it.

He'd made it, and he was alive.

He ran for the woods.

37

STONE BRIDGE MEMORIAL HOSPITAL
Thursday afternoon

Savich lightly touched the back of Erin's hand. He still remembered the searing pain he'd felt when a burning seat from an exploding van in Jessborough, Tennessee, had sliced into his own back. She lay on her side, still asleep, or drugged out, just as he had. He looked up at Bowie. "Tell me what happened."

Bowie did, adding, "She could easily have died if she hadn't acted so quickly. She jumped right out the door and rolled."

Savich said, "Answer me this, Bowie. Why the attempt on her life?"

Bowie dashed his fingers through his hair, making it stand on end. "Because, somehow, she's in the middle of this mess, only I don't have a clue how that could be, and I should. Sherlock knows, but she wants Erin to tell us when she's not under the influence of morphine. Do you know?"

"So Sherlock's figured it out, has she?"

Bowie looked angry at himself. "She has, yes."

Savich said. "Where's Caskie Royal?"

"I just spoke to Agent Clive Pohli. He and Agent Marty Torres are following the limo. They're on the Merritt Parkway, in Connecticut now."

Bowie's cell phone sang out "It's Beginning to Look a Lot Like Christmas." Bowie dug into his pocket, frowned, then spotted his cell on the side table beside Erin's bed.

He listened, said to Savich, "Pohli says the limo's at a rest stop, and Royal and Toms went to the men's room, then Toms came out alone. Pohli said a blind man couldn't miss Toms, he's wearing a lime-green tie with white stripes."

"Anybody else around?"

Bowie asked the question into his cell. "Maybe half a dozen in the Quick Mart, a couple in the parking lot outside the store. That's it. Hey, wait, Toms just opened the men's room door and now he's running around to the back of the restroom. Pohli says the limo driver just made them. They're all getting back into the limo and pulling out of the rest stop." Bowie raised his eyes to Savich's face. "Caskie Royal is no longer with them. It seems, for the moment at least, he's escaped."

Savich said, "I guess I'm not surprised. In his shoes, I might run too. Tell Pohli to pull the car into the parking lot where Royal can see it if he's still close. And tell him to look in the woods. Maybe Royal's ready to talk to us now."

Bowie spoke into the phone, then looked at Savich. "We'll save his hide, then we'll make him see reason."

Sherlock hurried back into the hospital room. "I brought you some tea, Dillon. Is Erin still out of it?"

"Yeah, still asleep," Bowie said. "I get the impression she's very sensitive to drugs. Sherlock, Caskie Royal's run off from the Schiffer Hartwin directors and lawyers at a

Merritt Parkway rest stop, of all places. Our guys are trying to find him in the woods."

There was a small sound from Erin.

Sherlock leaned over her, lightly smoothed her hair back from her face. "Wake up, Erin, time to talk to Mama about all your worries."

But Erin wasn't with it yet.

Bowie said, "I wonder if the directors are staying at our *Psycho* B-and-B."

"The answer is no," Andreas Kesselring said as he walked into the hospital room. He gave each of them a sharp nod. He just needed to add a heel click, Savich thought, to really make an entrance. He looked like he could step off the pages of *GQ* magazine, the German edition.

Kesselring waved in Erin's direction. "I see she is still alive. How badly is she injured?"

Bowie said, "Some bruises and contusions, a burn on her back, but not too serious. She was very lucky."

"A nurse told me her car exploded. It was a miracle she managed to get out in time."

"Not a car," Bowie said, smiling toward Erin, "a Hummer. It wasn't a miracle, it was her own quickness that saved her. What are you doing here, Agent Kesselring?"

Kesselring looked thoughtfully at each of them in turn. "I find myself wondering why all of you are here at your daughter's dance teacher's bedside. And then I wondered, Why would someone try to blow up a dance teacher? I am forced to conclude this must all somehow be connected to the investigation. I am right, am I not?"

"We don't know yet," Sherlock said. "We're waiting for her to wake up enough to tell us."

Kesselring walked over to the single chair in front of the single window in the room. "I will wait with you." He sat down, crossed his legs, and swung a foot shod in dark gray Italian soft-as-butter leather, the exact shade as his suit.

"Nice shoes." Bowie wished he could throw the guy out the window. They were on the third floor, a nice long way down. "Are they comfortable?"

"Not particularly," said Kesselring, "but they go well with this particular suit, so I suffer them when I have to. I'm in a foreign country, and I must try to look as respectable as I can."

Sherlock said, "What have you been up to today, Agent?"

Kesselring smiled. Again, Savich saw a flash of hot violence in his eyes when he looked at Sherlock, but his voice sounded amused when he finally spoke. "Nice of you to ask, Agent Sherlock. I was at Schiffer Hartwin's headquarters, learning very little of use. I was hoping Carla Alvarez would have something to say, but she didn't."

Bowie said, "I was just telling Agent Sherlock that Caskie Royal ran away at a rest stop on the way here from JFK with the Schiffer Hartwin directors. Our agents are trying to find him, but no word yet."

Kesselring looked startled. "You say he ran away from them at a rest stop? How very interesting. I cannot fathom why he would do such an odd thing, and in such a manner. Dr. Dieffendorf and Herr Gerlach must tell us what happened. One is tempted to conclude Mr. Royal ran because he's guilty of a crime, perhaps even of this murder."

Bowie said, "So you no longer believe it was a psychotic mugger who murdered Herr Blauvelt? Now you believe it was Caskie Royal? Why?"

If the light touch of sarcasm failed to float over Kesselring's head, he gave no clue, at least Sherlock thought so until she saw the glint in Kesselring's very nice green eyes. "Why else, Agent Richards, would Caskie Royal run?"

Bowie said, "I'm certain we will find out soon enough."

Kesselring looked at his elegant Piaget watch. "At any rate, the directors should be here in an hour or so. They will no doubt be tired. It is a long flight from Frankfurt to New York, and they are not young men. I understand their limo driver is taking them directly to their hotel. I suspect they will wish to rest tonight. If so, I will take you to see them at the Schiffer Hartwin headquarters in the morning."

"Don't forget the lawyers, Agent Kesselring," Sherlock said easily. "Perhaps they will be able to tell us what frightened Caskie Royal so very much he felt he had to run for his life."

38

Kesselring didn't rise to the bait, though it was meaty. He merely swung his foot, tented his fingers, and tapped them against his chin, smiling charmingly at her. But his eyes, his eyes. "I find this case a fascinating conundrum. And this abrupt departure of Mr. Royal is yet one more thread to unravel. Please remember I am here to help you do that." And he gave each of them a long look.

Erin made a little sound in her throat and opened her eyes, saw Savich, and smiled. "You're back. Hi. I'm very glad to see you."

"Hi, yourself, Erin. I'm glad to see that smile on your face. You okay?"

She queried her body, nodded. "Yeah, I'll live." She turned her head slightly to look at the strange man sitting in the lone chair. *A feast for the eyes,* she thought, *and would you just look at those exquisite Italian loafers on that swinging foot*. She wouldn't mind wearing them herself. Her father had loved Italian loafers, particularly the ones with the tassels. She didn't smile at him. "Who are you?"

Kesselring rose and walked to stand beside Savich at the foot of her bed. He gave her a sharp bow. "My name is Agent Andreas Kesselring. I was sent here from Germany to help in the investigation of Herr Blauvelt's murder. You are a dance teacher. Your name is Erin Pulaski. Why is everyone here with you and not out chasing down Caskie Royal?"

"I'm a very important dance teacher since I also take care of Agent Richards's daughter."

"His daughter? I did not know this, but that is hardly the point. Why are you important?"

Erin felt only a slight aching in her back,

but nothing terrible. It wasn't the morphine talking, either. Most of the stuff was already out of her bloodstream. She felt alert and stronger, and realized she'd been luckier than she deserved. *Bless you, Daddy.* Very slowly, she rolled over and sat up, ignoring Sherlock's hand. She felt a twinge in her back, but it wasn't anything she couldn't handle. She said, dropping her voice to a whisper, "I'm important because I know things."

"What things could you possibly know to make someone try to blow you up?"

She knew it infuriated this lovely man, but she asked Sherlock, "Is it all right to speak to him?"

"Feel free," Sherlock said, and patted her hand.

Kesselring said, his voice hard, "Come, tell us what you know that makes you such a threat to—someone?"

"I know what everyone in this room knows: namely, Caskie Royal is a crook. Schiffer Hartwin are crooks. Herr Blauvelt is dead, brutally murdered. He was a crook too."

"Those are scurrilous things to say, Ms. Pulaski. Hopefully they're also completely unfounded. Well, Herr Blauvelt is dead, but as for the other—"

"It's simple," Erin said right over him. "It's about corrupt pharmaceutical houses looking for every possible way to make money, and not caring who they hurt on the way. It's all about their bottom line."

"Where did you get these ideas, Ms. Pulaski? The drug companies have done amazing things, amazing. They've produced medicines that have eradicated diseases."

"I now believe any good they do is secondary to their goal, which is making money and more money."

"Come now, what does any of this have to do with a ballet teacher?"

Erin looked him dead in the eye. "Agent Kesselring, are you a crook as well?"

Kesselring studied her face a long silent moment, then said with great precision, "I am a ten-year veteran of the BND, Germany's Federal Intelligence Service. I have dozens of awards and commendations to prove it. I ask you again: How do you purport to know anything that would push someone to try to kill you?"

"I don't know anything about you, Agent

Kesselring." Erin turned to look at Bowie, wincing just a bit with the movement. "I am all right, I'm not lying to you. What I am is very mad. Someone tried to kill me. That someone blew up my Hummer. Get me out of here. I want to rent a car, then I want to go home."

"May I accompany you?" Kesselring asked.

"Like I said, Agent Kesselring, I don't know you, but let me hasten to add I do understand why Agent Cliff was so pleased to drive you in from New York."

He snorted, which was really quite charming, and she had to repress a smile. "She is a woman of excellent character and taste. No one wishes to see you hurt, Ms. Pulaski, especially because you are a dance teacher who knows something you shouldn't, and that, for heaven's sake, is what exactly?"

Erin slowly swung her legs over the side of the hospital bed. "What I know is that I'm dancing out of here."

39

MERRIAM BARTLETT HOTEL
STONE BRIDGE, CONNECTICUT
Thursday evening

"I will, of course, support you in whatever you decide to do," Werner Gerlach said to Adler Dieffendorf as he hung up his favorite light blue suit with its very narrow light gray pinstripes. The wool was so soft now that it felt like a cozy old friend. He spoke in German, since no one in this impertinent uncivilized country felt the need to speak another language, and so it was safe. He stroked the material a moment and left it carefully hung on a padded hanger in the too-small closet.

Dieffendorf turned from the window. "While you were in the bathroom, I called Agent Kesselring to tell him Caskie Royal had run away. He already knew. He had to agree it seems likely our own man, the CEO we trusted, murdered poor Helmut. It's a shock, but one keeps coming back to it—why else would he have run?"

Gerlach said, his head still in the closet, "Royal killed him because Helmut must have found Royal was involved with Renard, Royal probably planned the sabotage of the Spanish plant with Renard as well." Gerlach shrugged. "They must have fought, and somehow, though it is hard to believe, Royal got the better of him, killed him. I didn't want to believe it, but now? I fear there is no other conclusion." Gerlach looked around his miserly little room which connected to Dieffendorf's one-bedroom suite in the Merriam Bartlett hotel, the only superior lodging for gamblers at the nearby Indian casino. Dieffendorf's bedroom was much larger than his. He watched Dieffendorf as he sat down in a cream-and-green-striped wing chair next to a window overlooking a vast woodland, and drummed his fingertips together. "Royal must have connected with Renard, right? I wonder if he had the spine to call him, or if Renard called Royal? There is no way Royal could have pulled off the sabotage of the Spanish plant by himself, and in any case, why would he? Without Renard, there wouldn't be a profit. It even smells like Renard, don't you think?"

Gerlach shrugged, carefully placing padded shoe trees into another pair of shoes. "I know nothing more than you do, Adler."

"I do not know what to tell the family. They look to me to keep scandal away from the door. But now? I have failed." Gerlach knew Dieffendorf had always worshipped at the feet of the Schiffer family. They'd always insisted the managing director be a medical doctor, and Adler was, having earned his medical degree in endocrinology. What Adler really excelled at, Gerlach thought, was looking both wise and benevolent. Gerlach wondered how many people besides him knew Dieffendorf was the most ruthless man in the room. Gerlach had often wondered if Dieffendorf's precious Schiffer family knew how skilled their managing director was at subtly skewing data so the drug in question was seen as effective enough, or safe enough, to pass review. He was renowned for it, in fact, impressed even the staff writers hired to ghostwrite many of the review articles presented by physicians to the major U.S. medical journals, a longtime practice by the drug companies only recently discovered, causing much chagrin in the medical journal review boards. It was a pity. But Gerlach knew that when one door closed, another opened, like the American FDA's recent approval of drug testing conducted outside the U.S., where the pharmaceuticals would be able to do just about anything they pleased. Didn't the idiots realize this? Not only were they making it cheaper for the drug companies, it meant the bribing of local officials would increase exponentially. Who would care about illegal drug tests run on local natives in backward countries? No one cared now. Gerlach couldn't see anything changing. As long as Dieffendorf and Helmut Blauvelt kept the problems plausibly deniable, the results pleased the family more than their consciences would bother them. But now Blauvelt was dead. It didn't matter,

Dieffendorf would soon sniff out another Blauvelt. There were more Blauvelts in this world than anyone imagined. Gerlach said, "Helmut's murder really bothers you, doesn't it?"

"Why do you sound so surprised? I have known and trusted Helmut for ten years. There are others, of course, and I will be forced to rely on them, but I have never trusted anyone like I trusted and depended on Helmut."

"Yes, I too am sorry for it." Gerlach looked over at his boss of more than twenty years, the one always seated on the royal throne, the bastard. But there was one area where Gerlach was the king and so he dug out his knife. He smiled at Dieffendorf, and said in a complacent voice he knew Adler hated, "I miss my wife."

"I miss Claire too," Dieffendorf said, staring out the window, swinging his foot rhythmically back and forth until Gerlach wanted to kick him. "It is a constant ache." Dieffendorf's wife had died of breast cancer six years earlier. He'd even tried two experimental drugs. Nothing had worked.

"I know," Gerlach said as he turned back

to the closet to hang up one of his three Savile Row white dress shirts.

Dieffendorf looked over at Gerlach now, his voice meditative as he said, "It was such a shock when your precious Mathilde was struck by that hit-and-run motorcycle driver last year. I remember you couldn't stop crying at her funeral."

"Yes, it was very difficult. It was good to have all my friends there to support me."

Dieffendorf paused a moment, then added, a drip of acid on his tongue, "Laytha, your wife of eight months, is your son's age, Werner." Beneath the drip of acid there was a note of disapproval in his deep resonant voice, but he was masking his envy, Gerlach knew it.

And envy was what Gerlach had wanted to hear. "Actually, Laytha is younger than Klaus by nearly a year," he said comfortably, and gave Dieffendorf a sly smile. "I told you she has a sister who is also very lovely, and very well educated. I believe she just turned twenty-five."

"I prefer not to agitate my children, all of whom are older than this sister." Dieffendorf pushed himself up to his feet. It seemed each year slowed down some other part of him. He saw himself in fifteen years with no moving parts at all. It crossed his mind that when everything stopped moving, he'd just fall over and die. That would be preferable to cancer.

"Why are we talking about your wife? Good grief, Werner, we must decide about our interview with the American FBI agents we'll see tomorrow."

Gerlach shrugged. "There is no other choice but to tell them part of the truth, which, I suspect, they probably believe themselves—Caskie Royal is responsible for the Culovort shortage in the United States, he pressed forward on his own authority. He may also be responsible for the murder of Helmut Blauvelt. They know nothing about Renard. I see no reason to enlighten them.

"If they find Royal, they can surely extract a confession from him, discover why he planned the shortage, and that he acted on his own. You are skillful, Adler, you will steer them away from considering any company involvement. They will close their case. Then we will go home and I will be with Laytha." Gerlach calmly hung up the third shirt.

Dieffendorf gave him a sharp nod and walked back toward the suite. He turned in the doorway. “The Culovort papers are Schiffer Hartwin documents. If they surface, it will hardly be as easy as all that.”

40

ERIN'S APARTMENT
Thursday evening

"Is Georgie asleep?"

Sherlock nodded to Savich, watching Erin as Bowie handed her two aspirins and a glass of water. After she'd taken the pills, Sherlock added, "I only read her two pages of Nancy Drew, and luckily, she was down and out." She turned to Erin and Bowie. "She said to give you both a kiss. If you like, I'll pass on that."

Sherlock sat down beside Dillon, and Bowie moved to join her. Erin realized she was sitting by herself, the three of them sitting opposite her, together, silent and waiting. She was in the dock. Confession time.

Sherlock said, "Georgie's asleep, the dishes are washed and put away, you've got aspirin on board. It's time, Erin. Tell us why you broke into Caskie Royal's office and printed the Culovort papers off his computer."

Bowie froze. Sherlock wondered if he'd guessed this was Erin's secret, but seeing him staring at Erin, shock clear on his face, obviously he hadn't.

Sherlock lightly laid her fingertips to his arm. "I can't let this go on any longer, Erin. Not only don't I want to see you killed, what you know is critical to our investigation."

Bowie stared down at Sherlock's fingers on his arm. Was she afraid he was going to start screaming at Erin? Maybe leap up and strangle her?

Bowie couldn't believe it, simply couldn't. "Yes," he said, his voice perfectly pleasant, "please tell us everything."

Erin didn't look at him. She knew she'd see his dawning sense of betrayal, and she couldn't bear it. Sherlock was right, there was too much on the line now to hold back any longer. She said, "Yes, it's past time. How long have you known I was the one who pulled off the break-in, Sherlock?"

"I wondered about your level of interest. I thought it was really over the top, your intensity, the way you were so very focused on every word we said. And the clincher was our witness, who described you perfectly."

Savich sat forward, his hands clasped between his knees. "You were friendly, Erin, you were charming, but you didn't act exactly right around the three of us, particularly Bowie."

"What do you mean? I acted weird around Bowie?"

"I didn't say weird," Savich said. "You just acted off. Bowie would have seen it for himself if he hadn't been so caught up in the investigation of Blauvelt's murder, and, naturally, his worry about his daughter.

"Of course I checked you out," Savich continued. "And that led me to your dad. You'd told us about his being a consultant to law enforcement for the last twenty years of his life, but not the nitty-gritty details like the specialized skills he taught—building security for the new millennium, situational and strategic planning—like what to do if you're caught somewhere you shouldn't be, whether behind enemy lines or in a CEO's office. Oh, yes, I should mention he was known to be able to pick any lock in the known universe. You were lucky there were thick bushes below that bathroom window to break your fall."

Sherlock said, "I bet you learned everything from him, including lock picking. Time to get it all out, Erin. Tell us all of it."

Bowie remained silent. Erin wanted to punch him, make him say something, anything. "I don't want to go to jail, Sherlock. Am I going to need a lawyer?"

Bowie said, his voice too calm, too controlled, "I'm going to see to it you have the greenest public defender in Connecticut."

"I'll just say it would be a good idea for you to cooperate," Savich said. "I assume that you didn't kill Helmut Blauvelt? That you don't know anything about his murder?"

"No, I only heard about his murder on TV the next morning."

"Then there are the Culovort papers, Erin. Who is your client?"

Erin got to her feet and walked to her fireplace, removed the brick and pulled out a sheaf of papers. "You already know all of this, Dillon, you homed in on the Culovort shortage on your own. These are simply Caskie Royal's detailed plans for shutting down the supply from the plant in Missouri. He couched it as a profitable upgrade, but again, I think you might have nailed it. There wasn't much money in it for him unless he colluded with Laboratoires Ancondor in France for a share of their profits when cancer patients were forced to switch to their expensive oral drug, Eloxium.

"I don't know how he was paid, he doesn't talk about that in the papers, but maybe stock options, maybe some under-the-table kickbacks paid outright to Royal by the CEO of Ancondor when the huge bucks started rolling in. I'm not all that smart when it comes to finances, but I suppose there have got to be more ways to make this work for him.

"Others in Schiffer Hartwin have to be involved as well, people who were responsible for the sabotage of the Spanish plant. You'll see there's no mention about the Spanish plant in the papers either.

"Royal's plans are meticulously laid out. And that's what my client needed to take to the media to pressure Schiffer Hartwin into starting up Culovort production again."

"Who is your client, Erin?"

"I can't tell you, Sherlock. I want to protect him. It was so important that he have the Culovort for his father, he's in chemotherapy for colon cancer, and his oncologist told him her supply of Culovort is running out—"

Bowie said, his voice sharp as nails, "So that gets him off? He pressured you to be reckless. He encouraged you to break the law."

"No, he didn't know what I was going to do. There was no pressure."

Bowie rose slowly. "When you were in the bathroom, you got a call on your cell. I took it. The guy wouldn't give me his name, wouldn't leave a message, and believe me, I asked. It was your client, right, Erin?"

"Yes, it was. I'll tell you what, I'll call him, tell him you guys know everything. You'll find him anyway, I know that."

"You want to speak to him? Fine, you can do it here and now. Where's your cell?"

"I don't want to speak to him with you hanging all over me. He's my client. I don't want him to feel threatened."

"Give. Me. Your. Cell."

Erin began walking backward, her eyes not leaving his face.

"Savich, would you please hand me that leather purse of hers that's nearly big enough to cover an entire cow, and dig out her cell phone?"

Bing Crosby sang out "Jingle Bells." Bowie felt around for his own cell phone in his pants, then his jacket, and frowned, trying to follow the sound of Crosby's perky voice.

Erin said, "It's under those papers on the corner of the table."

Bowie's cell phone went silent.

Erin grabbed her purse, ran to the guest bathroom, and slammed the door. They heard the lock click into place.

"Well, Bowie," Sherlock said, "I guess you either break the door down or let her make the call in private."

Bowie returned to the sofa, sat down, and didn't say a word. Savich calmly began reading the Culovort papers.

A few minutes later, Erin walked back into the living room. She said without hesitation, "Dr. Kender is a professor of archaeology at Yale University. I told him about my Hummer blowing up, and he agreed it was time to bring you guys into it. You can talk to him whenever you wish."

She drew in a deep breath. "He wants to know if he can release the Culovort papers to the media tomorrow?"

Sherlock said as she watched Dillon place the Culovort papers in his briefcase, "This concerns the Department of Justice, so we need to show them the papers and ask them how they think it best to proceed. We'll let you know tomorrow, Erin."

Sherlock shot Bowie a look, but didn't say anything. She gave Savich a light punch on the arm and rose. "I think it's time Dillon and I took our leave. Why don't you guys thrash this out between you."

They were out the front door in under a minute flat.

When the front door closed, Bowie stood in the center of the living room, still silent as a stone. If he'd had a stone, Erin thought he'd probably have hurled it at her.

"I'm sorry, Bowie," she said. "I really am."

"Are you? Are you really? You must have thought you'd won the lottery when I showed up on your doorstep and asked you to watch Georgie."

"I said yes because I wanted to help, because I'm very fond of her. All right, yes, I also wanted to learn more about the case. Really, Bowie, I'm sorry."

"But you'd do it again."

"I don't know. Well, yes, I probably would do it again. I wouldn't have any choice. I guess it's looking to you like I've betrayed you."

"You think?" He walked away from her, nearly tripped over the big red beanbag, and after windmilling his arms, finally made it to the window, his back to her. She saw he was stiff, knew in that moment he was trying to keep control of himself. He said without looking at her, "I couldn't for the life of me figure out why someone would want to kill you. I mean, I figured it had to do with Blauvelt's murder, but I couldn't make my way through the maze."

He turned quickly, steering clear of the beanbag this time. His anger had slipped its leash. "You did betray me. You've been playing us. Curse me for an idiot since I'm the one who invited you right in, encouraged everyone to speak to you openly. We told you every single thing you could possibly want to know. Sherlock even took you on an official interview with Jane Ann Royal."

He grabbed her arms and shook her once, just a little shake to make sure he had her full attention, not to hurt her. "Dammit, Erin Pulaski, you betrayed me!"

She felt tears coming and swallowed. "Bowie, I'm sorry, really. I didn't know what to do—"

"Oh, yes, you did, you knew immediately what you were going to do."

"All right, but I didn't think I had a choice. I don't know how the person who blew up my Hummer knew I was involved."

"I'll bet whoever it was followed you to your lunch with Dr. Kender. That's who you had lunch with on Wednesday, right?"

She nodded. "Yes, but who do you think followed me?"

"Probably Caskie Royal."

"Or it could have been Carla Alvarez. I overheard her and Royal speaking before they came into his office. He'd brought her into it, Bowie."

"Something else we didn't know. It occurs to me we need to sit down and talk, right now." He sat down on the sofa, folded his arms over his chest, still royally pissed, and motioned for her to sit in front of him. He eyed her and then said, his voice sharp, "I want you to start again, at the beginning. And don't leave anything out."

Twenty minutes later, Bowie leaned back. "Is that all of it?"

"You asked me that three times."

"Is it?"

"Yes, I've told you everything."

"I don't want you killed. I don't want my daughter in danger. There's only one way I can keep you safe now. Even though I've got two agents outside in a car across the street, I'm staying here." He nodded toward the sofa.

"And I'm thinking when this is over, I may just have to haul your butt to jail."

Bowie heard Georgie give a sound, a yip that sometimes came out of her dreams. No, there was no way he could hear her if she was in bed asleep. He slowly dropped his arms to his sides and turned. Georgie wasn't in bed. She was standing in the doorway, her thumb in her mouth, only half asleep, and she looked scared. She yipped again.

41

NORMAN BATES INN
Thursday night

Sherlock was gliding smoothly in a half-pipe on her skateboard, Sean behind her, laughing, when her cell phone woke her up at exactly three o'clock in the morning. "Yes?"

"Agent Sherlock? Help me, you have to help me!"

"Jane Ann? What's wrong? Come on, calm down. Talk to me."

"Someone's in the house, I-I can hear them, I—"

"Is it your husband? Is it Caskie?"

"Caskie? No, Caskie would call out to me, he'd tell me right off he was here. No, it's a stranger, it's someone here to hurt me. Help me!"

"Do you have a gun?"

"What? Yes, it's in Caskie's bedside table."

"Get it out and get yourself in a closet and close the door. I'll be right there. Don't shoot me! If it's your husband, don't shoot him either. Stay calm, Jane Ann, and get moving!"

There was sharp intake of breath, but nothing more from Jane Ann Royal. The line went dead.

Savich was already out of bed, pulling on his pants, Sherlock behind him, grabbing clothes.

As they ran to the small parking lot behind the B&B, she shouted, "I'll drive, I know where she lives. Do you want to call backup?"

"No, not yet. Let's wait and get the lay of the land first."

As they swerved out of the parking lot, Sherlock said, "It's my fault. I put her in danger by simply visiting her. I drew a circle on her back, and someone knows I met with her at her house. That same someone is afraid of what Jane Ann Royal told me. Or might tell me." She banged her fist against the steering wheel and took a corner too fast. "Is it Caskie there in the house? Maybe he's hiding and Jane Ann simply doesn't know it? Is he the one she heard?"

Savich lightly touched her leg. "Cut the guilt or you'll piss me off. Now, tell me about the house, everything you can remember. I don't want to go in there blind."

Sherlock talked nonstop, describing what she'd seen of the Royal house as she sped through the dark streets toward that lovely neighborhood with its big graceful houses and huge grounds, repeating herself, she knew, but she didn't care. "It is my fault if something happens to her," she said again. "You can't jolly me out of it."

Savich said sharply, "Of course I can. I'm your boss, you have to follow orders. Cut that nonsense out, right now."

She screeched into the large driveway. The house was dark, completely and utterly dark, not a single light on inside.

The alarm system wasn't on. Sherlock

was breathing fast and hard, praying for all she was worth. Savich turned the doorknob. It was open.

He swung the door back, smoothly and silently. He went in high, Sherlock low, something they'd done often, both in and out of Quantico, their movements practiced and fast.

Savich started to flip on a light switch then stopped cold when he heard a scratching noise off to his right.

He slipped his penlight out of his jacket pocket. Together they moved silently toward the living room, the beam from the penlight sweeping back and forth in front of them. After six steps, they stopped, listened.

Nothing now, only dead silence. Savich nodded. Sherlock yelled, "Jane Ann! Where are you?"

Nothing. Then they heard a whimper, a human being's whimper, coming from up the stairs.

They ran up the wide staircase, crouched over nearly double.

Someone fired at them from the landing, one shot, then a fusillade from an automatic weapon. Savich slammed Sherlock down onto the stairs and came down on top of her, covering her body as best he could. Bullets riddled the plaster on the wall two feet above his head, broke it apart and splattered it on the back of his head.

A painting fell, one sharp edge striking the stairs as it plunged down. It slammed the bottom stair and struck the tiles, sliding across the entrance hall.

There was another shot, this one from off to the right. He reared back and fired his SIG blindly toward the shooter.

Sherlock managed to get her arm free. When the next shot nicked the lovely mahogany stair railing, both of them fired toward the direction of the sound.

There was a shuffling sound, not like they'd shot someone, but something else, like someone was moving fast. Yes, he was running down the hall.

Savich was up in an instant, grabbed Sherlock's arm, and pulled her up. He fiddled with the penlight and it flickered on again, carving a narrow beam through the inky black. He whispered against her ear, "We've got to take this real slow. We'll be blind up ahead, and whoever it is could be circling back, waiting for us to come up."

They spread out across the stairs, each to one side. Crouching, they made their way to the top.

They stopped and listened. There were no more running footsteps. Whoever it was, was long gone.

"Which way to the master bedroom?"

Sherlock shook her head. "Let's go right."

They didn't know which room was Jane Ann Royal's, which rooms were her children's.

Sherlock nearly froze. *Her two boys.* What if the killer had murdered the boys? Please no, not the children.

Savich opened each door as they came to it. The first was a small sitting room with a harp sitting next to the window. Jane Ann played the harp?

The next was a bedroom that obviously belonged to a preadolescent boy—two posters on the wall of David Beckham, a soccer ball rolled into the corner, a pair of filthy sneakers on the floor. No occupant, thank God. She opened the closet door and nearly got buried when a pile of clothes poured out. She looked inside the clothes.

There was no body. She closed her eyes and offered up a prayer.

Sherlock thought she'd lose it when they eased open the second door, another bedroom, and there was something on or in the bed, something substantial, something that didn't move. Was it was one of the boys, dead? Sherlock ran to the bed and saw to her blessed relief that it was a tangled pile of clothes. A desk filled most of the space along the wall. No soccer theme in this room but an incredible array of computer equipment, and a big stack of comic books. She opened the closet door. There was no child, only a collection of shoes and sneakers and a couple of bats and mitts.

"Jane Ann did send the boys away, thank God."

"Very smart of her," Savich said. "Okay, let's get to her bedroom."

There was another door that opened into a small office with a single closet, and Savich opened it. Copy paper, envelopes, supplies. No bodies.

The room at the end of the hall had white double doors. They were closed. Savich didn't have a good feeling about this. He turned the doorknob, pushed lightly. The door went silently inward.

Sherlock called, "Jane Ann? Are you in here?"

There was dead silence.

"Jane Ann? Everything is all right now. You can come out."

They heard a gulping sound, then a sob. "Is that you, Agent Sherlock?"

"Yes." Sherlock ran toward her voice. The closet door slowly opened. Savich turned on the overhead light.

Jane Ann Royal was sitting on the floor of the closet, a thick winter coat pulled around her, and she was as pale as death. She held a gun in her hand. Her hand was shaking so badly Sherlock quickly took it from her.

"Are you all right?"

"Yes, I am—" She shuddered, and lowered her head to her hands and began rocking.

Savich asked, his voice calm and low, "Where are the boys?"

She started at the sound of the man's voice. Sherlock said, "It's all right, this is Agent Savich."

Jane Ann Royal peered up at him through terrified eyes. "I sent them to my sister in Philadelphia, yesterday. They're safe."

"You're all right, Jane Ann. Take a deep breath and tell us what happened."

"It—it's hard. I've never been so scared in my life."

"I know, but it's okay now. You've got to tell us what happened."

Jane Ann Royal sucked in air, breathed, and managed to smooth herself out. "After I hung up with you, I got Caskie's gun out of the bedside table and I hid here in the closet, just like you told me to. I kept the door open a crack so I could see and hear if someone came into the bedroom. I heard some men, I don't know how many, but I heard them come up the stairs, real slow, like they wanted to be quiet. Then they were in the hallway and I thought they were coming to kill me." Her voice broke as she began to wheeze.

Sherlock gently stroked her arm, and waited. Finally, Jane Ann raised her eyes to Sherlock's face. "Then I didn't hear anything, for maybe two minutes. I started to get up, but I heard someone right outside the bedroom door. I scrunched into a ball and pulled a coat over me. I held out my gun, aimed it straight at the middle of the closet door.

"But no one came in. I heard the men talking, then I heard a single shot. It sounded far away, like it was down at the end of the hall in the laundry room. One of the men yelled, 'I got the bastard!' I didn't know what they were talking about. I was so afraid. I didn't know who'd fired or why—there was no one here but me.

"I heard someone open the bedroom door and I thought I'd die. Someone looked in, I could hear his breathing, but he didn't come into the bedroom. I heard him say, 'Come on, let's get out of here.' And one of them shut the bedroom door again. Then I heard shots, so many shots, then they stopped. I wanted to help you because I knew it had to be you. I had to do something! I ran to the door and opened it a crack. I saw them running down the hall away from me. I guess they went out the window at the end of the hall, where the laundry room is. There's a huge cedar tree out there and they must have climbed down. Then I heard you, but I wasn't sure it was you, I couldn't hear you clearly. I knew you were looking in all the rooms, and I was afraid they'd come back, to see if there was anyone else here and I hid in the closet again. Then you came in, Agent Sherlock, and you called to me." She raised a tear-streaked face. "I know who they killed." She put her face on her drawn-up knees and cried, huge gulping sobs. "Oh God, I know who they killed."

Savich said quietly, "Who do you think they killed, Mrs. Royal?"

"Caskie," she whispered through her tears, "it must be Caskie. He must have come home. He had to be hiding from me, just like you thought he would, Agent Sherlock. I think they killed my boys' father, they killed my husband."

Savich and Sherlock found Caskie Royal's body in the huge laundry room at the end of the hall, sprawled on a pile of dirty sheets and towels, shot through the head. The large window over the dryer was open, the white curtains flowing inside, pushed by the night wind.

There was blood everywhere.

42

Friday at dawn

Bowie said, "Mrs. Royal's Smith and Wesson hasn't been fired. And none of the brass the team found were from a Smith and Wesson."

Sherlock said, "If you'd found her hiding in the closet, seen her terror firsthand, I don't think you'd have bothered checking out her S-and-W." She looked over at Erin, who stood against the side of her rented Taurus, bent forward a bit, probably feeling the burn on her back. She'd parked as close as she could get to the front of the

Royal house. She looked shell-shocked. Sherlock said, "I told her not to come, but I'm not surprised she's here." Sherlock paused a moment, saw the blood in Bowie's eyes, and added, "She's amazing. She can't be feeling all that hot."

Erin wasn't feeling much of anything. It was just past dawn, so she could finally see all the people going in and out of the Royal house, beyond the glare of the huge spotlights. The coroner's van was still parked directly in front of the house, but not for much longer—two men were carrying out a large green bag that held Caskie Royal's body. *He's dead,* she thought—just like that—a living, breathing person is dead. *Just like you could have been, dead and in a green bag, if you hadn't jumped out of your Hummer in time*. Only a matter of seconds, close, too close— She realized she was shaking and forced herself to breathe slowly, in and out. She saw plainclothes agents examining the grounds surrounding the house, looking for footprints, she supposed, and Sherlock speaking to Bowie.

Bowie stared over at her. She could tell from thirty feet that he wasn't happy. Of course she'd awakened when "Jingle Bells" blasted into the silence at three-forty a.m. She'd wanted to leap out of bed and see what was going on, but instead, she held herself still and listened to him search around for his cell phone. She almost shouted to him that he'd left it beneath the sports section of the newspaper. She heard nearly a full verse before he found his cell and "Jingle Bells" abruptly cut off. She heard him talking to Sherlock in a low voice, then heard him moving around, and after a few minutes, she heard the front door close quietly. She swung her legs over the side of her bed, got to her feet, and nearly fell over. She grabbed the bedpost and stood there, hunched over. She swallowed a Vicodin, and that blessed wonder drug finally got her together. She called Sherlock, and when at last she'd felt able to drive safely, she'd carried Georgie to the car, her back cussing at her all the way, and headed for the Royal house.

Bowie stared at her, hands on hips, then trotted over. "You idiot," he said from four feet away in mid-trot. "I can't believe you even managed to get yourself out of bed at dawn and truck over here."

"I didn't truck, I Taurused," and she waved her hand at her rental car, and tried for a smile.

"Don't you try to jolly me out of being mad. Agent Lewis called to tell me you were on your way, and then he had the gall to tell me not to worry, said he and Tucker were right behind you and he'd keep an eye out for any bad guys. He told me not to worry about Georgie either, she was sound asleep."

He reached out his hands to shake her, saw she really wasn't in very good shape, and backed off. To cap it off, she was shivering beneath her black leather jacket. The early morning was cold, the sky filled with gray clouds pressing down signaling rain. He pulled off his own leather jacket and laid it around her shoulders. "No, be quiet. I'll be fine. Okay, Erin, this better be good—what the devil are you doing here? Where'd you stash Georgie?"

"Don't yell at me, you'll wake her up," and Erin nodded over her shoulder.

Naturally, he had to look into the back seat to see his daughter lying on her side, her face against her open palm, two blankets tucked securely around her, covering her to her ears. She was dead to the world. She was a good sleeper, his kid. "I've been wondering how you knew where to come."

She had the nerve to shrug. "No biggie. After you left, I called Sherlock and she told me what happened." She waved her hand toward the big house. "I'm sorry, I didn't want to disturb Georgie, but I had to come, and I knew I couldn't leave her. She never woke up, Bowie, and I worried about that, after last night when she was so upset with us for yelling at each other." She paused a brief moment, tried another smile. "I don't know how you thought of it so fast, but telling her I was an idiot and you were going to make me iron her clothes for her really calmed her fast. That was well done."

He opened his mouth to blast her again, but what came out was, "You wait, Georgie will hold you to it."

"Yeah, she just might." Erin said, looking back toward the house. "What happened here, Bowie, it's unbelievable. Jane Ann's husband, he was alive, you interviewed him, you even knew the minute he ran away at that rest stop. And now he's just—dead, like I almost was.

"I talked with Jane Ann Royal Wednesday with Sherlock, and she was open and smart and sophisticated. She knew what her husband was, and laughed about it, showed off her tennis instructor. All buff and young, she told us, that's how she liked them, but she loved her sons, Bowie, you could tell that right away."

She was talking really fast now, and Bowie let her. She was scared and shocked to her heels, and she needed to get it all out.

"I had to come, Bowie," she said again. "Sherlock only had time to tell me the basics because someone was calling her."

She shivered in his jacket and pulled it closer. He held on to his mad like a lifeline. "Then how did you know—" He kicked the tire on one of the local officer's patrol cars. "You heard my cell and you listened, didn't you?"

"It's not every night you jerk awake to Bing belting out 'Jingle Bells.' How could I not listen through the thin apartment walls? Actually, you didn't say all that much. I only heard there was trouble and that's why I called Sherlock."

He looked very close to snarling. "I don't

understand why it took you so long to get here. You should have been on my heels."

"I had to take a pain med, let it kick in, and there was Georgie. I'm okay now, really. Agent Lewis and Agent Tucker are right over there, standing against their car. They stuck with me all the way here. I'm not an idiot, Bowie, I wouldn't ever put Georgie in danger. Would you stop being pissed off and tell me what happened? Look at Chief Amos, he's coming this way. He looks pretty shaken."

Chief of Police Clifford Amos looked more than shaken, he looked like he'd been run over by a Mack truck. Two murders and a Hummer blowing up in his town in a matter of days. He'd followed Bowie out of the house, noticed him talking, of all things, to Erin Pulaski, his attempted murder victim. He was tired, and he was angry. "Here now," he called out, "what are you doing here? You're a civilian, you've gotta leave. You shouldn't even be able to walk, not after that Hummer of yours blew itself up all over one of my neighborhoods. You asking to get yourself killed?"

Bowie saw Erin was ready to smart-mouth the chief of police, and that was something he surely didn't need at the crack of dawn. He knew the chief was scared, as well as angry; he was scared himself. He said, "Sorry about this, Chief. I should have told you. I asked her to come. She's acting as a consultant for us. She and Agent Sherlock interviewed Mrs. Royal. We need her here."

Chief Amos wasn't happy to hear that, but he preferred standing here stripping the hide off this damned dance teacher to being back in that stomach-twisting blood-and-gore crime scene. At least Caskie Royal wasn't lying in the middle of those sheets anymore, his brains splattered on the washing machine. He felt bile rise in his throat just thinking of it. He hadn't puked when he'd seen that German guy, Helmut Blauvelt, naked, his face bludgeoned to bits, no fingers, just bloody stumps, but it was close, and he'd sure enough been off his feed for nearly a day. Now this. Seeing Caskie Royal was different because he'd known him. He was a snooty bastard, but now he was very dead, and his pretty wife was rocking back and forth on an antique chair in the living room, whimpering and crying, and nobody knew anything, including him. Why was this bloody nightmare happening in his town? The FBI had flown in here looking all smart and sharp in a black FBI helicopter and taken over, and their guy from New Haven had moved right into his police station, and what had they done? Big zero, that's what. That big guy Savich had played with his computer and the rest of them had just talked to people—talk, talk, talk, no action—and now there was another murder in his town.

And now this dance teacher was hanging around. Who would want to kill her? Nothing about anything made any sense. He said to himself more than to anyone else, "A female shouldn't drive a muscle car like that Hummer unless she can handle it, which you couldn't, now could you?"

Erin just looked at him. Thank God she didn't say anything. He was tired, knew he was tired, running off at the mouth like that, saying things that would get Loraine Briggs, one of his deputies, ratting him out to Corrine. That nearly made him shudder. It was time to apply himself, to get things straight, but he knew to his bones he didn't know how to deal with this case, didn't have a clue what to do next. He said to

Agent Bowie Richards, his voice belligerent, "I suppose you're going to tell me this is your case too, aren't you?" He knew he sounded intimidating, tough as nails, like The Man in Charge. Maybe he'd sounded too intimidating and Richards would fold, which was the last thing he wanted Richards to do. He waited, saying a little prayer. What he wanted more than anything was to go home and crawl into his bed and sleep until *Wheel of Fortune* came on tonight and his wife made him his favorite pot roast with new potatoes. He wanted to think about all this, but from a distance.

Bowie knew exactly what the chief wanted him to say. It wasn't Amos's fault, he knew the best shot at cleaning this mess up was to keep it with the FBI. The last thing any of them needed was Chief Amos and his people blundering around. He said, "I'm sorry, Chief Amos, sincerely sorry, but I really must insist we handle Mr. Royal's murder. There were shots fired at our own agents. I know you don't want to let it go, but you must admit it all looks connected."

Chief Amos rocked back and forth on his heels, his hands tucked into his wide belt. "Well, I don't like it, but yeah, okay, maybe we can work together. But you gotta get this thing figured out, Agent Richards, and fast. My town's gonna shake to its foundations when it gets out that Caskie Royal was brutally murdered, and everybody's gonna start yelling—at me."

"I understand, Chief. I really would appreciate your continued assistance. Your sending out your people to speak to all the neighbors is just what I need. If any of the neighbors saw anything, have your deputies report directly to me."

"Yeah, well, I guess it'd be okay for you to assign jobs to my other guys as well if nothing major comes up."

Yeah, Bowie thought, like somebody stealing clothes from Maude's Dry Cleaners or some idiot high school bad boys handing around a joint on the corner of Main and Randolph, but he said, "Thank you, Chief."

Erin was listening with only half an ear. She recognized that Bowie was jollying Chief Amos, but she didn't care. She just couldn't get past it—Caskie Royal was dead. Who was next? Was there anyone left to murder besides her? What about Carla Alvarez?

"Bowie?"

He didn't turn to her, simply said over his shoulder, "Yeah?"

"Carla Alvarez."

He didn't miss a beat. "Chief, would you send a couple of officers over to Carla Alvarez's house, make sure she's okay? And stick with her, round the clock for a couple of days? I'm thinking it might be smart to keep a close watch on her."

"Who? Oh, I see your point." The chief hiked up his pants and walked to a small knot of men and one woman standing next to a squad car, spoke quietly to them, then headed straight to his car, not quite at a run but close.

Erin looked after him, but she wasn't thinking about Carla Alvarez anymore, she wasn't even thinking about people who'd tried to blow her up in her Hummer, she was thinking how nice it would be to sit down in her car and go to sleep.

Bowie looked at her, not a dollop of sympathy in his hard eyes or in his hard voice. "You look ready to fall over. Why don't you let me drive Georgie and your own butt home and put you back into bed?"

43

Bowie didn't wait to see if she agreed, he turned on his heel to start for the car door. She grabbed his arm, and he turned back, more than willing to pin back her ears. What stopped him cold was the panic in her eyes. Given that someone had tried to blow her up, panic was probably appropriate. She said, her voice urgent, "Bowie, please tell me what happened here. Do you know who's doing this?"

He was still angry with her, but he was worried about her too. "No, not yet. Mrs. Royal says there were two men. I see you already know that. Did you hear they fired on Savich and Sherlock?"

She nearly fell backward against the Taurus, not a good idea with her back already unhappy. Dr. Kender was right. This was insanity. "They tried to kill Dillon and Sherlock? No, she didn't tell me that."

"Don't hyperventilate. Take some slow, deep breaths. No, keep my jacket on a while longer. Listen, they're both okay, which seems odd, but there you have it. Deep, slow breaths, Erin. That's it."

It took a few seconds but she managed to get herself under control again. "Sorry about that. It's not okay for a private investigator to lose it like that. What do you mean, it's 'odd'?"

"Look at this straight on. Two gunmen murder Caskie Royal with one shot right through the middle of the forehead, then they hear someone coming into the house. They wait at the top of the stairs until Savich and Sherlock are walking up the stairs, admittedly they're alerted, but still, even after firing off at least a dozen rounds, neither of the two gunmen manage to land a single shot."

Thank you, God, was all Erin could think. She looked over to see Dillon and Sherlock standing together, speaking to Agent Dolores Cliff. Erin looked back up at Bowie, saw he was staring back at her as if he was waiting for her to keel over. She lightly touched her hand to his arm. "Yes," she said, "you're right, that is bizarre. You're also freezing. Here's your jacket. I don't need it anymore." She tossed it back to him. "Doesn't sound like real professionals, does it?"

Good, she seemed back together. He said, "It's something to think about. Savich and Sherlock found Mrs. Royal hiding in the closet in her bedroom, clutching her husband's S-and-W."

He repeated the story Mrs. Royal had told, and added, "A good thing for her the shooters had found Caskie Royal first. She said the killers didn't come into the master bedroom—and that's another strange thing. Why didn't they?

"We found brass all over the place, a good dozen rounds from two different weapons. A painting was shot off the wall, wall plaster rained down, and stair railings were splintered and flew everywhere. It looks like a god-awful shoot-out, but as I said, neither Savich nor Sherlock was hit, which seems a miracle. Besides the brass from Savich and Sherlock's SIGs, all the other casings were from a Glock forty and a nine-millimeter Kel-Tec, which does indeed add up to two gunmen."

"Did Dillon and Sherlock hit anyone?"

"They don't know. We didn't find any blood, other than in the laundry room. We also found a jumble of footprints below the big window in the laundry room, looked like a dozen people rather than just two, but maybe the CSI people will figure it out. The laundry room where we found Mr. Royal's body is at the opposite end of the corridor from Mrs. Royal's bedroom. It was a huge mess. Our thinking is he was hiding in there and when the men reached the top of the stairs, they turned left instead of right, found him, and shot him dead."

"So if the gunmen had turned right instead, they would have found Mrs. Royal in the master bedroom. Is that luck, or what?"

"She said the men did come to the bedroom door, but didn't come in."

"Did Mr. Royal have a gun?"

"Not that we could find."

"That doesn't make sense, Bowie. Why wouldn't he have a weapon? Surely he was afraid they'd come after him, whoever they are."

"Mrs. Royal had his gun, the S-and-W."

"But still—"

"Agreed," Savich said from behind Bowie. "Maybe he thought he was safe enough in the house, just get his passport and some cash—which we found on him—and he'd be on his way to South America. Maybe he didn't want to face his wife. Or maybe he planned to take the gun just before he left."

Erin said, "On the other hand, maybe Mr. Royal had another gun and the killers took it with them after they killed him."

Sherlock shook her head. "There were no other casings in the laundry room except the one nine-millimeter we found from the kill shot, so Mr. Royal didn't shoot back. The laundry room door was locked, so while they were kicking it in, he'd have been firing if he'd had a gun. We think he must have been trying to get out the window, but when they crashed through the door, he turned back to them, and was shot in the forehead."

Bowie said, "Royal had to be very afraid making even this quick foray into his own house, yet he had no weapon at all to defend himself."

Sherlock frowned. "Now, why didn't Mr. Royal tell his wife he was coming back?"

"He couldn't face her, that's why," Erin said. "He was running and he wanted to run alone. He didn't want arguments or recriminations, he didn't want to take the chance that she'd call you guys."

Savich said, "And his kids—did he know they weren't there? I'll tell you, the last place I'd go was where my kids were."

"Where are the two boys?"

Sherlock said, "Jane Ann sent them to her sister in Philadelphia. To give Caskie fatherhood points, he might have seen them leave, knew only Jane Ann was there, and he decided to ghost it." Sherlock turned to Erin. "You okay? I gotta say your eyes look bright, but you're hurting, aren't you?"

"Maybe a little bit," Erin said absently, barely registering that her back was throbbing again. She said, "Seems to me Jane Ann had to know her husband was in the house, no matter how careful he was."

"Not necessarily," Bowie said. "He obviously didn't plan on staying long."

"What really bothers me is that the men who killed Caskie didn't seem to care about her," Sherlock said. "Wouldn't the killers be afraid her husband had confided too much to her, the reasons they were after him? She was an unknown, wasn't she? A loose thread? So why didn't they kill her too? One murder, two murders, who cares?" She shrugged. "I guess it's possible, but my gut is singing another song."

Savich hugged her to his side. "Maybe mine is, too. Or maybe your different song is from exhaustion and being too jazzed on caffeine."

Erin said, "But what would her husband have confided? That he'd murdered Blauvelt? If he did, then why kill him? He was going down."

"The someone who killed him was afraid Caskie would talk, that's why," Sherlock said.

Savich turned to scan the Royal house, the early morning light bathing it in a soft pink glow. If it weren't for all the cops standing around, it would look idyllic.

After agreeing to some sleep before meeting at the police station, Bowie held open the passenger side door and waited silently for Erin to slide in. She didn't want to, but finally, she did. She buckled her seat belt and looked over at him. He was staring straight ahead.

"After all that's happened, you should be over your snit by now, Bowie."

"Oh, no," he said as he drove the Taurus away from the Royal house. He gave her a quick look, his face hard. "I really can't believe you, Erin. You break the law, betray all of us who trusted you, and to top it off, you put my daughter in danger."

She didn't look at him. "I've already apologized ad nauseam. What else do you want from me? And I didn't put Georgie in danger."

His hands tightened around the steering wheel. In that moment, she realized what was really wrong—he was scared.

She laid her hand over his. "Thank you for staying at my apartment. I feel completely safe now because of you."

He still didn't look at her. "I don't want my daughter in any danger."

She grinned at him, lightly smacked his arm. "I don't believe I've told you I think you're the best cop I've ever met."

The breath whooshed out of him, even as he was shaking his head. "Yeah, sure, isn't that the truth. Another dead body right under my nose. Yeah, there's no doubt, I'm the greatest."

"Stop beating yourself up, it really pisses me off. I'm sorry, Bowie. Please, believe me. Just please don't be angry with me any longer. I can't stand it. And really, having you sleeping at my apartment, it means a lot to me."

He was stone silent for two blocks, then he said in an emotionless voice, "My wife, Bethany, drove into a bridge abutment. They told me she died instantly. She was drunk. Another driver saw the whole thing. He said her car was weaving in and out of her lane, and she just kept accelerating as she neared the bridge. He said she was doing at least seventy when she drove into the abutment. She was an alcoholic. This happened right after Georgie's third birthday."

Erin remembered her brief marriage, remembered how she'd felt lower than a slug since she'd been lied to, her heart stomped. But this? She couldn't begin to imagine such a thing. "I'm very sorry."

"It happened four years ago. All of it's faded now, for which I'm profoundly grateful. Georgie missed her mother for a little while, but then her nanny Glynn came. It was Glynn who told Georgie I loved her mother so much that I'd never marry again." He looked over at her, his dark eyes shadowed. "Glynn called me. She's feeling better every day. She wants to know when I need her back."

Erin said, "No time soon."

44

STONE BRIDGE POLICE STATION
Late Friday morning

Four hours of sleep did wonders for the brain, Bowie decided as he sat down at the conference table in the police station. He felt alert and focused. Erin didn't look bad either, what with a couple of aspirin on board to keep the throbbing down in her back. She'd refused Vicodin, said she wanted to be able to face the two Schiffer Hartwin directors with a clear head. He knew no one was going to like the fact Erin was here—this was an official meeting, after all—but she'd looked at him and said simply, "I've got to come, Bowie. Surely you see I've got to come."

He'd said nothing more, simply touched his fingers to her cheek, then nodded. Where'd she get all this grit, this bravery, in the face of all the bad stuff raining down on her? She'd even managed to keep Georgie in the dark, hard to do at any time, but she had, laughing with her, helping her dress, brushing her hair and French braiding it, something he did well himself. At least he'd put out the Grape-Nuts and made toast, with apricot jam, Georgie's favorite. They'd taken Georgie to school together, hugging her, telling her to have a nice day, and bless her heart, she'd been oblivious to her early morning car ride to a murder scene. They'd come back to Erin's apartment, Georgie never stirring.

It was eleven o'clock Friday morning before the four of them congregated in the conference room to await the arrival of Adler Dieffendorf and Werner Gerlach. Sherlock looked over at Dillon, wondering how he could look so well rested when he'd slept for only an hour after they'd gotten back to their B&B room with its *Psycho* posters. She'd awakened to hear his beautiful baritone in the shower, recounting the story of a cowboy named Ben who'd lost his horse to a bordello madam.

Bowie's cell played a very nice rendition of "Silver Bells." Bowie felt around in his pants pockets, then his jacket pockets, frowned, tried to track the sound as the song segued into the chorus.

Erin said, "It's under your briefcase."

He pulled it out, stared down at the ID screen, and looked harried. He looked like he was going to ignore it, then realized he couldn't. They heard him say before he turned away, "Dad? Listen, I've got to get back to you. I'm pretty tied up here—"

His dad? Erin watched Bowie's face as he listened. At first he looked utterly blank, then he started shaking his head back and forth, back and forth. Finally, he said, "This is incredible. I'll get there when I can, Dad."

He flipped off his cell, dropped it in the small tray that held pens in the middle of the table, blankly watched it settle in among the three Sharpies, and finally looked at them like he'd been kicked in the head.

Erin was at his side in an instant, her hand on his arm. "What's wrong, Bowie?"

"That was my dad. Alex Valenti—the vice president—he's in the hospital, just went into surgery. Dad doesn't know if he's going to make it."

Erin said, "What? The vice president? As in the United States? What happened? Why is your dad calling you?"

"I've known the Valentis since I was born. No blood relation, but he and my dad have been best friends from grade school. He's been 'Uncle Alex' forever. His son and daughter, they're like my cousins."

Savich said, "None of us has been listening to the news. What happened?"

They heard a shout and ran from Chief Amos's conference room to join the half-dozen cops on their feet in the bullpen, staring at a small TV screen. One of them turned up the volume.

A newscaster stood twenty yards or so from a black Mercedes sedan. The camera zoomed in to show the entire front of the car smashed against a huge oak tree, the impact so powerful the car had accordioned. He held a microphone to his mouth even as he turned his head toward the mangled car.—*Vice President Valenti was driving to his daughter's house in Jessup,*

Maryland, some eighteen miles north of where I'm standing, to attend a birthday party for his six-year-old granddaughter, Patty. The police aren't yet certain how this happened, only that it appears the vice president lost control of his car and hit a tree head-on. The EMTs left with the vice president minutes ago.

They switched to footage of an ambulance driving away, siren wailing. The camera panned back to the crushed car once again, then broke to a woman newscaster standing in front of Washington Memorial Hospital. She said, in a subdued voice that just barely managed to contain her excitement, *A hospital spokesman has announced that Vice President Valenti is in surgery. There has been no word from his doctors as to the extent of his injuries. His family and friends have been gathering inside to hold a vigil. President and Mrs. Holley, we are told, will remain at the White House, awaiting word. No one in the family has been available for comment. Wait! Here is Senator Carl Blevins from Florida. Senator Blevins, can you tell us anything about the vice president's accident, or his condition?*

They watched the elderly senator pause

to allow the newswoman to stride up to him, and looked into the camera. *All I know is there's been a terrible accident. I'm joining his family, all of us will be praying for Vice President Valenti's full recovery.* And he walked toward the hospital without looking back. *Senator, sources are telling us this wasn't necessarily an accident. Do you know what happened? Do you think he will die?*

The cops cheered when the Secret Service barred the hospital doors to keep the newswoman and the cameras out.

The coverage returned to the newsroom where four talking heads were already gathered, looking sad and shocked, but not sad enough to keep them all from talking. It only took them a minute to speculate about who President Holley would pick as his vice president if Alex Valenti died.

Bowie stood there shaking his head, looking shell-shocked, unable to take it in. He took a cup of water from Savich as they went back into the conference room, stood silent as he drank it down. "I can't believe this is happening. Georgie and I were visiting my folks in Chevy Chase two weekends ago and we had dinner with Uncle Alex and Aunt Elyssa. His son and daughter, and their spouses and their four kids, all of us were there. One of the kids wanted me to tell them an FBI story and so I told them about a bank robber we caught in L.A. a couple of years ago who was using some stolen bills to light his stove. When he was questioned about this at his arraignment, he told the judge they were only twenties.

"Uncle Alex really liked that story, laughed his head off. Listen, this is a guy who takes care of himself. Sure, who wouldn't be stressed, with the job he has, but I was surprised how upbeat he was, joking about how he'd nearly made an eagle on hole fifteen, just a bad roll that made it end up a bogie." He looked around at them, not really seeing them. "No, this can't be right. The thing is, Uncle Alex is an excellent driver. He's always loved cars, used to be his own mechanic until he became vice president and didn't have the time. He taught his kids how to drive, pounded safety into them. He even kidded my dad that he should teach me how to drive since my dad had had three fender benders in that many years. No, this just can't be right."

Savich's cell pounded out Michael Jackson's "Thriller." He frowned when he saw who was calling, turned and walked out of the conference room into the police station hallway, empty except for a single teenage boy who was sitting on a wooden bench scratching his head, his mother standing over him, her arms crossed over her chest, looking pissed.

"Savich. What's up, sir?"

Five minutes later, Savich returned. "That was Mr. Maitland." He paused a moment, frowning down at his thumbnail. "Vice President Valenti is still alive. He's been in surgery for about two hours now. The doctors have told the family that besides several broken bones, he has critical internal injuries. I'm sorry, Bowie, Mr. Maitland said they've stopped the bleeding, and he might make it, but it doesn't look good. Everyone agrees it's a miracle he survived the crash at all.

"He was doing at least eighty miles an hour, maybe faster, before his car hit the tree head-on. He was driving on a two-lane country road, no cars in front of him and no cars behind him except for the Secret Service. There were no skid marks, no sign at all that he ever tried to turn or swerve to avoid the collision. Mr. Maitland said it's as if he aimed the car right at the oak. The tree was some eight feet off the road on fairly level ground.

"The vice president had been in a meeting with his staff, left them to drive to the birthday party in Jessup." He looked at Sherlock. "Turns out he and Senator David Hoffman are longtime friends, and both are car freaks. The vice president had arranged to borrow Senator Hoffman's new high-end Mercedes Brabus, the E V12 Biturbo, to drive to Jessup to his granddaughter's birthday party. He wanted to see if all the hoopla was true, that's what Senator Hoffman told Mr. Maitland. Senator Hoffman said his last words to Vice President Valenti were 'Don't wreck my baby.'"

Erin said into the silence, "I'll bet the vice president was on a back road because he wanted to play. It was early in the morning, no one would be out driving around, so he could let her rip."

Savich nodded. "Mr. Maitland said Valenti's Secret Service agents were maybe twenty yards behind the Mercedes, trying to keep up. The agents say they heard a metallic popping sound, and a crash. They came around a bend in the road and saw the Mercedes smashed against the oak tree, smoke billowing out of it. They got the vice president out of the car real fast because they were afraid it would catch fire and explode.

"That wasn't reported and probably won't be unless questions are raised about why the Secret Service was so far behind while the vice president was nearly getting himself killed."

Bowie said, "Did they see anything else, like another car nearby? Anything suspicious?"

Savich said, "No. The car is being taken apart and examined thoroughly. Mr. Maitland said it's a hell of a mess. He wants me back in Washington as soon as possible."

Bowie said, "Georgie and I will go down, hopefully this weekend, but that's for personal reasons. Why you?"

Savich said, "Thing is, since Senator Hoffman is involved, Mr. Maitland believes I should come back. There's what you'd call a problem here, and I'm already involved in it."

Erin forgot about her throbbing back and stared hard at Savich. She said slowly, thinking her way, "Dillon, are you saying that case of arsenic poison at the restaurant in Washington is related to the vice president's accident?"

Sherlock said without fuss, always a smooth liar, one of the skills Savich most admired in her, "Not a clue, but Dillon has to go check it out since Senator Hoffman's already asked for him personally once. Bowie, we're really sorry about Vice President Valenti. It will be all right that Dillon's in Washington for a couple of days. I'll keep digging here."

Bowie's cell phone started up "Silver Bells" again. He looked wildly around for his cell. Erin dug into the tray and handed it to him.

When he punched off, he said, "That was Agent Kesselring. He's on his way. The two directors from Schiffer Hartwin aren't far behind him." He shook his head. "I almost forgot about them. Savich, Sherlock, you guys with me on this?"

"Oh, yes," Sherlock said. Savich smiled and nodded.

Bowie turned at the light knock on the conference room door, then watched Andreas Kesselring stride in.

45

Andreas Kesselring, looking polished as usual in a gorgeous pale gray suit, a pristine white shirt, and a subdued skinny-striped gray and black tie, stood a moment in the doorway of the conference room until all their attention was on him. He said to Bowie, his voice low to show the depths of his displeasure, "Why did you not call me? I had to find out about Mr. Royal's murder from three waitresses talking to each other when they brought my breakfast in the hotel dining room."

Three waitresses brought him his breakfast? Sherlock thought it was odd that he lowered his voice when he was truly angry. He sounded so finely controlled, though his anger was so hot it nearly glowed. "I called Agent Painter, the FBI agent you assigned to me, but he was unavailable. His cell phone didn't appear to be turned on."

Sherlock gave Kesselring her sunny smile. "Good morning, Agent Kesselring. To be perfectly honest here—and that is always my motto—no one thought about it. So much has happened in such a short time, you see, and since all of us were about to fall over from exhaustion, we had to get just a bit of sleep, not that much for any of us, only a couple of hours. But you are here now." She looked down at her watch. "I hope the directors will arrive soon."

Kesselring said, "They will be here any moment. I was told their driver is escorting them, but they decided not to bring Mr. Bender and Mr. Toms. They are hoping for a more personal conversation, perhaps for some rapport and understanding with you.

"Both Herr Doktor Dieffendorf and Herr Gerlach are very upset about Mr. Royal's murder. We are all anxious to learn the details, since none of you chose to call me."

Kesselring strode to the conference room

table and slapped both palms down right in front of Bowie. "I request that you tell me right now what has happened. The directors are reasonable men, but they fully expect me, an agent of the BND sent here to help, to know something useful. If I am to contribute to this case, I cannot be purposefully kept in the dark. I do not intend to fail in my assignment here. My career in the BND is very important to me."

Bowie put his hands behind his head and leaned back in his chair. He smiled up at Kesselring.

"Well?"

"I'm thinking," Bowie said.

Kesselring cursed—at least Sherlock thought he was cursing since it was in German. Then he threw his hands up. "On top of that, I heard your vice president crashed his Mercedes into a tree and will probably die. Everything is falling apart, and here you are, Agent Richards, sitting here, *thinking!*"

Bowie said, "Okay, thinking time is over. Here's what happened." He told Kesselring about the alarm being turned off at the Royal house, about how Mrs. Royal had awakened, heard the single shot that killed her husband. He left out Savich and Sherlock's part and a bit more as well. No reason for Kesselring to know every little single detail. ". . . Since Mr. Royal's murder is all part of this case, the FBI will be in charge, not the local police department."

"This is very distressing," Kesselring said after a moment of silence. He turned to Erin. He didn't look happy. "Why are you here?"

"Surely you remember that someone blew up my Hummer yesterday, Agent Kesselring. The FBI wants to keep an eye on me."

The door opened and Dr. Adler Dieffendorf marched in, looking for all the world like a king on the hunt for his throne. He said without preamble, "Agent Kesselring, are these the FBI agents who are supposed to capture poor Helmut's murderer and explain Caskie Royal's death?"

"Yes," Kesselring said in an emotionless voice, "they are."

46

The great man paid Kesselring no more attention and immediately strode forward, his hand extended. "Ladies, gentlemen, I am Adler Dieffendorf, managing director of Schiffer Hartwin Pharmaceutical. This is my director of sales and marketing, Werner Gerlach."

Bowie made introductions, then waved Dieffendorf and Gerlach to their chairs. Kesselring remained standing, his arms crossed over his chest, and he leaned against the conference room wall.

Dieffendorf sat forward, his long face

concerned, his elegant hands clasped on the table in front of him. "I will tell you, Agents, it came as a tremendous shock to us yesterday when Mr. Royal, our longtime company CEO, literally ran away from us on our drive here to Stone Bridge.

"Then, this morning, we were told Mr. Royal was murdered last night! The murderer was himself murdered? It seems too incredible to be true. Who could have killed him? Was he associating with violent criminals?

"I would have more readily understood if Mr. Royal had taken his own life, out of remorse, perhaps, or to make amends for a wrongdoing, but Agent Kesselring assures us he was murdered. We are over our heads, Agents. We do not know what is happening here. It seems his murder and that of my good friend, Helmut Blauvelt, must somehow be connected, but we do not know how or why. We have asked Agent Kesselring to assist us, but he seems to be unable to be of much use. We very much need your help in these matters."

Nicely presented, Bowie thought, looking from Dieffendorf's sincere, concerned face, to Gerlach's, who also looked back at him openly. But Gerlach looked pale, and his lips were seamed tight.

Bowie had imagined Dieffendorf would have charisma; to hold his position as managing director of Schiffer Hartwin for so many years, he'd have to have something going for him. He'd never had any major missteps, until now.

He'd also shown he could be self-deprecating, always an engaging stance, and he seemed charming and fluent. Bowie suspected he'd rehearsed his eloquent monologue, but perhaps not. The man was intelligent and smooth. He was a respected figure in Germany and in the world of drug companies. He was, Bowie noted, well dressed, but not flamboyantly so, like Kesselring and Herr Gerlach. He appeared quietly dignified, a man to be trusted.

"It is our intention to solve these cases," Bowie assured him. "Would you like to add anything, Mr. Gerlach?"

Gerlach blinked, then slowly shook his head. "Not at the moment. I believe my colleague has expressed our sentiments very well."

Werner Gerlach was a small man, exquisitely dressed, his suit even more expensive than Kesselring's. He looked very tightly wound, held together by sheer willpower. The man had his own powerful position in Schiffer Hartwin, overseeing the sales and marketing of all their drugs, and he'd been there for as many years as Dieffendorf. Gerlach, Bowie saw, never looked away from Adler Dieffendorf for long.

Sherlock smiled and said to Gerlach, "I hope you and Herr Dieffendorf slept well last night? No jet lag?"

Gerlach said with only a slight accent, "One always tries, naturally, but with all the uncertainty surrounding our trip here, no, I did not sleep well. I usually don't in a foreign country."

Dieffendorf looked at Savich. "I have heard of you."

Savich arched a dark eyebrow.

Dieffendorf continued, "I have heard of both you and Agent Sherlock. I have met Quincy and Laurel Abbott. I knew their father. I was shocked to hear what they were accused of doing."

Sherlock said, "I myself am hoping they will go to jail for such a long time they'll build a wing with their names on it."

"That is clever, Agent Sherlock. If they are guilty, I trust they will."

Bowie said, "Both you and Herr Gerlach speak excellent English."

Dieffendorf said politely, "Thank you. We still have a bit of an accent, one does, you know, when one doesn't learn another language until one is older. Both Werner and I attended Columbia Business School here in the early 1970s."

Bowie leaned forward. "Mr. Dieffendorf, Mr. Gerlach, you do realize that you, Mr. Bender, and Mr. Toms were the last people to see Mr. Royal alive? Since you freely admit he ran away from you, it would seem obvious he must have been afraid. Of you?"

"Naturally not!" Mr. Dieffendorf immediately calmed himself. He pulled back, drew a deep breath. "That is absurd, Agent Richards. Mr. Royal had nothing to fear from us."

"Then why did he run? Tell me, what exactly did you discuss with him?"

"We made it clear we wanted the truth from him about the papers, that we would hold him accountable for his actions at the production plant in Missouri. He swore to us there were no so-called Culovort papers, that it was absurd that he, the CEO, would purposefully shut down this drug's production. He assured us there had simply been miscalculations during a planned expansion at the Missouri plant that had adversely affected production. He claimed he knew nothing about our production problems in Madrid, that he could not possibly have predicted that.

"He also said he knew nothing about Herr Blauvelt's murder, that his shock was as great as anyone else's. But then this grown man, our own American CEO at that, suddenly runs off from our meeting—at a rest stop for heaven's sake! It was the most astounding behavior from a man of substance I have ever seen in my professional career. As if he were a schoolboy, trying to escape a scolding. It was dishonorable and undignified."

"Then why did he run, Mr. Dieffendorf? Was he afraid of what you would do to him?"

"How could he be? I made no physical threat. Why would I? You see, I knew he was lying, but when I taxed him with it, he still would not admit to any wrongdoing. I suppose he knew, in your American slang, the jig was up. He must have feared we would expose him to the police and that is why he ran. He did not want to go to jail. He doubtless planned to leave the country."

"That would have resulted in a scandal," Bowie said. "Schiffer Hartwin would have been exposed as the company that pulled production on a necessary cancer drug. You surely wouldn't want that, would you?"

"We could have contained any scandal. I would not have allowed Mr. Royal to harm the company's reputation."

Savich said, "I understand the company's reputation is very important to you. Where were you and Mr. Gerlach early this morning, about two a.m.?"

Dieffendorf's white eyebrow shot up. He looked appalled and baffled, and turned quickly to look at Kesselring, but Kesselring merely nodded. "It is an appropriate question, Herr Dieffendorf, albeit insultingly delivered."

Dieffendorf turned back to Savich. "You are considering that Mr. Gerlach and I murdered our own CEO?" He gave a sharp laugh. "You are desperate, Agent Savich. I must say I find this amusing," and he flicked a dismissing glance at Savich. "Just think, Werner, Agent Savich is referring to us as suspects. That is a diversion I did not expect."

"Why?" Bowie asked. "Agent Savich is speaking openly. It is his job, part of establishing a workable dialogue. Isn't this what you wanted, Mr. Dieffendorf? To resolve all these questions?"

Dieffendorf shrugged. "What does it matter? We were both trying to sleep. We never left the suite. Now I will ask you a question. What motive could we possibly have?"

Savich said easily, "Other than preventing a scandal for Schiffer Hartwin? Perhaps because you yourself ordered Mr. Royal to shut down Culovort production, Mr. Dieffendorf, but with the theft of the Culovort papers, you were afraid Mr. Royal would, as we say in American slang, rat you out."

"That is absolute nonsense!" Dieffendorf was on his feet now, outrage bringing violent color to his face.

Kesselring stirred against the conference room wall, but he didn't say anything.

Bowie said, "Surely you realize you and

Mr. Gerlach had motive and opportunity to kill Mr. Royal."

Dieffendorf's fast heavy breathing was the only sound for several moments in the conference room. He finally nodded slowly. "Yes, of course, you had to inquire."

Bowie nodded. "Did you ask Mr. Royal if he knew anything at all about Helmut Blauvelt's murder?"

"He said he knew nothing about it." He paused, tapped his fingertips together. "Do you know, he lied about everything else, why not about Helmut as well? His running from us, his co-workers"—Dieffendorf shrugged—"as much as it pains me, it makes the conclusion almost inescapable. But even if that is true, even if he did murder Helmut, the question is why, exactly?"

Bowie said, "Tell us why Helmut Blauvelt was here."

"I don't know, Agent Richards. Of course I have wondered. Perhaps it was personal business. I did not send him. I do not know whether his murder is connected to Mr. Royal's or to the break-in. I frankly would not be surprised if it were, at this point, but I have no direct knowledge of that. Have you made any progress yourself in solving Herr Blauvelt's murder?"

Bowie nodded. "We expect everything will come together shortly. Tell us about the sabotage of the Spanish facility."

Dieffendorf said, "Whoever carried it out contaminated our chemical production vats and tubing. The entire facility has had to be shut down for a thorough decontamination. It has cost us many millions of dollars already, certainly nothing anyone in our company would have an interest in doing. Thus far we ourselves and the Spanish police have no good idea who perpetrated that act. I can assure you if anyone in our company was involved, I will do everything in my power to help you find him."

Savich said, "It seems fairly obvious to me, Mr. Dieffendorf. The Culovort production was not only cut off in the U.S., it was also cut off in Spain. You have no other facilities, so now there is a worldwide shortage of Culovort. We understand a French company is garnering windfall profits."

"If you are speaking of Laboratoires Ancondor and their drug Eloxium, yes, they have profited handsomely from our troubles, of course everyone has noticed that. We have gained nothing from it. I have no proof of any complicity on their part, but if any of this was a conspiracy of some sort, they were certainly the ones who gained from it."

Savich said easily, "You know, Mr. Dieffendorf, sooner or later money transfers can always be discovered, contacts traced, if they exist. Would it surprise you to know that Mr. Royal had nearly a half million dollars stashed in an offshore account?"

Dieffendorf looked unimpressed. "Not a large sum for a CEO. But if it was ill-gotten, it would be a calamity. I do not look forward to what the Schiffer family would say, having their CEO of American operations not only murdered under suspicious circumstances, but now he was involved in a crime? That is even worse." He shook his head, trying to gather himself. He said finally, "It is certainly looking like Mr. Royal was involved in wrongdoing. Perhaps he was helping someone who would profit from the worldwide shortage of Culovort, perhaps he had a hand in planning it all. Clearly, there are vicious criminal elements involved, if they have murdered more than once. Now, gentlemen, ladies, is there any other way we can be of assistance?"

Bowie said, "Mr. Dieffendorf, would you be willing to send me all the threats Schiffer Hartwin has received since the severe cutback on Culovort production?"

"We will, of course, cooperate to the fullest, without jeopardizing our company's position." Dieffendorf added with a nice understated shrug, "There are always unhappy people, Agent, all over the world, who must blame a drug for their misfortunes."

Bowie said, "This list, sir, we would like it to include only those people who were unhappy about the unavailability of Culovort, no other drug."

Erin spoke for the first time. "Can you tell me when Culovort will be back up to full production, sir?"

"It is now a priority," Dieffendorf said, his head cocked to one side as he looked at Erin. He looked down at his watch. "I fear it is time we returned to Schiffer Hartwin. We have much more information to assemble before we can return to Germany." He rose, followed quickly by Gerlach. "Thank you, Agents. I am sorry we could not be of much assistance to you. If you will fill in Agent Kesselring, so perhaps he may contribute something positive to your investigation?

"Oh, yes, Agent Savich, if you have the Culovort papers, may we please have them back? They are the property of the company."

Savich smiled. "Those papers are evidence now, Mr. Dieffendorf. It is my understanding we don't have the only copy. I fear you must prepare yourself for their release to the media and the Department of Justice."

The two directors left, leaving Kesselring standing against the wall, looking like he'd get great pleasure from shooting them. "If I do not aid significantly in solving these murders, I will have failed for the first time in my career. It is possible that my career will be ended." He turned to Bowie. "You have my cell phone number."

He turned and left the conference room.

47

FIFTH FLOOR, HOOVER BUILDING
WASHINGTON, D.C.
Friday afternoon

Agent Ruth Warnecki steered Aiden and Benson Hoffman into the CAU. The large room was crowded with agents and staff, all talking on cell phones and landlines, while computer keyboards clicked away above the hum of hard drives. One agent was whistling. The noise was a din, hard to hear over.

Ruth smiled at the two men. “It’s a bit

hectic. What with the vice president's accident, we're all very busy."

Aiden Hoffman, Senator Hoffman's eldest son, stared around him. "Can you tell us why Agent Savich wanted to see us, Agent Warnecki?"

Ruth smiled. "As to that, I'll leave it to Agent Savich. Now, come with me, gentlemen." She led them down the hall to an interior conference room, opened the door, bowed them in, and closed the door behind her. Savich was standing beside the table, speaking on his cell phone. He studied Aiden and Benson as he rang off.

He motioned them to be seated at the table, then sat across from them. It was stone silent in this narrow, windowless interview room, locked down tight with the door closed, like a prison cell after the loud, busy unit Ruth had brought them through.

"Do we need a lawyer?" Aiden asked, his voice tense.

"A lawyer?" Unlike Aiden's, Savich's voice was calm and smooth. "I certainly hope not. I wished to meet with you both privately, and this seemed the best place. Thank you for coming on such short notice." Both men were buff and tanned, and reeked of good breeding, like their father. Unfortunately, neither son's eyes had their father's humorous twinkle or sharp intelligence. Despite their laid-back designer clothes, they looked scared. *Good,* Savich thought.

Aiden, the older at thirty-eight, was sitting forward, his hands clasped. He looked both sincere and apprehensive. "We wondered why you asked us here, Agent Savich. I mean of course we're concerned about Vice President Valenti, Ben and I have known him all our lives. But asking us here—what do we have to do with what happened? I mean, sure he was driving our father's car, but—"

Benson cut in on a nervous laugh. "It wasn't just a freaking car, it was a Brabus." Benson, thirty-six, wasn't as impressive a figure as his brother, either in height or looks. Clearly, he didn't have his brother's control either. Savich knew Benson was more in-your-face, less concerned with what others thought of him. Savich felt a barely banked temper roiling behind his eyes, ready to bubble over with the right provocation. At least he hoped so.

"Maybe you don't know what that is, Agent Savich." Benson tried and failed to keep his voice light. A note of contempt bled through.

"Why don't you tell me?" Savich said easily, amused by the barely veiled smirk on Benson's face.

"Ben," Aiden said quickly, "Agent Savich drives a Porsche Carrera. Our dad really enjoys driving Porsches, always had a new Porsche in the garage when we were growing up. He told us your last one got blown up."

Savich only nodded, watching Benson Hoffman's eyes go hot. Because Savich had made him look like a fool?

Aiden said, "When you called, I thought at first you wanted to ask us what we knew about Dana Frobisher, the woman who died at the restaurant. Then when you mentioned the vice president, we thought you must be trying to get some background, since Dad doesn't seem to want to talk to anyone except for calls from the hospital. He's taking this very hard. Our mom died three years ago, and now his longtime friend may die too, and he was driving Dad's car. I think Dad feels responsible."

Benson snorted. "He's mourning the car as much as Valenti. I hope he had it insured."

Aiden looked pained. He ignored his brother. "Look, Agent Savich, what can we tell you?"

"Why don't you tell me first about Dana Frobisher. Did you know her?"

Aiden shrugged. "We met her a few times at the house. Our mother worked with her on a charity board, and Mom talked about her quite a bit."

"Only at first," Benson said. "Then Mom didn't mention her again. I don't know what happened. We haven't seen her for what, Aiden, five years?"

Aiden nodded. "Something like that."

Savich said, "You said you've both known the vice president all your lives."

"That's right," Aiden said. "Valenti and our mother were very close once upon a time, high school sweethearts, the way she told it. When we were little, she'd tell us stories about adventures they'd had growing up, places they'd gone, then she'd look embarrassed and shut up. Later I heard her say that when Alex Valenti went off to Harvard and she went to Stanford, they didn't see each other much anymore, and that's when she met Dad."

Benson sat back in the uncomfortable chair, crossed his arms over his chest, and snorted. "I don't know why they let Mom into Stanford—on an academic scholarship—I mean, she never did anything with her degree, never made any money on her own. She did love her charities, though, joined every one she could find. Anyway, it's ancient history."

Aiden said, his eyes serious on Savich's face, "Alex Valenti and my mother kept up with each other, stayed friends, and after Ben and I were born, our families sort of merged."

"Yeah," Benson said, "the Valenti kids—always around, always welcomed by Mom whether we wanted them there or not."

Savich said easily, "I guess both of you know the Richards family as well?"

Benson said, "Oh yeah, we've all met. Even though Bowie's family's got tons of money, Bowie couldn't cut it, he ended up going to some police academy."

Aiden said, "Bowie's an FBI agent, Ben. He got promoted to Agent in Charge in the New Haven Field Office last year."

Benson shrugged again, a particularly irritating habit. "Yeah? Like you, Agent Savich? Well, I just know he's a putz. Maybe he didn't deserve what happened, but poor old Bowie ended up really getting the shaft, didn't he?"

"How's that?" Savich said.

Benson spit it right out with a smile. "Everybody put out his wife was killed in a plain old auto accident, and wasn't it tragic, but that wasn't what happened at all."

Savich realized he didn't want to know. This was private and had nothing to do with this case. He said, "Why don't we leave that for another time. What can you tell me about your father's best friend, Gabe Hilliard?"

"Another uncle forced down our throats," Benson said.

"He gave you a train set when you were eleven," Aiden said.

"Yeah, but after that, all he did was preach to us about the value of education. He was a pain in the butt, and now his son, Derek, is going to marry Dad's aide, Corliss. Isn't that a kick? I always thought Corliss wanted Uncle Gabe, not his dorky son."

Aiden said, "That's true. She's young enough to be his daughter, but when we've seen them together, there's this sort of embarrassment, you know? And they look at each other when they think no one else will notice. Old Uncle Gabe, I wonder what he thinks about Derek getting her rather than him."

Now this was interesting, Savich thought. "What about your relationship with your dad?"

"Our dad?" Benson said, a trimmed eyebrow shooting up at least a supercilious inch. "What do you want to know about that?"

"I understand your dad spoke to you about his odd midnight visitations," Savich said.

Benson snorted again, more contempt oozing out. "Oh, that. The visitations? Come on, I mean, get a grip here, Dad. Aiden and I could never figure out that little scam. He hasn't sung that song for a while now, I guess he's had his fun with us."

Aiden said, "He only talked about it to us one time. I don't know what he saw, but it must have been something that scared him good because he even suspected that we were the ones behind it. It isn't true, of course. To be honest, we nodded and looked interested because we didn't know what else to do. We even stayed there one night to check it out, but of course there wasn't anything."

"It's funny, really," Benson said, and both his eyes and voice were hot now. "So many people admire our dad, claim he's exactly what our country needs. I've heard people call him a genius. A genius?" Ben let out a bitter laugh. "Our dad claims to see an alien outside his bedroom window. Come on. I'll tell you, the only thing he's good at is being a politician. He's like all the rest of them, a self-serving clown. To this day he won't let us have what is rightfully ours, because we weren't good at slaving away at some low-class office jobs he picked for us."

Aiden said quickly, "It was a brokerage firm, actually."

Benson overrode him. "It was all bull, just like the positions we have now. Then my bitch wife divorced me for no good reason—and my father is so mean-spirited he gave her a sizable payment from my trust, and locked down the principal for both of us until we're fifty. Fifty! I can't even afford the maintenance on my seventy-five-foot StarBird any longer. Dad could buy a new StarBird, pay for it out of household cash, but of course he refuses. It isn't fair."

Aiden looked like he wanted to jump in and agree with his brother, but he was smarter than that. Savich said, "Neither of you considered this manifestation could be the work of a stalker of some sort, someone out to hurt him? You didn't consider that your father could be in any danger?" Savich watched the two men, saw them exchange a look. He felt a tug of pity for Senator Hoffman. He found himself wondering what Hoffman's sons were like at Sean's age. Had they already shown signs of becoming the self-absorbed whiners they were today? Or were they innocent and eager and smart, like Sean, then somehow, for whatever reason, they'd changed utterly into what they'd become?

Savich gave them a chance to jump in, but all he got were another couple of shrugs. He said, "All right, then, so you weren't worried that your dad was in any danger. I would like to know what you and Benson think about what happened to Vice President Valenti."

Aiden sat forward. "Ben and I talked about this while we were waiting for you. We've always known Uncle Alex to be a really good driver. Back before he won his first election to the House of Representatives, he and dad were drinking at our house to his last hurrah—and then he flew to France and drove in Le Mans. Dad said Uncle Alex could have tried his hand at racing professionally."

Benson picked it up. "Yeah, he was a great driver once upon a time. But hey, Valenti's getting up there, he must have pushed the Brabus faster around that curve than he could handle. We all saw what that tree did to the car."

"Your father told me on the phone that he doesn't believe it was an accident," Savich said. "He's scared and he's angry. He believes the car was rigged." He stopped, waited.

"What?" Aiden asked blankly. "You're saying someone wanted to *murder* Vice President Valenti? That doesn't make any sense. Why would you murder the Vice President of the United States? I mean, they don't do anything, for God's sake. Is that really what you think happened?"

Savich rose, splayed his palms on the conference table, looked at each man in turn, both older than he was but not yet grown men. He strongly doubted they ever would be. He said, "The FBI is examining what remains of the car carefully. We hope to know for certain what happened. Until then, I would appreciate your not adding to any speculation.

"The fact is, very few people knew your father was going to lend the Brabus to Alex Valenti, so the vice president is not the likely target.

"So, tell me, who, other than yourselves, do you think might benefit from your father's death?"

Benson Hoffman laughed. "Other than us? Not more than a thousand people, I imagine. As I said, he's a politician."

Aiden didn't disagree, just tried to look pained.

48

GEORGETOWN
Friday evening

Savich played basketball with Sean until he nearly fell asleep waiting his turn for a free throw. Savich lightly wiped a damp washcloth over his face, put him into his Transformer pajamas, tucked him into bed, kissed him, and turned out the lights. He stood a moment in the doorway, looking toward his son's bed with its blue dinosaur quilt. The dim light coming through the bedroom window outlined his small body, and Savich wondered again, had David

Hoffman looked at his sleeping boys and felt his heart swell?

He was making himself a cup of tea while working on MAX in the kitchen, when the doorbell rang. He glanced at his Mickey Mouse watch. It was nearly ten o'clock. Because he was a cop, before he opened the door he called out, "Who is it?"

It was Jimmy Maitland, and he looked harried and tired, near the end of his rope.

"No coffee for you, sir," he said, and steered his boss to the sofa. Maitland nearly tripped over Astro, just emerging from beneath a big easy chair.

Maitland leaned down and picked him up, settled him on his leg, and to Astro's delight, he began lightly rubbing his ears. He let out a big sigh. "The Valenti case is going to be a monster. I've spent all evening with the forensics team looking at what's left of the steering linkage. It was pretty cleverly done, a small charge tied in to the speedometer. They're still looking for traceable components.

"I'm glad you're with us here on this, Savich, even if Sherlock is still up in Connecticut. You've done a good job already with that, caught Schiffer Hartwin cold with that planned Culovort shortage. They'll probably end up paying out a year's profit. Dice said chances are after they pay the fine, it's back to business as usual, like all the drug companies."

Savich looked down at his clasped hands between his knees. "It's the murderer I want."

"I don't blame you. It's better to have hope about something you can control, right?"

Savich nodded. "Give me a murderer over a drug company any day. I have to say it's all coming together. Sherlock's got the bit between her teeth. You know Sherlock, nothing's going to stop her."

Maitland smiled, then fell silent. Astro gave a little bark and Maitland rubbed his ears again.

Savich eyed his boss, waited. "Tell me," he said.

"I guess you haven't watched TV tonight?"

Savich shook his head. "After an early dinner, I played basketball with Sean until I put him to bed. I was working on MAX. What's happened now?"

"Remember we were hoping for some time before the press got wind the VP was involved in more than a simple crash?

Well, that's not going to happen. They're already putting together Dana Frobisher's death and Valenti's crash as possible attempts on Senator David Hoffman's life. They're quoting 'a knowledgeable source.'"

"No big surprise. It was just a matter of time. Any idea who the 'source' is?"

Maitland stopped petting Astro. Astro gave a pitiable low moan and he started up again. "I was thinking someone in Hoffman's office, but I personally spoke to Corliss Rydle, his senior aide, and she swore she's continuing to avoid reporters and cameras. I asked her about the midnight visitor to Senator Hoffman, and she lowered her eyes to her shoes, embarrassed for her boss, I'd say. It was pretty clear she doesn't believe any of it, claimed no one knew a thing about that and never would, at least from her. She had no idea who had leaked to the media, but it'll come out eventually, it always does.

"So far, I'm thinking the media won't pick up on the woo-woo part of this deal anytime soon." He began to pet Astro faster. "I don't like how this might turn out, Savich. The vice president is clinging to life, but the doctors at Washington Memorial are still shaking their heads. The talking heads on TV have already got a short list for the new vice president. What did Hoffman's sons have to say?"

"They were surprised by the accident because Valenti was nearly a pro as a driver. When I suggested their father might have been the target, they bought right in on it, claimed there were a thousand people who might wish him harm, this after Benson had insulted his father, called him names, and whined until I wanted to kick him under the table."

"I'd just as soon not meet them, thank you very much," Maitland said.

Savich offered Mr. Maitland a cup of tea, but he turned it down. Astro was now splayed on his belly, four paws extended, while Maitland's hand swept over his back. Savich drank his own tea, and swung his leg thoughtfully. "I imagine the director has made a report to the president."

Maitland nodded. "Director Mueller called me, said no one wants to believe this leak about Senator Hoffman being the possible target—it's unverifiable, way out there, like some of those TV shows. He's not about to tell President Holley about

Hoffman's dead wife visiting him, and communicating with you. And who knows? Just maybe Frobisher's poisoning and Valenti's crash have nothing to do with Senator Hoffman."

"You don't believe that for a second," Savich said.

"Well, no, of course not. As you'd expect, President Holley is saying he wants us to shake every tree for hunkered-down terrorists, but he knows the truth about the accident, knows it's highly unlikely a terrorist could even have gotten to the car. He also knows there's not a prayer of keeping it quiet for much longer, and wants it all resolved two hours ago. Mr. Mueller said he'd rarely seen the president so angry. He also asked Mr. Mueller a very good question: Who would want to assassinate the vice president of the United States?

Savich said, "So, yet again, it comes back to Hoffman."

Maitland nodded. "The problem is, Hoffman's been around awhile, so it's no surprise Dane has already turned up a great many people you might call enemies. Before Hoffman was elected to Congress, he was a high-powered Wall Street lawyer, involved with the SEC's regulation of the investment industry. Talk about cutthroat. And there's lots of family money—that says it all.

"It's slow going. No one specific to grab onto, yet. Oh yeah, I got a call from a Gabe Hilliard, claimed he was a close personal friend of Hoffman's, wanted to know when we were going to get this resolved."

"I met him. Senator Hoffman plays golf with him every week. His son is going to marry Corliss Rydle."

"Small world," Maitland said. Astro yipped when Maitland bent toward Savich, nearly crushing him. "Sorry, dog. Any luck with Hoffman's wife?"

"No, unfortunately. I did try a second time, but I couldn't get through. It would have been so nice if she'd just spit it all out that first time, but Ollie came into my office, like I told you, and she disappeared. I don't know why she can't get through to me any longer. Maybe there are time limits on this sort of communication, I simply don't know. There've been no more manifestations outside the senator's bedroom window either. It's like she's just—gone."

"So you got a piece of her story at least.

Like you, I just wish she'd give us a name, and save us a whole lot of misery. My nightmare scenario," Maitland continued, "is Hoffman meeting with the president and there's another attempt to kill him." He picked up a sleeping boneless Astro in one big palm, gently laid him on a bright teal-blue sofa pillow, and rose. He started pacing and talking nonstop, thinking aloud, "You've got to speak to Hoffman again, and we've already got Dane and his crew eating and sleeping this thing. There's got to be someone in Hoffman's background we can tie in. Maybe it's a revenge thing, from long ago, you know that old saw—revenge is a dish best served cold? Yeah, that could be possible."

Savich said, "You know what I always come back to? How was it no one in the kitchen saw anyone put arsenic in the shrimp at the Foggy Bottom Grill? It means someone who works in the kitchen is lying, and that someone had to be paid off. But as you know, every employee at the Foggy Bottom Grill has been questioned, and in-depth background checks haven't turned up anything yet. And I'm sure Dane's been trying to run down who had access to the

Brabus. The small charge you described that blew out the steering was a sophisticated piece of equipment, and installing it wasn't easy. It was intricate work and would have taken some time."

Maitland said, "Senator Hoffman's driver, Morey Hughes, claims no one ever got close to the Brabus. He even took a lie detector, turned out clean as a whistle. Morey rolled his eyes and said, 'That car costs more than I'll make in a lifetime. Do you think I'd let anyone near it? No sir, that Brabus is guarded closer than Clinton's black book.'"

Savich looked down into his now empty teacup, at the mess of tea leaves at the bottom. He'd always enjoyed staring at the leaves and making out various shapes. He saw, oddly enough, what looked like a magician in a black top hat waving a wand.

Maitland said, "Have all the Foggy Bottom Grill employees had lie detector tests as well?"

"Not all, but we've scheduled them. No one's refused and demanded a lawyer."

"Let me know the results. Then I want to hear you've got it figured out."

"You'll be the first. Go home, sir, get some sleep."

49

Savich knew it often came down to clearing out his mind. It was a matter of believing that all the facts one needed were there, waiting to be put together properly, not all that different from a picture puzzle.

After Mr. Maitland left, Savich checked on Sean, who was sleeping so deeply a clap of thunder probably wouldn't have disturbed his dreams. Then he returned to the living room and settled down, only to have his cell phone belt out Elton John. When he slipped the cell back into his pocket, he leaned his head back in his chair, closed his eyes, and thought about nothing at all. And what came immediately to his mind was Dane's call.

One of the Foggy Bottom Grill sous chefs, Emilio Gasparini, who'd been passed over in the first wave of lie detector tests because he'd said he'd been sick in bed with the flu, didn't show up for his rescheduled test. Dane's gut had started to salsa when he discovered Emilio hadn't shown up for his shift at the Foggy Bottom Grill either. Dane told Savich he'd bet his new kayak they'd find a drug problem or maybe gambling debts if they dug deeper. Emilio hadn't prepared the senator's shrimp that day, but he'd had access, and anyway, it didn't matter, because all the other Foggy Bottom Grill employees had passed their lie detector tests with flying colors.

Emilio was long gone. His apartment manager cursed when he found out Emilio had skipped on two months' rent.

Dane was worried Emilio might be dead, murdered by whoever had put him up to this. And the individual responsible for all this suffering, whoever he or she was, was still shrouded in mystery.

Savich let the questions drift through his mind. Whenever he hit a brick wall, he simply backed up and let his brain drift. He kept coming back to Aiden and Benson Hoffman, to what they'd said, and he wondered if the answers were there, in their own words.

Before he fell into bed, he read the transcript of their interview. Then he cleared his mind, called to Nikki, who didn't come.

Nothing came to him that night, neither ghost nor inspiration.

50

WASHINGTON MEMORIAL HOSPITAL
WASHINGTON, D.C.
Saturday morning

Savich walked head down into the hospital, hoping no one from the media would notice him. He heard Jumbo Hardy of *The Washington Post* call out his name, but he didn't react, just kept walking. A Secret Service agent stood at the bank of elevators, first in a long line of agents on the way to the vice president. He showed the agent his creds and took the sole elevator that stopped on the third floor. He said nothing to the dozen family members and friends stuffed in the waiting room. He walked into the ICU, creds out, and stopped. Half of the ICU was given over to the vice president. Savich had expected there to be protection, but there were six Secret Service personnel stationed outside of Vice President Valenti's room, eyeing every person who came within twelve feet of them. It seemed a bit of overkill, maybe partly for show.

He spotted Secret Service Agent Alma Stone and pulled out his creds, flashing each guard as he passed.

"Alma, you've got yourself a fortress here."

"You got that right, Dillon. I was told you were coming to speak to Vice President Valenti. I'll tell you, he's barely conscious, but he wants to talk to you, insisted to his doctors when they dared to disagree. Those are two of his physicians now. These guys don't ever crack a smile, so don't worry about it."

She introduced him to two very serious-faced older men in white coats and scrubs, turned, and quietly opened the glass door.

The two doctors followed Savich into a

private cubicle with curtained glass walls, quiet except for the sounds of the machines that kept Valenti tethered to life. There were only chairs and the bed in the room, no flowers, no cards, and enough equipment to launch a rocket, all of it beeping or whirring or humming in random rhythms.

A man and a woman stood by the window, arms crossed over their chests until Savich came in, and they straightened, their hands going closer to their sides, and their weapons.

Savich waited for Alma to nod her okay to the other agents. Then she patted his arm and left the small room. Savich looked hard at the two doctors who stationed themselves at the foot of the bed, giving them silent notice not to interfere, and walked to stand next to Valenti.

Valenti looked ten years older, his handsome hawk's face waxy gray, his eyelids bruised, oxygen tubes in his nose, one of his legs in a cast. He was fastened to several IVs, including one in his neck. His breathing was slow, but not all that labored, which was a relief to Savich.

Alex Valenti was in serious but stable condition, the media had announced with special reports and streamers running along the bottom of TV screens across the country.

The talking heads were at a loss, with nothing much left to speculate about.

Savich leaned down and lightly laid his palm on Valenti's forearm, above one of the IV lines. "Sir, I'm here."

The famous green eyes opened slowly. It took Valenti a while to focus, but when he did, Savich saw awareness and the blaze of ferocious intelligence in his eyes. "Savich. Good, you came. Do you know who did this to me? Was it terrorists? Is anyone taking credit? I know it wasn't an accident."

"No, it wasn't an accident. The car was sabotaged, but we don't think it was political or tied to terrorists. Sir, while we have the opportunity, could you please tell me about your relationship to Senator David Hoffman?"

Valenti blinked. "David? Why?" Savich saw a flash of pain, a moment of confusion.

One of the physicians came forward and pushed the morphine button beside Valenti. "That will help, sir. You'll feel better in a few minutes." He placed the button in Valenti's hand, and curled his fingers around it.

They all waited, the physicians' eyes on Valenti, until he had it together again. "Okay, that's better now. All right, I'll tell you about David and what he did—he got that incredible Mercedes to rub my nose in it. He knew I'd be mad to drive it, since I'd never driven a Brabus before. He was right. All I could think was what an incredible machine, I was flying, that amazing engine purring, it was more than anything I'd known in a long time."

"Let's get back to you and Senator Hoffman. Are you still good friends?" Savich saw Valenti had to shift mental gears, that it wasn't simply automatic. He had to work at it.

"David and I are the best of friends. We've known each other for a thousand years, well, maybe a hundred is closer."

"Very longtime friends," Savich said, all of which he already knew.

"Yes, all the way back to just after we all graduated college. It was odd, really, now that I think about it. Both David and I knew—knew all the way to our bones—that we wanted to go into politics. We took different routes, though. David wanted Congress from the get-go but I preferred state government. I was reelected governor of Virginia the same year David won his first election to the Senate. He'd been a congressman for fourteen years before that."

"And you, sir, before you were elected governor?" Of course Savich knew every single fact about Valenti, but he wanted him thinking and focused.

"I started out local, mayor of Richmond, then moved to state government, worked up to governor. I hope I did some good, I tried. Three years ago, when I was in my third term as governor, President Holley tapped me as his running mate. I hadn't considered it, really didn't want it, but David was one of those who talked me into accepting the nomination. Of course my wife and children were great assets in the campaign, they still are."

"During these years, your family and Hoffman's family got together a lot?"

If the vice president wondered at the direction of these questions, he didn't let on. Savich imagined he was pleased to be able to talk and make sense.

"Yes, of course. I knew David's wife, Nikki,

ever since we both attended the same high school. Then Nikki went to Stanford on a scholarship—she was very smart and so sweet. I went to Harvard, a tradition in my family going back to my grandfather.

"Did you ever meet Nikki, Agent Savich?"

"Yes I did, in a way."

"Her death wasn't a shock, but I'll tell you, it was difficult for all of us, David in particular. I'll catch myself thinking of her even now, wondering what she'd have to say about this or that.

"Like all eighteen-year-olds, we thought we were in love, but of course when you're young, life is always nearly too serious to bear. Nikki went to Stanford and met David. At Harvard I met my wife, Elyssa. She was two years behind me, at Radcliffe. I remember it was Nikki who got us all together back then. We've been great friends ever since." Valenti tried for a smile and managed a small one. "Our families ended up living within driving distance of each other."

"You're also close to the Richards family, I know. Bowie sends his best wishes."

"Oh, yes, we all go back nearly to the

ark. Bowie's a cracker FBI agent. We were pleased when he came back east."

"What do you think of Senator Hoffman's sons, Aiden and Benson?"

Valenti closed his eyes and fell silent. He whispered, sounding so tired, it worried Savich, "I don't know what to say."

"The truth, sir."

"I don't guess it matters, everyone knows what they are. Frankly, both Aiden and Benson are disappointments. Nikki never got over how they turned out. They resent their father's tight hold on his own money. When Nikki died three years ago, David simply let them go. I remember he told me they're adults and there was nothing more he could do."

"Have you ever known them to be violent?"

"Yes, actually. With women. David hushed up a couple of assaults on women they were seeing, paid them off so they wouldn't press charges. Spoiled men acting out."

"I've spoken to both Aiden and Benson. They tell me you're an excellent driver. You've driven competitively in Europe."

Another smile brought on a dash of pain

with it. Savich watched the vice president press the button for another hit of morphine.

"Yes, Elyssa has always hated that passion of mine because it scared her so much. Now she wants desperately to say 'I told you so,' but since I'm down and out, she can't."

Savich said, "The two gentlemen standing at the end of your bed say you're not going to die, sir."

"I'm pleased, at least most of the time now." Valenti fell silent a moment, studying Savich's face.

"Tell me what happened."

Valenti gave Savich a small nod. "I see you have no doubts at all about this. Good, because there's no other way it makes sense. I was taking a turn hard, testing the cornering a bit, when something jostled in the wheel. Then the steering failed completely. I jerked the wheel back and forth, but it didn't work. Then it all happened fast. I hit the brakes, but I was moving too fast, must have been near eighty. I saw that tree and I hit it in the same instant. Then it was lights out. I didn't understand it, but I knew it wasn't an accident, even while it was happening."

Savich was bursting with more questions, but he realized Valenti was fading. He leaned close to the vice president's face and said quietly, "Rest now, sir. I will see you again, and count on it, I will find an answer for you." He nodded to the physicians and the Secret Service agents and left the room. Secret Service Agent Alma Stone was soon beside him, escorting him to the door of the ICU.

"You're on your own from here, Dillon. Do you know we caught a media yahoo up here early this morning? No idea how he managed to slip through this far, and he refused to tell us, babbled about the freedom of the press."

"Keep him safe, Alma."

"You can count on that. Give my love to Sherlock and Sean."

"If you need me for anything, Alma, I'll be down the hall speaking to Mrs. Valenti."

51

MILLSTONE, CONNECTICUT
Saturday

The Glenis Springs Country Club boasted a bitch of a course, club golfers were heard to remark fondly. Even though the clubhouse hadn't been updated since 1981, the course was buffed and polished and improved upon every year.

Sherlock bypassed the red stone and glass clubhouse and walked down a stone path, past the pro shop, toward the first tee. In the distance she saw a half-dozen tennis courts, all of them in use. It was a beautiful day, in the mid-sixties, and she hoped Mick Haggarty was giving tennis lessons on one of the courts. Surely Jane Ann Royal would not be here with Mick, not with her husband brutally murdered in her laundry room early yesterday morning. Surprise was usually a good thing.

She was frankly surprised she didn't find Mick Haggarty. She checked in at the pro shop and learned he had an appointment at the Royal house. Go figure that.

She called Bowie and Erin, en route to see Dr. Kender in New Haven, and told them she was off to Jane Ann's house.

She pulled into the driveway and parked behind two forensic vans, both FBI. Forensic teams were still working inside the house. She was just about to ask if the techs had found anything useful when her cell played "Some Enchanted Evening." She smiled because Dillon had programmed it in right before he'd returned to Washington.

"Sherlock."

"It's me."

"Hi, you, what's going on down there?"

"I'm out near Leesburg. They found Emilio Gasparini, the Foggy Bottom sous chef, dead in his car at the bottom of a ditch. The Virginia cop who found him saw the APB and called us. He says it looks like an accident, but you can bet Astro's collar it isn't."

"I'd make that bet. One more piece of the puzzle, Dillon. Our murderer is running scared. I don't want you being a hot dog, all right? I want you to be careful, you promise?"

"My middle name, sweetheart."

"Which word?"

He laughed. "No one's tried to gun me down lately. Now, tell me this, Sherlock, how could anyone have messed with Senator Hoffman's Brabus without Hoffman's driver, Morey Hughes, knowing about it?"

"How much time would it require?"

"I asked the guys who reassembled what's left of the device. They said someone experienced at it could install it in maybe twenty minutes of intense concentration."

"Morey's coffee break?"

"Could be, since Morey also does other things for the senator besides driving him and taking care of his cars, so it's not like he camps out in the garage. But he's still there most of the time. His other tasks—like delivering to FedEx, dropping off papers to another lawmaker's residence or office, getting take-out for a staff meeting—it's always different stuff, so anyone watching for a set routine would be out of luck."

"So our murderer already had the skill to both assemble and install a pretty high-tech device, or he's bright and learned how?"

"Or our murderer hired someone to put it together."

"Yes, that's what I'm thinking, too. We've put out feelers for someone here in D.C. or close by who would fit the bill. Demolition background, maybe. I'm also thinking the person would simply have to watch and wait until Morey Hughes left the Hoffman house, slip into the garage and install it, hope he wasn't spotted."

"That's a lot of risk," Sherlock said slowly. "Whoever did it would have to be really committed, or extraordinarily well paid."

"Yeah, and that keeps bringing me back to Senator Hoffman's sons."

"You really think they have the answer to this mess?"

"Sounds strange, I know. I guess they could be just a distraction."

"No, if that's your gut, I'd take it to the bank. You're trying too hard, Dillon. How many times have you read the interview transcript?"

"Three, four times."

"Don't read it again. In fact, try not to think about it, just let it simmer. I know you, you'll sit bolt upright in the middle of the night tonight and there it'll be, the answer, crystal clear." Sherlock could see his thoughtful expression, and smiled.

She said, "Speaking of distractions, I'm beginning to think there are plenty of them around up here in Connecticut. I'm off to Millstone again to see if I can't find Jane Ann Royal. I'm here at her house and her Audi isn't in the garage, so I'm thinking she's with her tennis pro. I'm going to drive to Millstone, that's where Mick Haggarty lives. I want to see the two of them together. I could be wrong, I mean, Jane Ann could have friends right here in Stone Bridge, but I have this feeling. . . ." She paused, then added, "We'll see. Later I'll be hooking up with Bowie and Erin."

"You be careful, you hear?"

"You can count on it. I've got that enchanted evening coming up, right? And I don't mean pizza with Sean, either. How about Sunday night? Maybe we can get this all ironed out today."

"Sounds good to me." And he laughed.

Sherlock was grinning when she readjusted her mirror a bit, waved to the crime scene techs, and pulled out of the Royal driveway.

She called Agent Dolores Cliff, got Mick Haggarty's address, and drove back to Millstone.

52

BISMARK ROAD, TWO MILES WEST OF LEESBURG, VIRGINIA

Savich and Dane stood beside the stretcher two paramedics were preparing to shove into the back of the coroner's van. Savich unzipped the green bag.

Emilio Gasparini looked like he was asleep, as if he could open his eyes at any minute, smile at them, and ask if they'd like one of his special omelets. But he wouldn't be opening his eyes. He'd never wake up again. Sous chef Emilio Gasparini was Cordon Bleu–trained, and only thirty-four years old. He had dark hair and an olive complexion. He was born in Florence, both his parents chefs. There'd been no infusions of money into his bank accounts, no signs of sudden affluence, like new clothes in his closet, a new car, nothing. So that meant the money was in a safe deposit box or hidden with a girlfriend. Or maybe he sent the money back to his parents in Italy. Savich still hoped they'd have some of the answers in a very short time. Dane was already on his cell, giving information to Ollie back at the Hoover Building.

Deputy Glen Phelps was looking closely at Gasparini's face, worry lines already etched on his twenty-four-year-old forehead. "If this is an accident, I'd like to know where all the damage is." His thick southern accent was like slow, heavy syrup. "I mean, a guy drives off the road into a deep ditch, something's gonna show, right? But there's not a bruise, a cut, not one measly scratch on his face, nothing at all on him. I'll bet he was already dead when someone put him behind the wheel of the car. Not much of an attempt to make it look like an accident, or maybe the guy who did him isn't all that smart."

"The guy's smart," Dane said, still looking down at the dead face, "I just don't think he cared. There's a deep well of arrogance in this guy, and disdain, so who cares about a chef? Kill him, dump him, brush your hands off, and go about your business. What he's doing now is taking care of loose ends."

Dane called out to the paramedics, "We're done here, guys. They're expecting him at Quantico." He turned back to Glen Phelps, who had his pants hiked up a little too high, Dane thought, smiling. "That's a good call, Deputy Phelps." Dane wondered how long Phelps had been out of the police academy. Phelps flushed a bit, then said, "Thank you, Agent Carver. Truth is, when I saw that car in the ditch I had this really bad feeling what I was going to find, and I'll tell you, I was glad I hadn't had lunch before I went down there. But look at him, there's nothing at all to see, like he just nodded off."

Dane said as he shook Deputy Phelps's hand, "Glad you called us right away. Hey, here's my card, you think of anything more, give me a call, doesn't matter what time it is."

Savich and Dane watched Deputy Glen Phelps take Dane's card and ease it with great care into his wallet, right behind his American Express card.

"I've got a business card, too," Phelps said, and blushed as he handed it to Dane. "I just got them, a gift from my mom. She said you just never know when you'll need one. I guess she thought it'd impress people, show what a professional I am." He beamed at them, still blushing as the coroner's van left. "Nasty business. I sure hope you figure all this out."

Savich said, "We will. Thanks again, Deputy Phelps. We've got some folks coming to take the car away. We'll check it over."

"Agent Savich, would you like one of my cards too?"

53

MILLSTONE, CONNECTICUT

Jane Ann Royal's Audi was parked at the curb in front of a red-brick Art Deco apartment building, vintage 1930s, set amid thick maples and oaks. It was a lovely old building, beautifully maintained, the greenery lush. Sherlock was thinking it was pretty nice digs for a young tennis pro.

The building was five stories, only six apartments on each floor. Mick Haggarty was in 2D, an end apartment. Sherlock whistled as she walked down the corridor with its thick dark red runner and Art Deco red sconces on the walls, fanning soft light upward.

She paused a moment outside 2D to listen. She heard voices, a man and a woman, but couldn't make out what they were saying. A pity. She knocked. The door was opened almost immediately by Mick Haggarty. He was maybe twenty-four, twenty-five at most, good-looking, no doubt about that, with a nice thin nose, tough square chin, and high cheekbones. He had dark hair, a deep tan, and startling blue eyes, darker than hers. *Black Irish,* Sherlock thought. He was wearing tennis whites and sneakers, which really looked good on him. All he needed was a racket in his hand and he could pose for the cover of a magazine.

He stared down at her a moment, then, "Who are you? What can I do for you?"

She smiled up at him. He was tall, nearly as tall as Dillon. She handed him her creds. "As you see, I'm Agent Lacey Sherlock, FBI. I'd like to speak with you and Jane Ann."

She watched him hesitate. She reached out her hand and patted his arm as she pulled her ID from his fingers. "No, don't lie, I saw Jane Ann's Audi downstairs and I just heard her speaking." She stepped around him and gave a little wave. "Jane Ann? It's Agent Sherlock. I hope you're feeling all right today. I wanted to give you an update on what's happening."

Jane Ann stood in the middle of a good-sized living room with small Persian carpets scattered on the oak floor. There were floor-to-ceiling windows on two sides of the living room that gave out onto manicured lawns. It was an elegant room with high ceilings and delicate moldings. Jane Ann looked right at home. There was a tray on the coffee table holding two cups and a carafe of coffee. She was wearing black yoga pants with a loose purple top knotted at her side, black ballet slippers on her feet. Her hair was loose around her face, shiny as the polished floor, but she looked pale, her skin tight over her high cheekbones.

"I'm strung out," Jane Ann said as she hurried through the graceful archway. She took Sherlock's hand. "Thank you again for saving me last night. You came so quickly. I knew, I just knew, that those men were going to come in and kill me."

"You had your gun, Jane Ann," Sherlock said. "My money would be on you."

Jane Ann gave her a wobbly smile. "You think? Well, thank you for the vote of confidence. But I don't know, Sherlock, I was so scared I was about to hyperventilate. You and Agent Savich saved the day before I was tested. I just can't stop thinking about it, you know?"

Sherlock lightly laid her hand on Jane Ann's forearm. "It didn't happen, so don't go there. You survived."

Tears sheened her eyes. "It's difficult. I was so scared. Here I am going on about how I felt, and they murdered Caskie. How must he have felt when they gunned him down? Please tell me you've caught them. Were they from Schiffer Hartwin?"

"We don't know yet who's responsible. Do you believe they were from Schiffer Hartwin? You think they sent killers to murder Caskie?"

"I was thinking they'd make Caskie the scapegoat. All they had to do was have him killed, and then he couldn't defend himself."

"Yes, that's true. And you're exactly right

about one thing, they're doing just that—blaming your husband for all of it, from the planned Culovort shortage, to the murder of Mr. Blauvelt in Van Wie Park. Who knows if it will fly in the long run. The thing is, Jane Ann, we've already traced two different accounts Caskie had in offshore banks. The sum came to just under four hundred thousand dollars, not nearly enough for a mastermind."

Jane Ann drew in several deep controlled breaths. "He had four hundred thousand dollars?" She closed her eyes a moment. "That bastard."

"I bet he was going to run off," Mick Haggarty said from his post at the front door. "I bet he was going to leave you and your kids high and dry, Jane Ann."

"Very probably," Sherlock said, not taking her eyes off Jane Ann Royal. "Can you think of anyone else, Jane Ann? Anyone other than someone from Schiffer Hartwin who'd want him dead badly enough to invade your home?"

"I still can't accept that my own husband was a criminal. But one thing I do know for sure, he wasn't a murderer, he wasn't, Sherlock."

"Maybe not."

"All right. Let me think about this. As far as I know Caskie didn't have any personal enemies—wait, unless you count Carla Alvarez, maybe. She's very passionate, about causes, politics, business. Caskie would say she'd fly off the handle and people would scatter. Maybe she figured out he was going to dump her and she sent some men over to kill him."

"Did you speak to Caskie about her, after you spoke to me and Erin Pulaski? Did he tell you he was breaking it off with Carla?"

"No, no, it's just his pattern. Like I told you, Caskie was a cheat, but he was a very predictable cheat. He always followed the same pattern—intense flirtation, romantic little hideaway dinners, lots of sex—no one could outdo Caskie's sex talk—then no more mystery, and he was out the door. Oh, I don't know, Sherlock, I'm just talking, trying to figure this out. But Carla's tough, tougher than I am, that's for sure. Nobody gives her grief because of that hair-trigger temper of hers."

"If not Carla, then how about the manager of accounting, Turley Drexel, I think his name is?"

Jane Ann said, "I hadn't considered him. Yeah, they slept together. I remember the night it all started. It was a barbecue at one of the manager's homes in Stone Bridge. Turley was all over Carla that evening, wouldn't let her out of his sight. I thought he'd even follow her to the bathroom. I remember thinking he was probably a real loss in bed, he just gave off that vibe, you know? I couldn't imagine he'd be of any practical use to her. He didn't even look particularly nice on her arm. I decided maybe Carla was desperate.

"I think it was Caskie who took Carla away from Turley. Maybe that left him gnashing his teeth, swearing he'd make the alpha dog pay. Of course it would have been Turley who made Caskie perk up and notice Carla in the first place. And Caskie did, of course. He couldn't stand not having what another man had, particularly if the other man worked for him."

Sherlock remembered overhearing the argument between Carla Alvarez and Turley Drexel the first time she and Dillon had visited Schiffer Hartwin. Had that been about her affair with Caskie Royal?

Jane Ann suddenly whirled around and

buried her face in her hands. "Forget everything I said. I'm a bitch, gold plated. I really don't know, I'm just blathering. Damn, this is so horrible, unbelievable really. Four hundred thousand dollars? I just can't believe it."

That Caskie had stolen the money, or that he wasn't going to share it? Sherlock said, "I know. It's a huge shock, the sudden violence and death, even the hidden funds. But you came through it. You'll deal with it, Jane Ann, you have to because of your sons. Your husband's body will be released for burial sometime in the next two days. I'll give you Dr. Ella Frank's phone number. You can call her."

Mick Haggarty said, "I remember now, I saw you a couple of days ago, Agent Sherlock, when I was giving Jane Ann a tennis lesson. You were with another woman."

Sherlock turned to face him. It seemed he hadn't moved since she walked in. "That's right. Is it all right if we all sit down, Mr. Haggarty?"

"Jane Ann didn't want to be alone," Mick said as he led them into the living room. He motioned Sherlock to a big easy chair, obviously his favorite place, with a fifty-inch TV six feet in front of it, the remote close by on the side table. On its very nicely polished surface, she saw the overlapping outlines of beer cans. He gave Sherlock a tentative smile as he sat down on the sofa beside Jane Ann, his feet planted apart as if he was holding his tennis racket between his legs.

"How long have you been a tennis pro, Mr. Haggarty?"

"Three years now. It's good money and I can pretty much pick my own hours. It helped pay my tuition at Belson."

"A local liberal arts college," Jane Ann said, not looking at him.

"What's your degree in?"

"I have my B.A. in film. I'm an actor, really. I did summer stock over at Belson—Shakespeare. I played Petruchio until two weeks ago. I sure hope acting in summer stock impresses everyone in Hollywood. It'd be better, of course, if I had an uncle or a parent who already knew people in Hollywood."

Jane Ann was sitting hunched over herself, her legs pressed tightly together, her hands clenched on her thighs. She shot Mick a look like, *Who cares, you putz?* She looked like a woman on the edge.

She asked Sherlock, "How did you find me?"

Sherlock was afraid she was going to have to push her over that edge. "Actually, I went by your house, but of course the crime scene people were still there. Then I realized you would need comfort after last night, and I thought of Mick."

"I'm leaving later to take the train to my sister's in Philadelphia. I've got to tell the boys their father is dead. How can I do that? How?" Tears formed in her eyes, and one big one slipped down her smooth cheek. She wiped it away, swallowed, and tried to pull herself together, but another tear slid down, then another.

Sherlock looked from Jane Ann Royal to Mick Haggarty. "It will be difficult. I'm sorry." She paused a moment, then said quietly, "I hate lies, Jane Ann, particularly when I can't see the reason for them. Tell me, how long have you been sleeping with Mick?"

Jane Ann Royal jerked as she dashed her hand across her cheek. "What? What a thing to say to me the day after my husband was murdered! I didn't think you were like that—"

"Like what, Jane Ann?"

"I expected kindness from you, but you're being cruel."

"Well, fact is, I'm a federal cop and I'm investigating a particularly brutal murder." Sherlock flicked her finger toward the bedroom. "I saw a dress on the floor in the bedroom. Mick forgot to close the bedroom door before he answered my knock. Or maybe it's another woman's dress, Mick?"

Mick looked like a deer caught in the headlights. "No, no, th-there is no other woman. We're not sleeping together. Poor Jane Ann was exhausted. She came over here, all upset, and so I let her sleep in my bed. I slept on the sofa."

Sherlock looked back and forth between the two of them. "Your salary, Mick, I checked. No way do you earn enough to afford this lovely apartment. You only moved in two months ago. Your former residence was far more basic than this one, on the other side of the tracks. Do you have many paying clients, or is it just Jane Ann who keeps you in comfort?"

Jane Ann Royal jumped to her feet, her face flushed, waves of anger rolling off her.

"I didn't lie to you, I didn't! But it wouldn't matter if I had. I did come to Mick for comfort, so what? What business is it of yours? It had nothing to do with anything.

"Look, I didn't want to hear all the nauseating pap I'd get from my girlfriends, they're idiots. I knew Mick would understand, he wouldn't just mouth platitudes, he'd care, and that's why I came here. It's the day after my husband's death, surely not the time to screw around with another man.

"I want you to leave now, Agent Sherlock. I'm not going to sit here and let you make crazy accusations. You've done nothing to find his murderers—those two men who also tried to kill you and your husband, if you'll remember."

Sherlock asked, voice mild, "Are you paying for this very nice apartment, Jane Ann? I really can't see you visiting the Merriam Bartlett down the road twice a week. Someone would recognize you, and then Caskie would have done something, wouldn't he? I know he had the money in the family, not you. You worried about a divorce? Losing your lovely lifestyle?"

"All right, okay. So what if I do trade the

cost of the apartment for tennis lessons? What's wrong with that?"

Mick Haggarty roared to his feet. "I wouldn't sleep with her. Do you think I'm insensitive? Jane Ann is in pain. I've done what anyone would do, I've given her shelter, a place to rest, what comfort I could."

"You and Jane Ann have been sleeping together how long? Three months, maybe a month before you broke your existing lease to move in here?"

"No! Never! I'm not interested. Jane Ann's too old for me. Who wants to sleep with his mother?"

His stark words rode a violent tsunami into the now silent living room.

Mick yelled, "Wait, wait! I didn't mean that. I mean Jane Ann is a great tennis player and I like her a lot, but I mean, I'm twenty-four years old and she isn't, she's a mother, for God's sake, and her husband was murdered and I'm her friend, really, that's all—"

"You puking little freak!" Jane Ann Royal roared at him and slammed her fist into his jaw. Mick fell back onto the sofa. He sat there, holding his jaw, staring up at her, pinned.

"All you can do is play tennis. You, an actor? That's a joke. I saw you in *Taming of the Shrew*—you were ridiculous, you hear me? All you did was prance around, and everybody could tell you're a no-talent little creep! You don't even have any talent in bed. You're a huge conceited bore!"

Sherlock jumped up and hauled Jane Ann back as she pulled and heaved toward Mick again. "Don't hit him again, all right? Or I'll have to arrest you. Listen to me, this is going to stop, all the lies, and especially this little drama you're enacting for me." *Drama*. Is that what all this was? Sherlock saw a flash of movement from the corner of her eye, but she wasn't fast enough.

A man's fist struck her temple hard and she fell to the beautiful Persian rug. She hit the edge of the coffee table as she went down. Pain exploded in her head, and then she didn't feel anything at all.

54

Sherlock heard Jane Ann Royal's panicked voice through a blinding fog of pain. "You idiot, she doesn't know anything! Dammit, she was just guessing, throwing stuff out there to see if we'd bite, that's all. Now look what you've done. She's a freaking FBI agent! What are we going to do now?"

As she listened to them fight, Sherlock knew she'd wondered deep down whether Caskie's murder really was part of a big conspiracy. When Mick wanted to show off his acting talent, it was all there, right in front of her nose, two greedy people who saw their opportunity to get rid of their big obstacle, and cash in.

She saw Dillon's face, sharp and clear.

She forced herself to focus on Mick's voice now, scared, defensive, thin as soup. "I'm not an idiot! She knew, I know she did. I saw it in her eyes when she looked at me. I didn't have a choice, I didn't. I'm not going to jail! It's not going to happen. The next Mel Gibson can't go to jail!"

"You're too tall to be the next Mel Gibson! You look like a pretty boy, he doesn't. Why am I even talking to you? I've got to figure out what to do."

Mick's voice faded in and out. Sherlock realized he was pacing the length of his lovely living room. He was saying, "We've got to be calm here. We can't lose it, not now. We've got to find out what she knows, then we can decide what to do with her. You've got to get me out of this, Jane Ann. You owe me."

"All right, all right." Jane Ann was taking slow deep breaths, smoothing herself out. Yoga breathing. "She isn't dead, is she?"

Sherlock heard Mick's footsteps crossing to her, felt his warm hitching breath on her cheek as he came down on his knees beside her. She felt his fingers on the pulse in her neck, smelled the sweat on him as he leaned over her. "I hit her pretty hard, but she seems okay. I've done that in my martial arts classes, but this is my first time I ever hit a real person." He sounded more pleased with himself now than scared.

Keep breathing, keep listening, stay unconscious. Do not puke. Sherlock felt nausea roiling in her stomach, and knew the not puking part could be a tall order. She tried to breathe slowly, lightly, like Jane Ann.

Sherlock knew Jane Ann was standing over her now; she smelled her too, a fresh jasmine scent. "I liked her, you know? I thought she liked me too, but it was all an act. She suspected something was off, but Mick, she really didn't know a thing. Oh, I wish you hadn't lost it—where's my cell?"

He rolled right over her, anger and aggression spilling out of his mouth, "Yeah? Well, she was going to haul you away, and me too, and I don't deserve that, I don't! You are nearly old enough to be my mother! Look what you've got me into. She's a federal agent. Why do you need your freaking cell? Who do you want to call?"

Sherlock heard the sound of Jane Ann's hard slap against his face. *Not smart, Jane Ann, not smart, he's nearly boiling over.* "I'm thirty-six, you fool. Don't you ever call me your bloody mother again!"

"You hit me! Don't you ever slap me again, Jane Ann."

Sherlock felt the air shimmer with violence, heard Jane Ann's harsh breathing. She heard a smack that sounded like Mick catching Jane Ann's hand when she would have hit him again, knew he'd twisted her wrist because Jane Ann moaned. They were face-to-face, their rage beating the air between them. But when Mick spoke, it was in nearly a whisper, but there was rage in his voice, deep and thick. "You hit me again, Jane Ann, and I'll knock your perfect teeth down your throat, you hear me? Poor old Caskie paid for those pretty teeth, didn't he, just like he paid for all your tennis lessons? Did you ever pay for anything in your life?"

Jane Ann jerked away from him, and, smart woman, she moved to the other side of the living room, cursing under her breath. Sherlock slitted her eyes open to see Jane Ann vigorously rubbing her wrist, trying to regain control of herself and the situation. "Listen, Mick, we're losing it. We have to focus here. None of this is important now. We've got to tie her up."

"Yeah, well, that's the first smart thing you've said."

Sherlock was dead weight when Mick hauled her up and laid her on her back on the sofa. "I know just the thing. I'll be right back. How long is she going to be out?"

"We'll throw some water in her face, that'll bring her back." Jane Ann was moving away. "I'll get some. Then we can find out what she knows."

Sherlock heard Mick coming back into the living room. She moaned and slowly opened her eyes to stare up at the young man who was sitting next to her, a roll of duct tape in his hand, studying her face.

She blinked and gave him a smile. "Mick? Is that you? What happened? Did I faint? Oh good, you stretched me out on the sofa. Thank you."

He froze. "You think you fainted?"

She frowned at him in confusion. "Didn't I? All I remember is you were telling me how you were an actor and then, well, I woke up here on the sofa. My head hurts a bit. Hey, I think it's low blood sugar. It's happened before, my blood sugar just bottoms out and down I go. Mick, thank you for making me comfortable."

"Isn't your blood sugar still low?"

"Well, yes, it is. There's usually a brief spike then it falls again. Do you think I could have a glass of juice? Or maybe a regular soda? It's got sugar in it, and that'll get me back to normal."

Mick called out, "Jane Ann, bring some orange juice in here. Agent Sherlock says it was low blood sugar that made her faint."

"*What?* Faint?"

"Yeah, she fainted. It's okay, really, just bring in the orange juice."

Sherlock's temple pounded where his fist had struck her. Her palms itched to flatten the jerk. She whispered, "Could you help me sit up, Mick?"

Automatically, he pulled her to a sitting position. "How do you feel?"

"A little woozy, but I'll be okay. Like I said, this has happened before."

"Jane Ann, where's the orange juice?"

"Just a minute."

Still, it was another couple of minutes before Jane Ann wrapped Sherlock's fingers around a glass. Sherlock smiled up at her. "Ah, orange juice. Thank you, Jane Ann." Sherlock drank down half a glass, then leaned her head back, closed her eyes. "Thank you both. This doesn't happen often, but when it does, I'm down and out for a minute. I'm very glad you had some orange juice. It acts really fast, and hey, it's better for you than soda."

Sherlock waited, opened her eyes again, and set the orange juice on the coffee table. She stretched and smiled at the two of them, both standing directly in front of her, both looking worried, both still a bit on the blurry side. She had a ferocious headache, but she wasn't about to tell them that. She hoped she looked nice and pale. She sure felt rotten enough.

They hadn't taken her SIG, it was still clipped to her belt.

She stuck out her hand toward Mick and he took it and pulled her to her feet. She held still a moment to make sure she had herself back together again. "Do you know, a couple of months ago, I was shot. They removed my spleen. I'm all well again, but sometimes, like now, where my spleen once resided, it aches. Isn't that strange? It aches now." And she massaged her side a moment, continuing to smile at the two of them. "Thank you both for taking care of me. Jane Ann, I'll see you when you get back with your sons. Mick, you're a great guy, I know you'll make it in Hollywood."

She walked away from them through the beautiful archway, breathing deeply, evenly, not hurrying. Once she was a good six feet away from them, she pulled out her SIG and turned to face them. "All right, you two, I hope you didn't have great plans for Caskie's money since you won't be able to touch it. It's called ill-gotten gains."

Mick's face went red with outrage. "You were playing us! You were making all that up! Low blood sugar? It was all an act?"

"Well, yes, I had to. You two did take good care of me. Thank you. You know, Mick, it's not all that difficult to shoot people if you have the high ground and two guns blasting away. Then again, you didn't want to hit either of us, did you? I mean you couldn't kill us since we were Jane Ann's perfect alibi. We wouldn't have been any use to her at all dead. Tell me, what did

Caskie do when you walked in on him in the laundry room? Did he even know who you were? Before you shot him in the forehead, did you tell him you were his wife's lover? Did you tell him it wasn't personal, you just wanted his money?"

Mick was shaking his head, back and forth. "Listen, Agent Sherlock, I don't know what you're talking about. None of what you said is true. I didn't do anything."

"This grand plan of yours, you both took a huge risk but I guess you thought the payoff would be worth it. We could have so easily killed you, Mick, and for what? For money? That was a very bad decision you made, but you know, I don't think it was your idea.

"You came up with it, didn't you, Jane Ann? You thought it all through, decided to call me so I'd give you the perfect alibi. I can see it on your face. You set up the cold-blooded murder of your own husband. I'd hoped I was wrong, hoped it was Mick here who was the grand manipulator. But no, it couldn't have been Mick's idea, he's too young, too self-absorbed, and frankly, he's not bright enough. But you made sure he was in so far he couldn't get himself out when he discovered how you'd used him.

"I did like you, Jane Ann, and I believed you—the poor terrified woman hiding in her closet, waiting for the vicious killers to find her and kill her, just as they killed Caskie. You're the actor here, not poor Mick. But the killers didn't come to find you, did they? And that really bothered me. Too unprofessional.

"What decided you? That Caskie was already in the line of fire? That Schiffer Hartwin would be the natural suspects, and Caskie's murder would look like the revenge killing of a scapegoat? They're rotten enough, but they were innocent of Caskie's murder.

"It was only about two greedy people who wanted money. You're both under arrest for the murder of Caskie Royal. You have the right to remain silent—" While she read them their rights, she tried to punch in Bowie's number on her cell phone as she spoke, but she was having trouble, her fingers didn't seem to be working very well.

Jane Ann said quickly, her hands out,

palms up, the supplicant, "Won't you listen to me, Agent Sherlock? Won't you let me defend myself? Okay, I didn't tell you the truth, couldn't tell you the truth because I was afraid. Caskie pulled a gun on me, said he was going to kill me, I wasn't any use to him anymore. He laughed at me when I pleaded with him. He told me he and Carla were going to leave the country, he had no other choice, not really, since the Culovort scam had blown up in his face, and those bastard bosses of his were going to make him the fall guy. I couldn't let him kill me, I couldn't let my boys be orphans. Mick came in. He saved me. He shot Caskie in self-defense. I had to set things up like I did. I had to think of my boys."

"You need more practice on that story, Jane Ann. It doesn't make a lot of sense." Sherlock couldn't get the numbers on the cell phone to come into focus. It was probably Mick's blow to her temple that was making her uncoordinated. She shook it off and finally got the numbers in. Heard the cell phone ring, heard Bowie say, "Agent Richards here."

Jane Ann broke off and took a step forward.

"Don't move, Jane Ann, really, don't move."

Jane Ann took a step back again, and simply stood there staring at Sherlock.

"Bowie?"

Jane Ann said quite calmly to Mick, "What is taking so long?"

What?

She heard Bowie's voice on the cell phone, saying, "Who is this?"

"It's Sherlock." Nothing else came out. She fell to her knees and keeled over onto her side. Her cell phone skittered across the polished oak floor.

55

Where was she?

In a closet maybe. It wasn't pitch-black, which was a relief, so no, not a closet. She lay quietly on her side, getting herself back into her brain, letting her eyes grow accustomed to the dim light. She realized her wrists and ankles were bound, probably with Mick's duct tape. She gave a couple of tugs, but there wasn't any give. There was a reason men swore by duct tape.

Her brain was only half plugged in. She felt punch-drunk and so tired she could barely keep her eyes open, and why was that? Jane Ann had drugged her, of course.

Jane Ann, no dummy, had realized Sherlock was playing Mick with the fainting and the low blood sugar, and she'd mashed some kind of pills into the orange juice. She'd thought she'd pulled it off, but she'd never fooled Jane Ann, not for a minute. She didn't think she was destined for Hollywood any more than Mick was. She didn't think he'd make it as an acting critic either.

At least Bowie knew she was in trouble. Her brain was woozy again. She felt the dragging sweep of drugs and tried not to go under again. She counted to ten a half-dozen times. On the fifth try, she knew she made it to ten without a single short circuit in her brain. She realized her mouth felt desert dry. She made another half-hearted attempt to pull free of the duct tape, but there was no movement at all.

Where was she? She could see in the dim light that she was in a large room. She made out clothes, lots of clothes hanging from a long pole rack. Clothes? More than street clothes—costumes, dozens of costumes, at least that's what they looked like. There were long gowns, yard upon yard of heavy material, short silk 1920s flapper dresses that her great-grandmother probably wore, even a couple of high-waisted Regency gowns that looked flowy and soft.

What was that huge round thing that looked like gold? A gong, she realized, she could just make it out now, its mallet hanging beside it. Who would have a gong? She saw two sofas, one flowery, one dark leather, a dozen chairs, some old-fashioned and frilly, others painfully modern, end tables, lamps, and three rolled rugs not far from her feet.

Was she in an attic?

No, not an attic. Everything smelled too fresh, with maybe a layer of lavender. The room was large, deep. She saw another clothes rack with men's clothes—capes, coats, lots of shoes—modern shoes, disco pointed toes, velvet shoes, boots of all sorts. Was that a ruff hanging over a hanger under that plastic garment bag? A ruff like the men wore in Queen Elizabeth's time? Didn't the women wear ruffs too? She simply couldn't get her brain around that. There were stacks of luggage, looking vintage 1920s.

Was that a guillotine set on the floor, its wicked blade pulled up, ready to whack through a neck with a pull of the rope? That made her shudder. She managed to get herself up into a sitting position. At her back was a—tree? She twisted to look at it. Yep, a fake tree that didn't look very real at all up close and personal.

A ruff?

She knew then where she was. In the storage room of a theater, probably the Belson summer stock theater where Mick had played Petruchio in Shakespeare's *Taming of the Shrew.*

They'd stashed her here until they figured out what to do with her.

She could feel her Lady Colt in its ankle holster. She was very glad they weren't pros or they'd have found it in a matter of minutes. She'd have to get free before it would be of use to her.

Sherlock saw a weapons array—guns, muskets, fake Uzis, a butcher knife, an axe, and a stiletto—all of them fastened to a board set against a wall twelve feet away from her.

She tried to stand up and promptly fell on her side. She tried several more times, but always ended up on the floor. Okay, then—she wriggled over to the weapons board. She stared up at the stiletto, leaned her back against the board and slowly pushed herself up. She felt the weapons digging in her back, but she just kept pushing, pushing, until she was standing straight up. She turned slowly, leaning heavily against the board. The stiletto was still way too high up for her to pull it off with her hands bound behind her back. She went up on her tiptoes and clamped the steel blade between her teeth. It tasted cold and metallic. Since it was a stage knife, it had to be retractable. She'd have to be careful how she used it.

She pushed her back against the board again and slowly sank down to the floor. She dropped the stiletto and twisted around until she managed to grab the handle in her hand. Her first try at poking through the duct tape made the blade retract instantly. Okay, she'd have to saw the tape, not try to punch through it. She was clumsy at first, but she kept at it, sawed away. She cut her fingers, and her hands cramped. The stiletto kept slipping but she forced herself to be patient and repositioned it, aware of the precious minutes marching inexorably forward, bringing Jane Ann and

Mick back to her. She couldn't hurry because when she did, the stiletto slipped and she had to start over again.

She stopped counting the times the stiletto cut her. There was slick blood now, making the task all that more difficult. *Keep going, just keep going. Focus now, whine later.*

Sherlock couldn't believe it when the duct tape suddenly split apart. She was free. She sat perfectly still for an instant, not really believing it. Forever, she thought, it had taken nearly forever, but she'd gotten the duct tape off. She stared down at her bloody hands—just like Lady Macbeth's. She drew a deep breath and shook her hands to get the feeling back, rubbed her hands on her pants. It hurt, but who cared?

She picked up the stiletto and went to work on the tape around her ankles. She cut through it in an instant. She was in business.

She stood and stamped her feet until she felt the pins and needles go away. Then she leaned up and pulled a butcher knife off its hooks. It was blunt, but nice and heavy. Best of all, it wasn't retractable. Evidently the actors had to remember not to hack anyone with it in the plays they performed. She held the butcher knife in her left hand and her Lady Colt in her right. She was good to go. She walked quickly through the shadows to the door of the storage room. It was locked, of course. Okay, now what? She had two bullets in her Lady Colt, she could shoot off the lock and—

She heard footsteps coming. Heavy footsteps. It was a man, and he was coming here.

Her heart stopped. They were back, to deal with her, probably to kill her. At least she wasn't lying on the floor, helpless. No, she wasn't helpless at all.

Sherlock eased behind the closely packed clothes racks, and waited. She heard him fiddling with the lock, and then the door was pushed inward.

56

Bowie shook his cell phone, as if it would give him more information. "It was Sherlock. Something's happened, I can't get her."

Erin took the cell phone from him, hit some buttons, listened. "It's still open on the other end, but no one's there. You're right, someone's got her, Bowie. Do you know where she was going?"

"I think she was going to see Jane Ann Royal, but there are loads of crime scene techs over there. I sent Kel and Joel over there to help work the house since you were with me. I know Sherlock asked them to check on the Royal telephone records. She's not there, she can't be."

"Call them, see what they say."

He took back his cell and speed-dialed Agent Kel Lewis's cell.

"This is Bowie. Have you seen Agent Sherlock? Okay, is Mrs. Royal there? I want you guys to keep an eye out. We'll see you as soon as we can. What? Okay, check out that telephone number right now and get back to me. Kel, put an APB out on Jane Ann Royal. Wait, Sherlock asked me where Millstone was. That's it, she went to Millstone. But—"

Erin grabbed his hand. "Georgie's out of school in ten minutes. We can't leave her standing there. What are we going to do?"

He thought a moment, then speed-dialed the police station. He looked over to see Erin rotating her shoulders, easing the strain. He said as the phone was ringing, "Erin, you've got to drive, that okay with your back? I've got lots more calls to make." When he connected with Agent Cliff, he asked quickly, "Dolores, do you have any idea where Agent Sherlock is?"

Bowie jumped into the passenger seat, tucked the phone under his chin, and managed to fasten his seat belt as Dolores said, "She said something about a Mick Haggarty, and I gave her his address in Millstone. Who is that, Bowie? She didn't tell me."

Bowie said, "Mick Haggarty?"

Erin nearly side-swiped a light blue Honda as she turned onto Maple Avenue. "Mick Haggarty is Jane Ann's tennis instructor, the one she told Sherlock and me she was thinking about sleeping with. Sherlock must think he knows something."

Bowie said to Dolores, "Give me Mick Haggarty's address. Okay, yeah, got it. Now, important—would you go to Winston Elementary School and pick up Georgie? Then take her back to the police station with you, keep an eye on her?"

"Sure thing, Bowie."

He asked her, "Who else is there?"

"Cody and Graham. Kesselring left maybe an hour ago. He said he had things to do and he didn't need any assistance, but he wasn't specific."

"All right. But I told Graham he was to stick close to Kesselring, not let him roam around loose."

"You could have asked me, Bowie. I've

got perspective now, really. He's just another pretty face, right? He's kind of stiff, too, charming because he knows that works for him, but that's on the surface. I don't think down deep he's really that friendly."

"Where are Dieffendorf and Gerlach?"

"They're at the Schiffer Hartwin headquarters with their lawyers and two DOJ attorneys. Do you want the local cops to go to Mick Haggarty's apartment in Millstone?"

"Yes, but have them wait outside for us. Erin and I are heading there now. If Agent Sherlock calls, have her call me pronto. And run a location check on Sherlock's phone. It's in use and I want to know where it is."

Erin took the backroads to Millstone. They were more than five minutes away when Bowie's cell phone belted out "Santa Claus Is Coming to Town."

"You and those Christmas carols." Erin shook her head. "Alvin and the Chipmunks, I haven't heard them in years." She listened to the chipmunks as she watched Bowie reach into his jacket pocket, come away empty, then dive into his pants pocket and pull out the cell.

"Thanks, Dolores. We're on our way." He shook his head, then punched off his cell and turned to Erin. "The phone's in Millstone. Somewhere near Haggarty's apartment."

Erin pressed down on the accelerator.

57

"Agent Sherlock? Are you here? Are you all right?"

It was Andreas Kesselring's voice. In that instant everything shifted into place in Sherlock's mind. She'd tried and tried to connect the dots, but they wouldn't fit together until she heard his voice and realized they'd all been suckered by another cop.

At least she'd had the sense to ask Kel Lewis to check Jane Ann's phone records—she'd had this gut feeling, she just hadn't realized the who. Too bad it was a little late now.

He called out again in his smooth deep

voice, "Agent Sherlock? Are you in here? Did those criminals tape your mouth? I got them both. You're safe now. You can come out."

Sherlock knew all he had to do was look over maybe twelve feet and he'd see the duct tape lying on the floor. She waited, silent as a stone, her Lady Colt at the ready, her left hand clutching the butcher knife. He had to come closer. *Come here, Andreas, come to Mama.*

"Ah, I see you got yourself free. That's great, won't you come out now? Why are you hiding from me? We'll go down to the police station and you can question Mrs. Royal and that tennis pro boyfriend of hers. I've got them restrained just outside. What a pair, they've been talking over each other, each claiming the other is to blame."

Sherlock peeked through the small space between two plastic garment bags. Kesselring wasn't wearing a beautiful Armani suit today, no, he was transformed, wearing a baseball cap and a dark blue jacket, jeans and boots, his arms at his sides. Was that a gun in his right hand, pressed against his leg? Yes. He had a much better chance of shooting her dead than she would have getting off any kind of shot that counted. Her Lady Colt was an up-close gun, and Kesselring was at least forty feet away. No way could she disable him enough from this distance unless she was very lucky. And at the moment, she didn't put much stock in her luck. He stood there, not moving, not stepping any deeper into the storage room. And Jane Ann and Mick Haggarty were probably waiting just outside that door, waiting for a signal from Kesselring. To tell them what? That he'd killed her? How was she going to get past them all?

She heard more footsteps. Kesselring turned back toward the door. She saw Jane Ann Royal walk in and immediately look over at the place she and Mick had left her. She grabbed Kesselring's sleeve. "She's gone! Tell me you know where she is."

Kesselring said to her, "I don't know how she did it, but our girl got herself free of the duct tape. She's good."

"She couldn't have! I checked her hands and feet, she couldn't move. What are we going to do? So she's already gone—"

Sherlock saw Kesselring looked impatient, harried. A bit of contempt came through his voice. "Your lack of guts amazes me, Jane Ann, after all you've done. The door was locked so she's still in here, hiding. Now, if you would look over at that weapons board, you will probably see that something is missing, not that it matters since all the guns hold blanks and all the knives are fake, which means she has nothing. She is somewhere in this room, probably hoping I'll come and search for her, and she can attack me. Not that it would do her any good. She's half my size and she's a girl. She knows I can break her neck with one hand.

"Don't be afraid, Jane Ann. Come on in. We will find her together. Then I'll take her away. Or, perhaps I will just end it here. We can lock her in one of those trunks. She wouldn't be found for at least a month."

"I don't know. It's Mick who knows the theater performance schedule. And what good would a month do us? What kind of a plan is that?"

Kesselring said after a moment, "When I came in, I called to her, told her everything was okay, but she didn't say a word, didn't jump out to welcome me. The truth is I expected her to leap straight into my arms when I came in. So that means she figured it out, which, I will admit, surprises me. It was a sound plan, well executed until she went to your apartment, and you and that idiot boyfriend of yours screwed it up.

"She's smarter than I gave her credit for. Can you imagine, an agent—a woman—who actually thought outside the box? Ah, I understand now. You told her, didn't you?"

"Of course I didn't!"

"All right, I'll believe you. When I first saw her, I knew in my gut she'd be dangerous to me. I wanted to strangle her. I knew she was smart. Much smarter than you, telling that gigolo tennis player all about this. Look what it's brought you."

Jane Ann was silent for a beat, then she said in a deadly cold voice, "Of course she's smart. And so am I. If I hadn't asked Mick to the house that night, would you have killed me, too?"

He laughed, he actually laughed. "Yeah, right, real smart. It took me all of ten minutes to convince you to get rid of that spineless greedy husband of yours, and another ten minutes to get your pants down."

Another beat of silence, then Jane Ann said, her voice vicious, "You didn't give me much choice about Caskie, so don't go believing you're the God of Persuasion. All of this was always for my boys."

"You're a fine human being and an extraordinary mother," Andreas said, the sarcasm so thick it seemed to Sherlock it should hang in the air.

"You're more to blame for this than I am, Andy. It was you and those money-grubbing criminals who wanted Caskie dead and buried."

"Don't call me Andy, you foolish woman! I wouldn't have to be here at all if you had the guts to take care of this agent yourself."

Jane Ann shouted at him, "Well, now it doesn't matter. Your whole grand scheme—bilking cancer patients out of billions of dollars, and all of you walking away with millions for your off-shore accounts."

"I am not getting millions," Kesselring said shortly, and he sounded pissed.

"Ha! You, the brilliant German agent with all your supposed charisma—what a mistake it was to sleep with you. You, Andy, are a pig in bed and your hygiene isn't all that great either. Caskie was a cheat, but he always smelled nice."

"You stupid Americans and your foolish fetish for scrubbing your bodies all the time. You're idiots, all of you!"

"At least you don't sweat all that much until you're heaving like a goat in bed. You wouldn't get anywhere with American women if you smelled up your beautiful suits. The German dry cleaners must love you."

Kesselring said, his voice gone dead and very soft, "Do you really want to speak to me that way when I'm holding a gun?"

Jane Ann stopped talking.

Andreas continued in that soft dead voice, "I have listened to you preen and crow enough, Jane Ann. Your greed is as great as mine, or your husband would still be alive." He stopped, looked at her with utter disinterest, and shrugged. "This is nonsense. We have a job to do here. I will succeed. And I will escape this."

"How?"

She saw Kesselring shrug again. "You will see I know exactly what I'm doing. Are you ready to help me?"

Jane Ann nodded. "She's got to be here somewhere, listening to us."

"At least you were smart enough to take

her gun." He glanced down at his belt line under his dark blue jacket. Sherlock knew at that moment he had her SIG tucked under his belt.

Sherlock watched Kesselring walk over to where she'd lain unconscious, trussed up with the duct tape. "She woke up from your pills, managed to get down a stage knife and saw the tape off, quite an accomplishment, given all the knives retract. It couldn't have been easy." He called out louder, "That was quite good, Agent Sherlock. You might as well come out now. There's no place for you to go. Mick is guarding the outside door, you can't get past him."

Sherlock took one step then another down a long row of plastic bagged costumes, toward the door. Her best chance was to get to the door, slam it shut, lock it. She could deal with Mick, he was an amateur. She didn't have a chance with Kesselring, not so long as he kept his distance. He'd shoot her in the head in a heartbeat.

One more step. *Easy*. A board creaked. Sherlock froze, then squatted down to peer through a long lacy sleeve of an

1890s ball gown hanging out of the plastic bag. She saw Kesselring whirl around on the balls of his feet, a pistol in his right hand, but he wasn't pointing it at her, it was aimed at least six feet away from her. He'd heard the board, but missed the location.

"Come out, Agent Sherlock," came his soft voice. "I don't have much more time to play with you." He didn't sound now like he believed her dangerous to him. He fired two rounds. A bullet splintered a hanger, and a long Victorian gown spilled out onto the floor.

"I see that you do have a weapon, I can see its outline on the board. Is it an axe? A knife? You've got to know that unless you're a circus act, it's not going to do you much good. If you throw it at me, if it even manages to strike me, it will simply bounce off. Come on out now like a good girl and we'll get this over with. Tell you what, if you show yourself, one professional to another, I won't kill you. I'll tie you up and take you to Van Wie Park and stash you in some bushes."

Yeah, like she'd believe that. He was enjoying this. He didn't realize this butcher knife could hurt him. Good. Suddenly Sherlock realized she wasn't going to be able to get to the door, because there was Mick standing in the middle of the open doorway, looking scared enough to vomit.

Smart man.

Time was her enemy. She didn't see a weapon in Mick's hand, but Kesselring was armed and quite ready to shoot her. It didn't matter, she had to act. Even with the distance and her Lady Colt, she might wound him. If she was really lucky, she'd hit an artery and he'd bleed out. She wouldn't be sorry about that. But if she didn't manage to disarm him, she was, quite simply, dead.

Sherlock was raising her Lady Colt when Kesselring walked quickly to Jane Ann, grabbed her wrist, twisted it, and jerked her in front of him, wrapping his arm around her neck. He brought his pistol to her temple. "Mick, come in now, or I will kill this loud-mouthed slut."

Mick Haggarty shouted, "I knew we shouldn't trust you! I told Jane Ann you were crazy, told her you had dead eyes, but she said she could handle you. Don't you dare kill her, you lunatic!"

Mick dove for Kesselring.

Kesselring calmly turned, pulled Sherlock's SIG Sauer from his belt, and shot him in the forehead in mid-leap. The force of the bullet slammed Mick Haggarty back against the wall. He slid down the wall leaving streaks of blood and brains in his wake, dead before he hit the floor. Jane Ann screamed.

Kesselring grabbed her around the neck again and began choking her. She was gagging, beginning to turn blue, her hands pulling at his arms, but it did no good. He yelled, "You stupid woman, I told you I had a plan!"

Jane Ann stopped trying to pull his arms loose. Sherlock watched her get it together, watched her rip her nails down his face and drive her elbow hard into his belly. Kesselring howled and cursed in German and slammed the barrel of his gun to her head. Jane Ann sagged in his arms.

No time. No time. Sherlock took careful aim and fired one of her precious bullets.

58

Bowie and Erin slammed through Mick Haggarty's apartment door, three local cops behind them, so excited Erin hoped they wouldn't shoot her or Bowie.

"No one's here," Bowie said after racing through the apartment. "They took her somewhere."

"Agent Richards!"

Bowie ran over to Deputy Henry Mote, who was bent over near the door. "Look, sir, it's a cell phone."

Bowie quickly punched in the first speed-dial number.

Savich answered on the second ring.

"Sherlock? Why didn't you call before now? What's going on up there? Are you all right?"

"Savich, it's Bowie. I'm on Sherlock's cell phone. We found the cell on the floor of Mick Haggarty's apartment. I wasn't sure whose it was so I speed-dialed the first number. Look, she's gone. We know Jane Ann Royal and Mick Haggarty have her.

"Sherlock figured it out, but they got her first. Yes, I understand. Have the helicopter drop you close to the police station in Millstone." Bowie listened a moment longer, then hung up. He turned to the deputies. "I'm going to call your chief. I was just talking to Agent Savich. I'll need you to get every single deputy on your local force out looking for Jane Ann Royal, Mick Haggarty, and Agent Lacey Sherlock. I'll have photos of them very soon, and the license plates of their cars."

Erin said, "So they took Sherlock's car, and Jane Ann has hers. Where's Mick's?"

"I don't know. Let me find out what he drives." It only took three minutes. He called Millstone's chief of police, Brenda

Crocker, who looked up the license plate numbers and got things rolling. Photos were on their way.

Within ten minutes Bowie had done everything he could think of. What else? There was always something else to do.

He sat down on the arm of a big easy chair, obviously where Mick Haggarty sat while drinking beer and watching baseball games. "I've screwed up big-time," he said to Erin.

"You? In what way?" she asked absently as she checked out some framed photos on the wall. An older man and woman, probably Mick's parents. Two young kids. His brothers? Then something else—Erin pulled down what looked like a gold-framed certificate of some sort, set by itself in the middle of the wall. A place of honor.

"Don't try to jolly me out of this," Bowie was saying, disgust in his voice. "I shouldn't have left her alone. I shouldn't have gone to New Haven."

Erin said. "They aren't idiots, Bowie. Listen, I'll bet they're thinking fondly of the Canadian border about now, maybe taking her with them as a hostage. Don't you think?"

Erin didn't believe that for a minute, but it didn't matter. "We've got everyone on the planet out looking for both of them." She paused a moment, took the certificate off the wall. "Would you look at this."

Bowie rose and went to her, looked down at the framed certificate. "It's an acting award from Belson College Summer Stock Theater." Bowie looked up, clearly impatient. "Mick got a special commendation for his role as Hamlet last year." He handed it back to her. "So what?"

"I've been to some of the plays they've put on during the summer at Belson College. It's a nice outdoor theater set off to one side of campus, smack up against the woods, all by itself. It's only got people around when there's rehearsal or performances. I've been picturing the theater in my mind, how you snake your way through the woods from the parking area. There are several buildings behind the stage, for the actors to hang out, changing areas, for stage settings, whatever. I'm wondering where they'd take Sherlock, and just maybe—"

He stared at her a long moment. “Mick and Jane Ann would know all about this area, know the buildings on the Belson campus. Only one way to find out, Erin. We can call for more help on the way.”

59

Kesselring grabbed the side of his neck as he fired toward her, once, twice, but Sherlock had fallen belly-flat the instant before he'd fired. He fired three more bullets, fast, all of them going well over her head. Had she been standing, any of the rounds could have killed her.

He dropped an unconscious Jane Ann to the floor and crouched down behind some luggage. "Where did you get that gun?" he shouted.

"Surprise, Andy."

"It's not your SIG—I'd be dead if your damned SIG weren't in my belt because you would have emptied your clip into me. So what do you have? Maybe a small ankle piece? One more bullet, right? Or was that your only one?"

Sherlock shouted back, "I guess it'll have to be one of life's mysteries, Andy, until it's too late for you." She knew it was dangerous to let him hear her, but it was her only chance.

"I hate a smart mouth on a woman. I'm going to find you and gut-shoot you, Agent, listen to you beg me to kill you. That's what I wanted to do to Royal but there wasn't time. I nearly kicked his ribs in. If it hadn't been for that damned private investigator who broke into Royal's office—"

Sherlock called out over him, "That damned investigator's name is Erin Pulaski. Fact is, it was Erin who brought all of you down, Andy. You found out who she was, fast."

"Did you think I would not realize who she was? Three federal agents hanging around her, so close to her none of you realized she fit the exact description of that witness, until it was too late. Or it should have been too late. She should have blown up in that stupid Hummer of hers, but it all went wrong. The device I planted worked perfectly, but somehow she knew there was a bomb. I couldn't believe it when I watched her jump, no hesitation at all. Just a couple more seconds and she'd be blown up. How did she know?"

"Another smart woman. We appear to litter the ground, don't we? You know what, Andy? A woman is going to bring you down."

Keep talking, Andreas. Spill it all out.

Kesselring yelled, "You're about as smart as Royal, that brain-dead slug, and this rapacious cow on the floor."

"Smart enough to shoot you in the neck."

"Do you really have one more bullet in that gun of yours, Agent? Or maybe you're bluffing me. You don't have any more bullets, do you? Is that why you're trying to goad me? Make me lose it and come close enough for you to jump me? Good luck, Agent. I could break your skinny neck with one hand."

Sherlock was elbow-crawling away toward the far end of the clothes rack as she called out, "Maybe I'll put the next bullet between your stone-dead eyes, Andy."

"Don't you call me Andy!" He was angry, really angry, but not out of control enough to pull the trigger wildly. But she wanted him to keep coming, get him out in the open, to keep shooting.

Rile him, rile him. She called out, "You don't think much of women, do you, Andy? Why? Is it that after a while women see beyond your good-looking face to the cold-blooded loser?"

He growled deep in his throat, she heard it, and flattened herself, face against the dusty floor. He fired once, twice, the second bullet coming too close. She elbow-crawled two more feet back. How many bullets did he have left? Three, maybe four? Did he have another magazine? Not that it mattered, he had her SIG, and he'd used it to kill Mick. Then Sherlock finally realized what this was all about. She called out, "You must have been really pissed when Jane Ann called you in a panic, told you what she and Mick had done to me. You thought you had everything under control, thought you'd won, and now this debacle. Is that when you decided to come and mop up? Remove all three of us in a big shoot-out? Now you think you're home free?"

He said, "I would have shot Jane Ann

when I killed her loser husband, but she must have guessed something wasn't right, which is why she had her boy Mick there. As insurance. I should have killed them both right there, but then the two of you showed up. It took you long enough to figure it out, Agent."

That was the truth, Sherlock thought. Mick had scrambled her brains good when he'd clouted her, and the drug Jane Ann had added to the orange juice hadn't helped. She did know one thing for sure—her only chance was to keep pushing him, to make him lose control. She paused a moment to look through the clothes. He'd stood up behind the luggage, trying to find her, fanning his gun from one end of the clothes rack to the other, his left hand still slapped against his neck. No way could she take the chance of shooting at him from this distance. If she didn't put him down with her second and last bullet, he'd walk over here and shoot her dead.

She saw blood oozing sluggishly through his fingers. Too bad she hadn't hit an artery, but it was a start. Should she dare try her only other bullet? She was tempted, she was a good shot. Just maybe—

Suddenly he grabbed a still limp Jane Ann, dragged her behind a leather sofa, then pulled her up in front of him like a shield. "You want to try again, Agent? Well, go ahead, this slut is no loss to the world." Without the pressure of his left palm, blood snaked down his neck into his jacket.

She didn't know where she found it, but she laughed. "Hey, Andy, what do you call a male slut in German?"

He fired once, lower this time, but still well above her head.

She laughed at him again. "You're not in such good shape now, are you? You're bleeding all over the place. Hey, who knows? Maybe you'll bleed out. Talk about no loss to the world, but hey, I'm willing to make you a deal, Andy. You leave Jane Ann alive, and I'll let you walk out of here. No one else has to die today."

"*You* will let *me* walk out of here? To run for the rest of my life? That's not going to happen. I'm the one in charge here, not you. When all of you are dead, my problems are over. You've figured that out, haven't you? All of you are going to hell. *Where are you?*" He raised his gun and fired two quick rounds. One was no more than six inches from the top of her head. *Too close, way too close.*

She could hear rage simmering in his deep voice now, whipping up a mad brew. "You are nothing but a dried-up butch cop! What you are is dead, do you hear me?" She watched Jane Ann's head loll against his chest as he shifted her, clumsily trying to keep her in front of him so he could press his palm against his neck again. Holding Jane Ann with his gun arm hampered him, not that it mattered, Sherlock wasn't about to risk shooting Jane Ann.

"To be honest here, Andy, at first I thought you were like a sore thumb—just sticking out there, this jerk foreign cop with nothing to do, bumbling around, but you had your own agenda. You only wanted to find out what we knew. You didn't spend much time with your assigned FBI buddy, did you? Nope, you had too much to do, too many places to go, people to see, bombs to plant.

"You better deal with me, Andy, or you won't come out of this alive. You've got to ask yourself, is time on your side, or mine? You want to be sent back to Germany in a metal box? Does it matter? Is there anyone back in Germany to mourn you, anyone to care at all if you're dead or alive?"

It was a disappointment when he called back, calm and controlled, "I will deal with you, Agent Sherlock, and it's going to be on my own terms."

Jane Ann moaned.

Be quiet, be quiet, for heaven's sake, Jane Ann, be quiet!

"Let me tell you my terms here, Andy, something you must believe—if you shoot Jane Ann Royal, I will kill you. Do you understand?"

A moment's silence, then he spoke, his voice indifferent, "You can try, I suppose, with that little pea shooter of yours."

"Won't you tell me how you murdered Helmut Blauvelt when you didn't arrive in the U.S. until the day after he died?"

60

He giggled. It creeped her out, the conceit in that giggle, the unmistakable whiff of madness. She felt his arrogance, his dismissal of her, when he said, "I was already here on a forged passport. After I killed Blauvelt, I quickly returned to New York and left on the red eye back to Frankfurt."

"Now you've depressed me. I guess we're just too trusting of our foreign counterparts. And I must say you arrived with a reputation as a straight-arrow cop, Agent Kesselring. Who would have thought you're really a stone cold murderer?"

"One does what one must." He sounded

calm again, and it scared her. The last thing she wanted was to have him thinking clearly.

Push him, push him. "Sounds to me like Schiffer Hartwin had a great duo working for them, you and Blauvelt. How many people did you kill between you? How many officials did you bribe to run Schiffer Hartwin's illegal tests? Africa is a particularly nice drug testing ground, isn't it? So what happened with Blauvelt? Why'd you kill him? What did he do?"

She heard him snort, but he didn't answer.

"Come now, what does it matter? Inquiring minds want to know, Andy. Hey, had Blauvelt simply had enough of the intimidation and killing? Maybe the Culovort scheme finally got to him? That's why he wanted out?

"Did Dieffendorf know he'd become a liability? Did he send you over here to make sure Blauvelt was dead and buried, no longer a problem? What, Andy?"

He said something to her in German, something low and vicious. He'd probably sent her right to hell. Was he about ready to boil over?

"You're afraid to talk to me, aren't you, Andy? You, the big hollow cop in the expensive Armani suit—you're actually afraid of a butch cop half your size? You've told me everything else, why don't you want to tell me why you murdered Blauvelt?"

Jane Ann moaned again.

Sherlock heard the slap of flesh against flesh, knew he'd struck Jane Ann with his open palm. Better than his fist.

She shouted, "You're a psychopath, Andy, but I didn't figure you for a coward, too."

Hallelujah, that did it. He yelled, "The break-in, you idiot! The pathetic little man found out too much. Once that damned Erin Pulaski stole the information on Culovort right off Royal's computer, I knew he'd tell the one person who could cut the cash flow. Blauvelt would not listen, so I had no choice. I would have been exposed. To him I was nothing.

"Well, I showed him he was nothing. Less than nothing. I even erased his damned face. He always liked to say he was the big fish. Well, he got himself devoured by a bigger fish, didn't he?"

"You didn't want him identified, did you?"

"Of course not, at least not until I was safely back in Germany. But once I started smashing his face, I realized I rather enjoyed it. Then I cut off his fingers, left the rest for the local yahoos to try to identify. I didn't know Van Wie Park was federal land. It was just bad luck Agent Richards realized Blauvelt had foreign dental work, and you found out who he was like that—" Kesselring snapped his fingers. "It was a much quicker flight back than I expected. I've always found that to be true. Going home is always faster.

"Still, it should have worked, all of it, except for Royal. He was the weak link, ready to roll over on us."

"Who could have stopped it all?"

He laughed. "Good try, Agent, but I will keep that close to my vest, isn't that your American slang?"

"You nailed it, Andy. Is that when you decided to visit Jane Ann?"

"Ah, Jane Ann. Now she was a surprise, I'll admit it." He gave that insane giggle again. "She was something in bed, I'll tell you."

"A match made in heaven. You and Jane Ann and Mick Haggarty?"

"Was that the boy's last name? What a waste he was, no guts at all. He was shaking so hard when I shot Royal I thought he would piss his pants."

"Then you and Mick were waiting for us, and you were careful not to hit us since we were Jane Ann's alibi."

Sherlock wondered if she could shoot above Jane Ann's head with her precious second bullet and miraculously strike him in the forehead. Time was running out. She had to bring him out, she had to bring him closer to her, she had to end it.

"Schiffer Hartwin isn't paying you what you're worth, are they, Andy? Not a share of the real profits like others are getting, you know, a big slice of the windfall profits from Laboratoires Ancondor? Sounds to me like you're the one who makes everything work. What good are they without you, these men you work for? Surely the whole company isn't in on this? Who's running this show? Who could put a stop to it?"

"They will pay me now, every single penny I ask for. Enough, Agent! There is no more reason to talk."

"I've got a surprise for you, Andy. Jane

Ann forgot all about my cell phone. I've got it in my pocket, and not only is it recording our entire conversation, it's giving out a nice sharp signal. We've talked so long now, there are probably FBI agents and local police officers in position around this place right now, just waiting for you to come out. Best not to kill Jane Ann, Andy, or you'll go down so fast you won't even know you're dead. You know how good our snipers are, don't you? Right through the forehead, and you're gone.

"You want to die here, Andy? Or do you want to deal with me and live another day?"

He dropped Jane Ann, jumped over the sofa, and ran toward the sound of her voice, and he didn't stop firing until the clip was empty. Then he pulled her SIG from his belt and kept coming, firing with every step.

61

"Kesselring! Stop right there or I'll shoot!"

It was Bowie. Thank you, God, thank you, God. She had a chance now. Her SIG had to be nearly empty, but he didn't stop, it was as if he couldn't—and he was looking her right in the face when he took his next shot. Sherlock felt the bullet whistle not an inch from her right ear, felt the sting of it, and smelled the cordite. She had no choice but to rise up and try for a kill shot with her only bullet. Then there were two quick shots from the door, and thank the merciful Lord, Kesselring fell hard to the floor.

There was a moment of dead silence.

Sherlock shouted, "Bowie?"

"Sherlock, you all right?"

"Miracle of miracles, I am."

"Sherlock?"

It was Erin.

Sherlock called out, "Is Kesselring down for good?"

Erin said with a good deal of pleasure, "Yeah, looks like Bowie shot out his hip. He's lying on his side, panting and moaning. Blood on his neck, too. Did you do that?"

"Yeah." Sherlock stood up slowly, glad her legs held her, and watched Bowie drop to his haunches beside Kesselring. He took his collar between his two hands and shook him hard, saw he wouldn't resist, and searched him for weapons.

"Bowie? Everything okay in here?" It was Agent Cliff.

He said over his shoulder, not looking away from Kesselring, "Yeah, we've got things under control. Call a couple of ambulances, would you, Dolores? Tell everyone outside it's over." He looked over at Mick Haggarty. "And call Dr. Franks, too."

Sherlock stared down at Kesselring's

pale sweating face. His jaw was working. She knew he was in major pain. She saw his hand hover above his right hip, as if he was afraid to touch it. Kesselring was finally down and out.

It was a lovely sight.

She called out, "Jane Ann? Are you okay?"

"Yeah," came a faint whisper from behind the sofa. "But my brains feel upside down."

Now you know how I felt after Mick clocked me in the head. "Just lie still. Agent Cliff's getting an ambulance for you."

Bowie saw Kesselring had passed out. He said to Sherlock, "We found you all because of Erin. She saw an award on Mick Haggarty's wall for his performance in *Hamlet*, and she remembered coming here to see some plays. She remembered how isolated this place is." Bowie paused a moment. "So Haggarty is dead."

"Yes, Kesselring shot him when he tried to help Jane Ann. He planned to kill all three of us, make it look like we shot each other."

Erin stared down at Mick Haggarty. "They played him. He didn't have a chance."

"Mick Haggarty was old enough to know

exactly what he was doing," Sherlock said. "Jane Ann made sure he was up to his neck, though. She was also using him for insurance, to protect her from Kesselring."

Jane Ann whispered, "It was the only smart thing I did. Poor Mick."

Sherlock said, "*Poor* Mick was there when Kesselring shot Caskie, just as both of them were at the top of the stairs, firing at us, not to kill us but to make us Jane Ann's alibi. That means Mick was up for first degree murder along with this clown. Jane Ann too.

"Thank you, Erin, for finding me. I owe you a prayer every single night for the rest of my life."

Sherlock looked down at Kesselring. "If he'd gotten off one more shot, I think I'd be singing with the angels. Did you guys happen to bring my cell phone?"

"Sure did," Bowie said, reaching into his jacket pocket. For once, he came out with his own cell. He tried his pants pockets. Nothing.

"Just a moment," Erin said, reaching into her bag and pulling out Sherlock's cell phone, bowing slightly as she handed it to her.

"Thank you. It turns out Kesselring murdered Blauvelt, too, after you, Erin, copied the Culovort papers off Caskie's computer. There's more. I just hope Andy here will repeat it all again."

"Andy?" Erin repeated, eyebrow arched.

"I wanted to push him," Sherlock said, looking down again at Kesselring. "Jane Ann called him Andy and it enraged him. He hates it."

The huge room was now filling with FBI agents and local cops. Sherlock heard sirens in the distance. She realized her heart was slowing, as her brain finally accepted that she'd survived. She wondered when her hands would stop shaking.

Kesselring moaned and opened his eyes to look up at Erin standing above him. She said, "You tried to blow me up. My Hummer's in the junkyard because of you." She kicked him in the knee.

He jerked and moaned again. He was panting as he said, "You are responsible for this, you interfering bitch, you're nothing more than a stupid girl."

"Yeah, right," Erin said. "What does that make you, Prince Charming?"

Kesselring was panting with the pain now. "I need a doctor, now."

Erin smiled down at him. "You didn't answer my question, Andy."

He said with pain-dulled eyes. "I'm a man, a man."

Sherlock went down on her knees next to him. "Look at me, Andy."

"Damn you, don't call me that!"

"Okay, Andreas," she said, her voice soothing, gentle. "Look, I know you're in terrible pain, but you've got to understand, you're headed for death row unless you cooperate. Tell me who's paying you."

He tried to spit in her face.

"There's an answer," Sherlock said.

Kesselring looked up at the two people who'd beaten him. He had failed. Through his roiling, unspeakable pain, his hatred of himself was nearly as great as his hatred of these American FBI agents. Odd how failure tasted sour in his mouth, how it made him want to vomit.

He suddenly saw himself as a little boy, his grandmother bending over him, bundling him up in the middle of winter so he could go build snow forts in the backyard.

She was telling him over and over not to hurt his sister.

The pain was coming so hard and fast now it was hard to think, hard to even know what was happening to him. No matter what he said, no matter what he did, Kesselring knew there would be no deal that would ever allow him to walk free again.

He said to the faces above him, all of them blurred now into the haze where the god-awful pain pounded all the way to his soul, “My grandmother is in a nursing home outside of Frankfurt.”

He saw his grandmother wrap two coats around his little sister Lisle so she could go outside and play with him. He was so excited, so impatient, and he really didn’t want to play with her, she was too little, and she always tripped over everything, and whined—she still whined too much now and she was twenty-eight years old. “I’ll never tell you anything,” he said, and closed his eyes.

62

Sherlock stood aside to watch the paramedics, two young men with grim faces, work on Kesselring. “Good grief, Agent, you shot him up pretty good. Neck wound too? How did that happen?” He craned to look up at Sherlock.

“It was quite a shoot-out, let me tell you, I’m very happy he lost.”

“He lost, all right,” the other paramedic said as he passed pressure dressings to his partner and untied the straps on the gurney. “I think he’s going to pull through but he ain’t going to be happy for a good long time.”

Dolores walked over and took Sherlock's hands in hers. "We're all so relieved you're all right. I've never seen this much shooting in my entire career. It's going to take the forensic team days just to find all the casings. But you're all right," she repeated, and ran her hands over Sherlock's arms.

Sherlock grinned at her, then reached for her SIG. She slipped in a new magazine. "Thanks, Dolores. Thank God, it's over." She nodded, then turned to make a call.

He answered on the first ring. "All I want to hear is that you're all right."

Sherlock kept her voice calm and clear. "Everything's okay here. Kesselring's alive, bound for the hospital. Bowie and I both shot him. Kesselring murdered Blauvelt—and he and Jane Ann plotted to murder Caskie. I've got lots to tell you about that. We've got Jane Ann in custody too, but Mick Haggarty is dead. If we're lucky, Kesselring or Jane Ann, if she knows, will roll big-time on whoever he was working for."

Savich felt his heart finally slowing. "You swear you're okay?"

"Yes, I promise. Tell me what's happening down there."

"What I really need to do is speak to Senator Hoffman, so how about I fly up to Connecticut later this evening?"

She said slowly, "You know, don't you, Dillon? You know the answer?"

"Yes, I do." He took a deep breath. "Excuse me now, sweetheart, I'm going to offer thanksgiving prayers before I do anything else."

63

Saturday evening

Savich met Senator David Hoffman in his elegant library in Chevy Chase.

He shook Savich's hand and said without preamble, "Tell me you've found out who's behind the attempted murder of Vice President Valenti. And don't tell me it was a terrorist."

Savich said, "No, I don't believe it was a terrorist."

"But you agree it's the same person or people who are trying to kill me who also murdered Dana Frobisher and sabotaged my car?"

"Yes, there's no doubt about that now."

"I see. Then you believe there is some—what, some madman after me, Agent Savich? And that I've been damned lucky he's missed me twice?" As he spoke, Senator Hoffman walked over and sat behind his mahogany desk. He motioned Savich to sit in front of him. The desk, Savich thought, suited the man.

"Yes, that is certainly how it appears."

"But who? I've thought and thought, you know that." Hoffman's voice suddenly dropped to a whisper. "You haven't discovered it was my sons, have you?"

"Your sons are many things, Senator," Savich said, "but I don't believe they'd consider murdering their own father. I could be wrong, especially about Benson, since he's not what you'd call a well-controlled, compassionate, or logical man. But you know that yourself."

Hoffman nodded. "Benson was only six years old when he started stealing lunches from other children, children who were smaller than he was, I might add. He became quite fat before I discovered what was happening and put a stop to it. He hasn't changed."

Savich said, "I think he could commit murder, if it were on the spur of the moment, a crime of passion. But I don't think he has the brains or the character to execute such a well-thought-out plan. Also, I don't think your sons like each other much, so I can't see the two of them planning anything together."

"Then who? The good Lord knows I've made enemies, impossible not to when you've been in a position of power for more than three decades. But who?" He exhaled and shook his head. "I'm repeating myself. Sorry." He stopped cold. "You can't have reason to suspect Corliss Rydle. She's been my most loyal employee, at least I've always believed she has."

"No, I don't think she harbors a grudge toward you, Senator. She's a rock. I understand she's marrying Gabe Hilliard's son."

"That's right. I thought he was interested in my wife once upon a time, but our friendship survived it. No, Gabe would have no reason to murder me, especially now that Nikki's dead."

"Your wife and Mr. Hilliard? I found nothing to indicate he's ever been interested in playing more than a round of golf with you."

"Forget I said that. Gabe has always been an excellent friend." Senator Hoffman ran his hand through his hair, making it stand straight up. "Just the thought that Gabe—well, I'll tell you, Agent, being the target of a murderer makes you question relationships you never thought you would. I don't think I could have gotten through this if Corliss and my staff hadn't been there for me."

Savich said quietly, "I find it curious that your wife, Nikki, has never managed to get through to me again, Senator."

Senator Hoffman shook his head as he said, "I've already told you, Agent Savich, that what you claim about Nikki is so beyond anything I could possibly accept, well, I—"

Savich said easily, "I understand it's hard to accept, Senator. Nonetheless, it is real, it did happen. It's like she had only so much opportunity to connect with someone, and then she had to leave. I honestly doubt she'll come again."

"So do you think God controls dead people? Lets them talk to us, then pulls them back?"

"I don't presume to know. It's just that in Nikki's case, she either couldn't connect with me anymore, or she wouldn't."

"That sounds ridiculous."

"It certainly makes you reexamine your beliefs."

"Did she ever tell you who is behind the attempts on my life?"

"No."

Senator Hoffman took a pen from its holder and began tapping it up and down. "It seems that is what people who claim to have psychic powers always say—the dead never quite get it done. They never show the psychic the one scene that would make sense of everything, they never convey the one critical fact that would solve the problem. Like Nikki. Life imitating art?"

He tapped his pen a half-dozen more times, frowned. "You would think that if indeed Nikki was really worried about me, she'd not only break through to communicate with you, she'd tell you exactly what you needed to know, but she's never managed to be helpful, has she? Don't you find that curious, Agent Savich?"

Savich said, "I did until I realized I needed to back up and do some thinking. Fact is, she did tell me exactly what I needed to know when she spoke to me that first time. I just didn't understand what she was saying."

"What, did she speak in tongues?"

Savich no longer had to pull out the paper from his wallet. "Perhaps you remember what she said, Senator. '*David's in such danger. He doesn't understand, doesn't realize what will happen to him. You've got to stop it, you've got to, he can't—*' You're right, I wish she'd told me more, but we were interrupted. It's a pity, because a woman is dead and the vice president could easily have died as well."

The dark library was silent. Hoffman finally said, "I wish she could have finished it, wish she could have told you who has it in for me."

"She was very frightened for you, Senator, that came through loud and clear."

"So death doesn't brush away the emotions one felt while alive?"

"Not in my experience."

"Well, my wife loved me."

"Yes, she must still, since she wanted me to save you. I'm going to do my best to do that tonight, Senator. Now, let me be specific. I've spent many hours checking into people who know you socially, who work for and with you, all of your colleagues, your political and personal rivals. I realized there was no one who seemed to have enough of a motive to go to such complex lengths to kill you.

"After my interview with Benson and Aiden, I realized I was too close, and so I got rid of all my preconceptions and biases. And do you know what? I finally realized the truth, Senator. I saw clearly what I needed to see in what Aiden and Benson said, and finally, in what Nikki had said. Everything fell into place."

Hoffman nodded. "I too have found over the years that sometimes a bit of perspective is exactly what one needs. Tell me, what is it that fell into place, Agent Savich?"

Savich steepled his fingers and lightly tapped his fingertips together. "Would you like to tell me why you poisoned Dana Frobisher and tried to murder Vice President Valenti?"

Hoffman laughed, sat back in his beautiful Moroccan leather chair. "Your reevaluation led you to this? Come now, Agent Savich, I don't have any idea what you're talking about, but what you're implying is ludicrous. Why would I murder a woman I scarcely know over lunch? And Valenti, he's been one of my best friends for years. This is even greater nonsense than your claim about talking to Nikki."

Hoffman slowly rose. "I am more than disappointed in you, Agent Savich, not that you ever afforded me much protection or assistance. You are a disgrace to the FBI. I will be speaking to Director Mueller, and I promise you, sir, you will be reassigned to the Anchorage Field Office, if not kicked out of the Bureau altogether. You are a professional, you are supposed to be thorough, to be sure of your facts before you act. Let me ask you—do you have a shred of proof for your allegations against a United States senator?"

Savich's voice was dark as night. "I may never find absolute proof against you. But I like my odds."

Hoffman said very precisely, "There's no proof to find because I did not commit either of these heinous acts. How can you possibly accuse me after you claimed my dead wife begged you to save me? Nikki knew I was in danger. I was very lucky, Agent Savich, and my being alive, here speaking to you today, has nothing to do with your help. I wonder if I'll be so lucky again?"

"You don't need to sing another verse of your victim's song, Senator. You and I both know the truth. The reason I came here was that I promised Nikki I would try to protect you. I have told you what I know to stop you from harming anyone else. It really would be best if you gave yourself up."

Senator Hoffman sat back down in his chair, his arms behind his head as if he were suddenly enjoying himself. "I thought you were smart, but I now I see that I was wrong." He laughed, a full, deep laugh. "You're whistling in the wind, Agent Savich."

"You said you hardly knew Dana Frobisher, but your wife worked quite closely with her. An old friend of Ms. Frobisher recalls quite a nasty split between them, something to do with allegations of embezzlement, but it was never pursued. Did you consider that Frobisher had committed an offense against your wife?"

"I don't know what you're talking about."

"It's interesting you invited her to lunch to discuss working with you on some charity when Frobisher hasn't been involved in any charity work in over five years, and you have never before shown any interest."

"How would I know that? All I know is what I wanted to do and I remembered her name. Nothing more than that."

"Senator, I attached GPS monitors to your three remaining cars, as part of my investigation meant to protect you. The Range Rover was in close proximity to Leesburg, Virginia, late last night. Emilio Gasparini of the Foggy Bottom Grill was found dead there this morning."

"I have nothing to say about that. I will not allow you to interrogate me in my own home."

"I imagine Emilio met you there last night expecting to be paid, but you killed him instead. Do you really believe we'll find no evidence of any of your dealings with him? Do you think Emilio didn't confide in anyone at all? A girlfriend? A boyfriend? There will be bank deposits, phone records, credit card receipts. I will trace them, Senator, and I will catch you. Count on it."

Savich rose to face him. "I also realized there was simply no one else who could have rigged the Brabus, Senator—only you or Morey Hughes. I will find the evidence if you did any research on how to sabotage that vehicle, or ordered the parts you needed. It doesn't matter if you deleted it, I will unearth it."

Hoffman shook his head. "Add this to your fantasy mix, Agent Savich. Morey leaves the house more often than you imagine. Anyone could have gotten into the garage and sabotaged the Brabus."

"Do you know what bothers me still? I don't have a handle yet on why you tried to murder Vice President Valenti. I know he and your wife were high school sweethearts, and Aiden and Benson implied that their mother still had strong feelings for him, telling them of adventures she had with Valenti when Aiden and Benson were children. Was it sheer obsessive jealousy, Senator, finally gone mad years after the deed, or something more?"

Hoffman laughed again. "I have been Alex Valenti's friend since before you were born. I have had enough of this conversation. Next time you speak to my wife, Agent, that is if some Being allows her to come back to earth a final time, tell her she went to the wrong person. She went to a buffoon who did nothing at all except try to destroy her husband. Now, get out of my house. I do not wish to see you again."

64

STONE BRIDGE, CONNECTICUT
Sunday morning

Adler Dieffendorf and Werner Gerlach walked to the conference room table, nodded to Bowie, Savich, and Sherlock, and sat down. Dieffendorf said immediately, "I elected not to have our lawyers here, but I will call them if you become in any way inappropriate. Do you understand?"

Bowie nodded. "We understand."

Dieffendorf said, "Good. As you know, Werner and I have been speaking to your Department of Justice attorneys. About this." He pulled a copy of the Culovort papers out of his briefcase and fanned the pages.

Savich saw his hands were shaking slightly, but his voice remained firmly in control. He closed his eyes a moment, then his shoulders squared again. "This has come as a grave shock to me, this well-crafted plan that my very own CEO Caskie Royal implemented to shut down the supply of Culovort in our Missouri plant. Let me emphasize that this was the act of a rogue employee. Nothing like this would ever be sanctioned by Schiffer Hartwin. The company's leadership is not to blame, and so I have told your federal attorneys. I have already informed the family, and we are in discussions concerning restitution.

"Now I will tell you that I suspected something was amiss, and that is why I sent Helmut Blauvelt here to find out the truth. No, I more than suspected, I'd heard rumors that I could not discount, and so Helmut, less than a week after his appendix surgery, insisted on coming, even insisted on making private travel arrangements so no one would find out. He was a bulldog, and Caskie Royal would not have managed to fool him for very long. Even I did not expect the truth to be this damning or to precipitate such dreadful acts. Helmut Blauvelt was more than a Schiffer Hartwin employee. He was a longtime friend of mine. I simply couldn't believe it when he was so brutally murdered. Then Royal himself was murdered. Still I did not know how damning it all was until I read the actual plan Royal implemented to systematically close down production, making it look like unfortunate occurrences had led to the shutdown. I was trying to find out the truth from him when he ran away. Neither Werner nor I knew what to think. It seemed to us everything had flown out of control.

"If I accept that Royal was a rogue employee, acting on his own, why then was he murdered? I don't understand, I simply don't know anything, except that these papers, these papers are a horror for the company." He shook the Culovort papers, then dropped them on the table. "Someone knew to copy these pages off Royal's computer. What is going on here?"

Bowie said, "Mr. Dieffendorf, did you yourself request Agent Andreas Kesselring of the BND to come here to assist in the investigation of Helmut Blauvelt's murder?"

Dieffendorf frowned at him, shook his head. "No," he said slowly, forcing his brain to refocus, "but when his services were offered by the BND, I gladly accepted. I checked. Kesselring has an excellent reputation. Why do you ask?"

"Agent Kesselring was sent here, sir, just as you sent Helmut Blauvelt. He was here to assess the situation and contain it. He was never here to assist us. He was never on your side, or ours. It was he who murdered Helmut Blauvelt because Blauvelt discovered too much of the truth. He also murdered Caskie Royal because Royal was trying to escape and Kesselring knew he'd be caught, and he knew Royal would confess everything to save his own neck. He did not murder Royal on his own. He had the help of Royal's wife and her lover. Yesterday morning, he planned to murder his accomplices and Agent Sherlock. He failed."

Dieffendorf stared blankly at Bowie, his face perfectly white. He'd aged ten years since Bowie had opened his mouth. "No," he said quite clearly. "No. This cannot be true. You are saying that an agent of the BND has betrayed us? Me? The company?"

"Yes, sir, he did indeed betray you and the company. I imagine you've wondered why Agent Kesselring hasn't answered his cell phone. He cannot, you see, because he's in the hospital, being treated for gunshot wounds."

Dieffendorf frowned. "Werner, you told me Kesselring wasn't answering his cell phone. You said you were concerned."

"That's correct. Yes, I was becoming worried."

Dieffendorf said to Bowie, "You swear to me what you've told us is true?"

"Oh, it's quite true," Bowie said.

Dieffendorf said to Gerlach, "Did you have any idea what Kesselring had done?"

"Of course not. I do wonder, though, if the FBI agents here are being completely accurate in their telling of these events. Where is your proof that Kesselring did any of these things? Did Kesselring confess it all to you?"

Savich said, "He has refused to tell us who he worked for. Let me ask you, Mr. Dieffendorf, do you think Caskie Royal himself contrived somehow to sabotage the Spanish plant?"

"I don't see how he could have." Dieffendorf stopped short, sucked in his breath. "You're saying Kesselring helped him?"

"I'm saying that Royal did not act alone."

Bowie pulled a cell phone from his pocket. "We took this cell from Kesselring's pocket. It's prepaid, impossible to trace to a specific buyer, only to the store where it was purchased.

"There are many calls on it, some to a number you know very well, Mr. Dieffendorf." Bowie turned to Werner Gerlach. "I find it particularly interesting, Mr. Gerlach, that Kesselring phoned you three times last Sunday night, around the same time as the break-in at Caskie Royal's office and Helmut Blauvelt's murder. Did he call you for instructions? Did you discuss whether he should kill Blauvelt?"

Werner Gerlach sat motionless, staring straight ahead. Dieffendorf leaned down and shook his shoulder. "Werner? What did he call you about?"

Gerlach slowly stood now. "All of this is the grossest sort of speculation, Adler. I know nothing of any of it. I wish to call our lawyers now. They will put a stop to this lunacy."

Savich said, "I have accessed your phone records, Mr. Gerlach. There are also calls from your number to Kesselring. A total of six calls until yesterday morning. Then you left three messages."

Gerlach crossed his arms over his chest. He stood stiff and as tall as he could. "This means nothing at all. Agent Kesselring was here to find answers, not commit crimes. Naturally I wished to communicate with him, to find out the status of his investigation. There is nothing more to it than that."

Dieffendorf said slowly, "I have known Werner Gerlach for more than twenty years. He is loyal to me, he is loyal to Schiffer Hartwin. He would never conspire in a fraud of this nature, never."

Savich sat forward, his hands folded. "I believe eight months ago you married a young lady named Laytha Guerling, aged twenty-six?"

Gerlach erupted, "What business is that of yours? Don't you dare bring up my wife's name!"

"Actually, it's much worse than that, Mr.

Gerlach. You see, your wife was hired by a man who knew of your first wife's recent death, who knew you were vulnerable. She was instructed to seduce you, and so she did. She's a professional, after all. When you asked her to marry you, the man she worked for was very pleased. She soon convinced you to collude with that man, didn't she? It must not have taken very long to convince you, Mr. Gerlach, since the shutdown of the Missouri plant and the sabotage of the Spanish plant happened eight months ago. How much money was promised you?"

Gerlach was breathing hard, his face turning alarmingly red. "I do not know what you are talking about. You will cease your slander of my wife, do you hear me?"

Savich said, "Do you wish to tell Mr. Dieffendorf who you've been working with? No? It was Claude Renard, the CEO of Laboratoires Ancondor, the man whose company has profited so handsomely from the skyrocketing sales of the cancer drug Eloxium, since you arranged for the shortage of Culovort to begin."

Savich pulled a photo out of his briefcase.

"This was just sent to me by the Frankfurt police." He turned the full-color photo faceup.

It was Laytha Guerling Gerlach, seated behind a young man on a motorcycle. Her arms were wrapped tightly around his waist, her long blond hair blowing wildly about her head. She was smiling.

"I'm sure you recognize your wife. The man is Rupert Snelling, your wife's lover since before you met her."

All the color drained from Gerlach's face. "No," he whispered. He reached out toward the photo, then slowly pulled his hand back. "No, that can't be true."

"Believe it, Mr. Gerlach." Savich picked up the photo and held it out to face Gerlach. "This photo was taken yesterday morning. How much of the immense profits is Renard siphoning off to you, Mr. Gerlach? We know Caskie Royal had over four hundred thousand dollars in an offshore account. Who recruited him? Renard? You?"

Dieffendorf roared out of his chair, knocking it backward. "You traitor! You mewling fool! I trusted you, I was even a bit envious of you when Laytha wanted to marry you!"

He grabbed Gerlach by his collar and jerked him forward. He shook him like a rat.

Sherlock took his arm. "Mr. Dieffendorf, you really don't want to kill him in front of three FBI agents. Let him go, sir, let him go."

"You betrayed me!" He shook him one final time and dropped him. It was only luck that Gerlach fell back into his chair. He swallowed, but remained silent.

Savich continued. "You and Mr. Renard have been very careful with your wire transfers. It will prove very difficult to track down those transactions, but your wife, Laytha, was not nearly so careful. She and Renard have a joint bank account, Mr. Gerlach. Someone has been making regular large deposits into this account. I've been working with the German authorities for the past day tracking their source in France."

Gerlach raised dead eyes to Dieffendorf. "Not Laytha, not Laytha. She loves me." He put his head between his arms on the table and wept. His sobs were the only sound in the conference room until Dieffendorf yelled, "You idiot, I remember when you met her! I'll wager her name isn't even real, you old fool!" He whirled around to

Savich. "Am I right? What is the woman's real name?"

"Gerda Wallenbach."

"Yes, yes, you see? I knew she was too good to be true, you bloody blind sot!"

Gerlach never raised his head. His voice was liquid with tears. "She played tennis, her education was paid for by a rich old aunt. She was refined, she adored Wagner! I loved her!"

Dieffendorf hit his shoulder. "And she demanded what? Clothes, shoes, trips? You couldn't afford all her demands, and you were afraid she'd leave you? You probably saw Renard as your savior, with enough money to convince your precious young wife to stay with you.

"It's not like you weren't paid a princely salary by Schiffer Hartwin," Dieffendorf said. "Given the bonuses, you are rich, do you hear me? Rich! You've worked by my side for years now, moving up in the company just as I've moved up, to garner great responsibility. Did your loyalty to the company, your loyalty to me, mean nothing to you? Damn you, how long did it take her to talk you into it?"

Savich waited a moment, then said, "Your

wife spent at least two hundred thousand dollars in the first month you were married, Mr. Gerlach. I have copies of bills from travel agencies, jewelry stores, fashion houses. Did you see financial ruin coming?"

Gerlach's head snapped up. He shouted, "None of this is true! It's all lies! It was Caskie Royal's doing, all of it." He strained to look up at Dieffendorf's furious face. "That is why I sent Kesselring here, to find out the truth. That is why there are phone calls between us. I had no idea you had also sent Blauvelt for the same purpose. I did not know!"

Dieffendorf shouted down at Gerlach, "When all's said and done, the truth is, you're a greedy little bastard who has to wear two-inch lifts in your shoes! I'll bet you couldn't wait to sign on with Renard. You know what? I can see your precious Laytha and her boyfriend laughing about what a preening little cock you are!"

Dieffendorf frowned down at him, then said slowly, "No, wait. No one held a gun to your head, did they, Werner? Not Laytha, not Renard. You wanted all that money for yourself, didn't you? How much was Renard paying you?"

Gerlach didn't answer. He was crying.

65

WASHINGTON MEMORIAL HOSPITAL
Sunday evening

"I would like to speak to the vice president alone, Agent Jarvis. Would you and Agent Paul wait just outside, please?"

"I'm sorry, sir, but you know we can't leave the vice president alone."

"Come, Jarvis, I've known him since we were very young men. It's a personal matter that is rather urgent. I need only five minutes."

Alex Valenti opened his eyes and his mouth widened just a bit in a smile. His voice was hoarse when he whispered, "It's all right, Agent Jarvis, I'm sure the man has already been frisked like a criminal. You can stay right outside the glass door."

Agent Jarvis continued to look uncertain, but he finally nodded. "Very well, since it's important. Senator Hoffman, the vice president is very weak, so please keep it short, all right? Press the call button if you need anything." He gave Hoffman a quick nod. "Thank you, sir."

"This won't take long, I promise," Senator Hoffman said, and watched Jarvis leave, closing the glass door quietly behind him. He looked down at a nearly motionless Alex Valenti, a man he'd known for—how many years was it now? Forty? He said, "I tried to see you earlier, but was told only family was allowed. I'm glad I could see you this evening."

Valenti's voice was hoarse when he whispered, "Dave, it's good to see you. They finally took that damned tube out of my nose, what a relief."

"Your voice sounds harsh. Is your throat sore?"

"A bit, along with everything else. Since I nearly bought the big one, I'll accept a sore throat without complaint. I'm pleased they let you in. The doctors are trying to make me bore myself to death. Even in the miserable shape I'm in, I can't sleep all the time."

"No, they want you to heal. They want to get full credit for saving you. No relapses allowed. I heard your wife and family were dancing around the halls when the doctors told them you're going to make a full recovery."

"They did indeed. Elyssa was grinning so big I could see her back molars. She wouldn't stop kissing my ear. She told me the waiting room was overflowing with family and friends. I didn't feel much like talking, but I told her I didn't deserve all the attention, and she had the gall to agree.

"I'm sorry about the Brabus, Dave. It was a beautiful machine, and now it's junk."

"Maybe you'll be the first vice president to get a year-end bonus for actually making headlines. Then you can buy me a new one."

Valenti gave a small laugh, barely a sound really, but he immediately regretted it. He pressed the morphine button, waited a minute until he could handle the slowly ebbing flow of pain. "Can you imagine the public outcry? Year-end bonus. That's funny, Dave. You're here one minute and already I'm laughing. It hurts."

"You survived, that's the only important thing. I spoke to Dr. Myller. He called you amazing, the force of your spirit, your will to live. He told me he wished all his patients had your strength, mentally and physically."

Hoffman fell silent, seeing the furrow of pain on Valenti's forehead. He watched him push the morphine button again, but it was far too soon for more of the drug to be delivered, and he had to wait, his eyes closed, for his last dose to kick in.

"Thanks for telling me that," Valenti said after a couple of minutes. "Sometimes the pain seems to spike. I'm okay now. The pain gets me every once in a while."

"Would you rather never have awakened?"

"I suppose if I'd died I wouldn't know any different, so the question is really irrelevant, isn't it? No, I'm glad I'm here and breathing even though my insides feel like they're on a death march. Agent Savich was here to tell me it wasn't an accident, which I already knew in my gut. He said someone sabotaged the steering linkage, set it to blow out. He said I didn't stand a chance. I've thought about who would want to kill me, Dave, but I was forced to admit that no one hates me enough to kill me in such a convoluted way. I mean, who would want to knock off a vice president? We're about as necessary as roll bars on a Volvo."

Hoffman laughed, couldn't help it.

Valenti waggled his eyebrows. "At least as a governor I was always busy—places to go, legislation to get through, enemies to make. It doesn't make much sense that someone would try to kill me now."

Hoffman looked toward the lovely big window with its view of the National Mall in the distance. He said over his shoulder, "Nikki came to me recently. Of course I didn't realize it was her, but there she was, nearly every night around midnight, in front of my bedroom window."

Hoffman heard Valenti suck in his breath. Was it pain or astonishment at what he'd so casually said about his wife?

"Truth be told," Hoffman continued after

a moment, "I believed it was a trick, I believed it was my sons, the worthless little sods, trying to drive their old man over the edge to get their hands on my money. I realized quickly enough that neither Aiden nor Benson has the imagination or the guts to pull off a stunt like that."

Valenti said quietly from behind him, "Nikki's been dead over three years, Dave. We both were with her at the end. We both held her hands. What are you saying? You really believe her ghost visited you?"

"Yes, you were there, weren't you, holding her hand? Did you know Agent Dillon Savich has a special gift, that he claims she spoke to him?"

"No, I didn't know. I do know President Holley thinks he's very bright, very intuitive. Now you're telling me he's a psychic?"

Hoffman waved his hand as he turned away from the window and walked back to Valenti's bedside. He said as he straightened the glass of water and the small cup of ice chips on the wooden arm, "Apparently. Who really knows?" He picked up the glass. "Do you want to drink some water, Alex?"

"No, not right now. To be honest, I don't think I could swallow it at the moment."

Hoffman set the glass back down. "Later then. Savich and his wife, Agent Sherlock, spent an evening at my house, and the next day Savich told me Nikki came to him to beg him to save me from some sort of trouble."

"What kind of trouble are you in? What is all this about?"

Hoffman laughed again. "You don't need to worry about me, Alex. You see, I'm quite sure it wasn't me Nikki was trying to save, it was you she was trying to protect, even after her death."

Valenti spoke, his voice barely above a whisper, but the shock was clear in his voice. "*What?* What did you say? Is this another one of your jokes, Dave?"

"No, I'm not joking. Do you know how long I've hated you?"

"*Hated me?* Dave, are you all right? What's going on here?" He glanced toward Agent Jarvis through the glass door, saw he was speaking with another agent, both of them looking directly back at him.

Hoffman leaned close. "Take yourself back, Alex, to when Nikki and I met at Stanford. She told me all about you, how you'd been her high school sweetheart, how you'd sworn your teenage undying love, but then you went off to Harvard, and Romeo and Juliet were separated. She laughed about it, but I wasn't fooled. She was still in love with you. Why did you leave her?"

Valenti said quietly, "It was a very long time ago, so long ago I can't even remember exactly how my father convinced me. He always had his ways to gain my obedience, you know that. You've locked horns with him a couple of times yourself over the years. Why do you care now? It's utterly unimportant, has been for years. Why do you hate me?"

"Because when the two of you met up again—Nikki and I had been married only six months—it started all over again. You started sleeping with her, Alex. Did you think you could divorce Elyssa and that I would divorce Nikki so you two could ride off into the sunset?

"Not going to answer that, are you? I don't blame you. When you and I held her hands as she was dying, I knew she wished she could have spent her life with you, not me. At her last breath, her last instant of life, it was you she looked at, Alex, not me."

Valenti stared up at the man he'd tried to protect from this for so many years, but he knew after all, he'd always known. It had been years ago when he and Nikki had decided to keep their families together, and he'd hurt so deeply he didn't believe he would ever stop regretting that this man was her husband and not him, that her name was Hoffman, not Valenti.

But the years passed, and the despair lessened, and what took its place was an abiding love for his own wife and his magnificent children. Now he was a grandfather, and he knew he was loved—Elyssa had danced when they said he was going to live. There was only Elyssa now, he thought, and he felt the power of his feelings for her press deep. He couldn't remember when she'd become the most important person in his life. He wondered what would have happened if he had left with Nikki all those years ago when their passion seemed the only worthwhile emotion in life, when giving in to what they felt seemed the only right thing to do? How long had that pain lasted? Valenti couldn't remember now. Nor could Nikki. They'd spoken of it when she knew her death was close, and they'd even laughed a bit about their star-crossed passion that had faded, of course, through the years. "Youth," she'd said, "youth is a wonderful dream that doesn't last. What is vital in youth doesn't stay as important as we get older, now does it?"

Then David had come into the hospital room and she'd died a few minutes later, with both of the men who'd loved her holding her hands.

What had Dave said? Something about how Nikki had looked at him, Alex, when she'd died and not at Dave?

"No," he said, "I remember clearly it was you Nikki was looking at the moment she died. She whispered good-bye to you with her last breath."

Hoffman sneered. "You have a convenient memory, Alex. How much does Elyssa know of your feelings for my wife?"

Valenti felt a great grief settle over him, a heavy grief because he knew it was Elyssa's grief and David's grief as well. They'd both known, they'd both watched, both waited. He said slowly, "At the beginning, all those years ago, Nikki and I decided to keep our families together. How can you believe Nikki wouldn't do that? She was filled with honor, with goodness.

"When she became ill, Nikki told me she'd come to love you more than she'd ever loved me, because your love for each other was real, not an old fantasy."

"You're a liar!" Hoffman straightened and nodded over to the Secret Service agents who were watching him.

Valenti said slowly, "Why do you think I would lie about that?"

"Because she told me, damn you to hell! I don't think she planned to, but she was weak and confused, even delirious near the end. She told me Aiden is yours, not mine. Nikki married me only because she couldn't have you. You'd already married Elyssa, but did that matter? Oh, no, she still had to have your child!"

Valenti slowly shook his head back and forth on the hard pillow. "No, no, that's impossible."

"You slept with her in high school, didn't you? Did you meet during college as well?"

"Back then we all slept with each other, you know that, Dave. Sex was as common as eating and sleeping, it was simple recreation. Surely you slept with college girls before you met Nikki? Before you married?"

"Yes, but you and Nikki, it was more between the two of you! Aiden was born a year and a half after Nikki and I were married. I've done the blood tests, Alex, I know for a fact I'm not his father. You are."

66

He saw the instant Valenti believed him, accepted it. The honorable, forthright man he liked to think he was had a bastard son. Valenti said slowly, "I didn't know, never even guessed. You believe I'm lying to you? You think Nikki told me and I decided to ignore it? Well, she didn't, never even hinted, never said a word, even during that brief time we wanted to go away together.

"My God, David, I've always thought Aiden looked like you."

"You know what, you bastard? Nikki did

come to love me, I knew it, and so I didn't punish her by forcing you out of our lives. I allowed all of us to become such close friends, your children and mine, like cousins. Two big loving families, and the Richardses too, all the boys playing together. I remember watching them and thanking the Lord they were my sons, mine and Nikki's, together. But of course they weren't. It was a fantasy.

"When she went into the hospital for the last time, I finally believed she loved me. But then there you were not even three days later, sitting beside her, stroking your hands through her hair, what was left of it, whispering to her."

David Hoffman stared down at him, wondered in that moment if he hated Valenti more than he'd loved his wife.

He gave a low laugh, one filled with pain at the sharp memory of her death. "You know what, Alex? When she came back, Savich believed she was trying to protect me, but it was you, always you. Even beyond death, she was trying to protect you, from me. I always came in second. I hated it. But then she spoke to Savich, and gave me a gift, an opportunity, so fitting, so perfect, it was too good to let pass. That's when I decided what I was going to do."

Valenti looked into his friend's eyes, but he simply couldn't accept it. "Are you telling me you sabotaged your own car? That you tried to kill me?"

David Hoffman slowly rose. "Ah, you're looking at me like I'm a monster, Alex. If only you'd died when the Brabus hit that oak tree. I would have given one of the most eloquent eulogies at your lavish funeral, reminded all the mourners of what a wonderful family man you were. And I would have been thanking Nikki for making it all possible. Unfortunately, you survived. I've lost to you yet again."

"There was never anything to lose. You've become obsessed, Dave—"

"Shut up, for once, shut up! There's nothing wrong with me, nothing. Listen to me. I came to tell you it was I who tried to kill you, but I will not try again."

Valenti felt nauseated, from physical pain, from the drugs, from this soul-leaching hatred, this obsession, yes, that's exactly what it was, and surely it was insanity too, and he was the focus of it. Had

Nikki really spoken to Savich? Had she really been trying to warn him? He whispered, "You know it will all come out, Dave."

"Eventually, perhaps. Agent Savich suspects some of it. Will he find evidence of what I did? I was very careful, but who knows?

"Now, Alex, I'm asking you not to tell anyone what I've told you. I don't ask it for myself, but for both our families, for Elyssa, for *all* of your sons, and for your own sake. This is not what either of us want to be remembered for, is it?"

Valenti wondered how his body could keep breathing. He couldn't believe this, just couldn't, and now David wanted him to keep silent? He asked him, "What would happen to you, Dave?"

"Do you know, I've decided to join Nikki. Since I won't try to kill you again, you'll probably live for a good long time and that means I'll have years with her before you show up."

"Why did you tell me in the first place, then?"

"You had to know," Hoffman said. "I wanted to watch your face as I told you why I wanted to kill you, why I've hated you more years than I can remember, wanted you to know the truth about your bastard son.

"You took everything that should have been mine, my wife, even my first-born son. I had to call you friend, had to laugh with you, I had to feign being sorry when misfortune struck you. That's all over now. When I leave this room, I have no desire to ever see you again." He paused, gave a sharp laugh, and added, "Please don't give a eulogy at my memorial."

The vice president looked at him, deep shadows in his eyes, memories ricocheting in his brain, memories and pain and what-would-have-beens. He didn't want to accept what David Hoffman had confessed because it meant so much of what he had cherished for so many years was a lie. Aiden was his son? He could barely get his mind around that fact.

He was tired. He hurt. He wanted Elyssa. She would know what to do. Above all, he was so sad he wanted to weep. He closed his eyes and saw Aiden's face in his mind. *Nikki, I'm so sorry.*

He heard the door open. "I won't even come to your funeral," he said, and heard the door close. He saw David Hoffman speak briefly to the Secret Service agents, then turn and leave. The tears he refused to shed burned his eyes and his throat. He swallowed, but the damned tears burned hotter. He raised his hand to pick up the glass of water.

"Sir, please give me that glass."

Valenti stared at Sherlock as she walked quickly from the small bathroom, stared at her hand as she quickly picked up the water glass. "You're not a Secret Service agent, are you?"

"No sir, I'm not. I'm FBI. I will ask your nurse to bring you water, all right?"

Sherlock saw realization dawn in his eyes, followed by a look of utter desolation. He looked, she thought, unutterably weary.

Valenti whispered, "He lied."

"Oh, yes." She lightly touched her fingertips to his forearm. "It will be all right, sir. I will tell your wife she can see you now, all right?"

Alex Valenti slowly nodded. "Yes, I need to see my wife. Thank you."

Secret Service Agent Alma Stone came into the room, carefully took the glass from

Sherlock, fitted a lid tightly over it, and wrote her name, the time, and the date on a card and taped it to the glass.

Sherlock nodded and walked quickly toward the ICU doors. She punched a single number on her cell. “Dillon? It’s done. The senator is on his way down. You can take him.”

She slipped her cell back into her jacket pocket, next to a small recorder.

Epilogue

GEORGETOWN
Monday evening

"Excellent pizza," Bowie announced when he'd finished off the last slice of deep-dish pepperoni with cheese baked into the crust. He looked over at the remains of Savich's pizza—artichokes, olives, peppers, onions, and just about every other vegetable known to man. He called out, "How about you, kiddo, you full yet?"

Georgie didn't hear him. She was on the floor with Sean and Astro, their slices of pizza cold and forgotten as they took turns designing their own houses on JumpStart World. They were busy arguing over Sean's selection of bright red shag carpeting in his living room.

Sherlock said, "Would you like to try the Big Dog's coffee, Bowie? I have to admit, Starbucks would pay Dillon big bucks for his skill with the coffee bean. Erin, how about you?"

Savich toasted Erin with his teacup. "This is a nice dark oolong, Erin. Would you like to give that a try instead?"

Erin sighed. "Yes, thanks, I guess I'd better go the tea route, otherwise I'll be bouncing off the ceiling half the night. I doubt if either Sean or Georgie will spare us in the morning."

Sherlock said, "Since Georgie's sleeping in Sean's room, maybe they'll play awhile before they drag us out of bed. For you and Bowie—" She paused a moment. "Well, there's a guest bedroom across from Sean's room. And this sofa pulls out into a double bed."

Bowie said easily, "We can decide about that later. Thanks for letting us crash, Sherlock."

They listened a moment to Sean telling

Georgie, "I don't think Astro's going to like you having a cat for your pet, Georgie. He might bite it good and you'd be mad."

"Astro won't try to hurt my cat. Crookshanks is a really big cat. She could bat Astro around, make him sorry he was ever born a little doofus dog."

"Astro's not a doofus! Papa, is Astro a doofus?"

"Not the last time I checked. Best beg Georgie to choose a kitten, though, Sean. That way, Astro will have time to train it."

Sean and Georgie were soon going at it again, this time over kitchen appliances.

Sherlock said, "Sean believes the purpose of a microwave is to present him with popcorn, so you can't do without one of those, Georgie." To Bowie, "You and Erin have had a long day, the flight down with Georgie, the hospital."

"There are more media there than patients," Bowie said, shaking his head, "trying to get in to see the family, the vice president's spokesperson, anyone who will step in front of a camera."

"Actually, it's the A Team," Savich said as he handed Erin a cup of tea and Bowie a cup of coffee that had Bowie smiling blissfully just smelling the aroma. "The B Team is hounding the Hoffman family and staff. This isn't going to blow over for a very long time."

Sherlock raised her cup. "At least our part in it is all over."

Bowie said after a moment, "Erin got to meet Uncle Alex."

"Poor man," Erin said, shaking her head. "I felt so sorry for him, but he was charming to me, said he wished they'd let Georgie in to give him a kiss." She laid her hand on Bowie's thigh. "The Valentis and your family are wonderful, Bowie."

"I think they sort of like you too."

"Ah, Bowie, your mom wants me to have lunch with her tomorrow."

Bowie's fingers froze on his coffee mug. "Lunch, you said? With my mom?"

"Yep. She asked me if I liked French. When I said I only ate fried snails under extreme duress, she heaved a sigh of relief and said she'd much rather eat Mexican."

"My mom isn't what you'd call subtle, Erin. Be prepared for nosy questions. Actually, she asked me if we'd like to spend the night with them. I said we'd already agreed to staying with Savich and Sherlock. I hope she didn't know I lied." He grinned toward Sherlock. "I hadn't asked you guys yet. Thanks again."

"Not a problem," Savich said.

Erin said, "Let me add my thanks. Since Dr. Kender promised me he'll never mention my name again, I guess I'm clear of all this, too. Bowie told me you all had made it official that the Culovort papers came to you anonymously."

"I wouldn't like Georgie to have to visit you in jail," Bowie said. "I hope this will be your last foray into the criminal world."

"Only the straight and narrow for me from now on," Erin said. She drank down the last of her tea, checked her watch. "It's past Georgie's bedtime. Bowie—"

He was frowning. "I forgot to pick up some stuff. Have you got a store nearby?"

While Savich told Bowie where to find the Shop 'N Go, Sherlock said to Erin, "Mr. Maitland seems to think the DOJ will force Laboratoires Ancondor and Schiffer Hartwin to make restitution to the cancer patients who had to switch to Eloxium when the Culovort ran out."

"I don't believe it."

Sherlock grinned. "Mr. Maitland says

the French will publicly blame us for the Culovort shortage, but privately, they'll slam Claude Renard really hard. We're talking huge fines here, maybe hefty enough that the industry will stop their corporate shenanigans for a while."

"I doubt it," Erin said, "they'll just get more careful."

When they'd gotten Sean down for the night, a major undertaking since he was so wired, Savich said to Sherlock, "Erin said she'd keep Georgie with her until Sean was out, then move her into his room."

"Probably a good idea. All Sean could talk about was Georgie. He said he might marry her instead of Marty. He's thinking hard about it. I told him Georgie was an older woman, that she might not believe he's serious. He smiled at me and said it was good she was older, that meant she could teach him things. Because he's five years old, I knew he didn't realize that what he'd said would make a mother's hair stand on end."

Savich laughed and moved over to lie against her. She rested her head on his chest, and he stroked his hand over her curly hair, winding the curls around his finger. "It was too close," he said, "just too close. It was like last time when you got shot. You could have died and I wasn't even there."

She lightly butted her head against his chin. "Bowie and Erin came blasting in to save the day. It's over and I'm okay. It's Kesselring who got shot up."

"You were very lucky Jane Ann and Mick were amateurs, and it didn't occur to them to check for an ankle gun. So many things could have happened."

"Isn't that true of just about everything in life? Dillon, we do the best we can, and keep moving forward. It's what we do. It's who we are, both of us."

"How are the cuts on your hands and wrists from sawing away on that duct tape?"

"Just fine." What he needed, she realized, was distraction, and so she slipped her hand down over his stomach. "Just little cuts, Dillon. Nothing more." Another couple of inches and he was thoroughly distracted.

There is a dark wind blowing. The camels shuffle about, pulling on their leads, ducking their heads up and down, making the plaintive sounds camels make

when they know something is wrong. The women press close to them even though the camels' breath is foul and their bites sharp. The women don't care because the camels are real and solid in a world that has become something they can no longer understand. They don't know that camels never bite when they are terrified, that they are struck dumb, even their feet stop moving, their humps stop swaying. Terrified camels hunker down. The camels are relieved the women are so close.

The women can't see, can't hear, can only feel the dark wind blowing, stinging their faces, and they know the wind is bringing something very bad. They wait. The camels wait with them. There is nothing else to do. But wait.

"Okay, kiddo," Erin continued in a whisper so as not to wake up Sean and Astro, "that's the beginning of our story. You chew that over before you go to sleep. I expect you to continue the story tomorrow night, all right?"

"Let me do it now, Erin, I know what the dark wind is bringing, let me tell you now."

"Shush, sweetie, you don't want to wake

them up, particularly Astro, he'll spend the next hour licking off your face." Erin brushed Georgie's hair off her forehead, leaned down, and kissed her small nose. "No more of our mysterious story tonight, it's time for you to sleep and dream about dancing in *Swan Lake* and that beautiful second arabesque you're going to hold flawlessly before you fly into a sweeping glissade."

Georgie giggled, then whispered, "But the dark wind blowing, Erin, I know—"

"Tomorrow night, sweetie," Erin whispered back. She leaned down and kissed her forehead, smoothed the covers to her chest, and rose. "Good night, Georgie."

"Good night, Erin. Kiss Daddy for me."

"I will."

Erin watched Georgie close her eyes and shut down.

She walked back downstairs to the Savich living room. The house was quiet, too quiet for her. She thought about the dark wind in her story and wondered if a dark wind was blowing outside. She decided that wouldn't be good because she didn't have any camels. She realized then that her story was excellent fodder for a nightmare.

Oh dear. But Georgie had laughed, excited to continue the story. She'd have to be more careful in the future.

She grinned as she looked through the front bay windows over Dillon and Sherlock's lovely lawn, currently covered with piles of raked autumn leaves. A wind was rising, she saw. They'd had no time to bag them up. The dark wind would whip them all over the yard again.

She looked at the houses still lit up across the street. So many families—kids and parents, pets, getting ready for bed. Maybe telling stories to their kids? And she thought of Bowie Richards, FBI Agent Bowie Richards, and of herself, Ms. Erin Pulaski, Polish-Irish-American dance teacher and private investigator, who'd severely crimped the bottom line, for at least a year, of two major drug companies.

She hoped there was a dark wind blowing for those conscienceless men. She hoped it would blow on them for the rest of their lives.

She heard a car pull into the driveway. It wasn't the low roar of Dillon's magnificent Porsche, it was the smooth sound of

Bowie's rented Taurus. Where was the Shop 'N Go? What had taken him so long?

Life, she thought, waiting for the front door to open, held great promise. Who could have guessed all this would happen when she took the huge, and really stupid, risk of breaking and entering into a CEO's office? Life was amazing. She wouldn't even go to jail. That in itself was amazing enough.

Bowie came in, something in his hand. He closed and locked the front door, set the alarm, and turned to face her. He wouldn't show her what he'd bought, but he was grinning.